Hope McIntyre was born in London and spent her childhood in Africa and Paris. She has worked in the film industry in London and Hollywood as a producer's assistant and in story development, as an editor in publishing, and as a journalist contributing to *Condé Nast* publications and several national newspapers. She now lives at the beach in Amagansett, Long Island, where she runs First Base, an editorial service for authors at the beginning of their careers.

To find out more about Hope McIntyre, visit her website of her alter-ego at: www.carolineupcher.com

Killer Date

Previously published in hardback as
How to Cook for a Ghost

Hope McIntyre

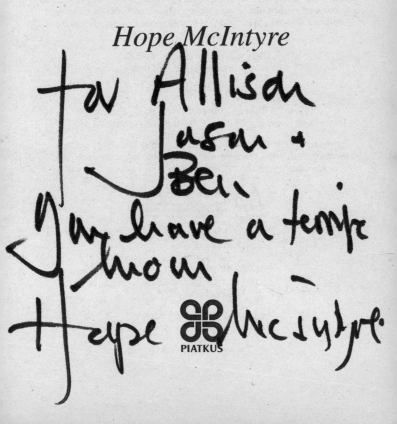

To Allison
Jason +
Ben

you have a terrific
mom -

Hope McIntyre

PIATKUS

PIATKUS

First published in Great Britain in 2008 by Piatkus Books
This paperback edition published in 2009 by Piatkus Books

Copyright © 2008 by Caroline Upcher

The moral right of the author has been asserted

All characters and events in this publication, other than
those clearly in the public domain, are fictitious
and any resemblance to real persons,
living or dead, is purely coincidental

A CIP catalogue record for this book
is available from the British Library

ISBN 978-0-7499-3901-4

Typeset in Times by Phoenix Photosetting, Chatham
Printed and bound in the UK by CPI Mackays, Chatham ME5 8TD

Papers used by Piatkus Books are natural, renewable and recyclable
products made from wood grown in sustainable forests and certified
in accordance with the rules of the Forest Stewardship Council.

Mixed Sources
Product group from well-managed
forests and other controlled sources
www.fsc.org Cert no. SGS-COC-004081
© 1996 Forest Stewardship Council

FSC

Piatkus Books
An imprint of
Little, Brown Book Group
100 Victoria Embankment
London EC4Y 0DY

An Hachette Livre UK Company
www.hachettelivre.co.uk

www.piatkus.co.uk

In memory of Tess McCoy

And for the real Bartholomew sisters, Alison, Lindsay and Kate, whose friendship has been the longest in my life, dating back to when we were all at school together *many* years ago.

And for Colin Murray, who likes Lee, 'girly' or not – for inspirational editing.

My thanks also go to the following cooks whose help was invaluable in restaurant research. Ellen Airgood, Rick Guth and David Zechmeister of the West Bay Diner, Grand Marais, Michigan; David Barber of the Three Square Grill, Portland, Oregon; and a cook in Devon who wishes to remain anonymous. She knows who she is and if at first she doesn't, I hope she will make the link later on.

I should also like to thank my favorite booksellers in the United States. They are:

Chris Avena of Bookhampton, East Hampton, NY, Bonnie Claeson of Black Orchid and Ian Kerr of The Mysterious Bookshop, New York, NY, and Tammy Domike, Janine Wilson and everyone at the Seattle Mystery Bookshop.

Finally, I want to acknowledge the many authors I have met at Bouchercon, Left Coast Crime, Malice Domestic and MWA events, whose work I have read and whose company I have enjoyed. They are: Cornelia Read, Julia Pomeroy, Gwen Freeman, Ann Parker, Julia Buckley, Harley Jane Kozak, Martin Edwards, Pari Noskin Taichert, Marshall Karp, Anthony Bidulka, Polly Nelson, Meg Chittenden and Neil Plakcy.

Chapter One

When I learned that my cousin Gussie was suspected of poisoning someone while working in a restaurant in the wilds of Devon, I simply didn't believe it. Gussie can't boil an egg. No one in their right mind would hire her to work in a restaurant.

Although Gussie was in south-west England and I was in London, I learned about Gussie's predicament from America, where I had been living until recently. I had a frantic call from my mother, a born-again New Yorker, who said she'd heard the news of Gussie's alleged restaurant disaster from Gussie's older sister, Cissie. Cissie, a successful designer of silk, high-end knitwear, the kind of slinky covering that would allow a boil on your bottom to protrude, and who had recently opened a store in Manhattan, had called my mother in a panic.

'You know your cousin Cissie, she always was a bit of a drama queen,' said my mother, and I imagined I could hear the transatlantic wires crackling as she geared up for a bit of spite. It would only be an indirect swipe at Cissie. The real venom would be aimed at Cissie's mother, Aunt Joy, whose breathtaking beauty, even at the age of seventy-one, always caused the green monster to rise within my mother. 'But, Lee, I knew it had to be seriously bad news when Cissie told me Gussie had called her. Gussie hasn't called *any*one in her family since her divorce. And it really does sound worrying. Someone died and

Gussie was the only member of the staff at the restaurant. No wonder they think she might be responsible. Who knows what they'll do to her. Someone has to go down and be with her.'

I didn't know how my mother had the nerve to accuse Cissie of being a drama queen. By the time she'd finished, I had visions of Gussie with her back against a wall. Which only added to the guilt I'd been feeling about the mysterious email I'd left unanswered in my laptop. Just three words and I'd almost missed them as I'd skimmed wearily through the day's mail at midnight. *Where are you?*

'Why can't Uncle Bobby or Aunt Joy go?' I said.

'Because,' said my mother with a finality that made me suspect they didn't even know about Gussie's predicament, 'Gussie asked for *you*. Her head was in such a muddle, she thought you were still living in America. That's why she called Cissie in New York and asked her to try and track you down.'

My mother's call prompted me to think about another communication concerning Gussie that I'd had about a month earlier from my ex, Tommy Kennedy.

Tommy is neither my ex-boyfriend nor my ex-husband. He is my ex-fiancé. I have a bit of a problem with marriage – not from personal experience because I have never been married. My dilemma is that I cannot make up my mind whether I want to be or not. For years I didn't. Poor old Tommy, bless his shaggy blond hair, his ever-increasing beer belly and his seemingly inexhaustible readiness to put up with my neuroses, was my boyfriend for nine long years, banished to live at the opposite end of London and told repeatedly that a wedding was out of the question.

I'll give you the long-story-short-version of why I finally changed my mind. Let's just say it involved me realizing that having a live-in partner snoring beside me every night would make me feel less paranoid about the imminent arrival of all the psychos out there who had a chainsaw with my name on it.

But you know what? At the last moment, he was the one who chickened out. I spent months arranging the wedding

2

and then he let slip over breakfast one morning – while munching noisily away on his scrambled eggs (made with egg substitute – I *had* to get his cholesterol down somehow) – that he'd had second thoughts. And his reason? He claimed that I was less needy than I was when he first knew me. To be translated: he felt superfluous to requirements. Now I had finally grown up a little, now I no longer needed a shoulder to lean on – not quite so much, at any rate – he was removing said shoulder altogether. Can you freakin' believe it?

Later, once I had fled to New York to ghost the memoirs of an aging rock star – because that's what I do, I'm a ghost-writer, the 'as told to' or 'written with' you see underneath the celebrity's name on the cover of their autobiography – I discovered that in fact Tommy had lost his job as a sound engineer at the BBC and he didn't think I'd want him anymore. Pathetic, right?

Anyway, he pulled himself together and came after me in America but then, just as we were beginning to plan a new wedding ceremony, I had to come back to London to get a new visa. And while I was there something happened that made me realize I couldn't marry Tommy.

So that's where we stand, separated by an ocean – Tommy stayed in America and started a new career as a karaoke disc jockey – and in fact we hadn't been in touch for almost a year when his email popped up out of the blue. *Hi Lee, I'm forwarding an email from your cousin Gussie. All best, Tommy. PS I've perfected a mean Faith Hill.*

'All best, Tommy.' We'd been together for nearly nine years, we'd almost married. Twice. And it boiled down to 'All best'? And God help me, what did he mean, he'd perfected a mean Faith Hill? *Please* let it *not* mean that he had become a karaoke drag artist. A 250 lb man with the giant paws and the trusting face of a Labrador, huffing and puffing into the micro-phone and trying to pass himself off on stage as a blonde of slender proportions. Not a pretty sight.

I digested Gussie's email to him – *Darling Tommy, where on earth is Lee? She hasn't replied to an email I sent her. I need her, Tommy. Please tell her to get off her butt and get in touch. How are you and what are you up to and when are you coming back to England? I miss you. All my love Gussie* – and was sitting there, slightly shell-shocked to realize that Gussie didn't appear to know (a) that I was back in England and had been for almost a year or (b) that Tommy and I were no longer together. Gussie had always been a big fan of Tommy's. She had been almost as devastated as I was when he called off the wedding. How on earth would she react when she discovered I'd subsequently done the same thing?

So Tommy was on my mind as I found myself haring out of London down the M4 on the first day of February en route for Frampton Abbas in Devon, glancing nervously at the speed cameras located at alarmingly regular intervals by the side of the road. According to the lone postcard Gussie had sent me when she'd moved there well over a year ago, Frampton Abbas lay 'in a bowl between soft green fields and lots of wonderful woods full of gnarled old trees, offering protection and habitat for the abundant wildlife; ideal conditions for wild flowers and fauna.' Gussie, who balked at writing anything more than her name by hand, had clearly copied this out of a guide book. Further investigation on my part had revealed that Frampton Abbas was an old market town nestling in a valley below Exmoor. But what interested me most was the mention of a river running through the town and the fact that it had been a convenient fording place for travelers in prehistoric times.

I'd come on a bit disgruntled to my mother about being the family's designated Gussie-carer but the truth was that I was secretly thrilled to be getting out of London. I'd always had this romantic dream about living in the country, that it would be the perfect life for me. Idyllic, peaceful, just the sound of birds chirping and ducks quacking to disturb me. A far-off tractor chugging through a field, leaves rustling in the wind. No, strike wind. I didn't want wind. Nothing disturbed me more than a gale. And I didn't want chickens or roosters crowing at dawn and waking me up. I was happily drawing up a mental list of what I would or wouldn't have in my fantasy rural existence when something made me start so abruptly that I nearly drove the car off the motorway.

It was the sound of a bird actually in the car.

It took me a second or two to realize that it was the ringer on my new mobile phone, *Chirrup-chirruping* away inside my bag on the back seat. I leaned back, struggling to keep the car on course with one hand on the steering wheel while I fumbled to retrieve the phone.

'Hold on,' I yelled as I struggled to get my earpiece in place so I could keep both hands on the wheel.

'Bad news, I'm afraid.' My agent Genevieve's voice was faint.

'Can you speak up, Genny?' I said.

'I said it's bad news. There doesn't seem to be a single celebrity on the planet who wants to tell their boring life story this week.'

Fine by me, I thought, *I could do with a break.* I didn't share this with Genevieve, of course, but the truth is there are moments when I feel I never want to hear another celebrity's story. If you want a job that makes you feel totally unappreciated, try ghosting. Sometimes, after I've sweated for months writing about their tortured childhood (mostly, I suspect, fabricated), and their struggle to overcome addiction, they barely acknowledge my existence. Sometimes I see them sitting there, bold as brass on national television, swearing that they've written every single word while I munch away on my granola, knowing for a fact that they haven't even *read* the book let alone written it. I'd once had extremely satisfying proof of this with an actress who'd always claimed she was ten years younger than she was. I'd included her real date of birth and I was ecstatic for a week following the sight of her shocked expression on breakfast TV when she was asked why she'd finally chosen to reveal her true age.

'Well, you know, Genevieve,' I smiled at the thought of her sitting in her immaculate office in Covent Garden, not a hair out of place or a tiny wrinkle in her clothing, 'it really doesn't matter because I'm on my way to the country for a while.'

There was a deafening silence. Genevieve doesn't *do* the country. The image of her in green wellies – or even jeans – is unthinkable. Genevieve favors crisp business attire, although she has an alarming tendency to select pastel shades of lavender or pink. She has an extremely pretty face with dainty features – a cute little turned-up nose, a rosebud mouth, that sort of thing. But from there down she is a disaster, spreading out more and more the further south you travel, until her thighs – which she usually keeps hidden behind her desk – confront you like two pregnant whales. Yet there's a cuddly aspect to her that's undeniably attractive. We have always had a tacit understanding that we will stick to business and not discuss our private lives so I've never had the skinny on her lovers. But one of these days I plan to take her out and get her drunk and find out what goes on behind her oh-so-efficient exterior.

'I hope you're not having one of your dotty dreams about moving to the country,' she said finally. 'You won't like it, Lee. All that grass growing makes a terrible din.'

'Let me be the judge of that,' I said a mite huffily. 'Who knows? I might even find some work down there.'

'Well, don't go near any pigs. They might start flying in your face. Where exactly are you going anyway? I hope it's somewhere where they've heard about the Internet.'

'It's a small town called Frampton Abbas in Devon. In the foothills of Exmoor. It's—'

But Genevieve cut me off. 'Yes, I know Frampton Abbas.'

'You've been there?' I was amazed.

'No, absolutely not. No way! I just know someone who moved there, that's all.'

'Who?' I started to ask but I could hear Genevieve clicking away on her keyboard, a sure sign that she was preparing to wind up the call.

'I'll call you if anything comes up,' she said and was gone before I could say anything else.

As I drove further into the West Country, I began to wonder about Frampton Abbas. When my mother had told me that Gussie had moved there after her divorce, my heart had leapt in recognition at the name. Note I say my *heart*.

Even though Tommy might be on my mind, for about the past year my heart had belonged to Max Austin. I can barely stand to say anything more about him without beginning to shake, so I won't. Suffice to say that I remembering him saying – because I remember *everything* he ever said to me – that he had an uncle in Devon, and that this uncle was a farmer who lived near a place called, you guessed it, Frampton Abbas. I might pretend to myself that I was going there out of love and concern for my cousin Gussie – and to a certain extent I was – but the real reason I was venturing forth from my reclusive inner-city existence was that she had fetched up on a dot on the map near Max Austin's uncle. It was a hell of a stretch, but these days it was all I had.

I was so caught up in thinking about Max, and Tommy, and then Max again, that I forgot to come off the M4 and drove all the way to Bristol by mistake. I switched course to drive across country, over the Quantock Hills and along the foot of Exmoor to drop down into the Exe Valley, finally arriving at Frampton Abbas at around six o'clock in the evening.

I was looking forward to seeing Gussie. She was the youngest of my three girl cousins, Flossie, Cissie and Gussie Bartholomew, the daughters of my father's eldest brother Bobby. Uncle Bobby was an artist and Aunt Joy, with her fine-boned beauty, had always been his muse. They lived in a rambling – and crumbling – old house on the coast of Northumberland and throughout my childhood school holidays had been punctuated with visits by one or other of the cousins to our house in Notting Hill. My mother always claimed Aunt Joy was hoping that a veneer of what she called 'London gloss' would rub off on at least one of her daughters.

Unlike her sisters – Cissie (Cecilia) was in fashion and Flossie (Florence) was a midwife – career wise Gussie (Augusta) was a disaster. When it came to marriage, however, she had outdone her sisters. To everyone's complete astonishment she had hooked Mickey Beresford, a charismatic lawyer with a five-storey townhouse in Belgravia. But the marriage was doomed from the start. Mickey turned out to be a first-class shit. Although not a patch on her mother or Cissie – but infinitely better looking than the plain, big-boned Flossie – Gussie, with her mop of russet curls and eyes the color of sapphires, had always drawn admirers. But it soon became clear that Mickey saw her as not much more than an adornment at his dinner table. He entertained constantly, but, unfortunately for him, not only could Gussie not boil an egg, she also did not have the first clue how to brief caterers. Unfortunately for her, *he* was a divorce lawyer. Gussie didn't have a prayer. I could never understand why I could pick up the paper and read about million-pound settlements and there was poor Gussie crawling miserably from her marriage with possibly even less than she took into it.

And then she had disappeared, flung cruelly out of London society and beetling down to bury herself and her humiliation in deepest Devon. Yet judging by the sporadic – and almost illiterate – emails I had received from her, her love life seemed to be thriving. As far as I could make out, she had a new boyfriend every month. And when I parked the car and trudged down the main road running through the center of Frampton Abbas looking for the number she had given me during a hasty conversation on the phone, I was surprised to find myself in front of a beautiful double-fronted Georgian house with very pleasing lines. The facade still had the original stone and high sash windows, and with a feeling of sudden anticipation I raised my hand to grasp the gleaming brass door knocker.

I waited a good five minutes, knocked twice more and then eventually the door opened the barest crack and Gussie peeped through it. Her mop of dark red hair was so unruly I couldn't see her eyes, just her little nose pointing at me like a hedgehog's.

'Lee-Lee!'

It was her childhood name for me, her interpretation of Nathalie when she was still learning to speak. Everyone else had shortened it to Lee but Gussie stuck with Lee-Lee.

She reached out and embraced me quickly, glancing up and down the street, and I was startled to see that she was wearing a satin Chinese robe of garish emerald with dragons all over it – and apparently nothing underneath. Had she been asleep? Was that why she had taken so long to open the door?

I was shocked by her appearance. Her stunning midnight blue eyes, when she revealed them by shaking her fringe, had been reduced to slits by the puffiness below them and her abundance of freckles, contrasted with the sickly pallor of her skin, was more pronounced than ever.

But if Gussie looked run-down, her house – from my first impression – was spectacular. I gazed in awe as I was presented with a view from the front door along a stone-flagged passage all the way to the back of the house where, through a corresponding half-glazed door, I looked straight out up the valley to the hills of Exmoor in the distance.

'Cup of tea? Glass of wine? Or do you want to check out your room first?' She relieved me of my laptop and my bag and stood looking at me expectantly, her robe falling open to reveal the freckles spotting her chest.

'Gussie, this house is staggering! I had no idea you lived in such grandeur. I imagined you snuggled up in a hovel at the end of a muddy lane. I'm impressed.'

'I'm not *completely* hopeless,' she said and we both laughed. It was an old family joke. Gussie, younger than me by five years and very much the baby in her own family, seemed to have been born with an inferiority complex. For some reason we could never quite fathom, she always felt slighted by her older sisters. She had started protesting in the playpen. Yes, she *could* keep up if they went on a long walk and of *course* she was old enough (aged six) to stay up for Cissie's fifteenth birthday party. Until it became so ingrained in her that when, in her adolescence, we started to compliment her on her appearance, her jokes or indeed anything at all, her stock response was a churlish *I'm not completely hopeless.*

But the truth was that I'd always had a soft spot for Gussie because she was the one person in the family who *was* hopeless – or, more to the point, even more hopeless than I was. Or so it appeared. Yet in a way Gussie had the edge on me because while she didn't have a career and had failed in her marriage, she did have an ability that I severely lacked.

Gussie was comfortable having people around her.

It's an odd thing being a loner. It's not the same as being lonely, not at all. In fact it's quite the opposite. If you're a genuine loner you actually don't *want* people around you. You tend to shoo them away because you crave your own company and no one else's and everybody thinks you're a cranky self-obsessed misfit.

Which of course you are but it's not a quality you want to acknowledge in yourself. Looking at it objectively I can see it sounds mad. You want friends but you don't necessarily want to see them. You want a man but you don't want to live with him. You want children but – oh God, I hadn't thought that one through. Would they have to raise themselves?

'Lee-Lee, don't stand there on the doorstep. You haven't even seen the rest of the house yet. And by the way I got it dirt cheap because of the river.'

'The river,' I repeated, bewildered. I had noticed on arrival that the house was adjacent to a bridge, which meant one side of it bordered the river. Surely that was a plus?

'It floods,' said Gussie.

'How often?'

'Time will tell. I've been here over a year and it's never got further than the first step down to the garden. Look, why don't you take your bags up and then come down and join me in the kitchen? Your room's at the top of the stairs, turn left and it's the door at the end of the passage. It's about three miles away from mine. I take it you're still a fully paid-up member of the Polar Bear Club?'

My friend Cath had once likened me to a polar bear – they live apart and only come together to mate – and I'd subsequently announced the formation of the Polar Bear Club, maintaining there were millions of people all over the world who craved solitude as much as I did. So far I was the only member.

But Gussie had always accepted me for exactly what I was and I loved her for it. And I positively adored her when I saw the room she'd given me. It ran the length of the building from front to back and it was huge with a welcoming fireplace at one end.

It did not, however, have any furniture except for a king-size bed and a table and chair. And a cursory check on my way downstairs revealed that the same went for all the other rooms. Great space, wonderful proportions, all the original moldings but virtually empty.

Except for the kitchen, which was crammed with an odd assortment of second-hand junk and was clearly where Gussie spent most of her time.

'I've been asleep all day,' she said as I accepted a glass of Beaujolais, 'and I'm afraid I've done absolutely nothing about dinner.'

'Well, let me take you out,' I said, 'what about that restaurant you work in? Or do you have to work tonight?'

She rolled her eyes at me. 'Of *course* I don't have to work tonight. They've closed the place down.'

'Who has?'

'The council, what are they called? The Health and Whatsit authorities. There's nothing wrong with the kitchen, it's all perfectly clean, no rats running around or anything but they won't let us re-open until the results of the post-mortem are known, until we know why the person died. Although everyone's assuming it was because she was allergic to peanuts.'

Peanuts! My mother hadn't said anything about peanuts.

'Well, isn't there somewhere else we can go?'

'I'm not setting foot outside my front door.' The sudden hounded look on her face shook me. 'I don't like the way people have been staring at me since the restaurant was closed. As if it was *my* fault.'

'Well, we'll stay in and I'll cook you a meal,' I said gently. I opened her refrigerator door and shut it in a hurry. A desiccated lemon and the stink from a bottle of sour milk. That was it. Suddenly I felt depressed. When had she last eaten?

'Gussie, I didn't drive all the way down here to starve. Are there any shops still open?'

'There's a Spar at the end of the street by the church, I don't think they close till seven. They have a deli section at the back with some rather good local sausages,' she added hopefully.

It was only half past six but there was no one else on the street as I walked up the road past a Post Office, a butcher's and a greengrocer's, all firmly closed. I was walking through the center of Frampton Abbas but it might as well have been three in the morning. The place was deserted and the scarcity of street lamps made for a distinctly murky atmosphere that gave me the creeps. It was with some relief that I turned a corner and came upon the glaring neon illumination of an establishment that announced it was The Frampton Fish Bar. *Fish 'n' Chips,* I thought. *That's what we'll have.*

'Where does the cod come from?' I asked the youth behind the counter. He glared at me and said nothing.

I'd had it drummed into me by my mother – all the way from New York – that eating cod was a conservationist minefield. Everywhere was over-fished – the North Sea, the Irish Sea, the east Baltic, Norway, you name it. But as far as I could remember anything line-caught in British waters and Iceland was OK.

12

'The cod,' I repeated, 'that's in the batter. Where does it come from?'

'The kitchen,' said the youth. Now he was looking at me as if I were insane.

'Just give me haddock and chips twice, loads of salt and vinegar.' My mother had never said anything about haddock.

I found the little supermarket nestling incongruously beside the church. I picked up a carton of what I called some 'designer soup', cheddar and broccoli, and, thinking ahead to lunch the next day, I asked the man behind the counter if he had any local sausages.

'Sold out this morning.' His tone wasn't helpful.

'Well, I'll just take these,' I said after I'd wandered back down the three short aisles. I handed him half a dozen eggs, some mushrooms and a bag of salad. 'And maybe a sliced wholewheat if you've got it. '

'Over there.' He didn't move, but called after me. 'Will you be wanting a bottle of wine at all?'

His tone was marginally short of hostile. I paid and left in a hurry. I had almost made it back to Gussie's when a door across the street from her opened and an old woman stepped out into the street. I was about to nod politely to her when I saw that she was clad only in her nightdress. I thought of Gussie greeting me in her dressing gown. Was this how people lived their lives in Frampton Abbas? Ready for bed by six thirty?

But then I saw that the woman had bare feet and she had begun to hobble with grim determination up the street.

It wasn't even one of those prissy Viyella nighties that you buttoned up all the way to your chin to keep out the winter cold. It was a flimsy knee-length cotton affair, sleeveless and, I was horrified to see, totally transparent when the old woman passed under one of the pathetic quota of street lamps.

She had the bandy-legged walk of the aged and infirm and I watched mesmerized as she suddenly lurched off the pavement into the middle of the road and came to a dead halt. I heard the sound of a vehicle approaching the bridge behind

13

me and I leapt into action, dumping the shopping on Gussie's doorstep and charging up the road to shepherd the old woman to safety.

I could have lifted her up in my arms, she was so shrunken and frail, but her voice when she turned to speak to me was strong and robust, with just the merest hint of a quaver, and I could hear it easily above the roar of the delivery lorry thundering by.

'They never brought my dinner so I had to go shopping. I was on my way to the bank. Where are you going?'

Her smile was rapturous and I was almost certain that the teeth she flashed at me were her own. Her hair was a mist of snowy white fluff like cotton wool and looking down on her I could see the bald patches where her scalp glowed pink in the cold.

As we stood there, I was aware that she was wheezing and shivering. I had to get her inside as quickly as possible before she froze to death. I placed a hand under her elbow and guided her back across the road towards the house she had come out of. Pray God the door was still open.

It was and I ushered her inside. I grabbed a shawl from the floor and wrapped it around her shoulders. Exhausted, she collapsed in a wing chair by the fire with paroxysmal, shaking chills. They appeared almost violent and her teeth chattered. As I laid the palm of my hand against her feverish forehead, I took note of the wing chair. It was no ordinary piece of furniture. I'd once taken a course in antiques and I placed it as early eighteenth century, walnut with padded back and sides and those curious outscrolled arms that I'd only ever seen once before. There was a rumor going around that the bottom had fallen out of the antiques market, but if it hadn't this chair would fetch over a thousand pounds easy. I looked around and saw that the small square room was crammed with treasures. I spied a Victorian rosewood button-backed chair on turned legs with casters, a mahogany secretaire bookcase whose top brushed the ceiling – probably George III and worth at least three thousand pounds – and her ancient box TV set was perched precariously atop a demi-lune mahogany cabinet with a marble top whose origin I couldn't quite place.

She seemed to have a slight fever but it hadn't suppressed her appetite.

'I'm hungry,' she said and now her voice had sunk to a pathetic murmur.

'Stay there,' I told her, 'don't move an inch. I'll be right back.'

I propped the door open, raced across the road and returned with the fish 'n' chips. I shut the door, waved at her and went through to the back of the house to look for the kitchen.

There was an oak dresser with stained pine back and base-boards, probably eighteenth century Welsh, but apart from that everything seemed to be coated in the original 1960s Formica, including the small rectangular kitchen table over by the window. There was linoleum on the floor and an old fridge whose doors had rounded edges stood in the corner emitting a deafening hum. A peek inside told me it was completely empty. Her electric stove was covered in grime and I averted my eyes in disgust as I unwrapped the fish 'n' chips and popped them in the oven to warm them.

While I was waiting I sneaked a look around. The house was much smaller than I had at first thought, just the front room and the kitchen on the ground floor, no dining room that I could see. I couldn't help comparing it with Gussie's just across the road, about five times as large and virtually empty and yet this little two up, two down was chockablock with stuff.

I opened the back door and looked across the yard to an outhouse with a door that was freshly painted. Intrigued, I wandered over only to find it locked. I peeped through the adjacent window and instead of the gardening equipment or garbage cans I had expected to find, I saw a table with a large computer on it, a chair and a bright red filing cabinet. A pad and a mug holding pens stood beside the computer and it was all very neat with a waste-paper basket placed just so on the floor beside the chair. The orderly image was slightly marred by a laptop placed in a haphazard fashion at one end of the table with a cluster of loose papers to one side of it. The brickwork of the walls had been whitewashed, there was a piece of rush matting on the floor and I couldn't for the life of me picture what the old lady I had just left would get up to in here.

I suddenly remembered the fish 'n' chips in the oven and ran back to the kitchen to retrieve them before they burned to a crisp. The old lady was waiting patiently for me and I was treated to another ravishing smile as I put the plate of fish 'n' chips on a tray, laid a blanket over her knees and placed the tray on her lap.

Her eyes were bigger than her stomach. She ate a few bites with apparent relish but soon pushed the tray away and sank back in the chair. I kneeled down and gently fitted her bare feet into the slippers under the chair and then sat back to watch in silence as she picked up a chip in her fingers and brought it, trembling, to her mouth. I'd read about how social workers asked elderly people with dementia a string of mundane questions to test their memory.

'Who's the prime minister?' I asked her when she'd swallowed the chip.

'I am,' she said happily and I almost groaned aloud.

'Are you here all on your own?'

She nodded.

'What's your name?'

'Maggie.'

'I'm Lee,' I said, 'I've come to stay with my cousin. Gussie Bartholomew. She lives across the road from you. Do you know her?'

The old lady's face lit up. 'Gussie,' she repeated. 'Lovely.' Then after a beat she added 'red' and pointed to her own hair.

'Who normally gives you your dinner?' I asked her.

'Gussie,' she said. 'Red.'

Could this be true? Gussie, who couldn't boil an egg and didn't have a thing in her own fridge. Surely not.

'There's a computer in your outhouse,' I said. 'Did you know?'

She looked at me and smiled. Maybe she didn't know what a computer was or was I being patronizing of the elderly to think that? Or maybe she thought it was presumptuous of me to imagine she didn't know what she had on her own property.

But her reply, when it came, surprised me.

'It's my son-in-law's,' she said quite distinctly. 'He takes care of me.'

Not very well, I said under my breath. I wondered when she'd last had a bath and whether I should offer to help her. In the end I decided it would be encroaching a little too quickly on her privacy and asked instead what she planned to do with her evening.

'Tired,' she said and then with surprising agility, she got to her feet and pushed aside a chenille curtain to reveal a narrow staircase leading out of the room.

'Bye-bye,' she said and with a cheerful wave she disappeared.

I cleared away the plate, rinsed it off and left it on the draining board. I was tempted to go upstairs and check she was all right but I had sensed a certain amount of pride lurking beneath her frail exterior and I didn't want to overstep the mark.

I made my way back to Gussie's wondering whether I had enough for supper now we no longer had the fish 'n' chips. Mercifully, the rest of the shopping was still sitting on Gussie's step. I could never have got away with that in London, I thought, as I let Gussie's knocker crash down with a resounding bang.

Once again she didn't answer and I began to wonder if she had returned to bed. After all, I hadn't exactly come straight back with the shopping. But then I heard her faint cry from within. 'It's open.'

She was collapsed at the kitchen table – oak, farmhouse, circa nineteenth century, my mind was still in antique mode –

her head in her hands. When she looked up at me I could see she had been crying.

'Oh Lee-Lee.' I dropped the shopping in a hurry as she got up and came towards me with arms outstretched, flinging herself against my chest and clinging to me.

'What on earth has happened?'

'Sylvia called,' she stepped away from me, still clasping my hands.

'Who's Sylvia?'

'She's the owner of the restaurant where I've been working.'

'What's the problem? Why have you been crying?'

'She called to tell me they've told her the results of the post-mortem. The woman who died, it was as everyone suspected. She had a peanut allergy and when they did an examination of the contents of her stomach, they found she had ingested something with a peanut trace – maybe peanut oil.'

'Did she tell you about her allergy when she ordered?'

'Not exactly,' Gussie shook her head. 'She just said *I'll have a green salad. No nuts!* She was quite emphatic about that so I figured she had a problem with them. But it's not as if we'd put nuts in a green salad anyway.'

'Well, was there anything on the menu that might have had a trace of peanut?'

'Nothing!' said Gussie defiantly.

'So what's the problem? She can't have eaten whatever it was at the restaurant.'

'No one was with her when she died and she hadn't seen a doctor in ages so there's going to be an inquest. It's what Sylvia said that's got me so upset. She said I would have to face the music at the inquest – that's how she put it: *face the music*. Because if there was any question that the woman had been given peanut oil in the restaurant, then it was my fault whether I was there on my own or not.'

'But why?'

18

'Because I make the salad dressing. That's just about the only thing I'm allowed to do and then we keep it ready made in a jug. And it never has peanut oil in it. Sylvia knows that yet she made it quite clear that this time she thought I must have accidentally added some.'

'But you didn't?'

'Of *course* I didn't!' Gussie was on the point of tears.

'Well then, that's what you have to say at the inquest.'

'There's something else,' she whispered, 'something I haven't told anyone.'

I looked at her and waited.

'The morning after – the peanut woman had been in the night before but we didn't yet know what had happened to her – I went in around eleven as I always do to begin my prep work for lunch and I noticed that the salad dressing had been thrown away.'

'And normally it wouldn't have been?'

'Oh, yes. I make a fresh dressing every day but *I'm* always the one who throws it out and I usually don't do that until the next day. This time someone else had got rid of it the night before. I probably wouldn't have thought twice about it but when I went to the cupboard to get the olive oil to make a fresh dressing, there wasn't any. We buy it in bulk and decant it into this big plastic bottle.' She mimed pouring it from one container to another.

'One of my jobs is to take out the garbage and I saw this bottle poking out the bag and it wasn't quite empty. Sylvia's always going on about not letting anything go to waste so I thought I'd use this last bit in the bottom of the bottle to start the fresh dressing. And I could tell immediately that it smelled different.'

'Peanut oil?' I said.

Gussie nodded. 'In a dressing, the olive oil would mask the smell but on its own it was quite prominent.'

'So why haven't you told anyone? And what did you do with the bottle?'

19

She reached under the kitchen table for a bag from which she produced a plastic bottle. She handed it to me and I took the top off and sniffed.

'Gussie, I can definitely smell peanuts.'

'I know,' she said. 'That's what I mean. But it was wet when I found it. It had been washed on the outside – you know, wiped clean of prints. The only ones on it would be mine and I haven't shown it to anyone else because I know no one would believe me. I was alone when I found that bottle in the garbage. Sylvia's as good as pointed the finger at me anyway. You see, what really frightens me is that we just don't have peanut oil in the kitchen. Someone brought that bottle in and it wasn't me.'

'Gussie, are you saying what I think you're saying?'

'I think I am.' Gussie looked at me in horror. 'I think whoever it was knew about her allergy and added the peanut oil to the dressing deliberately. I think what I'm saying is that—'

'Whoever it was intended to kill her,' I finished and we both sat down at the kitchen table with a bump.

Chapter Two

Next morning the place was buzzing.

I was woken at the crack of dawn by what sounded like a tank regiment rolling through the village and when I staggered out of bed to the window, I saw a procession of farm vehicles and Land Rovers trundling over the bridge. I opened the window in what I thought was true country spirit, ready to breathe in some healthy fresh air and was met by a blast of pig manure.

And then my head began to pound with one of the worst headaches I'd ever experienced and I remembered the copious quantities of wine Gussie and I had sunk the night before. Gussie might not have a thing to eat in the house but she had enough wine to flood the river.

Once I'd calmed her down a little, I had set about making her a mushroom omelette.

'I'm sorry I was such a long time,' I said, 'but I saw this old woman wandering along the street in her nightdress and bare feet. I wound up taking her home – she lived right across the street – and then she said she was hungry so I gave her the fish 'n' chips I'd bought for us.'

'Oh my God! Maggie! I forgot all about her.' Gussie's tone was mortified.

'She said she was the prime minister.'

'It's not as crackers as it sounds,' said Gussie. 'Her name's Maggie Blair and everyone's always kidded her about it. But she must have been *starving*! She probably hasn't had anything to eat since the restaurant closed.'

'She eats *there*?'

'Don't be daft,' said Gussie, 'she's senile. She shouldn't be living on her own but she refuses to move out of that house. No, we take her one meal a day. We run across the road from the restaurant every evening before we get going. It's a kind of gourmet Meals on Wheels. Her daughter set it up, the daughter that can't be bothered to come down and see her, that is.'

'It must cost the earth or does she get a special rate?'

'Sylvia giving someone a special rate? You have to be joking.'

Talk of Sylvia had Gussie returning to her usual animated self, I noted. Clearly she wasn't a fan of her employer.

'I can overlook quite a few flaws in people,' Gussie went on, 'but the one thing I can't stand is meanness. In all the time I've worked there, I've never known Sylvia offer anyone a free drink or anything on the house, not even her regular customers. She doesn't know the meaning of the word goodwill. She owns the restaurant, right? All the profits go straight into her pocket but she always divvies up the tips so she gets a share of them too. I feel dreadful about Maggie. It's typical of Sylvia to forget all about her but *I* should have remembered her.'

'Where is this restaurant?'

'Just up the road, right opposite Maggie's house. You must have seen it. It's called The Pelican.'

'*That?*' I recalled seeing some tables and chairs behind a window. 'It looked like just a cafe.'

'Well, it calls itself a bistro but I'm telling you, they come from far and wide for the food.'

'And you worked there, Gussie?'

'I know, I know. How could anyone employ *me* in a restaurant? Well, I did the grunt work. I washed up, laid the tables, waitressed sometimes, took the bookings. They never let me anywhere near the food – except for that night.'

'You'd better tell me what happened.' I reached for the largest cafetière I could see. I had a feeling it was going to be a long night. 'Is Sylvia the chef? Was she there that night?'

'Not at first. That was the problem. And no, while she takes most of the credit, she doesn't cook much because the truth of the matter is she doesn't really know how, not in a busy restaurant kitchen anyway.'

'So why did she open The Pelican?'

'It was a classic case of someone thinking "it would be so nice to have a restaurant." Gussie's face registered contempt. 'Apparently all her friends told her that her dinner parties were so wonderful, she should set up somewhere where they could come and have a night out. But why she picked that building is a mystery. It's a disastrous place for a restaurant. There's nowhere near enough space.'

'For the tables?'

'No, in the kitchen. There's no room for a big six-burner range, we've only got an electric stove, an extra oven and a microwave. There's no gas mains in Frampton Abbas, only Calor gas and there's no room in our kitchen to store the bottles. That's why we have to have electric. And there's not even a yard outside to store the rubbish. We have to negotiate with the neighbor to keep it in his garden until we lug it up the alley on collection day.'

'It sounds like the most Mickey Mouse operation I've ever heard of,' I said. 'So if Sylvia can't cook, who does?'

'She really got lucky. There was this guy turned up about nine months ago looking for some part-time cooking. For cash. André Balfour. This man, Lee-Lee, I tell you, he cooked like a dream so of course she asked him to stay on.'

'So he's the chef?'

'Well, yes, he is but he keeps a low profile. It really worked out well for Sylvia. She swans about doing front of house and taking all the credit while he slaves away in the kitchen, saving her bacon if you get my meaning. But it's weird, he has zero interest in making himself known. He talks to us but he never says a word to the punters, discourages people from coming into the kitchen. He just wants to lie low by the looks of things and that suits Sylvia fine.'

'Have you any idea why?' I was curious.

'There's a woman comes in now and again to help out as a pastry chef and she got him talking once. She reckons there's an ex-wife somewhere in the picture. Could be she's after him for alimony.'

'So he was there the night when—'

'No, he *wasn't*, Lee-Lee. No one was there. I was on my own for the first part of the evening. That's why everything went pear-shaped. André had the night off.'

'And Sylvia?'

'She was supposed to be there. I'd gone home for a nap after lunch and I was back there around four thirty to sweep up and lay the tables. Sylvia usually arrives about five to get the starters sorted but she called me in a panic and said she'd had to go to Exeter, didn't say why, and she'd be late getting back. In the meantime I'd have to open up, greet everyone, take the orders and get the starters going.

'Well, by this time, Lee-Lee, I was almost shitting myself, I was in such a panic. Sylvia talked me through what I had to do but she got all sarcastic when I didn't grasp something first time round and asked her to repeat it, began pronouncing everything really slowly as if she were talking to an idiot.'

I could picture it well. Gussie could get seriously flustered if she thought someone was getting impatient with her.

'The line-up for the starters wasn't too bad that night, as it happened. Potted shrimp. Sylvia had made that after lunch before she left, which was a shame because it's the one thing I know how to do. It's just shrimp and—' She looked blank for a second. 'What else do you put with it?'

'Clarified butter?' I suggested.

'That's it, and you put it in little pots. Well, they were all ready sitting on the top shelf of the fridge, Sylvia told me. All I had to do was get them out. How hard was that?'

'And what else?'

'Chicken salad, and here's where I had to pay attention. It wasn't the lettuce and stuff. That was easy. I can wash a lettuce as good as anyone and I just had to lay it out on the plates so it looked nice.'

'A *bed* of lettuce, isn't that what they say?'

'There you go,' Gussie smiled. 'Well, all I had to do was lay the chicken on top of that. And then there was soup. Cream of carrot and something. All I had to do was heat it up. Sylvia would take over as soon as she arrived.'

'And did she?'

'Yes, but by that time it was too late. Luckily we weren't too busy, it *was* Sunday night after all. We can do twenty-seven covers. Imagine if they'd all turned up! In the end there were only sixteen.

'Four people had the chicken salad. Then three people had the soup and that was my first big problem. I ladled it into bowls with every intention of popping them into the microwave at the last moment and then I realized I had no idea how to work the microwave.'

'What happened?'

'I came clean, didn't I?' said Gussie with disarming candor. 'And a young man came into the kitchen and showed me what to do. People can be so nice sometimes, can't they?'

I'd seen Gussie's effect on people. She could be irresistible without even knowing it.

'So that's seven. The rest all had the chicken?'

'Oh, no, only three. The peanut woman just had a green salad, as I said, but loads of people didn't have a starter at all. I remember being worried that Sylvia would say I hadn't pushed them enough. But then something happened that got me in an even worse state.'

'What was that?'

'Just as I'd given everyone drinks and was laying everything out in the kitchen ready to serve, I turned on the tap to wash my hands and no water came out. Would you believe it?

25

I had to call Keith the plumber and for the rest of the night we had to step over him as he lay on the floor fiddling under the sink. His stomach, Lee-Lee, it was disgusting. His shirt was pulled right up over it and it was like a big fat jellyfish lying on the floor.'

'So what was she like, the peanut woman? Who was she having dinner with?'

'Well, that's what was so strange. Nobody else showed up. She was the first to arrive and she was all edgy. She said her name, Rosemary Waters. Anyway, she wanted to know if anyone had come in asking for her.'

'How old?'

'Oh, I'm hopeless at ages. Probably early thirties,' said Gussie. 'She'd made the reservation for two people and while she was waiting, she looked up expectantly every time someone came in. And I have a funny feeling she didn't know the person she was waiting for because if a man came in on his own, she stared at him until he joined someone else. But what was really weird,' Gussie looked at me, 'was that she suddenly decided she was going to go ahead and order and when I said didn't she want to wait for whoever was coming, and that it was quite all right, she came over all surprised and said she wasn't expecting anyone and couldn't she come in and have a quiet meal on her own?'

'And that was when she ordered her salad with no nuts?'

'Right, and I think I know who she was waiting for.'

'You do?'

'Well, I don't know his name but my guess is she was on a blind date, probably someone she met online. And then when he didn't show, she was embarrassed and pretended she was on her own. Didn't want me to know she'd been stood up.'

'Clever old Gussie. How'd you work that one out?'

Gussie laughed. 'Easy. Takes one to know one.'

I remembered the emails she'd sent me about a new boyfriend every month.

'You've been meeting people online?'

Her face lit up. 'I'm totally addicted. Exmoormates.com. I meet the most amazing men, Lee-Lee. They're farmers, mostly. Country guys, that's the point of this particular service. We chat for hours and some of them are really good-looking if their photos are anything to go by. I fall in love every week!'

'So you go out on dates all the time?' I had a fleeting vision of Gussie lying atop a haystack, tenderly removing a blade of straw from someone's mouth before she kissed them.

'No!' she said emphatically. 'I don't. That's what I mean when I said it takes one to know one. I've had loads of men interested in me but I've never actually met one. We have a great correspondence, sometimes for months, and we know absolutely everything there is to know about each other but then I always get cold feet about The Date.'

'And you stand them up?'

'Yes.' She flashed me a guilty look. 'Is that dreadful?'

'I think it's very wise,' I said. 'I don't approve of Internet dating.'

'Oh, you're so stuffy, Lee-Lee.' Gussie leaned across the table and tapped my forearm playfully. 'And you're a scaredy-cat. You always think something terrible's going to happen to you.'

She was right, of course. I'd always had an almost pathological fear of being murdered. I mean, I don't imagine anyone actually runs around begging for it unless you count that man who answered the online ad posted by an urban cannibal who wanted to chop up someone and eat them for his dinner. An *online* advertisement. I rest my case. Bad things happen online.

But I had to admit that I was a bit paranoid. If I got on the tube at Notting Hill and there was only one other person in the carriage with me, the minute we entered the tunnel I immediately assumed they were going to come over and strangle me before we got to High Street Kensington. I'd actually get out and try to find a carriage with people in it, even if it meant waiting for the next train.

The thing was, I only had to read about an attack happening *some*where in the world and I immediately started assuming it would automatically happen to *me*. And I'd read about bad things happening to people via the Internet. And on blind dates.

'Well, maybe,' I conceded. 'But what I really don't get about dating online is that the whole point of meeting someone is that knock-out punch you get when you first lay eyes on them. That's what it's all about in my book. Chemistry. And photos don't do it.'

Gussie was looking at me wide-eyed.

'Beginning a relationship by email is so *false*!' I went on, warming to my theme. 'Real love has to have a basis in physical attraction. It's not about whether you've both seen *Lost in Translation* twenty-five times or you both have the same favorite color. You've got to see the way he looks at you. Eye contact is everything.'

I had no idea why I was banging on so knowledgeably since my own love life was in such a hopeless state. I think Gussie sensed as much because she tossed me a sly look.

'I was furious about you dumping Tommy,' she said and when I opened my mouth to protest, she held up her hand to silence me and continued, 'but I'm more furious with you for not telling me. How could you not call and say you were back in London? If I hadn't contacted Tommy when I was trying to find you, I'd never have found out.'

'Gussie, I'm truly sorry,' I said. Why was it that whenever I genuinely wanted to express remorse, I always wound up sounding trite? *I'm truly sorry.* It was more like whining – but I had to try and make her understand. 'I'm sorry I didn't tell you. I'm sorry I wasn't here to see you through your divorce. I'm sorry I've been such a—'

'—such an invisible polar bear? I don't know why I'm even bothering to mention it, Lee-Lee. You *never* call me. You never call *any*one. I was so surprised when you phoned and said you were coming down to stay with me, I completely forgot to tell you I'd spoken to Tommy.'

'What did he say?' I found I was suddenly extremely nervous to hear the answer. 'About me, I mean?'

'Well, this'll shake you.' Gussie wagged a finger at me. 'He didn't say anything about you beyond telling me that you weren't together anymore and that you were back in London. I tried desperately to get him to open up – you know how I love Tommy – but he wouldn't budge. He said I'd have to ask you.'

So I told Gussie the whole story – well *almost* the whole story. I told her that I'd worked it out in my head that I didn't want to get married. Ever. Not to Tommy, not to anyone. I was a polar bear. I could only function properly on my own. And that then I'd done something I'd always regretted. I'd hopped on a plane back to England and left him a letter trying to explain. Just a stupid, inadequate *letter* that I'd been working on for months before I actually decided I couldn't go through with marrying him. At least he'd had the guts and the decency to tell me face to face when he'd changed his mind. But that was Tommy all over: decent, kind, dependable and then there were those times when he was like a little boy lost, his bottom lip quivering with hurt because I'd been so crabby with him, as was my wont.

But, I confessed, I missed him dreadfully. No one knew how to handle my neurotic, quirky moods like he did – except maybe Gussie and I couldn't very well marry her. But what I missed most was his tenderness, the giant bear hugs and the Eskimo kisses he insisted we share when I was being a particularly difficult polar bear. All we did was rub noses but it never failed to send an erotic charge through me.

'I haven't heard a single word from him since I left America,' I said. 'I don't know if he's angry and bitter and deeply hurt or if he's managed to become totally indifferent to me by now.'

'Well, I'm afraid I can't tell you,' said Gussie. 'So have you moved on? Is there anyone in your life? Are you in love?'

'Yes. No.' I said hastily. I *was* in love – or rather I was in *obsess* – with Max. He was the reason I'd come back to

England but I hadn't heard anything from him for months so, as far as confiding in Gussie was concerned, there wasn't much point in going there.

'Well then, maybe you'd like to join Exmoormates with me and we could go on double dates?'

'But you've just told me you don't go on actual dates,' I pointed out.

'Not yet,' she said, 'but I'm going to soon. Definitely. There's a bloke I'm really excited about. I've got a date with him next week. I think I'm going to keep it. I'll show you his profile in the morning.'

'Tell me, Gussie. Do you want to meet someone just to get back at Mickey or do you genuinely think you'll find Mr Right?'

Her answer when she finally whispered it moved me. 'I just want to know that I'm attractive again. You have no idea how much it shook me when Mickey threw me out. I felt like I was the most undesirable, useless female in the universe. I just want to be able to say I'm not completely hideous as well as not completely hopeless. And that's why I always balk at actually meeting them. I'm so worried they'll take one look and run a mile.'

It had taken another bottle of wine to hear the whole sorry tale of the disintegration of Gussie's marriage – yet again I cursed the fact that I'd been in America and unable to be there for her – and by the time we both staggered up to bed we could hardly walk.

Now every step I took down the stairs seemed to reverberate throughout my head and the sight of several empty bottles scattered all over the table made me feel even worse.

There was no sign of Gussie. The least I could do was get the dishes from last night's meal into the dishwasher before she came down.

But there wasn't a dishwasher, not in the kitchen nor in the scullery next door. And judging by the array of Gussie's underwear and nightdresses hanging over the Aga, there wasn't a washing machine either. No furniture, no appliances. Poor Gussie clearly hadn't a bean.

I had got as far as making a pot of coffee and was about to collapse at the kitchen table when I heard Gussie coming down the stairs. But before she appeared my head disintegrated into a million tiny shards of pain as someone banged the front door knocker so hard I half expected to go into the hall and see a hole through to the street.

I heard Gussie scuttle back upstairs. I peeked through the window and saw a woman in a gray duffle coat with one foot on the doorstep and her hand raised. I didn't think I could weather another bang so I opened the door.

The thing about fake smiles is that they never reach the eyes. And I remain innately suspicious of anyone who smiles at me for longer than a minute. Especially when I'm hungover.

'Gussie?' I called hopefully up the stairs. 'Someone to see you.'

The woman stepped into the hall and peered up the stairwell behind me in time to see Gussie mouthing *Tell her to go away. Say I'm not here* and flapping her arms in a dismissive gesture.

'Good morning, Gussie,' said the woman, the too-brilliant smile never leaving her face, 'I need to have a little chat with you.'

'Oh, hi Sylvia,' said Gussie. 'Right now's not very convenient, I'm afraid. My cousin Lee has just arrived. I'll catch up with you later, OK?'

'Well, later isn't all that convenient for me,' said Sylvia and that's when I knew that she was the sort of person who enjoyed delivering bad news with a smile.

Poor Gussie was at a distinct disadvantage. She appeared to be in an even worse condition than I was and in her disheveled state it was all she could do to prop herself up against the Aga, holding her dressing gown tightly around her as if to protect herself from Sylvia's onslaught.

I offered Sylvia a cup of coffee and was rewarded with a furious look from Gussie.

'Would a cappuccino be possible?' said Sylvia, making it clear she had never been inside Gussie's house before.

'I only have instant,' lied Gussie and I moved quickly to stand in front of the cafetière on the counter.

'In that case, perhaps not.' Sylvia gave a little shake of her head. She had mouse-colored curly hair shot with early gray and cut short. She reminded me of a wire-haired fox terrier, the kind that growl and snap at your ankles while wagging their tail at the same time. I watched Gussie flinch as Sylvia went over and put her arm around Gussie's shoulders.

'Gussie, sweetie, I think you know what I'm going to say, don't you? I'm afraid I'm going to have to let you go.'

I have always hated that expression. If you're going to get rid of someone, just do it, just say *You're fired!*

I was proud of Gussie. She didn't scream or protest in any way. She just shrugged, very cool, as if it really didn't mean all that much to her. But in the next couple of minutes, as Sylvia's tone became strangely self-congratulating, I had to restrain myself from ripping the tartan scarf from around her neck and throttling her with it.

'I could have phoned, Gussie,' she said, 'but you know I have integrity. I knew I must come and tell you this face to face. It would be cowardly not to.'

'But *why*?' I yelled, unable to stop myself. 'Why does Gussie have to go? She didn't do anything?'

Sylvia was still smiling. I think that was what made me lose control. Now she turned to me and spoke with exaggerated patience, as if talking to a child who didn't understand English. 'A customer died. Lee, is it?' I nodded. 'And now we know it was due to her eating something contaminated with a peanut trace. All right, so it's the customer's responsibility to see that they don't order anything with nuts in it if they have an allergy but supposing there was something in my restaurant that accidentally got into the salad that poor woman ate?'

She turned to Gussie and by now her smile was horribly condescending. 'Gussie, do you remember that Thai evening we had last summer. I did those Pad Thai noodles and Justine made satay – that's made with peanuts, isn't it?'

I looked at Gussie. *Justine?*

'Justine's my pastry cook,' said Sylvia before Gussie could open her mouth. 'But she's ever so good at all sorts of things. Anyway, what I'm saying is there could have been something peanutty left over from that time and maybe you used it accidentally, Gussie.'

'Satay isn't made from peanut oil,' said Gussie and I glared at her. Why did she have to bring up peanut *oil*?

'I never said it was,' said Sylvia. 'And peanut oil's something we've never had, have we? André's got something against it, hasn't he? André's my chef,' she said before I could appeal to Gussie again. 'I'm sorry, Gussie, I really am, but everyone knows you were the one who served Rosemary Waters whatever she ate that night and I think if you stay there, it's going to make people nervous. I really do.' She turned to me. 'You do see my point, don't you? I have my reputation to think of. I can't risk keeping her in my kitchen.'

'André's kitchen,' muttered Gussie and for an instant Sylvia's smile faded a little.

'Well, they'll want to hear from you at the inquest as well as Gussie,' I said, 'it'll be your overall responsibility.'

Sylvia's smile had now hardened considerably. 'Are you in our business, Lee, *by any chance*?'

'Lee's a writer,' said Gussie. 'She's a famous ghostwriter. She helps celebrities tell their stories.'

Sylvia's face relaxed instantly. '*Do* you? Really? That must be so interesting. And in fact it's also rather fortuitous – is that the right word? You have to watch what you say around writers, don't you?' She winked at Gussie. 'Because you know I've been thinking about doing a book myself. Now that The Pelican's beginning to get quite a reputation. It's either a book or a TV show, I don't know which should come first.'

The look of sheer incredulity that appeared on Gussie's face told me that Sylvia was severely delusional.

'I'd be interested to talk to you about ghosting the book,' Sylvia turned to me. 'I was brilliant at English at school and everyone always told me I'd be a wonderful writer but I really don't have the time. I'd need help, I know I would. Anyway, Lee, it was nice meeting you and if you'd like to have a think about my offer for you to ghost my book, give me a call and we'll have a little chat about it.'

And I'd like to wipe that complacent *little* smile off your stupid face, I thought.

'Perhaps we'd better see if you manage to get your restaurant re-opened first.' I tried to sound ominous.

For a split second Sylvia's smile vanished altogether. It was not a pretty sight. Terriers could be mean, I reflected, but I was beginning to see myself as Gussie's guard dog and I'd make sure my breed was big enough to take Sylvia on. I ventured an exploratory growl and Gussie giggled.

'Oh,' said Sylvia, 'I'm opening again any day now. Closing me down was only a formality. Now they know she died as a result of her allergy, they can't blame it on the restaurant. And with Gussie gone, they've got nothing on me, really, now have they?'

I had the front door open and when neither of us said anything, she backed towards it. She hadn't even taken off her duffle coat so it didn't take long to get rid of her. As soon as she was gone Gussie let rip.

'That woman is the biggest pain in the butt I have *ever* come across,' she yelled. 'But it's her word against mine and there's nothing I can do about it. I bet she's been telling everyone in Frampton Abbas it was my fault. I can tell by the way they look at me whenever I stick my nose outside.' She slipped her arm through mine and leaned her head on my shoulder, 'I want to stay here, Lee-Lee. Until this happened I loved living here. I was beginning to feel settled – and safe. And then Jesus! All that talk about a book and a TV show.' She began moving about the kitchen, clearing up after last night with a lot of angry banging and clattering. My head started to pound all over again. 'Who does she think she is? She can't even cook. If anyone should do a book, it's André. He's the only chef around here and I have a feeling his story might be pretty interesting.'

'I just can't stand those kind of women who go on about how people are always telling them they're so great at something, they should turn professional.' I joined in, '*I can write a book, I can open a restaurant. It's as easy as pie. I don't have to sweat blood and pay my dues like everyone else. My friends tell me I'm good at something so that entitles me to jump on the bandwagon just like that.* She hasn't a fucking clue how hard it is.'

'Right. She just gets other people to do it for her,' said Gussie, 'me, André and now you by the sounds of things.'

'And anyway she can't possibly fire you just like that. It's almost as if she's doing it on a whim.'

'Yes, she can,' said Gussie looking decidedly glum.

'No way,' I said, 'you've got rights, Gussie, you—'

'No,' she said, 'you're wrong. I haven't. I'm paid cash in hand. I'm not on the books. I've got no benefits, no rights at all. She can do exactly what she wants with me. But speaking of work, tell me Lee-Lee, what are you working on at the moment? I never asked.'

'Nothing as it happens. I need to find a job. But forget about that, what we need to do is sort you out. You know it works both ways. She'd probably be in trouble if the Inland Revenue were to find out how she's paying you. We can probably use that somewhere down the line but first we need to find out what really happened with that peanut oil.'

'But how?' Gussie looked defeated. 'I'd love to be in that kitchen and figure out how it was done but I can't go back.'

'But I can,' I said. 'How about this for an idea? She wants me to do her book. When the restaurant is re-opened, why don't I offer my services as your temporary replacement? I need to be in there, to see her in action so I can make her story authentic, and also I might be able to figure out how the peanut oil got into the kitchen. I could pretend it would be valuable research experience for me for writing her book.'

'Do you have any idea what you'd be letting yourself in for?' Gussie sounded skeptical. 'It's hard work running around at everyone's beck and call in that kitchen, Lee.'

'If you can do it—' I stopped.

'If I can do it, how hard can it be?' Gussie grinned. 'But hold on a second, Lee. Do you remember what we said last night? We reckoned someone laced the salad dressing deliberately. We even went so far as to mention the M word. You want to go and work in the kitchen and see if the murderer comes back?'

'We were pretty drunk when we came to that conclusion,' I pointed out. 'There's probably a perfectly reasonable explanation.' I made sure to keep my tone cheerful and light but inside I felt pinpricks of unease begin to fester. Was I really volunteering to walk into what might turn out to be a crime scene? Right now everyone was probably thinking Gussie might have made a deadly mistake. I had to prove otherwise even if that meant starting a murder investigation of my own.

'The other thing I'm really worried about,' said Gussie, 'and this is where you could help out too – is Maggie Blair and who's going to deliver her meals. If you do go and work in the restaurant, you can take her food from there but in the meantime we'd better provide it ourselves.'

'What about her son-in-law?' I said, remembering how the old lady had said he took care of her. 'She said he keeps his computer in her outhouse. Is he a writer like me? And doesn't he take her food?'

'Be a bit hard,' said Gussie. 'Poor old Maggie. Did she really say that? Her dementia must begetting worse. Her son-in-law's dead. He was killed in a car accident four years ago.'

Chapter Three

Maggie Blair, as it turned out, must have been popping up and down the High Street in her nightdress on many a cold night because she succumbed to pneumonia shortly after my visit. When Gussie and I went round the next day with a plate of food, we found her coughing up rusty phlegm and Gussie called the doctor.

I was disheartened by the interminable time it took the ambulance to arrive and somehow I knew as Maggie was lifted into it that she would not be coming back. Gussie went with her to the hospital and, alone in Maggie's house, I wandered into the kitchen and a noise in the yard made me look through the window.

The door to the outhouse was open, banging in the wind. *The computer!* I thought and rushed outside.

The outhouse was completely empty. No table, no computer, no chair, waste-paper basket and no laptop. And no papers either. Everything was gone.

Had there ever been a computer there? Had I imagined it? Maggie had sounded so convincing when she had said it was her son-in-law's, the son-in-law who had been killed four years ago. But Maggie had been suffering from dementia and seeing the empty space on the table where the computer had been, I began to wonder if I was too.

I turned the handle of the door to the outhouse and it opened. I stood in the middle of the brick room and noticed that the paintwork on the windowsills and skirting boards was fresh, and low down on the wall behind the table and beside an electric socket there was a phone jack. Who needed a phone in an outhouse?

But I didn't get a chance to delve further into the mystery of the outhouse because Maggie was gone before we knew it.

'She died last night,' said Gussie, bursting into the kitchen a few days later after a lightning dash to the Post Office. Since my arrival she was beginning to make little forays outside, venturing further afield with each new day. 'They were all so busy talking about it in the Post Office, no one even bothered to glare at me. The funeral's at the end of the week and she's being buried in the graveyard behind the church. You'll come with me, won't you, Lee-Lee? Here,' she handed me a flimsy newspaper, 'they wrote about Rosemary Waters in the local rag. *Her* funeral's this afternoon so I'd better keep my head down.' She tapped the front page. 'Sylvia's going to love this. Normally she's ecstatic when The Pelican gets a write-up in the *Frampton Gazette* but judging from the headline she'll go nuts when she sees this. Have a read and tell me what they say while I put the kettle on.'

I had forgotten who Rosemary Waters was but I remembered soon enough when I saw the headline. **EXMOOR FARMER'S DAUGHTER DIES FOLLOWING MEAL IN LOCAL RESTAURANT.** I scanned the article quickly and learned that Rosemary Waters had been thirty-two and living in a converted barn adjacent to her parents' farm. She had worked in an estate agent's office. I stared at her picture and saw a buxom-looking woman, slightly overweight, lank curtains of straight black hair falling either side of an anxious face. Another photograph showed her distraught parents with their farm in the background. It looked like a pretty remote part of the world. I read the mother's quote. *Throughout her childhood we lived in fear of this happening every single day.*

She had one attack when she was tiny. First her ear turned red, then a rash spread to her neck, her chest. Soon there were these terrible welts all over her body and she could hardly breathe. And all because she'd had a peanut butter sandwich at a playdate. After that I could hardly bear to let her out of my sight but when she made it out of her teens, I began to relax. She was such a responsible girl. She knew she had to be vigilant and she always told people about her allergy. That this should have happened now – just when I was beginning to think she was safe.

I had been reading this out loud to Gussie but I stopped short and surreptitiously slipped the *Frampton Gazette* out of sight under a cushion. Gussie could do without hearing the last few lines.

Augusta Bartholomew, thirty-five, was working in the restaurant on the night of the tragedy and served Rosemary Waters her last meal – a green salad. There is speculation that the salad dressing could have contained the fatal peanut oil although Sylvia Leach, the manager of The Pelican, stated that peanuts were not normally staples of the restaurant's kitchen. She confirmed that Miss Bartholomew would not return to the restaurant when it re-opened. Miss Bartholomew was not available for comment.

Miss Bartholomew, I noted, not Mrs Beresford. Had Gussie even told anyone in Frampton Abbas that she had been married, I wondered?

'Now come along, Gussie,' I said, adopting my bossy older cousin mode that never failed to provoke Gussie into action, 'we've got to get to the bottom of this. Sit down and tell me who was in the restaurant that night. What kind of customers do you get in a place like that in the depths of the English countryside?'

'Oh, you'd be surprised, we get all sorts in there,' said Gussie, plunging her hand into a paper bag and bringing out a doughnut. 'Want one? They had them at the Post Office and I couldn't resist. No? You'll regret it. Well, I say all sorts but the young tend to go to the pub so I suppose it's mostly middle-aged people. Well-heeled, it's not cheap. There's quite a few retired accountants and bank managers who live on a modern estate just outside Frampton Abbas. It'd only be a five-minute walk for them but of course they insist on driving here in their Rovers and cluttering up the High Street.' A trickle of synthetic-looking red jam had escaped from her doughnut and her tongue darted out like a snake's to scoop it off her chin. 'Then there's the London crowd who've got second homes round here but you see them in the summer mostly. They stick out a mile when they come in because their clothes are all this century's. The rest of us are a bunch of frumps.' She pulled self-consciously at the shoulders of her bottle-green velour sweatshirt. 'Dressing up for us means taking off our tracksuits and putting on our jeans. Lee-Lee, it's terrifying how quickly you stop bothering what you look like when you move down to the country. You'd never think I'd ever worn Prada and Versace, would you?'

Where was it now? I wondered. Stashed away in Mickey Beresford's basement?

'So by the sounds of things Rosemary Waters wasn't a typical customer?'

'Well, in a way she was. You haven't been in the restaurant yet, Lee-Lee, but it's got quite a romantic atmosphere surprisingly enough given it's Sylvia's place. And it's where couples go if they want to celebrate something special, anniversaries and that. You should have seen the place on Valentine's Day last month. Packed to the rafters. So it's sort of perfect for a first date – even if it was a blind one.'

'So who else was there that night? You said there were sixteen people.'

'Ah! What I didn't tell you was that eight of those people were a family party. The Mortimers. They always come in en masse whenever they have a celebration. They fancy themselves as foodies, do the Mortimers, so any excuse will do. I forget what this one was but it wasn't a birthday or we'd have had to get Justine in to do a cake. She's the pastry chef.'

'The one who got André to talk?'

'Right. So the Mortimers came barreling in, the old man and his missus, their two sons and *their* wives and two brats, not sure which couple they belonged to, one of each maybe. I nearly had a fit when I saw them because they're all so large, they have to pull their chairs much further apart than most people so the aisles become that much narrower and waiting tables is a nightmare.' Gussie shuddered at the thought. She stood up and waddled to a chair, sat down and splayed her legs out wide to show what she meant and I laughed. 'But I have to tell you,' she went on, 'when Rosemary Waters saw them she nearly got up and left and that's when I had a feeling she was meeting someone out of the ordinary.'

'Why?'

'Because old Ma and Pa Mortimer rent a house on the Waters' land and I think Rosemary probably didn't want old Mrs Mortimer eavesdropping on her conversation with whoever she was meeting and then telling Mrs Waters what she'd heard. The two old biddies are quite tight, so I hear. It was well known that Mrs Waters kept poor Rosemary on a tight rein although I suppose it was understandable under the circumstances. She was so worried about what might happen to her. Apparently the poor girl didn't move into the privacy of the barn till she was over thirty – and that was only about twenty minutes ago.'

'So you think the Mortimers are in the clear?'

'Definitely. They've been in the restaurant a zillion times, everyone knows them. The two sons and their families live in Exeter and Taunton but they grew up round here.'

'So who else?'

'Well, Rosemary Waters and her date who never showed up, that makes ten. The other six were three couples. There was a married couple who live at the other end of Frampton Abbas, he's a doctor at Exeter hospital and I think she is too. Dr Jenkins. I think his wife's called Virginia.'

'And the other two couples?'

'Ann Bates and Monica Massey. Two middle-aged women who live together in a rather beautiful Georgian house. It's set high above the road to Tiverton as you leave the village. Must have a stupendous view across the valley. They've lived there for years and keep themselves to themselves. They were very nice to me when I first arrived, kept asking me to go and have a glass of sherry but I never went. I've heard some rather sala-cious rumors about them being lesbians, but who cares? That wasn't what stopped me. I was just so miserable about Mickey, I didn't want to see anyone and they've never asked me since. Pity, really. They're rather jolly.'

'And not likely to have spiked the salad dressing in order to poison Rosemary Waters?'

Gussie looked very solemn. 'You really think that's what happened?'

'It just doesn't sound like the sort of thing that could happen accidentally in a kitchen that never normally had peanut oil in it. I think it looks as if someone spiked the olive oil in your back-up plastic bottle in the store cupboard with peanut oil.'

'So I *did* make the dressing with peanut oil. I am to blame after all.' Gussie was beside herself.

'Of course you're not because you didn't know it was there. You said yourself that olive oil would mask the smell of peanut. You only smelled it when it came to the dregs, which were probably more concentrated. And in fact we really should be focusing on anybody who was in the kitchen that night rather than the restaurant? What about the young man who helped you with the microwave? He must have come into the kitchen.'

'Oh my God!' Gussie groaned. 'He was so nice. You think it was just a ruse? That he slipped peanut oil in the dressing while my back was turned?'

'Who was he?'

'I've no idea. He wasn't a local. He was dining with another man and they had papers and official-looking stuff all over the table. They kept asking me to take things away like the flowers and the bottle of Perrier and the salt and pepper so they would have more room. I assumed it was a work dinner of some kind even though it was a Sunday. I didn't take their reservation but it'll be in the book.'

'So we've got eight Mortimers, Doctor Jenkins and his wife, the lesbians—'

'We don't *know* they're lesbians,' protested Gussie.

'And it's absolutely fine if they are,' I pointed out. 'It's just for purposes of identification, And then there's the business gents, the blind date who never showed and the victim.'

'*Don't* call her that,' shrieked Gussie. 'You sound like a police detective.'

'Well, we've got to *think* like a police detective if we're going to find out what happened. By the way, who's the local policeman? Do you know him?'

'There isn't one,' said Gussie.

'No one? No police station? What happens if you want to report a crime?'

'Well, first of all there's nothing to report unless you call kids going into old ladies' gardens and knocking off the heads of tulips a crime. And if anything does happen you have to call the central police HQ in Exeter. Although I wouldn't bother if I were you.'

'Why is that?'

'There was this story about a man in the next village who came home and found his house had been broken into and all his valuables taken. So he called Exeter and they said yeah, yeah, we'll send someone over but it won't be for a day or so because we're a bit busy at the moment.'

'No!' I was shocked.

'Yes, but wait Lee-Lee, it gets better. The man thought about it for an hour or so, so the story went, and he got himself so worked up he called back and said, "Listen, don't bother sending anyone because I've caught the bugger and whacked him over the head with my spade. He's dead as a doornail." Apparently the police were there within the hour.'

'He didn't really kill him, di—'

'Oh, for God's sake, Lee-Lee, of course not. What I'm trying to get across to you is that murder is just about the only thing that's going to get the police to pay attention.'

'And I'm guessing you don't have too many of those?'

'Actually,' said Gussie, 'there was one about five or six years ago. A woman's body was found under a bale of hay. She'd been strangled and dumped there but there was something fishy about it.'

'Something fishy about a murder, Gussie? Heavens, that's unusual.'

'Shut up.' She glared at me and I was transported back thirty years to the tormented little girl who demanded that her horrible teasing sisters and cousin take her seriously. 'Just listen to me for a change. She was strangled but there was something fishy *beyond* that. Of course I wasn't here then but someone told me all about it. The post-mortem revealed that she had a ton of sleeping pills in her stomach so it looked as if she had been drugged first. But the worst of it was the dog.'

'The dog,' I repeated dully. I knew I didn't want to hear what was coming but there was no way I was going to stop her telling me.

'She had a little poodle and it had been butchered. They found bits of it all over the field. Can you imagine?'

'Who was she?'

'Can't remember her name but she was black.' Gussie made an *Ooh, what have I said face*. 'Should that be Afro-Caribbean?'

'Well, not if she was American,' I pointed out.

She wasn't. I knew who she was – who she had to be at any rate – and she *was* Afro-Caribbean. Jamaican to be precise. Tall and flamboyant and in-your-face striking, to use the words of my friend Cath who had told me all about her. And her skin had been café-au-lait, not black, and she'd had great legs and a long neck and high cheekbones and—

And I wasn't going to go there. I wasn't going to tell Gussie I knew who it was because then I'd have to tell her that the woman had been Max's wife and I wasn't ready to tell her about Max yet.

'Talk me through who was in the kitchen the night the peanut woman was killed,' I said to get her off track, 'there was you and—'

'Me?' Gussie squeaked. 'I didn't do it. You know I didn't.'

'Of course I know you didn't,' I said patiently, 'but as I said, I have to approach this like a detective would. So who else? Sylvia?'

'Sylvia was there later. And Wendy. She's a young girl from the village who's just a miserable skivvy like I was, rushed off her feet at everyone's beck and call. She's a much better dishwasher than I am, poor thing, so she gets landed with that more often than not. Poor Wendy, it was actually her night off but I called her in when I saw the way things were going. She's terrified of André. He reduces her to tears virtually every night. If he shows the slightest sign of losing it – which is every twenty minutes – she starts blubbing. Sometimes I think she just adds Fairy Liquid to her tears and goes to work.'

'So who else came into the kitchen?'

'One of the Mortimer women came in to ask to use the phone to call her babysitter. Apparently they'd left the latest addition to the family at home. Monica Massey popped her head in to ask for another glass of wine. The businessman who was dining with microwave man wanted to know where the loo was. Fair enough. He'd never been there before. And someone did wander in off the street to ask for a reservation for the following night. They do that sometimes, they just don't realize how disrupting it is.'

'And that was it?'

'Except for Keith the plumber who fixed the water problem but he was under the sink for most of the evening. Oh and Mr Walker.'

'Mr Walker?'

'Local wine merchant. I think he quite fancies Sylvia because he's always dropping off a case of something he thinks she ought to try on his way home. I know, I know,' she saw my face, 'he must be desperate to go after her but listen to this. He's one of the men who has posted his details on Exmoormates.com. Of course you don't give your real name but I recognized him from his photo.'

'What's Sylvia's situation? She's not married, I take it?'

'I don't really know much about her private life. I heard she was with someone in Bath and when they broke up, she moved here to lick her wounds. Rather like me.' Gussie made a face. 'God, to think I have something in common with Sylvia. I hope her man wasn't a shit like Mickey. Actually,' she paused and shot me a mischievous grin, 'I hope he was. Serve her right. But, no, she's on the lookout for a man, all right, and my guess is that man is André. She's not too subtle about her interest in him. It's quite nauseating sometimes. Probably why she hired him in the first place. He can behave like a real asshole – get drunk, doesn't turn up for work, insults the customers if they come in the kitchen, he even yells at Sylvia – but she doesn't turn a hair. In fact, she's really rather pathetic around him.'

'She can't afford to lose him since you say he does all the cooking.'

'Right. It's a very odd set-up if you think about it.' Gussie frowned a little. 'She takes his verbal abuse and he lets her take all the credit for the success of the restaurant. Oh God, I just remembered!'

'What?' I looked at her, alarmed.

'The woman who came into the kitchen to call her babysitter, one of the Mortimer daughters-in-law, she had a cardigan slung over her shoulders and it fell off as she was making the call. She didn't notice and I picked it up off the floor. I meant to give it to her but I forgot. I've got it upstairs. I *must* return it to her.'

'Well, perhaps the day of Rosemary Waters' funeral wouldn't be the best time. You can't very well go running up and toss it to her across the grave. Actually,' I looked at Gussie, 'I've had an idea. Why don't we wait a few days and take it back to her in person?'

'Oh, I couldn't!'

'Yes, you could, Gussie. You've got to face these people some time and I'll be with you. And you know what? It'll give us an excuse to ask a few questions about Rosemary Waters. Like who she was supposed to be meeting at The Pelican that night.'

Gussie looked thoughtful. 'Maybe.' She didn't sound convinced. 'Couldn't you go on your own?'

'No I couldn't. We're in this together.'

'You make it sound like we're still ten years old and plotting to give your mother the slip so we can go on an illicit shopping expedition down Portobello Market.'

I smiled but inside I was jumpy. Gussie had always had a problem taking anything seriously while I would invariably worry something to death.

'So you'll come?' I asked her.

'OK but not until after Maggie's funeral on Friday. And in any case we'll have to wait for the weekend because the Mortimer sons are never there during the week and I'm not facing old Ma Mortimer undiluted by the rest of the family.'

And with that she got up and walked out of the kitchen leaving me to reflect on her state of mind. She was still so fragile, I realized, and the knowledge that she might have accidentally killed someone was going to make an even bigger dent in her confidence. From the little she had divulged about the extent to which she had come to terms with her new life, I sensed that she had accepted that she had been nothing more than a trophy wife to Mickey and that she was well out of the marriage. At first I had thought she was behaving in a cowardly fashion by escaping the bitchy rat-race of her former London world and burying herself in such a hick place as Frampton Abbas, but as time went by I saw that she was truly comfortable there. And it made sense. Of my three cousins, Gussie had been the only one who had genuinely loved her Northumberland country upbringing. Aunt Joy and Uncle Bobby had only sent her off to follow Cissie and Flossie to London because they had assumed that was what she wanted. But they had never actually *asked* her.

Cousins have a strange relationship. Gussie and I did not really have that much in common other than we were close in age and were both regarded by our families as annoyingly unconventional. But a cousin can fill the role of surrogate sibling in a reassuring and uncomplicated way if you don't happen to get on with your older sisters and that was what Gussie did for me. Or rather I for her since I was an only child.

So the one thing Gussie and I really did have in common was that our mothers felt we had let the side down. Gussie had a failed marriage and no career to speak of, while, although I had become a ghostwriter, it was not a profession my mother recognized because the very nature of it meant you were invisible and unlikely to receiving glowing reviews in the literary press. But perhaps my worst crime was that I still did not have a husband.

'She's been washing *dishes* for a living?' my mother spluttered down the phone at five thirty the following morning. Virtually every morning since I had been at Gussie's, I had been woken by the frenetic quacking of the ducks racing down the river to clamber on to a slab of stone just below my window. Here they assembled with much squawking and jostling for position to wait for Gussie to stumble out of bed and into the cold February mist some twenty minutes later and throw them some bread. I had had the presence of mind to start taking bread up to my room at night and chucking it out of the window at the first quack in the hope that it would shut them up and we could go back to sleep.

But my mother had beat them to it. Gussie shuffled blearily into the room with the cordless phone and handed it to me. I couldn't very well chuck my mother some silencing crusts down the transatlantic line so I rested my head sideways on the pillow and balanced the receiver on my ear to weather her onslaught. She had an annoying habit of coming back from parties on such a high that she was unable to sleep and thought nothing of picking up the phone. When she had still been in London I had been frequently awoken after midnight and now, with the time difference in New York, it was at dawn. I wasn't sure which was worse.

'And waiting tables,' I said without thinking. Too late, I was grimly aware that I was consolidating Gussie's lowly position in my mother's eyes. She pounced as I suspected she would.

'Does Joy have any idea her daughter has become a wait-ress?' Now she sounded a little gleeful.

'Mum, for God's sake,' I managed to snuggle further under the duvet without dislodging the phone – quite an art, 'isn't it more important that she's been fired because they think she accidentally poisoned someone?'

'Depends which way you look at it.' My mother was not deterred. 'If Gussie can't even be relied on to wash dishes, what can anyone ask of her? On the other hand, isn't it a good thing that she doesn't have to anymore?'

'Well, anyway, when the restaurant re-opens, I'm going to take her place,' I said with a certain amount of satisfaction, 'and if Aunt Joy ever bothers to call poor Gussie, I'll tell her that I'm going to be washing dishes while Gussie makes plans to become a rocket scientist.'

My mother spluttered something about it being much too late to make silly cracks and it was time we all got some sleep.

Gussie giggled. 'I got the gist of that. We are a pair, aren't we? But,' she added wistfully, 'at least Aunt Vanessa picks up the phone.'

'Downstairs,' I said firmly, sensing an impending early morning meltdown, 'Now. I'm making breakfast.'

It was weird for me getting up every day and having no work to do. Normally I would grab a quick cup of coffee and go straight to my desk. But by the time I'd made Gussie bacon and eggs and we'd had a second cup of coffee followed by a leisurely soak in the bath, it was barely nine o'clock. The day stretched before us.

'Gussie, why don't you show me the village? I've been to Spar and the fish 'n' chip shop and Maggie's cottage but other than that, I really haven't explored. I'd like to see it through your eyes. Let's go for a stroll.'

She looked at me as if I were mad but reached for her jacket and a woolly hat with a bobble on it – in which she would never have been seen dead in London – without a word. I followed her out into the street where, instead of turning left up the High Street, she went right over the bridge and marched me to an ugly modern wooden building looking decidedly out of place beside the old stone quaintness of the rest of the village.

'What's this?' I said with a sense of foreboding.

'It's the Village Hall,' she said with bewildering pride. 'I keep the key.' She produced it from her pocket, unlocked the door and we entered a musty-smelling room, empty except for a few folding chairs stacked against a far wall. 'I wonder if anybody needed to make a booking in the last few days,' she mused. 'I don't expect they wanted to come and ask me now my name is mud.'

'Oh, stop talking like that. It's not going to get you anywhere. And why on earth would anyone want to make a booking *here*? I can't wait to get outside.'

'*Loads* of things happen here.' Gussie sounded quite indignant. 'Coffee mornings, yoga classes, we have bingo in here in the evenings and the youth club used to hold their discos in here.'

'Used to?'

'There isn't much youth left in Frampton Abbas,' she said sadly, 'they all seem to leave as soon as they're old enough.'

'And you're surprised?'

50

I regretted it as soon as the words were out of my mouth. Gussie looked so forlorn. This was the world she had chosen, the life she was trying her best to make a go of and I was dumping on it from a great height. But after a while a rueful grin spread across her face as if she knew what I was getting at.

'Actually, it's a bit of a nightmare,' she admitted. 'I think they saw me coming when I volunteered to take over the running of it. The legislation they've got surrounding something as simple as a Village Hall these days defeats me – noise restriction, whether you can sell food or not, disabled access – which we don't have enough of apparently – you name it. Do you know, at one stage I was even thinking of having a speed-dating evening here.' She saw my face. 'Maybe not. Come on, let's go back to the High Street because that really is a bit of a success story.'

Maybe I was being unusually dim but I couldn't see why. On close inspection it looked pretty moribund to me. A garage, a baker's, two pubs – The Dog and Frog and The Prince Frederick – the fish bar, a butcher's, a greengrocer's, a hairdresser's that looked as if it would have a fit if it was required to do anything besides a blue rinse, a chemist with dusty bottles in the window and Spar, the mini supermarket. By contrast The Pelican's green and white striped awning, which I hadn't noticed in the gloom of my first night, positively gleamed with color as we passed it. There was a large CLOSED sign hanging in the door but below it a notice invited passersby to '*Enjoy a morning cappuccino by the fire.*' Do they even know what a cappuccino is in Frampton Abbas? I wondered.

I was, I told Gussie regretfully, so used to the high streets in London with all the chains to choose from – Marks & Spencer, Waterstone's, Woolworths, Dixons, Boots the Chemist. 'Where does everybody do their shopping?' I asked her. 'Where do you buy clothes? Electrical goods?'

'Lee-Lee, you have no idea. Except for that time you lived in America, you've been closeted in London all your life, haven't you? Everyone who lives in the country drives to those huge supermarkets in the middle of nowhere these days. They've diversified so much, you can get just about everything you want there now. It's actually pretty amazing that we still have our own butcher and baker and greengrocer here in Frampton Abbas, because the supermarkets sell all of that too. But we service all the farms that are still left on Exmoor and that's what keeps us going.'

I noticed the 'we' and once again her pride in her surroundings was apparent. She had a sense of belonging, I realized, and it was touching.

'Besides,' she said, dragging me by the arm into the Post Office, 'in here they make the best dairy fudge I've ever had and you wouldn't get that in London.'

No, you wouldn't, I thought as I watched a woman lift a section of the wooden counter top and step through into the main part of the shop, not in a Post Office anyway. She smiled at Gussie and chatted to her for a minute or two. In fact several people had greeted Gussie warmly as we were walking along the street and I began to wonder if maybe it had been Gussie's pathetically low self-esteem that had made her think people would automatically blame her for Rosemary Waters' death. No one who knew Gussie could ever think that, but her natural assumption that others were always judgmental created a constant barrier between her perception and reality.

And my mother's derision over Gussie's job was still shifting uneasily around my head. Gussie had had the benefit of an expensive education. Accepting work washing dishes was a sure sign that she thought she was good for nothing. Mickey Beresford had a lot to answer for and I resolved to restore Gussie's confidence in herself – miniscule at the best of times – before I returned to London.

We ventured back into the High Street and I was about to put my arm around her in a show of affection when the door to The Pelican opened and Sylvia came out, followed by a woman in a tight-fitting red overcoat with black frogging across her bosom, and high-heeled boots. Such an outfit was so incongruous in Frampton Abbas, I almost gasped.

'Oh God, it's Mona. Miss Mona-lot. It's all she ever does,' said Gussie not quite under her breath.

Sylvia gave her a sharp look that told me she had heard but then Sylvia was probably always giving Gussie sharp looks. The woman in the high heels waved at Gussie and began to cross the road. Sylvia followed with a look of resignation.

'Hello Mona,' said Gussie. 'Lee, this is Mona Richards. Maggie's daughter.'

'I'm sorry for your loss,' I said, aware that I was sounding rather stilted. It was an expression they used in America where I had been living for the past year. Over there people 'passed away' or were 'lost' rather than died.

But Mona didn't reply. She held her hand out to me – *wait a moment* – while she whisked a vibrating pager out of her pocket and checked her messages.

'Mona's a multi-tasker, just like me,' said Sylvia, squinting sideways at Mona's little screen.

Mona's an arrogant bitch who could learn a few manners, I thought, staring hard at her to show my disapproval. She had a sour face, rather like Sylvia's without the fake smile.

'Sylvia's been so wonderful, helping me organize the funeral and clear out Mother's house,' said Mona to Gussie. 'I don't know what I would have done without her.'

I was about to open my mouth to protest – *What about Gussie? She's the one who's been running across the road with meals for your mother and checking up on her* – but I felt Gussie's restraining hand on my arm. So I kept it short.

'Bit of a mess, was it?'

Mona snapped her phone shut and rolled her eyes. 'You have no idea! And I didn't have a clue how batty my mother had become. I just opened the weirdest collection of mail. She had catalogues for men's clothing! And get this! It's insane but she had an account with an online dating agency.'

'So she did have a computer,' I said without thinking.

'Of course she didn't have a computer.' Mona thought I was asking her. 'She barely knew what they were let alone owned one.'

I was about to mention what Maggie had said about her son-in-law owning one when I remembered what Gussie had said about him being killed in a car accident. Not the most tactful thing to say to his widow.

'Which dating agency was it?' said Gussie.

'Something called Exmoormates.com. Unbelievable. So, assuming she's allowed to, Sylvia's offered to open up The Pelican for a little gathering after the funeral if you want to join us, Gussie? And you too?' she added after an awkward pause. 'More than welcome.'

She couldn't have sounded less welcoming if she tried. She had a voice that emanated a constant state of extreme boredom. I turned to look at Sylvia. Surely she wouldn't condone Gussie setting foot in The Pelican for whatever reason, but before Sylvia could protest, Gussie said, 'Oh that's so kind, Mona. We'll be there. Do let me know if there's anything we can do.'

And then she took me by the arm and marched me away leaving Sylvia speechless.

'That woman has not been down to visit her mother in months,' said Gussie. 'How on earth could she know what state Maggie was in? Matter of fact she was always fine with me. And you said there *was* a computer there.'

'But joining a *dating* agency? And she said the computer was her son-in-law's and you said he'd been dead for four years.'

'I know Maggie's mind was far from reliable.' Gussie glared across the road at Sylvia and Mona. 'I just don't like the way everyone automatically wrote her off as if she was crackers just because she was old. Do you remember that awful story about the poor old woman who was taken home from hospital to the wrong house. She kept trying to tell the ambulance men she didn't live there and they assumed she was gaga. She broke her leg trying to escape. People should have more respect for the elderly.'

I heard the underlying subtext in the words *automatically written off*. Gussie had had some kind of unspoken affinity with Maggie Blair and when it came to dealing with the Sylvias and the Monas of this world, I didn't blame her.

I didn't know what to think. A state-of-the-art computer, an account with Exmoormates.com and a habit of wandering along the High Street in her nightgown.

Something about Maggie Blair just didn't add up.

Chapter Four

Maggie Blair was laid to rest on a glorious Friday afternoon. The little church of St Catherine and All Angels was packed but Gussie was miserable.

'They didn't ask me to come and do the flowers,' she grumbled to me *sotto voce* as we huddled in a pew near the back of the church. 'I'm one of the Holy Dusters, responsible for the housekeeping of the church and I *always* help do the flowers for funerals.'

I decided not to mention that she hadn't been asked to do the flowers for Rosemary Waters' funeral either. 'I wish the Holy Dusters could do something about the heating,' I whispered to her, 'it's a gloriously sunny day outside but it's freezing in here.'

Gussie frowned at me. 'Our heating apparatus dates back to the 1880s,' she said, 'it's of historic importance! You're sitting in an extraordinary church, Lee-Lee. The chancel walls and the tower are probably fourteenth century.'

'I don't care,' I moaned, 'it's still bloody freezing. Where's the vicar? I wish he'd hurry up.'

'It's a she,' said Gussie, 'the Rev. Milly Mulholland and she's a locum parson, you know. She's always rushing between us and the next village on her bike. I heard she had a christening over in Market Dutton this morning. That's bound to make her late.'

Maggie was already here, her coffin borne up the aisle by four strapping farmers' sons and deposited on to a trestle table at the foot of the steps to the chancel that looked as if it might collapse at any moment. Out of sight someone was plodding away at the organ with a mournful dirge and Mona was sitting in solitary splendor in the front pew with the rest of the congregation keeping a respectful distance.

Except for Sylvia who suddenly charged up the aisle to sit beside her in what I thought was a rather possessive manner.

And then the Rev. Milly arrived, a tiny figure in a billowing white cassock stomping up the aisle in fur-lined boots. She reminded me of a puffball with her frizzy fair hair bobbing up and down as she hurried to begin the service.

She wasn't the only one who was late. While the Rev. Milly was intoning in a high-pitched and rather squeaky voice *We brought nothing into this world and it is certain we can carry nothing out* the door clanged behind us once more. The clattering din of footsteps on the stone floors of the church caused everyone to turn and stare. The Rev. Milly continued, sounding more like Reese Witherspoon than a Church of England country parson, and I was about to point this out to Gussie when an imposing figure hove into sight at the end of our pew. He was a man who looked to be in his early forties with a mane of tangled ginger hair and as we looked at him he fished an elastic band out of his pocket and attempted to scrape his unruly locks into a pathetic little ponytail at the nape of his neck. At the same time he managed to gesture to Gussie to move up so he could sit beside her.

Our pew was packed and we all had to scoot down to fit him in, resulting in the last person having to get up and move to the pew in front. The newcomer barely noticed. He sat very close to Gussie, I noticed, his thigh pressed to hers and for a split second he glanced past her to look at me.

His eyes were green, of such an emerald brilliance that I wondered if he was wearing contact lenses. He had a big nose but it sat easily in the middle of his wide-planed attractive face. He was scruffily dressed. His clothes – black jeans and a designer anorak, also black – were not dirty but neither were they respectful apparel for a funeral. But it was the pair of shiny black clogs on his feet – the cause of the clattering – that prompted me to lean over and whisper in Gussie's ear.

'Who *is* that man?'

She looked at me in surprise, as if I should be expected to divine who it was. 'It's André, of course,' and then when she saw my puzzled look, she reminded me 'the chef at The Pelican.' Then she leaned back towards him and whispered something and he nodded at me and smiled briefly. But he wasn't really seeing me. Gussie had his real attention, I sensed, and the lack of space in the narrow pew wasn't the only reason he was pressed against her.

The Rev. Milly hadn't done her homework. All that cycling around the countryside probably didn't give her much time to look up who she was burying.

'She was a much loved member of our tiny community,' she squeaked from somewhere up above us. When she had spoken several sentences without actually mentioning Maggie's name, I realized she didn't have a clue who she was talking about. We were barely able to see her behind the lectern in the pulpit but we could make out her hands frantically rustling notes. Finally, after a slight pause, she announced triumphantly 'and she will be much missed by her beloved daughter Mona.'

And from the pew behind me I heard a voice say quite distinctly, 'her beloved daughter Mona, *my foot!*'

I turned around and choked. Max Austin was staring straight at me.

Max Austin was the man who constantly occupied my thoughts. Max Austin was the man whose wife had been found strangled under a bale of hay just over six years ago *in darkest Devon*, according to my friend Cath. Max Austin, I was once told, again by Cath, was besotted with me. I was the first woman in whom he had showed any interest since his wife had been murdered, she told me with great excitement, why didn't I wake up and smell his roses? OK, she didn't actually say that but she implied it.

I ignored her and when I re-encountered him a year later and suddenly got the full-on heart-stopping physical point of him, it was too late. But we shared one kiss and that was enough to keep me going. I believe that a kiss will do it every time – far more than a night of actual intimacy. If a man gets his tongue inside your mouth and, far from it being intrusive you feel as if your whole body is melting into his, then that's something you don't forget.

All right, I have to be honest here. You remember the kiss if you haven't actually *had* the moment of intimacy yet. You remember the kiss because it's all you've fucking got. And at the rate I was going, it seemed like it was all I was ever going to get.

I had walked away from Tommy Kennedy, my boyfriend of nine years and the man who wanted to marry me, because of Max Austin's kiss. I had left Tommy in America and come back to England just to be in the same country as Max.

And I hadn't heard a single word from him. Not a dickey. Granted it was partly my fault because I hadn't actually had the nerve to call him. But Cath was married to Sergeant Richie Cross and Max was his boss, so don't tell me Max wasn't aware I was back. What did it say about me that I went to sleep every night conjuring up the vision of a man I hadn't even seen for over a year? It said I was a sad and pathetic case who was clinging to an obsessive fantasy, and that Gussie, with her touching determination to forge a new life for herself after suffering a genuine relationship drama, could surely teach her older – and chicken-livered – cousin a thing or two. And of course this was why I wasn't going to breathe a word to her about Max until I absolutely had to.

59

And I didn't have to yet because of course it wasn't Max I was staring at. Max was in London investigating gruesome stabbings and stranglings and hounding people who cut up bodies and buried them in the garden or stashed them in washing machines. This was an older version of Max – by some twenty-five years from the look of him – but there was enough of a resemblance to give me a serious jolt.

This had to be Max's uncle.

He looked quizzically at me and at the same time I felt a sharp nudge in my side from Gussie.

'Turn round,' she hissed, 'we're at a funeral. You're supposed to be saying goodbye to Maggie and all that. What are you *looking* at?' She half turned her head. 'Oh, Jake the Rake. Stay away from *him*!'

I sat through the rest of Maggie's service feeling Jake the Rake's eyes boring into my back and I thought about Max and Tommy and I wondered why it was that I could never make up my mind about what I wanted. Why did I always crave one thing only to discover, once I had it in my sights, that I wanted the other? Had I not had this dream, ever since I could remember, of living in the tranquillity of the country? Yet after barely a week in Frampton Abbas I had found nothing but fault with it.

I glanced at Gussie. Would she grow old here? Would she have a similar fate to Maggie lying up there in her coffin, abandoned by her daughter and left to rely on the kindness of people like Gussie herself? But unlike me, at long last Gussie seemed to know what she wanted. Maybe Mickey throwing her out would turn out to be a lucky break because her fresh start in Frampton Abbas would appear to be the saving of her.

Providing we could establish that she had played no part in the death of the peanut woman.

When we were all filing out of the church and shuffling towards the freshly dug grave, I quizzed Gussie about Jake the Rake.

'He's a lecherous old farmer,' she said, 'hence his nick-name. That and because he looks like a rake, tall and skinny. Lives by himself on his farm way out in the middle of nowhere. Gives me the spooks.'

'What's his last name?'

'Austin. Jake Austin.'

Well, now I knew for sure. The resemblance was so strong it was almost uncanny. I scrutinized him as we stood on opposite sides of the grave. It was so unnerving seeing him standing there that it almost took my mind off the fact that I was witnessing a burial. I felt guilty enough about the unhealthy amount of time I spent worrying about when I was going to be murdered but every now and again I was forced to confront my horror of what would happen afterwards. The thought of being barbecued in a crematorium was too terrify-ing to contemplate – although I did at frequent intervals – but looking down into the depths of the trench into which Maggie was being lowered, I began to fret about that too. Because of course after I'd been brutally stabbed or stran-gled or bludgeoned or whatever, when it came to disposing of my body, I would be the one person in the world who wouldn't actually be dead when they piled on the earth. As the flames began to lick my coffin or six feet of earth was piled on top of me, I'd wake up and I'd scream and no one would hear me. Just as if I ever had to have major surgery – God forbid! – the anesthetic wouldn't work but I wouldn't be able to move and tell them and as the surgeon picked up his knife—

I emitted a tiny squeak of dread as Maggie's coffin landed in its final resting place, mercifully drowned out by the Rev. Milly's droning. *Man that is born of a woman hath but a short time to live, and is full of misery.* Gloomy words, I thought as I pulled myself together and glanced across the hole, but at this particular moment Jake Austin looked anything but gloomy. He was smiling broadly at me and suddenly I realized what was happening. He had mistaken my interest in him, he thought I was attracted to him and a little thing like a funeral wouldn't stop a dedicated pick-up artist.

I glowered at him until he looked away, bewildered.

But he was persistent and later, as I followed Gussie through the crush of people who were gathered to raise a glass in The Pelican to Maggie's memory, I could see him edging closer to me through the crowd.

All the tables had been removed and the chairs had been pushed to the edge of the dining room but even so my first impression of The Pelican's interior was of an interesting space. I sensed from the thickness of the walls that the building itself was several centuries old. The floor, what I could see of it beneath the throng of people, was comprised of large uneven flagstones. The walls were painted a kind of streaky burnt orange – I'd heard the term distressed used in association with interior decor – and the color gave the room a certain warmth. The lighting was discreet, emerging from half-moon sconces at intervals along the walls. In the center of one wall was a long slate fireplace and its striking contemporary design gave the room a refreshing slant, lifting it right out of the ubiquitous old-fashioned country restaurant niche and conveying an altogether more sophisticated message. I was impressed. The size of the room – maybe 20×15 – said cozy bistro but the modern touches hinted at a more intriguing dining experience. It was clever, warm and inviting but not at all *olde worlde*.

And you could see the kitchen. At the back of the room was a rectangular stone hatch through which I saw stainless steel glinting in pools of spotlight – again an incongruous sight against the ancient stone walls.

When we finally made it to the bar set up along the counter of the hatch, we were offered red or white wine or beer. Gussie made a face at me.

'I'm going to sneak into the kitchen and get myself a Red Bull and some vodka from the freezer. I'm not braving this lot without a shot of extra adrenaline. What about you?'

'Sounds great,' said Jake Austin materializing at my side. 'Can you introduce us, Augusta?'

'This is my cousin Nathalie,' said Gussie with equal formality, and disappeared into the kitchen.

'Jake Austin,' he said, holding out his hand, which I was obliged to shake. As I did so I nearly dislodged an unlit cigarette clamped between his long fingers. 'Come down for a bit of country air with your cousin, have you?'

'Something like that,' I said, not looking at him. I was watching Gussie in the kitchen. André was lifting trays of little pastry cases filled with something I couldn't identify out of the oven. As Gussie tried to get by, he waylaid her with a hot tray, backing her into the wall. He set down the tray and shot both arms out either side of her, palms against the wall, trapping her.

And she loved it. She stared straight into his eyes and for a second I thought they might actually kiss but at the last moment, she giggled and ducked under his arm. Well, well, well, I thought. Was this the real reason why, despite her lowly role as a dishwasher, Gussie had actually enjoyed working at The Pelican?

'It's OK, no one's watching,' said Jake and I flushed at the amused look on his face. I waited for Gussie to rejoin us and bring him his vodka and Red Bull but instead she made a bee-line for a group of people standing by the fireplace and I was stuck with Jake the Rake. He was twitching in a vaguely nervous way and I noticed him gazing with longing at a woman smoking over by the fireplace. Before I lost my nerve I asked him, 'Do you have a relation called Max, by any chance?'

For a second he looked a little startled then he relaxed. 'My nephew,' he said. 'My brother Sam's boy. You know him, I take it?'

'He's a detective in London and there was this arson case about eighteen months ago and a boy died in my summer-house and it turned out to be murder and Max – Inspector Austin, actually he's Detective Superintendent Austin now –

63

was the detective who investigated the case and he had to interrogate me about it.' Why was I wittering on like this?

'I'll bet he did,' said Jake with a knowing grin. 'The lady doth protest too much methinks. All I asked was *do you know him?* You could have just said yes. And I didn't know he'd got a promotion.'

'You're not in touch?'

'Not for a while. I rarely get up to London and he's not too keen on this part of the world.'

I raised my eyebrows.

He studied me for a moment and I sensed he was wondering whether to tell me something. I smiled in what I hoped was an encouraging fashion and it seemed to work.

'I assume you know what happened to his wife?' he said.

I nodded.

'Well, she was found near here. Max used to come charging down here as often as he could, trying to find out what happened to her – until they told him to keep well out of it. Poor bastard, a murder detective and he couldn't investigate the most important case of his life. He stopped coming after that. We speak on the phone now and then but I haven't actually clapped eyes on him for a couple of years.'

'Oh.' I didn't really know what to say but I wanted to keep him talking about Max. 'What was she doing down here, his wife?'

'Sadie? Well, if you really want to know – she came to see me.'

And then he turned away and signaled that he wanted a beer, making it clear that he wasn't going to say anything more on the subject. After he'd taken an initial swill, he looked at me again. 'So did you know Maggie Blair or are you just tagging along after Augusta?'

'I couldn't say I knew her but I did meet her. What about you?'

'Known her all my life. And hers.' He pursed his lips and I thought I was going to faint. Max had the exact same habit and it was one of the sexiest things I'd ever seen. Both he and Jake had the same cruel mouth that gave them a perpetual slightly sardonic expression and whenever they did something with those mean lips, it did something extremely unsettling to me. I had enough of my wits about me to realize that I was reacting to Jake's resemblance to Max rather than to Jake himself. Jake was probably only in his mid sixties but he looked decidedly haggard and his raincoat, which he hadn't taken off, and the dark suit underneath it were distinctly shabby. Now I had the opportunity to study it at close range, I could see that his face was Max's but with deep lines etched along his forehead and running down from his nostrils to his chin. He'd been wearing a cloth cap at the funeral, which he had now removed and his narrow head was almost bald. But his eyes were beautiful, chocolate colored and very deep set like Max's, but softer. Those eyes could weep, I found myself thinking as I stared at him.

'We grew up together, Maggie and me,' he said. 'I've lived round here since I was born and so has she. We went to school together for a bit – I say school, it was just an old biddy giving us lessons in a hall. She was a real tomboy, was Maggie. And fearless. She wasn't like all the other little girls who couldn't say boo to a goose. Maggie could pick up a rabbit by its hind legs and give it a side-of-the-hand chop—'

I stepped back hurriedly as his outstretched hand came towards my neck.

'—and the neck would be snapped, just like that. I couldn't do it, no more than I could wring a chicken's. And she'd be out with a scythe come harvest time along with folks three times her size. But it all came to an end with the birds and the bees.'

'What did?'

'Our friendship. Our *childhood* friendship, I should say, our innocence. She was quite a few years older than I was but she was a late starter. As I said, she was a tomboy running around with the lads until I brought an end to that. It was my fault, I won't deny it, although believe me, she was more than willing. I took her virginity – or rather she took mine – in the old barn up on Dorcas Tor – it was as deserted then as it is today – and it changed things between us. But I wasn't the one who got her pregnant.'

He looked at me, challenging me with his eyes to ask for more details.

'Maggie had a baby?'

He nodded. 'I was her first but after that she couldn't get enough of it and there were plenty of lads around, itinerant farm hands. Her parents sent her away to have the baby because it was a huge scandal in those days, getting pregnant out of wedlock, but she told me about it. Swore me to secrecy.'

'What happened to the baby?'

Jake shrugged. 'No idea. Adopted, I think, but I'm pretty sure Maggie had no further contact after the birth.'

'And who else knows?'

He looked at me, aghast. 'No one. *Absolutely* no one. I never told a soul. To be honest I forgot about the baby pretty quickly but hearing Mona described as her beloved daughter, I don't know, it just took me straight back to that time when Maggie was first a mother.'

'What about Mona's father?'

'Owen Blair? Waste of space. Don't know where Maggie found him but she brought him back here to her parents' farm after they died. Couldn't farm his way out of a window box and then he lost control of a tractor and ran into a tree. He was only going about five miles an hour but his heart gave out with the shock. Good riddance, I say, but Maggie was never the same afterwards.'

Jake's soulful eyes showed genuine sadness.

'I think that was when she started to go a bit doolally. I mean her dementia, it came on in her late sixties, a case of early onset if ever I saw one. Mona saw the way things were going and cleared out pretty sharpish. She went to London and

66

found herself a husband but then *he* was killed in a car accident. Only a few years ago actually. I had to laugh, serve her right. But did she come back here to check up on Maggie? No, she did not, unless one of us hounded her on the telephone. It was a disgrace and Maggie deserved better. But listen to me,' suddenly he looked so fierce, I felt distinctly nervous, 'don't you go saying anything. I think I only talked to you because you're a stranger and it was on my mind. What I've just told you, keep it to yourself. Maggie's in her grave, God bless her, and as far as she knows the secret's in there with her. I think she forgot she ever told me all those years ago.'

'What have you two been gossiping about all this time?' Gussie appeared at my side. 'Maggie looked forward to your visits, Jake. You seemed to be one of the few people she recognized towards the end. When was it you last saw her?'

But Jake didn't answer. I could see that talking about Maggie's past had shaken him. He stared at me for a second or two, standing there in his raincoat, then he fumbled in his pocket for his cap and turned abruptly to fight his way to the door. The last I saw of him was his lanky frame striding off along the pavement.

'Surly bugger,' said Gussie, 'I never could understand why he had such a reputation as a ladies' man. Not recently, mind, but there's talk of what he got up to in the past. Anyway, see that woman leaving now?' She pointed to a ruddy faced woman about to go out the door. 'That's Gilly Mortimer. I'm meeting her back at the house. She's going to come back and pick up that cardigan she left here. She's going on ahead. No prizes for guessing why. She doesn't want anyone to see her with me, so unless there's anyone else you want to bond with, you might want to leave now with me.'

'So you're tight with André?' I asked her as we walked back along the High Street. 'I saw the two of you getting pretty hot in the kitchen.'

'You did, huh?' She grinned. 'He's never made it a secret that he wants to get it together with me but I was never sure I

67

could handle it if I was working in his kitchen. It can get awfully steamy in there and there were a couple of things that always stopped me taking it any further with him. One was Sylvia. She made it pretty clear she disapproved. She used to snap at me – things like *Keep out of Chef's way.*'

'And you implied she had her eye on him too. What was the other?'

'I like him, Lee-Lee, but what if he just wanted a one night stand? How would I cope with that, working at such close quarters?'

I didn't say anything. Gussie was seriously bruised, I thought. She had practically convinced herself that every man was going to treat her as badly as Mickey had.

'It makes me sick seeing all those people packed into The Pelican,' said Gussie, waving at Gilly Mortimer who was already standing on Gussie's doorstep, 'bloody hypocrites, they never went near poor old Maggie once she started her decline. Sorry to keep you waiting, Gilly.'

'And I'm sorry to distance myself from you but my mother-in-law would never let it rest if she saw me talking to you,' said Gilly. 'We've got a bit of a divided household at the moment because old Father Mortimer is of the "accidents can happen" persuasion. He doesn't blame you, Gussie. He thinks it's a shame you were careless but he understands that you didn't mean to kill Rosemary. He reckons you'll suffer enough from your guilt, you don't need him and old Ma Mortimer on your back as well.'

Gussie and I stared at each other in disbelief. 'I didn't do it, Gilly,' Gussie whispered. 'If there was peanut oil in that dressing, I didn't know it was there. I swear to you that's the truth.'

Gilly Mortimer set her face in a stiff *I don't believe you but I'm not going to say anything* expression and turned her back on us to stomp ahead into the house. She was awkward in her thick-soled shoes and long woolen coat that nearly reached her ankles. As it fell open, I saw that she was pregnant again.

'Were you close to Rosemary?' I asked as Gussie went upstairs to get the cardigan.

'In a way,' said Gilly. 'We were both trying to get out from under Ma Mortimer's control. The old battleaxe felt she had the right to exercise as much control over her friend's daughter as her daughters-in-law. Do you know of any other sons who are required to take their wives and spend every weekend with their mother? And with Rosemary she always used the excuse of the allergy, implied Rosemary couldn't take care of herself. Rosemary told me she felt like Ma Mortimer was spying on her and telling Rosemary's mother everything she saw. The saddest thing, of course, is that Rosemary was just beginning to spread her wings.'

'Moving into the barn?'

Gilly nodded. 'But of course if she hadn't, she might still be alive.'

'Why do you say that?'

'Because although she'd been living in the barn for a couple of months, she still hadn't moved all her stuff in. There was so much of it scattered all over the farmhouse – where she'd lived for over thirty years! – and it was so close, she knew she could pop across the yard and get something when she realized she needed it.' Gilly was becoming visibly upset and I moved closer to her, pulled out a chair and motioned to her to sit down. But she declined.

'Rosemary must have come home from The Pelican and prepared for bed in the barn. She was in her nightdress when they found her. If only she'd gone into anaphylactic shock right there in the restaurant – but she didn't. It can happen as much as two hours later. So she was alone. And her epinephrine – she had a kit for emergencies, it was easily injectable – it'd been so long since she'd had an attack, she'd grown complacent. She'd left it in the house. She suffered the attack and she couldn't breathe and the life-saving syringe was just across the yard. Her dog must have sensed she was in trouble because he started barking his head off. He woke everyone up but it was too late. By the time they got to her, she was dead. I can't stop thinking about it.'

I patted Gilly's arm and she gave a little shake and smiled at me.

'But I have to, don't I? It's just that she was being so positive about her future. She was actively looking for a husband, someone who would take her right away from the farm. She'd joined one of those online dating agencies. It was perfect because her mother was terrified of the computer, didn't even know how to turn it on.'

'I told you,' said Gussie, overhearing as she came back into the kitchen with the cardigan, 'here you are, Gilly. I'm afraid I haven't had it cleaned or anything. So which agency was it?'

'Something called Exmoormates.com and she'd already had a few dates. But I know she was really excited about the man she was going to meet the night she died. She wasn't much of a looker, poor Rosemary,' Gilly said sadly. 'Her mother had done quite a job on her. In a way I don't think she really *expected* any of the men she emailed to be attracted to her.'

'What was so special about the one who didn't show up? Why was she excited about him?' I asked.

'Well, she'd chatted to him – emailed him, I mean – for a long time – a couple of months – and she said she really felt she knew him. She said she could tell him anything, she really trusted him. She said he sounded so gentle and understanding and he'd traveled the world and now he just wanted to settle down.'

'Did she show you these emails?' I was fascinated.

'No,' said Gilly, 'of course not. They were private. But I am going to read them one day. Not yet, it's too soon, I need to let it all rest for a while. I have her computer, you see. Her mother was going to throw it out but I asked if I could have it. Of course she had no idea what was on it. Rosemary was a bit naive. She wrote down her password so she wouldn't forget it, left it right by the computer. I can get in there whenever I

70

want. I thought I'd wait until I'm quite far gone with junior here,' she patted her stomach, 'when I don't feel like doing much more than stare at a computer screen all afternoon.'

'So you don't actually know who it was she was going to meet?' I said.

Gilly nodded. 'Oh yes I do. At least I know his name – his Exmoormates name at any rate. Rosemary couldn't stop saying it. She was the one who suggested dinner and she picked The Pelican and he said he'd meet her there. I told her she was asking for trouble but she wouldn't listen to me.'

'You didn't think she should be going for a date with someone she'd only met online?' I glanced at Gussie.

'I didn't think she should be going to meet him in a *restaurant*.' Gilly was getting worked up again. 'You have to understand she never went to restaurants. Can you imagine, thirty-two years old and she'd only ever eaten out where she knew it would be safe, at the homes of people who could be trusted not to accidentally slip in a peanut. But when she moved out of her parents' home, away from her mother's clutches, she started to become more adventurous. Complacent, as I said. I don't think she fully realized how serious her allergy was. So she ignored my worrying about going to a restaurant and she made the reservation.'

'And I took it from her,' said Gussie, 'I remember. She did sound excited. She even knew what she was going to order. A green salad. I remember her saying she couldn't go wrong with that. Little did she know!'

'So she made the reservation in her name?' I asked.

Gussie nodded.

'Well, it would have been amusing if she'd made it in his,' said Gilly, 'as I said, she only had his online name. He told her he wanted to save his real name for when they met.'

'So what was his online name?' I asked.

'You'll never believe it,' Gilly smiled. 'Mr Wright. With a W. It might have been his real name for all we know.'

There was an audible gasp from Gussie. We looked at her but she didn't say anything.

'Well, I'm off,' said Gilly, 'before Ma Mortimer comes looking for me. Gussie, if you ever come to Exeter during the week, look me up.'

'Yes, I probably will have time to come to Exeter now I'm no longer working at The Pelican.' Gussie had no qualms about rubbing it in.

'I'm sorry,' said Gilly. 'I really am. But Sylvia promised Ma Mortimer she would fire you and I suspect Rosemary's mother was the one who suggested it first. Even if it was a tragic accident, they had to find someone to blame and you were the nearest available scapegoat.'

'What do you mean *even if*,' shouted Gussie but Gilly was out the door. 'Lee-Lee,' she said, turning to me, 'it's pretty spooky.'

'What is?'

'What Gilly just told us. Rosemary was going to meet Mr Wright.'

'And she didn't. She died instead.' I pointed out.

'That's who my date is with next week. The one *I've* been emailing on Exmoormates.com, the one I've finally decided to meet. On his online profile, his name is Mr Wright.'

Chapter Five

'Oh look, Cissie's in the *Telegraph*,' Gussie called out as I staggered into the kitchen the following morning having once again been denied my full quota of sleep by the ducks. As a result I was half dead with fatigue.

It was always a bit of a shock entering the kitchen and being hit by the blast of steamy heat that was distinctly lacking in the rest of the house. Gussie had not taken kindly to my remark the night before that it felt as if we were camping. Because of the lack of furniture in our rooms upstairs, our stuff was sprawled all over the bare floorboards in little piles. Gussie kept her clothes in a series of cardboard boxes lined up underneath the tall sash windows in her bedroom. They were identifiable only by fabric. Wool, cotton, linen and, as an exotic reminder of her former London life, cashmere, *mousseline de soie,* duchess satin. 'Duchess satin?' I queried the first time I saw it. 'My wedding dress,' said Gussie and gave the box a defiant little kick.

She had laid a trail of towels from our rooms to the bathroom in an attempt to mitigate the shock of the cold floor first thing in the morning but they did nothing to alleviate the jangling my nerves experienced at the deafening rattling of the antiquated plumbing once we roused it into action. Every morning I stared at the rusty brown water trickling out of the taps, wondering whether it was safe to slap it on my sleep-encrusted face. And then the staircase had to be navigated, plunging halfway down the wall and then doubling back on itself, its stone steps having crumbled in places to a precarious state of disintegration. The fine lines that I had appreciated in Gussie's house on my arrival were, I realized, in need of hundreds of thousands of pounds of restoration. There were four bedrooms upstairs but only two of them, mine and Gussie's, had their ceilings intact.

The kitchen more than made up for the void in the rest of the house. Here Gussie appeared to have accumulated her entire life. A Welsh dresser meant to display china and glass housed her collection of paperback romances, baskets of assorted make-up and dusty hair products, DVDs and accumulated back issues of *Country Life*. A pale pink blanket, covered in the hairs of a dog that had probably died twenty years ago, was thrown over a seven- foot sofa placed under the window just inside the door. It was so low to the ground that the kitchen table towered above it and I realized that it had at one time served as a dog basket in the kitchen of Gussie's Northumberland childhood. One end of the sofa was hidden by more of the ubiquitous cardboard boxes, these as yet unopened, and perched on top of them was a DVD player with a TV on top of that. A bedraggled little velvet bedroom chair nestled close to the Aga as if it were trying to get warm. And in the far corner a rickety bamboo table buckled under the weight of Gussie's computer and a pile of phone books, comprising what Gussie called her office.

The sight of Gussie sitting at her computer invariably rankled for there had been a deafening silence from Genevieve, which meant that my own laptop was lying depressingly idle upstairs. I had welcomed a break but now I could feel myself going into my neurotic *why hasn't anyone called, I'll never work again* mode. The fact that Gussie couldn't even type properly and I had to watch her hunt and peck at the keyboard like a chicken made it worse. And I objected to the word 'office' because Gussie's computer was only used for one thing – and I refused to call it work.

She was sitting at it now reading the *Telegraph* online, another thing that infuriated me even though I found it hard to justify the satisfaction I got from holding cumbersome and messy newsprint in my hands.

'I'm reading about Cissie,' she repeated over her shoulder as I helped myself to coffee, 'she's over for London Fashion Week. Her knitwear's having a show. Oh bugger!'

'What?' I stood behind her, peering at the screen.

'I wish they hadn't used that pic of her.'

'Why ever not? Looks like it's quite a good one.' I was being careful to downplay it because *any* picture of Cissie was a good one. It was as if Gussie's tentative beauty had been fine-tuned to perfection. What must it be like to have such a paragon as a sister? As an only child, it was something with which I had never had to contend. But surely it must have contributed to Gussie's lack of self-esteem in some way? They both had red hair only Cissie's was a blissful concoction of strawberry blond to Gussie's russet mop. Cissie's eyes were glittering jade pools whereas Gussie's were midnight blue. And while they both had the same milky white skin, it was the only area where I had ever heard Gussie voice her envy. Unlike Gussie's, Cissie's skin was totally devoid of freckles.

Gussie clutched her mouse and stabbed at a few keys and a new page came up, again with the same photo of Cissie. I leaned closer and blinked.

Gussie had called up a profile on Exmoormates.com and it appeared to be Cissie's – until I read the details.

'Eye color: dark blue, Height: 5' 5", Marital Status: divorced, Has Children: No.' I tapped Gussie sharply on the shoulder, 'What's this all about? Cissie has twins. Date of Birth: 2 July 1971, that's not Cissie's birthday, it's—'

'Mine,' said Gussie quietly. 'This is my profile.'

It took me a minute to grasp what she had said.

'But Gussie, why? Why use Cissie's picture? Cissie's name?'

'Well, you don't want to use your real name,' Gussie shook her head firmly. 'Dangerous. And well, isn't it obvious? Cissie's so much prettier than me.'

'You're using Cissie as bait,' I said slowly, the pathetic truth finally dawning.

'And it's working, Lee-Lee,' said Gussie clapping her hands in glee. 'I've had loads of interest, I told you.'

'But what do you say when you meet them and they find out it's you, not Cissie?'

She didn't respond, waited for me to put it together.

'You don't meet them, do you? That's what you said. That's why you've been avoiding actual dates. You've been an ostrich, Gussie and it's totally pointless. You don't need to hide behind Cissie. You're a beauty in your own right. Look at you.' I hoisted her to her feet and dragged her over to a beautiful old gilded mirror hanging by the dresser – another relic I recognized from Northumberland. 'That's you, Gussie, and that's what you should be offering. There are plenty of men out there who'd be ecstatic with that face and they'd be bloody lucky to have it. Now,' I propelled her back to her 'office', 'you're going to remove Cissie's photo and post one of you. Go on, do it *now*!'

'I guess the game's up anyway if they're going to run this picture of Cissie all over the papers,' Gussie grumbled, 'someone's bound to see it.'

She might be a lousy typist but I couldn't help but be impressed by the dexterity with which she called up a picture of herself and somehow maneuvered it on to the Exmoormates.com site.

'Now move,' I said when I saw a head shot of Gussie's laughing face on the screen. It was a few years old, taken probably about the time of her marriage to Mickey before he began to torment her, but it was still an excellent likeness. 'I'm the writer and I'm going to re-write your details.' I sat down at the computer.

'You can't use my real name.' Gussie's voice registered alarm.

'So we'll give you a new one. Who do you want to be?'

'Oh, I don't know, you choose a name.'

'What's your favorite animal?'

'Chipmunk,' said Gussie without hesitation. 'Although I don't think I've ever seen one.'

I smothered a giggle. With her provocative overbite – rosebud lips parting over slightly protruding pearly teeth – Gussie looked a little like a chipmunk.

'I have,' I said, 'when I lived in America. It's perfect. Now, let's see how you've described yourself.' I scrolled down through the endless details – Exmoormates.com were certainly thorough. I stopped at Education: *A Level English and French. Read English as an undergraduate.* Gussie had left school at fifteen with no qualifications we'd ever heard about. I thought about it for a second and left it. But when I came to Sports and Exercise: *I work out regularly and go to the gym three times a week* and Books: *I like challenging reading, Dostoevsky, Salman Rushdie, Toni Morrison*, I looked up at her. 'Gussie,' I said, 'I had no idea you had such a talent for creative writing. Where's this gym you go to three times a week?'

'A gym? In Frampton Abbas? You *are* joking!' She grinned.

I pointed to the Mills and Boons lined up on the dresser. 'And you call that challenging reading?'

'I want a man to think I'm clever,' she said. 'Mickey always made me feel so stupid. One time when we had people to dinner he told everyone I thought Toni Morrison was a man and that I didn't know George Eliot was a woman.'

'You *are* clever, Gussie,' I said, 'look at the way you've made a new life for yourself down here. You're clever *and* you're brave. Not everyone's smart in the same way. You want someone to appreciate you for who *you* are, not who Mickey wanted you to be. That way you can enjoy being the Gussie we know and love.'

Gussie didn't look convinced.

'Where's the bit where you say how wonderful you are,' I said, 'and where you describe the type of man you're looking for?'

'I couldn't think what to put,' she said miserably. 'I am completely hopeless, after all.'

'No, you're *not*,' I said, 'Listen, I'll take care of the first part.' And I typed in *I am a warm, affectionate home-loving person with my own special brand of humor and sense of fun. I used to live in London but I find I am much happier here in the country where a simple life can feel rich in the abundance of home-grown vegetables and fresh air.'*

'Now you're indulging in creative writing,' muttered Gussie looking over my shoulder. 'I haven't planted a single vegetable since I've been here. Why don't you add *where ducks drive you crackers and people get poisoned in the local restaurant*?'

'Shut up,' I said, 'and describe the kind of man you want.'

I half expected her to come up with a flip description of a tall, dark stranger who would ride into town on his proud white tractor and rescue her from the ducks. But when she finally spoke after a few minutes of silent reflection it was with a quiet sincerity that surprised – and moved – me.

'I want a man who isn't perfect,' she spoke so softly I could barely hear her, 'who has flaws just like I do and who is not afraid to admit to them. I want someone on whom I can rely, with whom I can discuss my problems and *to* whom I can promise that I will always be there for him. I want an ordinary man whom I can make feel special. And I'd like him to do the same for me.'

I typed each word slowly, careful not to make a mistake and by the time I came to the last sentence I could feel a bit of a lump forming in my throat.

'See, you can do it if you try,' I said gruffly, not wanting her to witness my emotion. 'Now, let me take a look at Mr Wright's profile. I want to see if he matches up to your requirements.'

The first thing I noticed when she sat down and called him up on the screen was that there was no photograph. In the square where the picture should have been were just the words *All will be revealed.* As I read on, the details were few and far between. His marital status was separated, he didn't have children and he wasn't sure if he wanted any. Instead of the details about his hair/eye color, height and body type, again he'd put the irritating *All will be revealed.* He said yes, he drank and he'd smoked in the past. He loved animals, he'd been educated in Dublin but he didn't say anything about degrees, he wasn't overly interested in politics, he spoke French, Spanish, Italian, he liked jazz and blues, he never watched television, he never went to the movies, he had tried yoga and failed. He listed his Interests and Activities as *food, sleep, sex.*

I looked to see what his occupation was and found I was none the wiser.

I've had ME (Myalgia Encephalomyelitis) for the last four years and have had to take time out from work – but I'm now making steady progress in my recovery.

How come I just didn't believe that? Why did I immediately think it was the perfect foil for someone who didn't want to reveal what he did for a living until he had to? My answer was confirmed when I read what he said about himself.

I'm a chameleon. I can be anything you want. Meet me and find out for yourself.

'I know, I know,' said Gussie when I pointed all this out. 'That's partly why I didn't rush into a date with him. But another part of me couldn't help but be intrigued. All the other profiles are mostly country farming types banging on about their new Land Rover or how they rescued a sheep that had strayed on to the moors. I had visions of dates spent discussing whether or not to bring the hens into the house because of the threat of avian 'flu. It's all right,' she nodded earnestly when I looked at her, 'I do know avian 'flu's important. But this guy,' she tapped the screen, 'he sounded so different – even though he doesn't actually say what he does.

And it's very tempting to think someone will mould themselves to your wishes, even though you know they probably won't. But his emails, Lee-Lee, they were just so wonderful, he seemed to know exactly who I was and what I needed. He gave me such good advice, right down to how to deal with Sylvia. I told him all about how she infuriated me, how she made me feel so useless at The Pelican and do you know what he told me?'

'What?'

'He said I should flatter her. He said from the sound of her she was probably insecure and that she was jealous of my being younger than she was and that I should never show her that she made me feel inferior.' Gussie raised her eyes at the memory. 'He said I should rise above her carping and turn it around. He suggested I compliment her on something she was wearing, ask her advice about something, make like I was in awe of her. He said that way I'd secretly have power over her.'

She gripped my shoulders and I sensed her excitement.

'I didn't understand what he meant at first, Lee-Lee, but he was right. Sylvia *is* susceptible to flattery. She almost purred like a Cheshire cat the first time I told her the blue of her shirt really brought out the color of her eyes. She was actually quite nice to me for the rest of the day.'

'Can you show me these emails?'

'No,' said Gussie, 'I'm an idiot about saving them. I never remember.'

'Gussie, you know what you've got to do, don't you?'

'What's that?' She turned back to close down the Exmoormates.com site and I could tell she wasn't really listening.

'You've got to keep your date with him. We have to find out who he is.'

Gussie froze. 'Because you think he might have been involved in Rosemary Waters' death? Because he knew about her allergy?'

'When is your date?' I asked her.

'Sometime next week – we still have to fix the place. Come to think of it I haven't heard anything from him since Rosemary Waters' death. He's gone quiet.'

'Email him now and find out what's happening.'

'Maybe I'll never hear from him again,' said Gussie hopefully, 'but OK, I'll ask him. Oh, get that, will you?' she added as the phone rang.

'Is this – oh my goodness, I am so silly, I've forgotten your name. I thought Gussie would answer and I'd be able to ask her.'

I recognized the voice instantly. I could almost *hear* the fake smile in the patronizing tone.

'It's Nathalie.' I hoped she'd be stopped in her tracks by my curtness.

Not a bit of it. 'Oh, Lee, yes, of course. Forgive me. And how lucky for me because it's you I want to talk to.'

Sylvia waited for me to say something and I didn't. After a second she gave an irritating little giggle.

'I'd better get to the point, hadn't I? I wanted you to know that I've been given the all clear to re-open the restaurant and—'

'So Gussie can have her job back?'

'Oh no! Oh, I mean, I'm terribly sorry but that's just not possible.' She actually sounded quite flustered. 'We've been through this. You were there. I have to let her go but I'm calling because I want to offer *you* a job, Lee.'

'As Gussie's replacement.' I didn't even make it a question.

'Oh heavens, no! I want you to—'

'No, you don't understand,' I interrupted. I felt some kind of strong inner resolve to get the upper hand of Sylvia, 'I *want* to be Gussie's replacement. I know why you're calling. You want me to write your book. Well, this would be the perfect way for me to do research for it because I'd be right there on the spot. You wouldn't have to waste time telling me all about that side of things.'

I didn't quite know why I was talking to her so firmly. It wasn't the usual way I dealt with potential subjects for ghosting assignments. Normally I let them think they had the upper hand, pandering to their egos until I had extracted from them all the detail I required to get inside their personalities in order to be able to tell their story.

But if I stopped to think about it for a second, I knew I was just stringing Sylvia along. I had no intention of writing her book for her. I was just using her as a way of getting into her restaurant to find out what had happened the night the peanut woman – as I still called Rosemary Waters in my mind – had died.

'Well, yes, I suppose you would.' She didn't sound too sure.

I pressed my advantage. 'You must be rushed off your feet most of the time,' I said, 'it'd be a way for us to spend time together, time you'd otherwise have to squeeze into your hectic day.'

'Do you have any experience working in a restaurant?'

'None whatsoever,' I said cheerfully, 'but I can wash dishes and I'm a quick learner and you'll be there to show me the way.'

She batted the ball back and forth for a few more minutes while I wore her down with bare-faced lies like *I can't wait to find out how you started such an extraordinary venture, I called all my friends in London and they all seem to have heard about you, surely all the TV networks must be knocking on your door?*

'Let's give it a trial run,' she finally suggested. 'Today's Saturday. Can you be here Monday morning around ten?'

'You're insane,' said Gussie cheerfully when I put down the phone. 'You'll regret it within five seconds of signing on. Anyway, it's *your* problem. Now, when I logged on just now I found an email from Mr Wright. He wants to postpone our date until the week after next but we're on for the Sunday of that week. Odd day of the week for a first date but there you are. At The Longhouse, a pub where they serve really good food. It's a bit remote, it's right out in the country at the foot of the moors but it's cozy in the winter, they have a roaring fire and candlelight and stuff. I love it.'

She prattled on with a lot of girly talk about how she didn't have anything to wear and maybe she should call that woman who had wanted to hire the Village Hall for beauty makeovers.

I wasn't listening. My mind had strayed back to her description of her perfect man. I wished I could say that I would write the same sort of thing but I knew it wouldn't be true. My perfect man was someone who got under my skin and gnawed away at me, someone who focused all their attention on me one minute and barely seemed to know I existed the next. I yearned for someone whose capricious moods left me without a clue as to where I stood but whose approval – even *in absentia* – I sought in my mind for everything I did.

It was just as well I was terrified of seeking a partner on the Internet because the only thing I could honestly say about the person I was looking for would be *I want Max Austin. No one else need apply.*

Which was why I had not stopped thinking about Jake the Rake since he had made his hasty getaway from Maggie Blair's wake. Which was why I told Gussie later that afternoon that I was going out for a couple of hours to explore the countryside, something I'd meant to do ever since I'd arrived but had never got around to.

'Don't get lost,' said Gussie. 'It can get a bit blowy and snowy if you're going up on the moors. Don't want to have to come and dig you out like an old sheep at the end of the winter.'

'I've got a map,' I said, waving it at her as I left. It was a map on which I had scored a large cross marking Jake Austin's farm. Dorcas Farm. That was all that was given as his address when I looked him up in the phone book. I could have asked Gussie where to find him but then I would have had to give a reason why and I wasn't ready to tell her about Max yet.

Dorcas Farm was about seven miles away. With the map lying open on the passenger seat beside me, I drove along the Exe Valley with the steep banks of the moors rising either side of me, finally crossing the river over a bridge that ran along six stone arches. Then I began to climb from the lowland up on to Dorcas Moor itself. That morning the sky had been overcast and ominous but so far the rain had held off and I stopped the car to get out and savor the breathtaking view. A couple of ravens cawed above me and then a buzzard wheeled overhead making a weird plaintive call and I cringed instinctively, imagining that at any moment it would swoop down and attack me. Far away on the horizon a dark cloud was rolling in and I could feel the wind increasing all around me. As I stood there a herd of wild ponies appeared, wending their way in a long file over the gorse to seek shelter lower down the hill from the oncoming storm. I'd heard about the Exmoor ponies and I noted the way their red-brown coloring blended like a deer's with the heather and bracken of the moors. They seemed to be leading me over the hill and I got back in the car and followed them slowly along the road.

According to the map, Dorcas Farm was located on Dorcas Down, which fell away from the moor below Dorcas Tor. To reach it I had to drive off the moor road along a twisting lane that was barely more than a track. The clouds, pushed by the wind, were fast advancing and I was relieved to catch a glimpse of tall chimneys and a slate roof beyond a ridge up ahead. I proceeded cautiously along the track, by now slippery with wet mud, until I came to an abrupt halt, my path blocked by a herd of red cattle. They were massive beasts with curling hair and huge white horns and they surrounded the car like a pack of hungry press photographers, barely reacting when I tooted the horn. I inched the car forward, nudging them out of the way until I crossed the cattle grid and descended a sharp incline to the farm.

As I neared the farmyard I felt the car's wheels begin to turn in the mud and I veered off to park at the edge of a field. By the time I approached the house my boots were caked in dark-red dirt. It was a miserable-looking house, square and built of rough stone with small lead-paned windows. It faced north and I could imagine the dark depression that filled the rooms inside. The surrounding barns seemed to have been totally neglected. They were in such bad repair that much of the stone wall had collapsed into rubble. This is the country, I told myself as I squeezed through the gap left by a rusty iron gate that had fallen off its hinges, this is the reality. All this time you've been picturing an idyllic existence of rural bliss but you're an idiot. This is what it's like. Wet and cold and run-down.

But it'll be nice and warm inside, I thought. There'll be a welcoming Aga and Jake the Rake will make me a nice hot cup of tea. I knocked nervously on the front door but there was no reply and when I tried the handle it was locked. I waded through the mud around the back and was confronted by a hayloft obscuring the rear wing of the house. The tall double doors were slightly ajar and I crept inside, relieved to see that I could walk through to the doors on the far side and out to the house.

There were a few chickens squawking away. For some reason they weren't on the ground but had somehow flapped their way to a higher perch. I was looking up at them so I didn't see the messy trail of blood and feathers that lay directly in my path and I stepped right in it. The attack had been a massacre. At least seven chickens had had their throats rent and torn apart.

I screamed in shock. I went on screaming, registering the awful din I was making but not understanding it was coming from me for several seconds. I looked down. The dull red dirt on my boots was now mixed with the scarlet of the chickens' blood. I screamed again and then stood, silent, unable to move. No one came. I was alone here on the moors and a witness to carnage. Who was to say that my own throat would not be ripped out before I made it back to my car?

I lurched out of the hayloft straight into a mass of nettles and stumbled over to the house, trying the handle of the nearest door and finding it open. I entered without bothering to knock and shouted.

'Anybody here?' And then louder. 'IS THERE ANYBODY HERE?'

It suddenly occurred to me that maybe this wasn't Dorcas Farm, that I was trespassing on a stranger's property. Twenty seconds later it dawned on me that even if I was in the right place, I was actually trespassing on Jake's property. He hadn't invited me and he clearly wasn't here to receive me.

But then I looked down at the bloody footprints my boots were making on the stone floor and I knew I wasn't going anywhere in a hurry. I went into the kitchen, telling myself I was looking for evidence that I was in Jake's house.

There was an Aga – or a range of some sort – and an open fireplace in the wall opposite with a tall pile of ash smoldering in the grate. I nearly tripped over a rising pile of *Farmer's Weekly* on the floor. I could see no modern appliances but I could hear an electrical hum of some sort and peering through a door, I saw a washing machine in motion in a larder, whirring away below shelves of canned food, a cold roast joint congealing on a platter and a dish of hardened cheese.

The sink was filled with dirty crockery as was the wooden draining board either side of it. A microwave looked ridiculously modern on the counter beside a chipped enamel bread bin and what looked like a toaster from the 1950s. Empty milk bottles crowded the floor and their silver tops were scattered all over the kitchen table beside an unruly pile of unopened brown envelopes. Whoever lived here clearly wasn't in the habit of opening their bills.

It *was* Jake Austin, I discovered when I picked up one of the envelopes and suddenly I was curious to find out more about Max's uncle. And he appeared to have had company recently because there was an empty wine bottle on the table and two empty glasses beside it. Female company judging by the lipstick smear on one of the glasses.

There was a narrow staircase leading out of the kitchen and I went up it straight into a low-beamed attic. It was empty except for a wooden chair at a trestle table with a computer on it. I tried to step up into the attic and realized the ceiling was too low for me to stand upright. Jake was taller than me, I recalled. He must have to slither across the floor like a snake if he ever needed to come up here.

Coming back down I realized there was another staircase where I had entered the house. This one led to the upper floor of the main part of the house and I came across a couple of monastic bedrooms with single iron cots in them with the bedding folded up into a roll. The bathroom across the landing was ancient with sloping ceilings running almost to the floor and exposed copper pipes. There was a giant claw-footed tub below the window and the toilet's cistern was high up on the wall. To flush it you had to yank a long chain hanging down. It was a long time since I'd seen one of those.

It was pretty spartan up here, I noticed – just a towel hanging from a nail and a shaving kit and toothpaste and a brush beside the basin – but it was neat and clean. But the master bedroom – if you could call it that – was a shock because instead of the simple sleeping arrangement of a bachelor that I had expected to find, the room was filled with an ostentatious king-sized bed. It was voluptuous and inviting but also strangely lurid with a gaudy maroon eiderdown and black satin pillowcases. Other than a Bible and an alarm clock, there was nothing on the nightstand, no personal effects anywhere in the room as far as I could see and I found it unnerving. Who *was* Jake Austin?

I turned to leave the room and stopped dead. My boots had left a trail of bloody footprints across the floor. They must be all over the house, blatant evidence of my snooping. I flung open what I assumed was the door of a wall closet, hoping in my panic that I would find some sort of cleaning material but all I saw were three jackets and a lonely suit hanging forlornly in the dark space.

And then I heard the sound of a vehicle coming down the hill. As it pulled to a stop outside the house, I backed out of the walk-in closet and as I did so I caught a glimpse of some kind of poster taped to the inside of the door.

It was a pin-up of a woman lying on a bed, hair splayed out on the cover. She was naked and a slender line of black hair running from her navel to her crotch was the only detail I had time to take in before I slammed the door shut.

Randy old Jake the Rake, I thought, as I tore down the stairs, just reaching the bottom step when I heard him come in the back door. I managed to enter the kitchen seconds before he did.

He didn't say anything, just walked right past me to stand at the bottom of the staircase.

'Are you hurt?' he asked suddenly. He pointed to the remains of the chickens' blood and guts trailed by my boots up the stairs.

'Oh, no, not at all. I'm so sorry about the mess. I should have taken my boots off when I came in. Your chickens – outside in the barn – something's got at them, ripped them apart and I stepped in it. What was it, a fox?'

'Probably a mink,' he said, looking me up and down. 'So what took you upstairs?'

'I was looking for you,' I said. It was the first thing that came into my head and in a way it was the truth. I was looking for clues that would tell me more about him. 'I came here to see you, I wanted to ask you—' I faltered here, wondering how I could have been so stupid as not to prepare a reason for visiting him. Then it came to me. 'I wanted to ask you more about Maggie Blair.'

'Nonsense,' he said. He sounded brusque but there was an amused look in his eyes. 'You came here to ask me about my nephew.'

Chapter Six

'Why do you look so shattered?' He shrugged off his coat and tossed it over a chair. 'I'm right, aren't I? Something's going on between you and Max. You flushed bright red when you asked me if I was related to him at Maggie's wake.'

'Did *he* say there was something between us?' I asked in wonder.

Jake shook his head. 'I told you. I haven't been in touch with him recently. Want me to call him up and ask him? Oh God, now you're covered in confusion again. Calm down! And *sit* down. I'll make you a nice cup of tea and you can tell Uncle Jake all about it.'

He was teasing me and I wasn't quite sure what to do about it. That was the problem when it came to Max. Whenever his name came up, my feelings about him were written all over my face, as they say. And I couldn't quite make Jake Austin out. There was something lugubrious about him, an air of melancholy lurking behind a rather provocative front.

But the way things stood, he was my only link to Max and I couldn't afford not to exploit it.

'Tell me the truth about you and him,' he said, suddenly serious, 'don't hold anything back. My nephew's a tricky bastard and I can probably help you out with him. God knows, I've done it before. Tea or coffee? And it'll be instant or teabags. We don't stand on ceremony up here at Dorcas Farm.'

'We?'

He smiled, wistfully I thought. 'OK, *I* don't stand on ceremony. I'm all alone up here, as you've probably gathered.'

'You never married? And I'd love a cup of tea, please. Tetley's or PG Tips, if you have it.'

He reached for a tin on the back of the Aga and settled the kettle on the hob.

'No, I never married,' he said slowly. 'I'm a loner, if you really want to know.'

'Me too,' I blurted out and then regretted it. Did I really want to align myself with this strange man?

'Well then, you know what it's like,' he said. 'You might want someone in your life but you don't want them around all the time. I'm set in my ways now. I like it up here on my own. In fact, you're the first visitor I've had in a month or so. That's why I don't have any sociable biscuits to offer you with your tea.'

As he said this his eye rested on the lipstick-smeared wine glass and he plucked both glasses swiftly off the table and into the sink. I pretended not to notice.

I looked around the kitchen. What did he do about meals? I wondered. Did he cook for himself? Properly, like I did? That was the secret of living on your own, you had to behave just the same as if you were with a house full of people. No sloppiness, no allowance for the fact that no one was going to see you. No standing at the counter and wolfing down a sandwich. Lay the table, sit down to eat, pour yourself a glass of wine.

He saw me looking and pointed to the microwave. 'Changed my life,' he said, 'that and the Internet. You know there are millions like me all over the world, I imagine. Get up, go to work, come home exhausted, eat a microwave dinner, check the email, do your laundry watch TV, fall into bed, jerk off—' He saw my face. 'Sorry, but it's a fact of life.

I don't pull them in like I used to. Don't pull them in at all anymore actually.'

Was he talking about women? This wasn't at all the kind of conversation I had planned on having.

'You said *go to work*,' I said to change the subject. 'You have a job somewhere? I thought you were a farmer – here, I mean—' Actually I didn't really know what I meant but I couldn't quite see him getting up and putting on a suit and going to an office in Exeter or somewhere.

'And farming's not a job? I *did* farm, all right? I tried damn hard to keep it going when my father died.' He sounded almost belligerent, as if I'd accused him of shirking his duty. 'For going on fifteen years I got up in the morning – and when I say morning, most of the time it was still dark – and I went out there and I worked the land from dawn to dusk to try and hold this place together. But I failed. Where my father and my grandfather had succeeded, I failed. It's just a smallholding, you'd think I'd have been able to manage it, but no. I was a bloody failure. Mind you,' he said quickly before I could react to the note of self-pity that had crept into his voice, 'it wasn't lack of effort that was my biggest problem, it was the fact that I was so resistant to change. I grew up thinking that one day I'd be growing oats and hay and plowing the fields with a carthorse, But there's no haymaking anymore, it's all silage-making and science these days, farm work's been completely industrialized. I went away for twenty years to seek my fortune and I tell you, when I left we didn't even have a tractor!'

He shook his head in a *how could I have been so dumb* gesture.

'I was a fool,' he went on. 'I came back when Dad died, thinking *I grew up on the farm, I know what's what, I can just step right in and take over* but of course everything had changed beyond recognition. And I couldn't find anyone to hire. All the farm hands had left the area. Say what you will, the old traditional way of farming might have been slower and yielded less but it provided a heck of a lot more jobs and when

91

those went, so did the able-bodied men in the area. I should have gone right out and invested in machinery but I didn't and then it was too late. However,' he said, 'that's the downside.'

'There's an upside?'

'There certainly is.' Now his eyes were suddenly gleaming. 'It's called the European Union. I've brought this farm to an absolute standstill but they're happy to throw money at me because I have twenty acres so I still qualify as a farmer. You'd think they'd tie it to the amount of crop produced the way everyone's farming whatever grows quickest, but no, it's based on the amount of land owned. I just stick my hand out along with everyone else and bow down to a new deity: subsidy.'

'So what did you do? While you were gone, making your fortune?'

'Oh God, you had to go and ask that, didn't you? Of course I didn't make a fortune. I never even got to London. I was a night porter and a desk clerk in a seedy hotel in Bournemouth for most of the time. I don't even want to talk about it.'

'What about Max's father? Your brother? Did he leave the farm too?'

'Absolutely. Sam got away before I did. He was the successful brother. I mean he didn't make much money either but at least he could hold his head up and say he did the best he could.'

'What did he do?'

Jake smiled. 'You know what he did? He was a baker. I loved it because I could see some correlation between that and my dad growing crops. Sam baked bread and sold it in a little corner shop in Wimbledon. They even expanded it to include a tea room where he and Maisie – that's Max's mother – served pastries.'

Max's parents ran a pastry shop. Whatever next? 'Is it still there?'

Jake shook his head. 'Whole area was bulldozed to make way for a mall. Far as I can tell poor old Sam was ripped off,

92

and what he did make, he plowed straight back into Max's education. When I say Sam was successful, it was because he married such a delightful person as Maisie – she made him truly happy – and they had the gumption to see that they were raising a son who was a whole lot smarter than the rest of us. They saw to it that he went to university, the first in our family, imagine that!'

'They must have been proud of Max.'

'They were. He joined the police force and he was fast-tracked for promotion but sadly not fast enough. Sam and Maisie both died before he made detective, although I have to admit I'm relieved Maisie never knew about him dealing with those sadistic killers he goes after.' Jake shuddered. 'Coming into contact with filth like that, it's no wonder Max is such a misery. Now don't look at me like that. If you know him at all, you'll know he has problems. He's destructive.' Jake spat out the word. '*Self*-destructive. I'm talking about women here. He's never sustained a good relationship—'

'And you have?' It was out before I could stop myself.

He had the grace to smile. 'Point taken, but at least I never tried. Except once.' He had turned away so I only just caught the last two words. I couldn't see his face as he said, 'OK, I screwed that up.' And then after a second he murmured, 'Maybe it's in our blood.'

He poured the tea and motioned to me to sit in an old armchair with a blanket thrown over it where I would benefit from the warmth of the Aga. He settled himself into another armchair, which boasted bald patches on the armrests and whose leather was cracked and split in places, and fished around in his jacket pocket for something. He pulled out a flattened roll-up and stuck it in his mouth but made no attempt to light it.

'Gave it up a year ago,' he said when he saw me looking at it, 'but I've got to keep something in my mouth to remember.'

Go on, I told myself, *ask him who it was. Ask him what happened. You've started this. See it through.*

But I'd lost my nerve. Instead I said, 'You must have a dog to keep you company.'

He nodded. 'I've got a bunch of 'em outside but you don't allow dogs indoors. I'll bring Willow in next winter if she's still with us but only because she'll be fourteen and her arthritis is even worse than mine. But look, it's no good trying to get me off tack. I want to hear about you and Max.'

Well, I'd walked right into this one, hadn't I? I'd come here uninvited and what he was asking me to do was have the exact same conversation I'd anticipated as I'd driven over the moors to Dorcas Farm. So why was I being such a nervous Nelly about broaching the subject of Max?

I knew why. It was because I had a feeling I wouldn't necessarily like what I was going to hear.

I was right.

Once I'd taken Jake through my initial acquaintance with Max, the solving of the arson investigation, Cath's insistence that he was clearly besotted with me and his very tentative indication of this (which I had more or less brushed aside), I went on to describe how a year later I had run into him again at a dinner party at Cath's house.

'But he brought a girlfriend.'

Jake looked up. 'He did? Who?'

'Her name was Paula. She was a blonde airhead.'

'Oh, yes, he mentioned her at some point. She wasn't anything serious.'

'I know,' I said, 'but the minute I saw him with her I was jealous and that's when I realized I felt something for him. I just hadn't been aware of it until that moment. Anyway he asked me to lunch the next day and as I sat across the table from him, I could barely stop myself from reaching over and grabbing him.'

Jake grinned. 'So we can safely say you were attracted to him? Did it go any further?'

I nodded. 'Just a little. One kiss, and it came right after I'd nearly been attacked by a maniac. We were in a room and there was a body lying in a pool of blood just the other side of the door. I'd solved a murder for Max – a case that had been cold for fourteen years – and he was in a state of total exhilaration. He just grabbed me and kissed me and I haven't been the same since.'

'What about him?' Jake had a wry expression on his face as if he knew what I was going to say.

'He hasn't said a word to me – at least not on a personal basis. We had to meet again for him to tie up loose ends with his investigation but he wouldn't look directly at me. And he never returned any of my phone calls. And yet,' I said, lowering my voice in humiliation because what I was about to tell Jake would no doubt make me sound ridiculous to him, 'I went back to America, where I was living, and broke off my engagement to my boyfriend of nine years. And I subsequently returned to London just to be in the same city as Max. I'm besotted with your nephew but he barely seems to remember I exist.'

'Don't you believe it,' said Jake and I stared at him in amazement. 'He probably thinks about you at some point every single day. I know Max and one thing I do know is that his approach to women is completely different from mine. I'm interested in anything that moves for at least twenty seconds – or I used to be at any rate – but Max is picky. If he's not planning to embark on something serious, he doesn't even waste time looking in a woman's direction.'

'But that's exactly what I mean,' I said, aware of a plaintive note creeping into my voice. 'He hasn't looked in my direction for months.'

Jake held up his hand. 'Slow down. Let me finish. From what you've just told me, he did pay quite a bit of attention to you at one stage and based on that, trust me, he's as smitten as you are.'

'But why didn't he follow up on it? Why ignore me?'

'Who the hell knows? That's Max all over. It seems as soon as he wakes up to the fact that he's interested in a woman, he starts backing away. You wouldn't be the first.'

'I wouldn't?'

'Why do you think Sadie came down to see me?'

Now he really had my attention. 'But Sadie was his wife.'

'Precisely. He played games even once he was married. All lovey-dovey one month and then just as she was convinced he'd finally settled into the relationship, he'd scuttle away again, didn't speak to her, pleaded too much work. He was just incapable of getting close.'

'But I don't get it,' I said. 'I heard she was down here on vacation. A week in the country sort of thing.'

'That was how she pitched it to Max. But it wasn't like that at all. She called me up one day and said she couldn't take Max's moods for one more minute. She was on the point of walking out on him, could she come down here and talk it through with me? She didn't know who else she could discuss him with and it not be an act of betrayal.'

'And while she was here she was murdered?'

'You're dying to know all about that, aren't you?' I was but he looked unbelievably sad so I didn't say anything, just prayed he'd go on and tell me.

'You know she was half-Jamaican?'

I nodded. 'She was black.'

'Well no, she wasn't really,' he corrected me. 'She had light caramel-colored skin but they did float the idea that it was some sort of hate crime. They found some members of a splinter faction of the BNP who had rented a farmhouse not too far away and there was a cache of firearms in one of the bedrooms.'

'But she wasn't shot?'

'No, she was strangled – and there was evidence she'd been drugged first. Her stomach was full of barbiturates and there was a ton of alcohol in her blood. But her dog had been cut up into pieces and scattered around a field.'

I winced at the thought of it. 'And it happened soon after she arrived? Do you think whoever killed her had followed her from London? Was it connected to one of Max's investigations?'

'It happened months after she first came down.'

'Months? I thought she was only here a week.'

'That was the original plan. But she came back after about a fortnight in London and then she stayed for a long time and it was during that time that she started thinking about leaving Max.'

'Didn't he come down and see her during all that time?'

'What have I just told you? Sometimes he never went near her. Of course he said he was tied up with a case when she was down here but it wasn't as if he even picked up the phone that often.'

'And you couldn't talk her out of it?'

He didn't say anything.

'What about her murder? I mean, how did it happen?' I persisted, 'Did she go out for a walk or something and not come back?'

'Or something,' he repeated. 'Listen, do you mind if we don't talk about this. I'll tell you anything you want to know about Max but I get a bit jittery if I dwell on Sadie's death for too long.'

'Of course,' I said, 'sorry.' *He feels responsible – she died while she was staying with him,* I realized suddenly. *Maybe he even feels guilty in some way.* Except he was the one who had brought her into the conversation and of course now all I could think about was her relationship with Max, which was now presumably off limits. 'So are you saying I'm better off not getting involved with Max – even if I had the opportunity?'

He smiled, rather fondly I thought.

'Not really. If it's going to happen, it's going to happen has always been my view. Not a lot you can do about it. Lord knows, I've had enough women here I should never have gone anywhere near.'

'You have?' My mind flashed to the king-sized bed upstairs and the black satin pillowcases. All it needed was a mirror on the ceiling above it.

'Sure.' He chuckled, back on more cheerful ground. 'I'm the archetypal bachelor, got a bit of a reputation, I shouldn't wonder. I used to just go down the pub and chat up a girl, bring her back up here. Then I learned how to use a computer and I just looked for them on the Internet, ordered them like a takeaway pizza. Brilliant! Those were the days.' He chuckled again.

'They came up here? Aren't you supposed to have the first date in a public place, just for safety?'

'Listen, darling, the girls who answered my emails, they knew what they were coming here for, believe me. I made no secret that I was looking for a shag. Why waste time? I was well enough known round here that no one thought it was dangerous to come to Dorcas Farm.'

'And you're still at it?' I remembered the computer in the attic.

He shook his head. 'Haven't got the energy, to tell you the truth. I think about it now and again and my profile's still on DirtyFarmers.com so I still get the odd email.'

'DirtyFarmers.com?'

'That's what I call it because that's what it is, a bunch of horny farmers looking for action. No, it's called something like Exmoordates.com. You should try it, my dear, before you think about wasting any more time on that morose nephew of mine but you'd better do something about your appearance before you do.'

He was joking, right?

Apparently not.

'Well, look at you. You're not giving out any vibes at all. Dressed all in black, ratty jeans, filthy old raincoat, your skin's as dull as dishwater and God knows when you last washed your hair. I'm in better nick than you are. You haven't thought about sex in quite a while, have you?'

I stared at him, completely dumbfounded.

'I thought so,' he went on, 'in your head you're "saving" yourself for Max. You're not even entertaining the thought that you might be available to anyone else you might meet and it shows. Big mistake! Supposing Max walked through the door right now. He'd barely notice you. The only time I've seen you remotely come to life was when you were watching me across Maggie's grave and I'm guessing that was because I reminded you of him.'

'You're very perceptive,' I commented, trying not to sound too surly.

'I'm a dirty old man is what you're really thinking,' he laughed. 'Listen, I like women. I've observed their behavior for years. I know what makes them tick – which is more than Max does – and I'm telling you, you've shut down because of him and we've got to do something about that.'

'You're not to tell Max I'm here. Oh *please* don't tell him you've met me. He'll think I came here deliberately, to meet you and ask you about him.'

'Well didn't you?'

'I mean to Frampton Abbas. He won't believe it's a coincidence that my cousin happens to live there.'

'He might,' said Jake thoughtfully. 'You'd be surprised how many people are hiding in this neck of the woods. A lot of the old farms round here have been bought by people from London who have turned them into second homes. Natives like me are few and far between these days.'

'Promise me?' I pleaded again.

But he just grinned at me.

Suddenly I wanted to get away from Jake fast. As I sat there listening to him I began to think that if I persisted in being a loner, this was how I'd wind up. It wasn't a pretty thought. There was something pathetic about old men on their own but who was to say it wouldn't be the same for a polar bear like me in years to come?

As I stood up to make my excuses and leave, the phone rang.

Jake reached out for the cordless on the kitchen table. 'Marjorie, what's up?'

My neighbor, he mouthed at me, *the farm just over the hill.*

'OK, *OK*! Calm down.' He pointed to the phone and rolled his eyes. 'There's no point getting all worked up. She probably just stayed the night at a friend's. Did she really? No. No, I haven't seen her. *Marjorie!* Give me a break. Why would I lie to you? If I tell you I haven't seen her, then I haven't seen her, OK? Absolutely. You'll be the first to know.'

He disconnected and slumped down in his chair.

'Trouble?' I said.

'Marjorie Mackay. Frets herself stupid night and day. If I ran down there every time she called me with a problem I'd have worn my legs out by now.'

'What's happened?'

'Nothing, more than likely. Her twenty-nine-year-old goddaughter Melanie comes down from London to stay with her on a regular basis. God knows why, there's bugger all for her to do around here. Anyway she didn't come home last night and Marjorie's got her knickers in a twist, thinks she's been abducted by aliens or something.'

I smiled but at the same time I felt a trickle of unease. But then I was another Marjorie, fretting away whenever I could.

'Take it from me, Melanie was screwing the socks off some guy she met on Dirty Farmers.com.'

'Exmoormates.com?' I stared at him.

'The very same. I turned her on to it myself last year. If anyone was after a dirty farmer, it was Melanie. And don't look at me like that. I admit I was tempted but I had the sense to realize I was at least twenty years too old for her taste. But I enjoy seeing her. She keeps herself fit by hiking over the moors from Marjorie's to the quarry every day and that takes her right past my door. Often as not she'll drop in for a cuppa or a glass of wine.' He nodded towards the sink where he'd deposited the glasses I'd noticed before. 'She'll probably turn up any minute if you hang around. She could show you a thing or two about how to get yourself in shape for Max, could Melanie.'

Now I really had to get out of there before he hammered my self-esteem into irretrievable pulp. I walked purposefully towards the door but he didn't try to stop me going.

'I expect you'll be back,' was all he said as I reached for my raincoat – he was right, it *was* filthy – and stepped out into the yard. He didn't seem to care about the bloody footprints my boots had left all over his house. His own rubber boots with their giant feet and rounded toe area curling upward stood where he'd discarded them on his return, caked with mud by the back door. He started to put them on, mumbling something about accompanying me to my car.

'Please don't worry,' I said, 'but if it's OK, I'd like to leave by the front door. I can't face walking past those chickens again.'

'You wouldn't last long down here, would you?' He smiled at me, not unkindly. 'You're probably better off getting back to London. But I expect I'll see you again,' he repeated, 'and sooner rather than later.'

As I slowed down to cross the cattle grid I saw something that the herd of red cattle had hidden from my view when I'd arrived. A dead sheep lay by the roadside and one of its eyes had been pecked out, probably by one of the buzzards circling overhead.

As I stared at the gaping socket I wondered how long it would be before Jake towed it away.

Chapter Seven

When I turned up at The Pelican a couple of days later to start work, the door was locked. Sylvia had asked me to be there at nine so I could observe the lunchtime prep work while I was instructed in my duties as kitchen slave.

I knocked tentatively on the glass pane and when there was no reply I went around the side, under a stone arch linking two buildings and along an alley until I found a side door Gussie had told me about.

'It leads directly into the kitchen,' she said, 'sometimes they don't unlock the main entrance to the restaurant until they're ready to open. Kitchen staff come and go via the alley.'

Like the door to the street this one was also half-glazed and I rapped on a pane.

Nothing.

In sleep-deprived irritation – once again the ducks had awakened me far too early – I kicked hard against the lower part of the door, rendering a series of thuds. Maybe someone was in the back and hadn't heard me. I pressed my face to the glass, my breath leaving a blurry mess in the cold air, and peered in but after a few seconds there was still no sign of life.

I was about to give up in disgust when I sensed a tiny movement on the staircase leading up out of the kitchen. It was a big toe – and then another one – on the end of gnarled and encrusted feet.

And then I looked away quickly because what followed were pale legs sprouting tufts of hair and above them two swollen gooseberries and a bobbing frankfurter.

Had their owner seen me? For a moment I contemplated running back up the alley rather than be caught spying on a naked man at nine o'clock in the morning.

But it was too late. The door opened and André stood there looking at me blankly. Mercifully, he had donned a large butcher's apron – navy/white striped – on his way to the door.

'We're not open for breakfast,' he said and the *breakfast* was mangled because his mouth widened as he said it to deliver a cavernous yawn. His voice was so soft in any case that I could barely hear him. And raspy. When he sneezed suddenly and followed it up with a paroxysm of coughing, I realized he was sick.

'I know,' I said quickly, motioning to him to turn around and get back inside out of the cold. I followed him in before he could say anything, closing the door behind me, and was confronted with the sight of his naked butt. Oh shit! I don't know why but I'd automatically assumed he'd have found a pair of boxers lying around the kitchen and put them on, along with the apron, before opening the door to me.

'Docsn't sound like you're in great shape,' I said. 'Hadn't you better put something on before you catch cold?'

He looked down at his apron as if to say *I've got something on* and then his whole body convulsed with an explosive sneeze.

'I've already caught cold.' He smiled disarmingly.

And I became aware of something I hadn't registered when he'd first spoken to me.

'You're American,' I said. Somehow this small detail had escaped Gussie's portrait of him.

'Yeah, I know,' he said, 'but I've caught a freakin' *English* cold.'

103

'Seriously,' I said, 'I really think you ought to put some clothes on. For decency.' I smiled to show I was only pretending to be a prude. And ruined it all by blushing scarlet as I noticed when he turned round to face me that his hands were plunged into the large boat-shaped pocket of his apron at the level of his penis.

'First you mind telling me who you are?'

It was a fair question but it was also a bit of a disappointment that he didn't remember me.

'We've met before,' I said, keeping my eyes steadfastly at chest level, 'you know. In church?'

'In *church*?' Now he was giving himself a good scratch.

'At Maggie Blair's funeral.'

'You knew Maggie?'

I nodded. 'I was sitting in the same pew as you. Right next to Gussie. I'm her cousin.'

'Gussie!' His face, unshaven and still puffy with sleep, was jumpstarted into animation. 'You know Gussie?'

'I just said, I'm her cousin. Lee Bartholomew.' I held out my hand.

He stopped scratching his balls and shook it.

'André Balfour.'

Standing close to him I was aware that he stank of old fat, of onions, of faded spices and my nose wrinkled in revulsion.

'Any chance you could take a shower while you're at it?'

It was downright rude of me. I'd only just met him and I was in what was to all intents and purposes *his* kitchen but he gave me a good-natured grin and nodded. His green eyes whose brilliance had impressed me when I'd first seen them were actually quite soft, I noticed, bringing a gentleness to his face, less feral than might have been suggested by the otherwise scabrous figure he presented.

'You had breakfast?' he asked, and before I could reply, *Yes, I'd had some coffee and a bowl of Raisin Bran* he'd bounded back up the stairs, yelling behind him.

'Stay right there. I'll make you breakfast when I've had a shower.'

He lived above the restaurant. I hadn't known that. And he must have held the world record for speedy showering because he was back downstairs again in just over five minutes, dressed in a pair of navy sweatpants and a light gray hoodie. His feet were still bare and he went around the kitchen, tentatively poking his toe under the counters until he located his clogs and kicked them into view. He bent forward so that his mane of tangled wet curls almost touched the floor and then straightened without warning to toss them back, spattering me with a shower of droplets. When it looked like he was going to do it at least ten times, I backed into a corner.

'Good way to dry my hair and exercise at the same time,' he said, finally remaining vertical for more than ten seconds. He retrieved some coffee from the freezer, busied himself with the espresso machine for a minute or two and then slipped a CD into the player.

'Schubert,' he told me, as the sound of piano filled the kitchen, '*Die späten Klaviersonaten. Drei Klavierstücke. Trois pièces pour piano. Tre pezzi per pianoforte.* Or three piano pieces to you and me. I tell you, you could learn languages from music notes.'

'Good idea,' I said. 'Sylvia's not here?' I was beginning to think that maybe I had got the time wrong.

He looked pained. 'No,' he said, and then, speaking very slowly and quietly, 'she is *not* here and I wish to God you had not mentioned her name and ruined my morning. I went to bed at four. I could have slept till noon but you woke me up and no,' he held up his hand, 'don't apologize, I'm glad you did. It means I can spend a little downtime in my kitchen before that woman gets here. A little piano, a cappuccino, an omelette, a quiet chat with Gussie's cousin.'

'I could have sworn she asked me to come at nine.'

'Sure but that doesn't mean *she'll* be here then. She demands that people dance to her tune but that doesn't mean she'll get her own act together. She'll be here ten thirty at the earliest so you've got time to let me make you an omelette. Sit down.' He pointed to a bar stool below the hatch to the restaurant. 'But hey, tell me something. Why are you here anyway?'

'I'm reporting for work,' I said. How come he didn't know if it was his kitchen?

'This doesn't sound good,' he said, handing me a frothy cappuccino, 'we don't need anybody.'

'I'm replacing Gussie,' I said nervously.

He looked shocked. 'Where'd she go?'

'Nowhere.' I nodded my head in the direction of Gussie's house up the road. 'She's at home. Sylvia came round and told her she wouldn't be needed anymore.'

He had his back to me and he stiffened. Without saying a word he reached for a black steel frying pan and set it on the stove. I noted that the pan was dirty but he didn't wash it. Instead he turned the heat up high under the pan and then scoured it with some coarse sea salt.

There was a stillness in the kitchen punctuated by the Schubert blending in with the hiss of the gas on the stove. André beat some eggs with a fork. 'Look,' he said, 'aerated. Very important.' Then he beckoned me to stand beside him as he seasoned the eggs. He gestured for me to open a giant fridge and pointed at the butter, which he chopped into little pieces and mixed into the eggs.

'Now watch,' he whispered. 'That steel,' he pointed to the pan into which he splashed a tiny bit of oil, 'is now *very* hot and when I pour the eggs in – like this – I'm going to stir as fast as I can so they won't curdle. I'm going to stir with the fork, see? And I'm going to keep moving the pan with my other hand at the same time – the eggs go one way, the pan goes another.'

He had begun to whistle softly in tune with the Schubert.

'Aren't they beautiful?' He nodded at the eggs. 'They're still runny and now I'm going to tap the pan on the burner so that they spread out everywhere, and I'm going to lift the pan

– like this—' He grabbed the handle and flipped the omelette once, and then again on to a plate that he had conjured up beside the stove without my even noticing.

'And here's your breakfast,' he said, propelling me back to the hatch and setting the omelette down in front of the bar stool that I had left for less than three minutes. When he'd made his own, I saw him toss the pan back on the shelf and knew that it would not be touched – let alone wiped – until he next made an omelette.

'Thank you,' I said, 'that was the best omelette I've ever eaten.' And it was.

'*De nada,*' he said, 'but listen are you really going to work here? This is not a normal restaurant kitchen,' he added suddenly. 'Most kitchens I have worked in do not have a window, do not have light. Until I cooked at The Pelican, I worked seven days a week without ever seeing daylight. *That* is normal. This,' he pointed to the weak winter sun that was beginning to filter in through the window, 'this is paradise. Or it would be if it were not for Sylvia. How could she get rid of Gussie? *Why* did she get rid of Gussie?'

'She's putting the blame on her for the peanut oil getting into the salad dressing – because it's looking pretty likely that that's what killed Rosemary Waters.'

He lowered his head on to his hands and his damp curls spread out over the counter like the tentacles of an octopus. They were red, I noted, not unlike Gussie's and indeed the patch of pale skin on his chest that could be glimpsed in the opening of his zippered hoodie was not unlike hers either, a mass of freckles on a white background.

'I know what's in my kitchen and there isn't any peanut oil, any peanut butter, any peanuts of any kind whatsoever.' His voice was muffled and I strained to hear. 'And you want to know why I'm so certain of that?' He looked up at me. I widened my eyes. *Why?* 'Because I knew a kid in high school who was allergic and we had it so drummed into us as kids by the teachers that she MUST NOT BE AROUND PEANUTS.

107

You don't forget, let me tell you. I mean we don't even serve French fries in this joint because they should be cooked in 375 degree peanut oil and I'm psyched to not having it in the place.'

He tipped his head back and downed his cappuccino and then shook his head vigorously as if it were tasting medicine.

'Anyway, whatever happened, Sylvia was ultimately responsible. She should have fired herself. Gussie should *never* have been allowed to open up on her own. That was sheer insanity. But as it was, you know, she really did a great job. The fact that she'd got everyone who wanted one a starter of some sort by the time Sylvia bothered to show up tells you what a trouper she is.'

Gussie a trouper? I smiled at that and made a mental note to tell her what he'd said.

He sneezed again, quite violently this time, and followed it up with another bout of coughing.

'Hadn't you better go back to bed?' I said. 'Your chest sounds bad.'

He stared at me. 'I'm the freakin' chef. Chefs don't get sick. Kitchen staff don't get sick. You never take a day off, *ever.* We're re-opening today, there's no way I can go back to bed. I was out last night taking advantage of my last night of freedom. I drove home from Exeter and I fell into bed around four. The inside of my head feels like it's in a blender set to ice crush yet there's no way I'm going to take off from work. I'm a professional.'

I supplied the unwritten subtext without even thinking about it. *I'm a professional – and Sylvia isn't. She hasn't showed up for work yet. She let Gussie open up on her own when she should have been here.*

'You show up, no matter what,' he continued, 'nothing can stop you getting to your kitchen. Even if the thermometer hits 150 degrees and you're sick to your stomach, you still gotta stand there at least five hours. And that's *after* taking care of a few hours' prep work. How come you don't know that if you work in restaurants?'

'I've never worked in a restaurant in my life,' I told him. 'I'm a writer. A *ghost*writer, to be exact. I'm going to help Sylvia with her memoir about getting The Pelican up and running and we thought if I worked here, it'd be a good way to learn the background to the book.'

'You don't *look* insane,' he said, 'in fact from my brief experience in your company, I'd have said you were perfectly normal. You already have a career, why would you want to be a cook?'

'I don't,' I said.

'You *don't* want to learn to be a cook.' His strange emerald eyes had fixated on me so intently that I was starting to feel uncomfortable. There was something mesmerizing about him. I wasn't attracted to him, he wasn't my type – I'd never gone for red-headed men – yet I couldn't deny his magnetism and this was when he was unshaven and hungover. God only knew what he was like when he felt 100 per cent.

'You have no plans to be a chef?'

I shook my head, *no plans whatsoever.*

'And yet you're volunteering to work your fingers to the bone, *literally*, by washing dishes, scrubbing pans, cleaning mushrooms, dicing tomatoes, peeling potatoes? Because don't kid yourself you're going to be doing anything else. Oh, wait, maybe you'll get to mop the floors and take out the trash. But that'll be a bonus.'

'If that's what I have to do to earn a place in this kitchen, then fine,' I said, sounding a lot more confident than I felt. 'I need to observe what goes on around here. Besides,' I added, 'I don't think Gussie had any plans to become a chef and she managed.'

'Gussie's different,' he said without explaining why although I had a pretty good idea it was because he liked having her around. 'She did OK. The only thing she couldn't handle was Sylvia and that was because Sylvia was never off her back. Gussie's one of those people who do just fine if you leave them alone to get on with whatever it is. She's a lot more competent than people realize. She copes pretty well when it gets crazy in here – and believe me, even though we're a tiny operation compared to most restaurants, it can get super stressful. I've noticed she only gets flustered if she thinks someone's judging her and that's what Sylvia does for kicks. *Why are you chopping the carrots* that *way, Gussie? Why don't you do them this way?*'

I was thrilled that he obviously got the point of Gussie. I wondered whether I should take him into my confidence and tell him that the real reason I wanted to work in his kitchen was to obtain proof of how the peanut oil had found its way there and thus clear Gussie's name.

'Is Sylvia a good cook?'

He stared at me. 'I'll pretend you didn't ask that question.'

Obviously not. 'So she doesn't do any of the cooking?'

'She does lunch,' he said. 'I do dinner. That's the deal. She runs this place, she has to do something. She makes her silly little quiches and her boring roast chicken and thinks she's Julia Child and I cook serious food in the evening. Don't tell Sylvia but in London I don't think they even know we're open for lunch.'

I didn't get it. Why would this man, who sounded as if he'd had some experience in cooking at establishments far superior to The Pelican, choose to bury himself in a one-horse town like Frampton Abbas.

'Where are you from in America?' I asked him.

'New Hampshire,' he said, 'north-east. So, Gussie, she married, divorced or what?'

'She's divorced,' I said, wondering which surprised me more – that he didn't know or that he would ask such a question out of the blue.

'So she's living in that house up the road all alone?'

'Well, I'm there now,' I pointed out.

'So you're here to stay a while?'

'Well, no, actually, I'm not. I'm just here to be with Gussie to help her—' I stopped. I dearly wanted to discuss with him the state Gussie was in. I sensed he could be a valuable ally. But I couldn't go gossiping about Gussie with someone I'd only just met.

'As I said, I'm here to help Sylvia with her book and that's why I'm going to be helping out at The Pelican. I'll be gone as soon as I've done enough research.'

'*Helping out,*' he repeated, shaking his head, '*research.* I just can't get my head round the fact that Sylvia's even thinking about a book. Because you know what? It won't be a book, it'll be a book*let*. No, it'll be a short story because if she has anything to say about her role in The Pelican's success, it'll be pure unadulterated fiction. Believe me, I'm the one you need to talk to. I can tell you everything you need to know. About Sylvia, about The Pelican, but essentially about *cooking*, about *food*, about *running* a *restaurant.* Anything Sylvia tells you will come straight out of her ass.'

'That's what Gussie implied,' I said, 'although she didn't put it quite like that.'

'And what is she *doing* getting rid of Gussie? I mean, no offense,' he held up his palms to me with a smile, 'but it's not exactly a plus that you've never worked in a restaurant. She *can't* do that to Gussie. We need *her* back here, not someone who's just *helping out.* No offense,' he repeated quickly.

I wondered what I should do. His anguish about Gussie was bordering on raving. I wanted to ask whether or not I should wait for Sylvia but I suspected that another mention of her name might possibly drive him into a further state of rage.

When the Schubert came to an end and he paused long enough in his ranting to put on another CD, I quickly made my excuses.

'André, you've been more than kind and thank you for the omelette but I don't want to take up any more of your morning. I'll run back home and come back in an hour or so.'

'Say hi to Gussie. Tell her I'll call her,' he said, making no move to detain me.

On the walk back to the house I found myself relaxing with every step and realized that while all the time I had spent with André he had spoken softly and, until I had mentioned Sylvia, quite gently, I had at the same time been aware of how wired he was. I came to the conclusion that I had been subconsciously waiting for him to explode at any second.

I sensed that nothing got past him and once I got to know him better, I planned to sit him down and interrogate him about the events in the kitchen leading up to the fatal peanut poisoning.

And how many other people had I come across who knew instinctively what made Gussie tick? *Something's going to happen,* I told myself. *He's interested in her and he's clearly one of those people who goes after what he wants. But is he right for Gussie? Can she handle someone like him?*

I was pondering all this when I let myself into the house, anxious to tell Gussie what he'd said about her, but she wasn't there. There was a note on the kitchen table. *Gone to Exeter to see Gilly Mortimer. Back in time to have a post-mortem about your first day (I hope). xxG*

Suddenly at a loose end, I went upstairs and turned on my computer. I'd been spending nearly all my time with Gussie who, despite her assurance that she would leave me alone, always found some excuse to seek me out. *Lee-Lee, can you help me take the washing down? I've hung it in the yard out back to dry and now it looks as if it's going to rain any second.* Or *Lee-Lee, I've bought a chocolate cake for tea. It was half price at the baker's and I thought, why not? Come down and have some. Pleeeeease, Lee-Lee.*

Normally these sort of trivial interruptions would have driven me mad but I told myself firmly that it wasn't as if I had any work to do – yet – and besides, I was getting a kick out of observing Gussie come back to life. I was secretly rather proud of the fact that she had blossomed since I had been there, her translucent skin once again taking on its luminescent glow with her freckles resembling little dots of cinnamon sugar sprinkled over it. She was laughing again and her fridge was brimming with fresh food for which she ventured out to shop with apparent pleasure. She didn't cook it – she didn't know how – but I did and I looked forward to pottering around her kitchen, preparing our evening meal while she leaned against the Aga with a glass of wine.

But would this all change now I was about to start work? Would I have the strength to perform in her kitchen after slaving away in André's?

And then I stopped thinking about Gussie and my fingers hovered in surprise above my keyboard as I saw that I had an email from Tommy. Just one line and it resembled a hasty text message – his passion – rather than a carefully worded email.

R U being a good polar bear?

I was shocked at how easily the tears came. His use of *polar bear* instantly brought to mind our Eskimo kisses, rubbing noses and giggling. Why had he picked this moment to contact me, just when my thoughts of Max had been reawakened by meeting Jake? And just when the lump in my throat was beginning to subside I remembered Jake's words about how I had let myself go, how I apparently no longer gave out any signals that I was available. *Ouch!* I knew he had been cruel to be kind but the truth invariably hurts. And here was contact from the very person to whom I ought to be available and I should be overjoyed. But all I could do was burst into tears at how sad it was that I felt almost nothing.

I didn't respond to Tommy's email. I told myself *I* was being cruel to be kind. I had no inclination to send him a long chatty reply full of news about Gussie and me. And a curt *Yes, I'm fine* would be more hurtful than anything. So I did nothing.

I went downstairs and made myself a cup of coffee. There was a newspaper article lying on the kitchen table, which Gussie must have clipped that morning. Bending closer I read the headline with a sinking feeling. **LADIES! DIVORCE IS THE WAY TO GET RICH.**

Two men in the City had divorced their wives, discarding them, in a sentence underlined by Gussie, *much as they discard spent assets*. The piece went on to report that one woman was to get 250,000 pounds out of the 750,000 her husband made a year, while the other would clear the fantastic sum of five million.

I sat down, feeling dejected. This was the last thing Gussie needed to read. But then my eye traveled down the page to another line she had marked. *Maintenance payments tend to be set according to the woman's needs plus an equal share of the family home.* Gussie had filled the margin with a heavy score of !?!!???? Having read this she must be feeling devastated, I thought, not least because it was her own fault she had left her marriage to Mickey with nothing.

And yet it wasn't. Not entirely. Gussie was an innocent and Mickey must have known she wouldn't have a clue as to how to go about claiming what was due her. And her shame at the failure of her marriage had made her keep her impending divorce a secret from her family. Once again I cursed myself for being so caught up in my own paltry troubles with Tommy that I hadn't been there for her. My only consolation was that in all non-financial areas of her life, I felt she was better off without Mickey.

While reading, I had been fiddling idly with the corner of a buff-colored folder lying on the table and seeing that I had made it grubby, I tried to straighten it out but only succeeded in making it worse. In the end I upended the documents it contained on to the table and turned the folder inside out so the ragged corner was less visible. I picked up the papers to return them to the folder.

I didn't meant to pry. And when I read the letter on the top of the pile, I almost wished I hadn't. It was a foreclosure letter from the bank. Gussie had fallen behind with her mortgage payments and was in danger of losing her house.

I sat for a while in a state of shock. Gussie's recent good spirits were a front. She must be worried sick and yet she had not said a word. And I couldn't confront her because she must never know I had been snooping.

A second reading told me that she had only received the first warning letter but even so I knew that now I had to come up with a plan not only to clear her name but also to secure her an income.

Forty-five minutes had gone by. Surely Sylvia would have arrived by now?

As it was, when I approached The Pelican I saw her coming out of Maggie Blair's house across the street.

'Sylvia!' I yelled, my concern about Gussie giving my voice a harsher edge than I had intended. 'I thought you said to be there at nine?'

She seemed flustered that I had seen her, but not, it appeared because she was late to The Pelican. She was wearing her gray duffle coat fastened with wooden toggles and she grasped the handles of a wheelbarrow standing outside Maggie's house and began to push it across the road towards me.

'I've been giving Maggie's house a top-to-toe blitz.' She seemed to think it necessary to give me an explanation. 'The junk in there, you wouldn't believe. But it's spotless now.'

A peevish *couldn't you have told me* formed in my head but I caught it just in time.

'Wouldn't Mona take care of something like that?' I asked instead. The bottom of the wheelbarrow was covered with Brussels sprouts, celeriac, beetroot, cabbages, onions, and leeks.

'You'd have thought,' Sylvia sniffed. 'I do the fruit and vegetable shopping locally every day as you can see. We're so small and cozy, it's not worth ordering in bulk from a supplier. I'm putting bangers and mash on the lunch menu, it's just what they need in this cold. But it's celeriac mash instead of potato, so much more healthy, bound to be popular, don't you think?'

I didn't actually. If people ordered bangers and mash, I thought, they'd expect sausages and potatoes. But I didn't say anything.

'Now we go in the side entrance,' she said and I didn't bother to explain I'd been there earlier. 'Down this alley.'

We heard the music the minute we turned the corner off the High Street into the alley. Led Zeppelin's *Whole Lotta Love* blasting off the stone walls and reverberating in our faces, heavy metal hyper-amplified and punctuated by the thud of shiny black garbage bags flying out of the door and hitting the pavement.

'*Oh* dear,' was all Sylvia said in a sing-song voice that I could barely hear above the racket. 'I've asked him time and again not to play it so loud.'

'Sounds like you'll have to re-name it the Hard Rock Café,' I said.

She didn't get it. She was wearing little rimless granny spectacles and she just stared at me through them, her thin lips pursed into a forced smile but there was nothing going on in her eyes.

I was beginning to wonder how we'd make it through the door without being knocked sideways by a garbage bag. But Sylvia had brought the wheelbarrow to a halt. And just as well she did because the next item to be thrown out the door was a microwave oven. It hit the stone wall on the other side of the alley and smashed into pieces.

'André.' Sylvia's voice was just a squeak. He couldn't possibly have heard it. 'You *are* naughty.'

She sounded like a kindergarten teacher referring to a wayward four year old but I had to admit that hurling a microwave oven out into the street did indicate someone was having a childish tantrum.

'I'm not having that thing in my kitchen another second.' André came outside and kicked the microwave. Then he coughed and spluttered all over it. 'People come here to have food *cooked* for them, not heated up. It's a restaurant, not some dinky little diner. When will you get that through your head?'

'It's *my* restaurant so I've had it in my head for quite a while actually,' said Sylvia evenly. 'Your cold doesn't sound

116

much better. Maybe you'd better go and have a lie-down.'

'That's what *I* sa—' I began and then stopped, remembering his reaction.

'What's this crap?' André was looking in the wheelbarrow. 'Where's the lamb?'

'Oh, I've not had time to go to the butcher yet.' Sylvia looked quite affronted at the thought.

'Every day it's the same fucking story.' André towered menacingly over her rather bird-like frame but she didn't seem in the least bit nervous. 'You won't let me take care of my own ordering, you insist on shopping locally but you NEVER get me what I need early enough. So I tell you what,' he backed away from her and began to play some energetic air guitar to the Zeppelin inside, 'from now on don't bother *having time* to do any of the shopping. From now on I'm taking care of everything, d'you get it? That's what I should have done from the minute I started at this place.'

'It's my restaurant and I'll—' Sylvia protested.

'No, you won't,' André interrupted. 'You can make your happy-snappy lunches – what are you giving them today? You've got some leeks in there, I see. So what's it to be? Leeks *au gratin*? So exotic. They won't know what's hit them. No, from now on, I don't want you involved in the dinner menu in any way whatsoever. And by the way, you might want to make a note of this. Every night there'll be just one menu. One starter, one main course, one dessert. No choice. I cook what I want and they like it or lump it.'

'I think that's a very bad idea,' said Sylvia, smiling at him but sounding very worried, 'they're not going to like that round here. They'll—'

'Tough,' said André, 'that's the way its going to be. If it's a problem, find a new chef. I'm going to start a Pelican website – it's ridiculous we've never had one. And I'm going to post the menu for the day – and the following day – on it and people can take a look and decide whether they want to come.'

'But supposing they don't like what's on the menu?' Sylvia's smile tightened a fraction.

'Well then, they won't come. They'll come another night when they do. But if they have merely the slightest appreciation for good food, they'll want everything on every menu. I'm going to use only the best ingredients – *and I'm going to order them myself!'*

He emphasized the last sentence with a mammoth sweep of his air guitar and disappeared back inside.

'He'll never get around to it,' said Sylvia, confidently, 'he's always having these little ideas. He thinks he's being creative.'

She'd said it loud enough that he could hear her. He turned up the volume on Led Zeppelin. Sylvia turned it down. André turned it up even higher and stood in front of the CD player so she couldn't get to it.

I sensed someone behind me and turned to see a faintly pretty girl with the worst skin condition I'd ever seen – greasy, pimpled, severely off-putting. She was in a drab woolen overcoat, which she shrugged off to reveal a sweatshirt and jeans. And all the while she was crying. Then, without a word, she suddenly hurled herself into Sylvia's arms.

Sylvia signaled to André to lower the music and, to my relief, he did, not much but enough for us to hear ourselves speak.

'Wendy, pull yourself together, dear.' Sylvia was recoiling slightly from Wendy, as if she feared close contact might ruffle her appearance. 'You've upset her again, André. I expect she saw you throwing the microwave out and making all that noise. It's all right, Wendy, he's just feeling a bit poorly.'

'For Christ's sake, Sylvia, will you cut it out? All I'm doing is trying to upgrade this place before you become a total laughing stock. But if you want everyone to go lie down every time they have a little headache – which would mean nothing would get served to your customers – then fine, go right ahead.' He was shouting at her, advancing upon her and the trembling Wendy, who burst into a fresh bout of sobbing.

'Now see what you've done to her. You've got to calm yourself, André. It's not good for you, getting all worked up like this.'

'The only way I'm going to calm down is if you get OUT OF MY KITCHEN.' André seemed on the point of going berserk.

'Then what would we do about lunch?' Sylvia seemed determined to madden him. 'I'm not leaving Wendy with you in this state.'

'It's not André.' Wendy's voice was unexpectedly high and clear through her sobbing. 'I'm not crying because of him. I've had a shock, Sylvia. My Dad took the dog for a walk up to the quarry and he found a woman lying at the bottom of it. She was smashed to pieces,' Wendy wailed into Sylvia's chest again, 'just like the microwave.'

Chapter Eight

Throughout my first day at The Pelican, 'the body in the quarry' was all anybody talked about.

Except for Sylvia. I was standing at the sink on my second day, trying to peel off a pair of slimy rubber gloves so that I could answer the phone and take a reservation – one of the menial tasks with which I had been entrusted – when I actually heard her say the words *I've got better things to do than sit around talking about dead bodies*.

The big question that seemed to be running through everyone's mind was whose body had been found? Everybody seemed to be accounted for in Frampton Abbas so it had to be a stranger. I scored a minor triumph when I blurted out that I had heard that Marjorie Mackay's goddaughter Melanie had gone missing.

'Where'd you hear that?' André muttered as I squeezed past him to get to the sink.

'Jake Austin. He's a farmer I—'

'I know who he is,' said André, grinning. 'Old Jake's probably got her stashed upstairs with her wrists and ankles tied to his bedstead with scarlet ribbon.'

I remembered the satin sheets, the pin-up of the nude body inside Jake's closet door and the lipstick-smeared glass and I hoped he was right.

Apart from that brief exchange, I barely registered André that day as I worked. Wendy, once she had recovered from her shock, wasted no time taking me under her wing. I realized this was because she had suddenly discovered that there was now somebody in the kitchen who was even lower than her in the pecking order. She immediately relegated to me her worst responsibilities, which meant that the only food I came into direct contact with was the stinking waste I carried out in the garbage or the remains I scraped off the plates or scoured out of the pans it was my duty to clean. Every time either André or Sylvia was done with a pot or a pan or a dish or a cooking utensil of any kind, I had to wash it, including taking apart the food processor several times and meticulously cleaning it. As I unloaded the dishwasher for the umpteenth time, I thought my back was going to break and, as much as I hated to be in agreement with Sylvia, I longed to smash André's boom box into smaller pieces than the microwave as UB40 pounded the headache mounting inside my skull.

'Me and my boyfriend, we go up the quarry sometimes of an evening,' Wendy told me on my first day as she peeled potatoes beside me at the sink, 'but of a *summer* evening. I don't know why anyone would want to go up there in the winter.'

'I hear the view's quite something from up there,' I said.

'The view,' Wendy repeated dully, sounding as if she didn't quite understand the word. 'You mean maybe she wandered up there for a stroll and walked over the edge in the fog?'

'Or someone could have pushed her?' I suggested.

'No they couldn't,' said Wendy firmly.

'Why is that?' I was intrigued.

'Well, it's too horrible to think about, isn't it?' said Wendy, as if that settled it.

'So you don't think anyone brought peanut oil in here and put it in the salad dressing the night Rosemary Waters died?'

'I don't make the salad dressing,' said Wendy, shaking her head and slightly missing the point. 'That's Gussie's job. I'm

121

not allowed. Much too fancy for me, salad dressing. I don't get the point of making it, we get ours out of a bottle at home. It's Gussie's job to see there's enough made to dress the salads in this place. If anyone put peanut oil in it, she did.'

Ah, well, good to know where Wendy stood then. A bit of hierarchical resentment would surely guide her finger to point at Gussie.

'So when did Gussie make the dressing on the day the woman died?'

'Like I'm going to remember?' Wendy raised her eyes. 'It was like a nuthouse in here that day because of the fire.'

'You had a *fire*?'

'No, of course we didn't.' Wendy sighed in exasperation. How much longer was she going to have to deal with a thicko like me? 'Does it look as if there's been a fire in here? The alarm went off, that's all, and we all had to go out into the street. André was making ever such a fuss. He had something in the oven and it was going to be ruined.'

'André was there? I thought it was his night off?'

'This was lunchtime, stu—' She caught herself just in time.

'*Lunch*time? You're saying the salad dressing was made at lunchtime?'

'Of course. Always. There's enough made for the lunch salads and the evening.'

'So who was here?'

'Everyone. Me, Gussie, Sylvia, André, Justine might have been if there was a cake or a tart to be made, I don't remember. We're always here at noon because that's when André takes us through the menu and then he hangs around, mostly just to get in Sylvia's way while she does the lunchtime shift.' Wendy glanced behind her to make sure no one was listening. When she continued, it was in a whisper that was curiously louder than her normal voice. 'He's always poking fun at what she does, I don't know how she stands it. She made this lovely soup the other day, carrot and ginger she called it, thought it up all by herself. She's ever so clever.' She smiled at the memory. 'I watched her do it and you know, I went home that night and made it for me dad. It was so easy. Just carrot and orange and what's it called? Tabasco? Didn't see no ginger come to think of it. Bung it all in the blender and you're laughing. Well, sneezing actually. It's quite spicy, me dad said it repeated on him something terrible. But André, he took a sip and he spat it out in disgust, right there in front of us. And the customers could see him too from the restaurant. None of them ordered it. Sylvia was ever so upset.'

I was beginning to get the picture. Gussie might have been André's pet but Wendy was definitely in Sylvia's corner.

'So André was here that day at lunchtime?'

'Oh yes, definitely. Around two o'clock he starts cooking for the evening and we all get involved in the prep work. As he was going to be off that night he was making pancakes so Sylvia could stuff them with chicken or whatever. He must have made about sixty.'

'Sixty!'

'Oh, we keep them in the fridge and use them when we need to. He stacked them up and wrapped them in a dry tea towel. I had to wait for them to cool and then wrap them in cling film and put them in the fridge ready for her to use.'

'So when did the fire alarm go off?'

'While I was waiting for them to cool. That's how I remember. While I was outside, I thought *I hope the bloody fire doesn't go and warm them up again.*'

'But it was a false alarm?'

'Not the first time it's happened,' Wendy grumbled, handing me her potato peelings to dispose of with what I couldn't help noticing was a certain amount of satisfaction.

'You never mentioned that the fire alarm went off the day Rosemary Waters died and you didn't tell me the salad dressing was made at lunchtime,' I snapped at Gussie when I finally made it home, dog tired, at ten o'clock that night. She was nursing a glass of wine at the kitchen table and I noticed she'd already got through half a bottle. 'Pour me a glass of that, would you? Sorry, I sound like I'm accusing you of a crime. I don't think I've ever felt so tired and achy.'

'It'll get a lot worse,' said Gussie ominously. 'I think it took me about three weeks to start getting used to being on my feet all day. And why would I mention the fire alarm? First it was a false alarm and second it was at lunchtime.'

'I don't know,' I said, sitting down and literally slurping my wine. 'I just feel it's significant but at this precise moment I can't tell you why. Gussie, you've had your hair cut.'

I still sounded like I was blaming her for something but I was resentful of the fact that while I'd been slaving away, she'd been off pampering herself. Then I saw her face fall and at the same moment I noticed the folder with the letter from the bank lying beside her wine glass. 'It looks great,' I added hastily.

And it did. Her unruly mop of curls had been clipped to follow the shape of her head and brushed away from her face to show off her cheekbones to their best advantage. Her long white neck was accentuated and it was extraordinary how much more elegant she looked.

'Thought I'd better do something in honor of my big date with Mr Wright at the end of the week,' she said. 'There's this great place in Exeter. You ought to try it some time.'

I remembered with a jolt Jake Austin's disparaging comments about my appearance but I didn't see how I was going to find the time to make an appointment. Which reminded me, so far no one had said anything about my day off. I had a funny feeling we were all supposed to work every day except when The Pelican was closed on Sundays. The new Sunday closure was something André had instigated, much to Sylvia's fury, in memory of Rosemary Waters – who had of course died on a Sunday.

'So did you have time to see Gilly Mortimer?' I asked Gussie.

'I certainly did. She gave me an early supper. I've only been back half an hour.'

'And?'

'She showed me the emails Mr Wright sent to Rosemary,' said Gussie. 'In fact she went one better and printed them out for me. Here, you can take a look for yourself but not before you've given me a blow-by-blow of your first day.'

'It's just a blur,' I groaned, 'a blur of pain and heat and being jostled by everyone's backside, a blur of cooking smells and garlic and sweat, a blur of André's boom box and Sylvia's squeaky voice sucking up to the customers – I can't believe how it travels all the way back to the kitchen above the noise in the restaurant and André shouting at us.'

'Tell me about it,' Gussie grinned. 'So what was on the menu?'

I told her about André's new plan to offer no choice and serve just one thing.

'He played it safe the first night. Just guacamole as a starter, steak, salad and *pommes dauphinoises* as an entrée and Justine had made a lemon tart for pud. Even he said it was boring. But nevertheless there was a drama.'

'Ooh goody!' Gussie rubbed her hands in glee. 'Tell me all about it.'

'A woman asked for her steak well done.'

'Uh-oh! I know what's coming.' Gussie nodded.

'He went over to the hatch and asked Sylvia to point her out and then he stood there and glared at her for what seemed like minutes on end. I thought he was going to march out and strangle her.'

'But he cooked it – well done?'

'Oh yes, but guess what? She sent it back.'

'*No!*'

'And do you know what he did? He took a cooked ham that was in the larder and he cut a large slab of it and he charcoaled that on the grill until it was like a bit of black shoe leather, *totally* unrecognizable – and that's what he sent out to her.'

'And she ate it?'

'Like a lamb. And he watched her chew every mouthful. So what about Wendy, Gussie? Creepy little creature, isn't she?'

'Oh she's not so bad,' said Gussie charitably and I felt guilty. Gussie was so much more tolerant than I was. I decided not to mention that Wendy had fingered Gussie for the peanut oil.

'She's a big fan of Sylvia in case you hadn't noticed,' I said instead.

'Lee-Lee, you've got to understand, Sylvia's the boss and Wendy needs to keep her job. Her mum ran off years ago and she's got her unemployed dad to look after, and her little brother. So what did everyone have to say about the body in the quarry?'

'André said he never even knew there was a quarry nearby. I heard him asking a delivery person about it – André's taken over the ordering of the produce and such, by the way. Sylvia acted like she wasn't interested but I think I sensed her ears flapping every now and then. Wendy had her own little freak-outs at the sink but it was hard to know if they were about the body in the quarry or André yelling at her. She actually said she didn't think the woman was pushed because "it was too horrible to think about."'

'Sounds like Wendy. What about the customers?'

'Sole topic of conversation from what I could hear.'

Gussie yawned. 'Don't know about you but I've had it. I'm going to bed, see you in the morning. Are you on duck patrol or am I?'

I took the printouts of Rosemary Waters' emails up to bed with me. It was a touching correspondence with both parties showing caution in the beginning and gradually progressing to the stage where they were clearly comfortable with each other. *Yet they had never met!* I had to admit I was surprised by how naturally they opened up to each other, just as if they were sitting face to face in a restaurant, but I couldn't help noticing that Rosemary's emails were considerably longer and much more revealing than Mr Wright's.

It was his reaction to her information that she was allergic to peanuts that seemed to do it for Rosemary. Mr Wright was clearly perceptive. He sensed immediately how important it was for her and he seemed remarkably well-informed about the allergy.

Wait a second! This wasn't necessarily a good thing. It could mean he knew exactly how to attack her vulnerability. But after his response there was no stopping Rosemary. She poured out her repressed and lonely heart to him, barely aware that he was only responding to one in five of her emails.

There was something else. Very near the beginning of their correspondence, Rosemary told him her real name – her Exmoormates name was *Peanut2000* – and asked for his. But he never gave it to her, proffering his irritating *all will be revealed* line.

When? she asked. *When we meet*, he replied. *When will that be?* She pestered him about this but he succeeded in evading her, always holding out hope but never actually committing himself to a date.

I looked at the photo of Rosemary. I'd never met her but I'd seen another photo of her in the *Frampton Gazette* and I knew she had been plain. The picture she'd posted on Exmoormates.com flattered her but even so it was clear she was no beauty. As I read on, I could see what Rosemary had not been able to. Mr Wright was friendly and understanding but there wasn't anything deeper going on. As far as I could see he had had no intention of ever meeting her. And of course he hadn't shown up to their date.

So why had he even agreed to it?

I turned to the last few emails. Suddenly, without warning, he seemed to have a change of heart.

Sure, why not, let's meet for dinner this week.

The line came out of the blue in response to Rosemary's perpetual demand for a face-to-face. Rosemary's torrent of emails after that, bombarding him with gratitude and excitement and *are you quite sure?* was embarrassing. And I could tell she was nervous too. *I feel I should tell you that I never go to restaurants – for obvious reasons. Maybe we should just take a walk.* But Mr Wright persisted, gently, persuasively, so that she wound up saying, *Well, I guess I could find something to order that couldn't possibly have any nuts in it.* And he suggested, *What about a green salad? You could specifically request no nuts and it'd be hard to hide them.* And that appeared to have convinced her, to the extent that she wrote back *How about The Pelican? 7.30 Sunday night. I'll book us a table.* And he replied *Fine, see you there. Mr Wright.*

Shortly after Rosemary asked him his real name and he withheld it, she started addressing him as 'W' as in 'Dear W' or 'Hi W!' And he began signing off with 'take care, W' or 'later, W'. And from then on she always responded with an effusive 'xxxx R.'

But in the brief flurry of emails before the date, he reverted to the more formal 'Mr Wright' – the handle he had used at the beginning of their correspondence.

I fell asleep trying to work out why.

Gussie and I were so exhausted, we both slept through the ducks.

But not for long.

Around eight o'clock the hammering of the front door knocker resonated throughout the house.

'Maybe it's Sylvia come to beg me to return because you did such a lousy job yesterday,' said Gussie, appearing on the landing in a shapeless T-shirt.

'Well then, you should go down and answer,' I retorted and retreated to the warmth of my bed.

Again not for long. I heard muffled voices downstairs – a man talking to Gussie – and then she was back, poking her head round my door.

'Friend of yours to see you,' she said and there was no mistaking the sarcasm in her voice. 'And he's brought you a present.'

128

I flung on my jeans and a sweater and a pair of thick socks and set off downstairs, intrigued. Halfway down my right foot slipped, I lunged for the banister and missed and then hurtled down the last few steps on my back, landing agonizingly on my behind at Jake Austin's feet.

'Fastest way to break every bone in your body, coming down the stairs in just your socks, but I'm pleased you were in such a hurry to see me.' He hauled me to my feet. 'Haven't taken my advice about fixing yourself up, I see.'

For a second I contemplated going right back up the stairs and leaving him there but he was way ahead of me. Before I even knew what was happening, he had propelled me into the kitchen and picked up the kettle.

'Why don't you make me a nice cup of tea to warm me up? It's blowing a gale out there this morning.'

I barely heard him. I was too busy recoiling at the sight of a skinned animal lying on the kitchen table. It was headless and glistening and so utterly disgusting that I nearly threw up on the spot. Beside it lay a larger animal complete with fur and head. It looked like a hare.

'I know, I know, I know,' he said, 'I shouldn't be disturbing you so early but I couldn't get any joy at The Pelican. I had a call from that André fellow yesterday saying he was on the lookout for some game. Sounds like he's taken matters into his own hands over there – and not before time. I told that bitch who runs the place when she first arrived in Frampton Abbas,' the look on his face told me what he thought of Sylvia, 'I said that if she ever wanted me to bring her anything, all she had to do was holler but she sent me away with a flea in my ear and all the time she had this sickly smile on her face as if she was doing *me* a favor.'

'These are for André?' I pointed, stabbing a finger in the direction of the table but keeping my eyes averted. 'Why didn't you take them straight there?'

'I just told you,' said Jake, 'I couldn't raise him. I wondered if you could drop them into him later on this morning. I've got to be in Tiverton by nine. I've skinned the rabbit for him – did it about half an hour ago. Off with his head and his feet, chop chop, and then his pelt came off in a flash like he was wearing a little vest. He's clean as a whistle. His stomach and his entrails came out easily and I wiped him inside with a damp cloth.'

I made it to the sink just in time to retch but to my surprise nothing came out.

'I thought you backed away from killing rabbits,' I said when I had recovered a little. 'Didn't you tell me Maggie Blair had no problem delivering the *coup de grâce* to a rabbit's neck but you couldn't face it?'

'That was then,' he said cheerfully, 'I was just a lad. When I became a man I put away childish qualms and from the looks of things, it's about time you did too.'

'I'm not planning on becoming a man,' I said. 'So is that a hare?'

He nodded. 'Tell André he's been hung for five days. See, if you give his back legs a prod, they'll move, they're not stiff anymore so he's ready for a bit of culinary action. All the blood's out of him and here,' he reached into a bag on his shoulder, 'I've brought him a carton of it. It makes a great sauce.'

This time I did puke a little and as I did so the kettle boiled. When I straightened up again, Jake handed me a mug of tea.

'What are we going to do with you? Tell you what, why don't I just leave them on the ground right outside the door in the alley? He'll find them in due course. You won't get two steps down the High Street with them if I leave them with you. He's going to have to butcher the hare, of course, but he likes that, does André. We've had many a good chat about the best way to use a cleaver. What you need to know is—'

'*Stop!*' I yelled. 'Please, Jake, spare me. Yes, you take them along and if he hasn't found them by the time I go to work, I'll let him know they're there.'

'Did you say work? You're *working* there? You can't stomach me talking about it, what are you going to do when André starts butchering right in front of you? Because he's going to have to if Sylvia's no longer going across the road to the butcher's for the meat. Marjorie was right, by the way.'

The switch was so abrupt I didn't register what he was talking about for a moment.

'The body in the quarry. It *was* her goddaughter, Melanie. I stopped by there this morning on my way here. Believe it or not the police made a rare appearance. Whoever it was who found the body tipped them off and they found a mobile in the woman's jacket pocket. Marjorie's phone number was on it, top of the list so they called her to try and get an ID. Her son and daughter-in-law are with her, they had to get the doctor out to sedate her, poor thing.'

'And is foul play suspected?'

'Foul play! You mean was she pushed over the edge deliberately? Not as far as I've heard. At the moment I think they've put it down to an accident but I don't know what they've got as the time of death. Look, I've got to be off. Tell André I'll call him with what he owes me. Bye for now.'

And then he poked his head back round the door. 'Put some lipstick on at least.'

'Don't ask,' I said when Gussie appeared a few minutes after he'd left. 'When I was out on the moors the other day, I ran into Jake Austin. End of story.'

'That's just it. It never is with Jake,' she muttered. 'If he bothered to come round here, he's up to something. You haven't seen the last of him.'

I was fretting about her foreboding as I walked up the High Street to work later that day, my lips sporting *Rose nocturne*. I'd had to scoop it out with an orange stick, the container was so old, and apply it with an eye-shadow brush.

I turned into the alley and looked around for the rabbit and the hare but there was no sign of them. The kitchen door was open with a hose running into it from a tap in the wall outside.

I stepped inside to find André hosing down the kitchen floor with a vengeance.

'Hey, how you doing?' He was sounding very American today. 'This is the only way to get the floor totally clean. It creates a bit of a flood and Sylvia freaks every time I do it but you know what? That's part of the fun.'

He was wearing his double-breasted chef's jacket with the stand-up collar and a pair of baggy pants with a garish tropical-fish motif all over them. He sported clogs and a navy paisley bandanna tied around his head that gave him the look of a ginger-headed pirate.

'Did you find something outside the door?' I said.

'A rabbit and a hare? There was no note in the bag but I'm guessing they were from Jake. You know something about this?'

I explained. 'He said to tell you he hung the hare for five days and he's already cleaned the rabbit for you.'

'Yeah, well I've got to tell him not to do that,' said André.

'Why?' I was astonished.

'Because the only way I can tell a skinned rabbit from a skinned cat is by the kidneys and he's removed them. How do I know that's not a cat I'm going to serve the customers? I wouldn't put it past old Jake to bring me a pussy and charge me for a bunny.'

My stomach began to feel queasy again.

'But the hare's OK?' I said nervously.

'Looks fine to me but I'm going to freeze him. I'll paunch him and chop him up and you can put the joints in cling film and prepare them for the freezer.'

He disappeared into the cold store room used as a larder and returned with Jake's delivery. He hefted the hare on to a chopping block and reached for a cleaver. I backed away in alarm as he raised it above the hare's head. I turned my back and waited, stupidly, for the squeal of pain – what if it wasn't quite dead? – but instead there was just a dull thud as the cleaver sliced through the neck on to the wood.

132

'What's the matter?' André laughed. 'Get over here and watch. You might learn something. I'm just trimming away the belly flaps so I can remove the kidneys. Uh-oh!'

'What? It's a poodle instead of a hare?'

'Very funny. No, it's the liver. It's all blotchy, which means it's probably diseased. I can't use this hare. Butchering lesson over for today. Just as well I know better than to depend on Jake. OK, let's get this rabbit – or cat or whatever it is – into a casserole. You can watch me chop him up instead and you can get me the ingredients for the marinade. I'm going to need you to zest me a lemon, and you can strain the juice, and when you've done that I want half a cup of an onion, *finely* minced and another cup of sliced onions and a *finely* sliced carrot and you'd better defrost some chicken broth, a cup will do it and—'

'How many times do I have to tell you we don't measure in cups over here?' Sylvia was standing in the kitchen doorway, weighed down by a couple of bags of shopping. 'I want you out of here, André, so I can start preparing lunch.'

'Well, I've got news for you,' said André in a breezy tone and I saw Sylvia stiffen. 'I've decided we're going to close for lunch until the summer and then I'm going to re-think the lunch menu. If this place has any chance of building up a decent reputation it's going to be on my cooking – and my cooking *alone*,' he growled suddenly as she opened her mouth to protest.

'Hey, I just found out who the body in the quarry is.' I was hoping to defuse the growing tension in the kitchen.

But Sylvia ignored me. 'You can't just close for lunch without warning,'

'Already have,' said André. 'Go take a look in the window.'

Sylvia dashed back up the alley and I followed. Pasted to one of the panes in the front door was a piece of paper with The Pelican logo at the top – a drawing of a very fat Pelican sitting at a table holding a knife and fork, a satisfied grin on its face – the same stationery used for the menus.

From today The Pelican will be open only for dinner. A single menu will be offered, no choice. Please review our daily menu by checking this space from 11 a.m. or visiting our website at PelicanDevon.com. We will re-open for lunch at the beginning of May. We apologize for any inconvenience.

Below was another piece of paper with the menu for that night. *Chicory, beet and walnut salad. Beef barley stew. Apple pie and ginger ice cream.*

For the first time I saw Sylvia forget to smile. The hard line of her mouth matched the permanently humorless expression in her eyes.

'This isn't going to work,' she told André who had come to open the restaurant door to us, 'they're not going to be happy with no choice. And today's Tuesday and everyone expects fish on Tuesdays and Fridays. Frank the fish man will be here any minute. Who the hell knows what beef barley stew is and where is everyone going to go for lunch?'

'To the pub,' said André cheerfully, 'where the food is probably a darn sight better than what you've been giving them. I've already rung Frank and told him not to call here anymore. He never seemed to understand that F stood for freshness as well as Frank. I'll be ordering the fish elsewhere from now on. And beef barley stew is an old recipe of my grandmother's – short ribs with onions, celery, turnips, green beans, courgettes, tomatoes, you name it. Just what you need on a winter's evening. They're going to love it.'

'You mean oxtails. You won't find short ribs in Frampton Abbas,' said Sylvia darkly.

'Of course I won't and that's why I'm ordering my meat elsewhere as well as my fish.'

'Well, we won't survive without the lunchtime income,' Sylvia retaliated.

'Sure, it might be a little tight to begin with,' André conceded, 'but I'm willing to bet that before too long we'll have a full house every night instead of empty tables like we often do – and that'll make up for the shortfall. Plus I'm going to put the prices up because I have a feeling we'll soon be attracting a more discerning type of clientele who'll be prepared to pay more.'

'Well *I'm* not putting the prices up,' said Sylvia. 'Wendy, you need to start laying for lunch. Here's the bread. Get it chopped up and into the baskets.'

'How can she lay for lunch when we're not serving lunch anymore?' said André and his voice had dropped. He seemed to have only two levels – a lion's roar or the gentle, almost silky, pitch he was adopting now. 'Wendy's busy prepping the ingredients for the beef barley stew and then she's going to peel the apples so they're ready when Justine comes in to make the pies. She won't have time for anything else just yet, will you, Wendy?'

I held my breath. What he was doing was brutal. How could he put Wendy in such an awkward position?

But while Wendy might be the most stupid person at The Pelican, she was, as I came to understand in the next ten seconds, also the most political. Her stupidity enabled her to succumb to André's silky tone, to dry her puffy little piggy eyes as if she'd turned off a tap and to become his instant slave, no questions asked. Sylvia had gone shopping leaving Wendy as her acolyte and returned to find her a traitor. And Wendy herself probably wasn't even remotely aware that she had caught the drift of a redirection of power in the air and gone with it.

'Sorry, Sylvia. Bit up to me elbows here,' she said without even looking up.

Sylvia turned on me in a flash.

'Before *you* get too busy, Lee,' and I cursed myself for not seeing it coming, 'why don't you come upstairs so I can fill you in on a few things.'

Without thinking I looked at André for his approval but he just grinned. 'I'll call when I need you, Lee.'

I followed Sylvia up the stairs, my curiosity overriding the embarrassment I felt at what I had just witnessed. At a glance

I could see there were two rooms upstairs and at the end of a corridor I saw a bathtub through an open door. The stairs led directly into a large space – the first room – that was clearly used for storage. Two giant freezers stood against the far wall rising oddly from the carpeted floor. On another wall were two refrigerators and a line of steel shelving packed with cans and packets and bottled water.

And on the floor in the middle of the room was an unmade mattress with a boom box, an open laptop, an empty bottle of wine and an alarm clock beside it.

'I tell him every day to make his bed but does he listen?' Sylvia tittered. 'And he never turns his laptop off after he's checked his emails in the morning. Even though he rarely has a chance to come up here till he's finished work.'

I couldn't believe she could be light-hearted after being so humiliated downstairs. But what she said next confirmed a repetition of her bizarre – almost maternal – reaction when André had hurled the microwave against a brick wall.

'He's *such* a naughty boy. Now, come, let me show you my office.'

It should have been André's bedroom. It was an unexpectedly charming room, warm and cozy with a view up to the top of the wooded hills surrounding the valley. On a cheap stripped-pine table stood a computer, nothing else except for a ceramic jar full of pens. Sylvia's anal desk, about as far removed from my cluttered workspace as you could get. She booted up the computer and called up something on her screen.

'Take a seat.' She pointed to a folding chair leaning against the wall.

'Did you hear about the woman in the quarry?' I tried again. 'She was the goddaughter of someone called Marjorie Mackay. She was down from London and—'

I stopped because Sylvia didn't appear to be listening to me. Still staring at her screen, she spoke as if she were informing me, rather than the other way round.

'The Mackay farm is over by Dorcas Tor. Silly woman probably went for a walk in the mist and fell into the quarry.'

Then without warning she began to read from the screen in a dull monotone.

'I grew up in Loughborough, near Leicester. My father's name was Roger and my mother's name was Michelle. We had a dog called Patrick. He was a bull terrier. Our house was in the round bit at the end of a close, the same as all the other houses. I went to Loughborough High School and I got 7 O levels and English A level. I was always very good at English.

'When I was twelve my parents took me to a restaurant for the first time. It was called The Boulevard and it was by the cinema. We had steak and French fries. My father had ketchup with his. We had a salad with French dressing. When we got home I asked my mother to show me how to make French dressing but she didn't know how so I went to the library and read cookery books till I found a recipe.' She turned to look at me. 'You don't have to take notes because I'll print this out for you.'

It was so pitiful I felt compelled to summon up a weak smile for her. I had been so exhausted by my first day at the restaurant, and so consumed with the thought that I must watch for clues as to how the peanut oil had got into the salad dressing, that I had completely forgotten that I was supposed to be observing everything for the ghosting of Sylvia's book.

'We need to start at the beginning, don't we? With my childhood?' Her eagerness was pathetic. 'How do you work? I've got fifty pages here. Do you want to take them away and re-work them or do you think they'll be fine as they are from the sound of this first page?'

Here I had a dilemma. If I told her they were fine, that she didn't need me then I'd be spared having to deal with this leaden depiction of her totally unpublishable life. But then what excuse would I have wanting to work in The Pelican kitchen?

'You can give me the pages,' I said, 'and while I'm here you can show me what you do so I can make sure all the details are included. People love behind-the-scenes details.' I smiled encouragingly.

'Oh,' she paused, 'then I'd better show you how I do the ordering online. But first let's print up the menu for tonight.' She called up another page and typed today's date. 'Frank the Fish man's got some nice skate for us.'

I leaned over to look over her shoulder and watched her type the words *raie au beurre noire with haricots verts and pommes purées*.

And with a shiver I suddenly understood that she was totally in denial, about André and what he was doing, but most of all about herself.

Chapter Nine

André called upstairs.

'Lee, I need you down here. Now!'

Sylvia closed her eyes very tightly for a second, as if to blot him out, and taking my cue from her, I ignored him. I wanted to probe a little further and try to find a reason why she seemed to be impervious to André's behavior, to provoke her into a reaction, *any* reaction, other than the self-satisfied little smile that played constantly on her face.

'Can he do that?' I asked. 'Can he change the menu just like that without consulting you? Surely not. It's your restaurant, isn't it?'

Now it was my turn to be ignored. Her only indication that she had heard me was a little toss of the head. She continued to stare at her screen.

'Here's my book-keeping,' she said. 'See? I have to come up here and total everything every night before I can go home. And I'd better make a note – last night I didn't give us all our credit card tips because I didn't have the cash. Which reminds me, I have to go to the bank. Or maybe you could do that for me?'

'No, she couldn't. I need her in the kitchen. Didn't you guys hear me?'

I glanced to see if André had slipped out of his clogs to nip so silently up the stairs. He had come into Sylvia's office and was standing behind me.

'And I need her to go to the bank.' Sylvia didn't even turn her head. 'Lee works for me, André. It's my restaurant.'

Oh, so she had been listening, after all. The printer whirring into motion beside me made me jump.

'And here's tonight's menu.' She handed him a page. 'Frank will be here soon with the skate.'

André took it and tore it into pieces and I was unable to suppress a gasp.

'I called Frank, I just told you. He's not coming.'

'Oh, but he is,' she said, finally readjusting her position to look at him, 'he called me on my mobile after he'd spoken to you. He wanted to say how sorry he was and to ask me why I hadn't mentioned I wasn't happy with his service. So I told him I was very happy and that it was all a silly mistake. He'll be here in a minute.'

'And I'll be gone,' said André. He was in the process of unbuttoning his chef's jacket. 'Plenty of jobs in Bath or Exeter, London too for that matter. I had a call only last week.' He left the room and Sylvia jumped up and ran after him. I followed and saw him pick up a suitcase beside the fridge and throw it on the mattress. He folded his chef's jacket and laid it carefully in the bottom and then moved to a chest of drawers at the top of the stairs. I ducked as several pairs of boxer shorts flew over my head in the direction of the suitcase.

Now I got my reaction from Sylvia and immediately I felt ashamed for having wanted it. Her face crumpled suddenly and she looked as if she was going to burst into tears. It was momentary but I caught it. For the first time I saw emotion in her eyes.

'No! You can't go.' She wasn't telling him, she was pleading with him. 'I'll tell Frank we just want to try someone else for a while.'

André stopped packing and I knew instantly that this was a ploy he had used many times before.

'And I'll decide the menu from now on – the *single* menu?' He had retrieved his chef's jacket and was dangling it from one finger.

'Well, we can see how that works out.' She was frozen, waiting for his response.

'OK,' he shrugged his way back into his jacket, 'come along, Lee.'

Oh no, I wasn't going to let him make me part of this. Now I had witnessed that she did indeed have *some* feeling, I was experiencing a tinge of sympathy for Sylvia. I was beginning to understand that her denial of the way he undercut her was the only way she knew how to deal with him, but was it worth it? It was *her* restaurant and so OK, while he *was* the chef, he worked for *her*, he had come in as a part-time employee if I understood Gussie correctly, and yet somehow he had maneuvered his way to a position of autocracy. But Sylvia didn't have to put up with it. She could fire him and hire someone else so why did she?

'Yes, off you go, Lee.' I nearly fell over. Sylvia actually sounded meek.

I opened my mouth to protest and then I remembered just in time what she had done to Gussie. I remembered that she practiced fake charm and that she couldn't be trusted. I remembered that André got the point of Gussie and that, if he left, there would be no hope whatsoever of Gussie getting her job back.

So I gave Sylvia a *Sorry, but what can I do?* shrug and followed André downstairs to await instructions.

There was a small boy standing on an upturned crate at the sink. He was peeling onions, manipulating the peeler in a skillful manner I would not have thought possible in one so young.

'Well, you're not going up there anymore. In fact I don't want you going out the door without telling me where you're off to.' Wendy had her back to him – she was standing at the island, measuring barley into a jug – but as she spoke to him, she reached out and tapped him smartly on the shoulder. 'Hey, you! Are you listening to me?'

'Who have we here?' My voice jangled with false jollity.

'This is my little brother, Taylor,' said Wendy. 'He's giving us a hand.'

When she saw my look, she added. 'It's half term. What else am I supposed to do with him? My dad's too far gone to mind him and I'm worried about what he gets up to when I can't see him. He was up the quarry the other day, weren't you, you little turnip? We don't want *him* going over the edge and all.'

'And he doesn't mind?' I rolled my eyes in André's direction.

'Him? No. Not at all, providing Taylor keeps out of his way. No, André's good with him, says he's planning to make a chef out of him. And Taylor's very interested in food, aren't you, Taylor?'

This much was abundantly clear. I wasn't sure I had ever seen such a fat little boy.

'It was her upstairs,' Wendy continued darkly, raising her eyes to the ceiling 'who said she never wanted to see Taylor in here. But now things have changed – I asked André if I could run across the road and get him and he said sure. I mean, I've had him peeling spuds since he was a nipper so we're not worried about him slicing his finger off. Now Lee, do me a favor and keep an eye on him while I take the garbage out.' And then, after the tiniest beat, 'Actually, that's your job now, right?'

I was trying to squeeze past André with two huge stinking sacks in each hand when the door to the alley opened and a man with a florid face and a less than spotless white overall stood there. He didn't have to introduce himself. The reek of fish that preceded him told me instantly who he was.

'Hello Frank,' I said, 'they're expecting you.'

I would have dearly loved to have witnessed how André – or Sylvia – or both – dealt with him, but it was dustbin day and I had to drag the bins from where we stored them in the neighbor's yard all the way up the alley so they wouldn't miss the collection.

I was in the process of rolling the last bin into place when Frank the fish man came striding into the street. A few seconds later I heard the kitchen door slam and Sylvia ran up the alley. I said her name but she waved me away and as she ran past me I saw that while she held her head high, her eyes were glistening with tears.

She didn't reappear for the rest of the day and by the time we were ten minutes to opening for dinner, I could tell by his furtive glances towards the door that even André was worried. Wendy had whispered to me in the larder that the showdown between Sylvia and André, following André's definitive dismissal of Frank the fish man, had been explosive.

'She was ever so upset, Lee. She all but bared her teeth at him, she was so angry. But he saw her off. She won't be back here in a hurry.' Wendy sounded quite triumphant, as if it had been she who had ejected Sylvia.

But Sylvia did come back. She made it only seconds before the first customers walked through the door and I marveled at the way she stepped automatically into front-of-house mode. But at the end of the evening she slipped away without saying goodnight to anyone.

Gussie was engrossed in a DVD and barely acknowledged me when I walked in the door.

'It's a remake of *The Parent Trap*.' She glanced up after a while. 'I've been told I'm the spitting image of Lindsay Lohan but I have to confess, I don't see it. Just because we both have red hair—'

And because there's almost a twenty-year age gap between you I thought, but didn't say anything. Gussie didn't need reminding that she was getting on a bit any more than I did.

143

I picked up the remote and pressed PAUSE. 'Gussie,' I said, looming over her, 'listen to me for a second.'

And I told her what had happened between Sylvia and André. I had assumed she would be riveted by the news that André had taken over the ordering and was clearly rebelling against Sylvia, but Gussie merely shrugged.

'He's the chef, Lee-Lee. In a *normal* restaurant,' and there was no escaping the note of irony in her voice, 'he'd be doing all the ordering and he'd most certainly decide on the menu. *And* he'd be doing the hiring and firing of the kitchen staff. Everything you say he's doing now, he's completely within his rights. I've never understood why he's deferred to her as much as he has up to now. Nor do I get it why she lets him get away with such outrageous behavior.'

'How *do* you explain it?' I asked her.

'I'm not sure I can,' she shook her head. 'When he first arrived she couldn't take her eyes off him. It was pathetic. And I noticed she even tried to touch him quite a bit. You know? Tapping him on the arm to make a point, squeezing past him to get to the stove. But that didn't last long. I mean, how could it? The way he talks to her sometimes, it's embarrassing to listen to it.'

I was about to sit down with Gussie for a good old gossip about The Pelican over a glass of wine but she grabbed the remote from my hand and pressed PLAY.

For a second I was secretly devastated. I found that I couldn't just come home and go straight to bed after working at The Pelican. I needed to unwind and relax for an hour or so but it was clear that tonight I would be on my own. *Fine*, I thought with childish petulance, *Gussie would rather watch a movie than talk to me, see if I care! I'm a polar bear. I'd rather be on my own anyway.*

But there were moments when I did need people and now was one of them. I wanted some kind of acknowledgement from Gussie that she appreciated that I had come down to be with her. I was only working at the damned restaurant for her sake and now she didn't even want to talk about it. Tiny seeds of resentment were beginning to germinate in my head. While I was wearing myself out every night, she was a lady of leisure, lounging on the sofa even as her house was on the point of being repossessed. Which I was not supposed to know anything about. I was wasting my time, I reflected, I might as well pack my bags and go back to London.

I was overtired and I knew that if I allowed this rancorous attitude to fester, I'd regret it so I ran myself a hot bath and climbed into it to soak my bitterness away.

And while I soaked I read Sylvia's pages because, as I quite rightly predicted, they would be guaranteed to put me to sleep.

Yet while her prose might be soporific, Sylvia the woman was beginning to intrigue me. After what Gussie had said about The Pelican not being a normal restaurant, I started to think that there was something a little *ab*normal about Sylvia and André's professional relationship too. What I had witnessed so far told me that he had a hold over her in some way and I wanted to know more.

I didn't have to be at The Pelican until noon the next day so I called Sylvia on her mobile on the pretext that I had some questions to ask her about her pages.

'Now?' She sounded subdued. 'You want to meet now?'

'If it's convenient. I'll come to you,' I added hastily. After a second or two of silence on the end of the phone, I said nervously, 'Sylvia? Are you there?'

'I'm not at home,' she said by way of response, 'I'm over at Maggie Blair's house giving it a clean. I suppose you could come over here?'

I said I'd be there right away and, as I crossed the road, I remembered that I had encountered Sylvia returning from cleaning Maggie's house only the week before. Why did she feel it necessary to do it again? Maybe it was an outlet for her anger, a way of channeling her frustration with André?

When she let me into Maggie's house, I emitted an audible gasp.

'What's the matter?' she said.

'Where's all the furniture?' I said. 'Her antiques?'

'In the outhouse in the backyard. Cheaper than putting it all into storage.'

I opened my mouth to say, *What gives you the right to say what happens to Maggie's possessions* but at the last minute I realized that I had no right to ask such a question.

'However did you get it all in there?' I said instead. 'Did Mona help you?'

'*Mona?*' The puzzled look on her face made me wonder if I had remembered Maggie's daughter's name correctly. 'Good Lord, no. I haven't heard a peep out of Mona since the funeral.'

'So is that where it will stay? In the outhouse?'

'Pending further instructions,' she said curtly.

From whom? I wondered, but didn't like to ask. I thought it odd that she and Mona didn't seem to be on speaking terms anymore given their apparent rapport at Maggie's funeral.

'Come into the kitchen,' said Sylvia, 'there's still a couple of chairs in there and I could probably offer you a cup of tea.'

She intimated that it would be such an effort on her part that I declined. As I followed her into the kitchen and noted that the oak dresser was still there, and the table with the Formica top, I wondered if I should mention André. The electric stove had been scrubbed and was now spotless and as Sylvia motioned to me to take a seat, I decided I would leave it to her to bring up his name.

'Do you like my story?' she asked in a coy tone that implied that she expected me to.

I chose my words carefully. She couldn't help the banality of her early life, echoing that of millions of others raised in a small town in the Midlands. She couldn't help the predictability of her inevitable procession from school to domestic science college to waiting tables to taking a book-keeping course. She had stayed in Loughborough until she was thirty, working in shops as a sales assistant, culminating in a job as a duty officer in a supermarket. While there she had been approached by one of the suppliers to become one of their sales representatives and this had led to *travel*!

Sylvia had typed the word in italics and added an exclamation mark and I envisaged trips all over Europe, maybe as far as America. But I quickly understood that she had spent the next ten years traveling the West Country collecting orders for pork pies. There was a moment when I wondered if she had ever been to London. She had finally made the move from the Midlands to a small house on the outskirts of Bath where she had, she wrote breathlessly, started to give Dinner Parties. Capital D, capital P.

And that's what led me to open The Pelican. Everyone said my cooking was so amazing, I had to start a restaurant were the last words of what she had written so far.

'Well, it's an incredible story,' I lied. 'The fact that you made the leap from duty manager at the supermarket to the other side of the counter, so to speak – that's very interesting.'

Her look of pleasure and gratitude was so pathetic I felt sharp pangs of guilt attack me and it dawned on me that maybe nobody paid Sylvia much attention these days. Could it be that no one had shown any interest in her present recently, let alone her past? And, I mused charitably, there was no denying that she must have some organizational talent to have started from scratch a restaurant that was still going nearly two years later. I wondered how many other people knew the extent to which she had advanced from what were relatively modest beginnings. Hers was not a sophisticated background and I began to wonder if maybe her fake smile was a front for a tightly wound attempt to present herself to the world as someone she was not. I had overheard her gushing to the customers in the restaurant, laughing too loudly at whatever they said, pandering to their whims, but once a quick glance in her direction had shown me that as she laughed and chatted, her hands were shaking.

I smiled at her gently. 'As I told you when we were sitting in your office, I'm going to need you to fill in some details.

You stayed in Loughborough for quite a while as an adult. Were you living with your parents?'

'Until I was thirty, yes,' she said, as if that were perfectly normal behavior. 'Then I was traveling, of course, until I moved to Bath.'

'And why did you decide to move to Bath then?'

'My father died.'

'Oh, I'm sorry.' I said, 'And your mother?'

'Well, she was all right then.'

Too late she realized what she had said. She tried to look composed but she gave herself away with a sudden frown. What was it that made it 'all right' for the mother once the father had died? Whatever it was, Sylvia hadn't meant to refer to it, however obliquely.

'Tell me about your parents.'

'My parents?' She looked bewildered. *What do you want to know about them for?*

'Yes. Were you close to them? You said your father took you to your first French restaurant. Tell me about him – what else did you learn from him, about food? Did he cook?'

She shook her head. 'My mother did all the cooking.'

'But she didn't know how to make a French dressing?'

Sylvia frowned. 'Why would she? My father didn't eat salad.'

'But he liked *steak/frites*?'

'He liked steak and *chips*. With ketchup.' She laughed. 'When they didn't have it at the restaurant, my goodness, did he shout at them!'

'What did you and your mother do when he shouted?'

'What did *we* do? Well, my mother probably laughed and said something like, *Oh Roger, if you want ketchup, looks like you'll have to go out and buy it yourself.* You know, something to humor him, like she always did.'

'Like she always did?'

'When he shouted.'

'He shouted a lot? And what did you do?'

I was aware I was starting to sound like a therapist but a picture was forming in my mind of this awkward trio with the father yelling for ketchup and the mother trying to jolly him out of it and Sylvia sitting between them, twitching.

'Nothing,' she said, and the fake smile returned.

Just like it did when André shouted. She'd learned from her mother how to deal with tantrums, never rise to the bait, always act as if it were all a joke, remain passive-aggressive at all times – and drive the person into an even greater rage.

'So your father was an angry man? Was he disappointed with the way his life had turned out, do you suppose?'

'I don't know what you're talking about.' The clamp-down was instant. The eyes were dead. Even the fake smile was fading. She wouldn't be drawn any further but I didn't mind. I'd had my glimpse. I'd know where to stick the needle in next time.

A couple of days later as André was taking us through the evening's menu, a large bear of a man walked into The Pelican followed by a woman who was almost as tall as he was. She was wearing a shapeless skirt down to her ankles and a baggy anorak. Her face bore such a sour expression that she made Sylvia look positively radiant.

André swore under his breath. He loathed people who thought they could just pop in and interrupt him in the kitchen. But when the man introduced himself, André leapt to his feet.

'My name is Neil Mackay and this is my wife Katharine. Forgive us for intruding but my mother asked me to pay you a visit. As you may have heard, we've had a tragedy. Her goddaughter—'

'My condolences, man.' André gripped his upper arm. 'Can I get you something to drink? A beer? A shot of something?'

I could feel Sylvia bristling beside me and then Taylor surprised us all by waving a copy of the *Frampton Gazette* at Neil Mackay.

'Have you seen her picture?' he said. 'Why isn't there one of you?'

Neil Mackay stared at Taylor as if unsure what to do.

'Taylor, come here,' said Wendy.

'Does Taylor know him?' I whispered to her.

'Well *I* don't so I don't see how he can. Who is he?'

But before I could reply, Katharine Mackay approached Sylvia. 'I don't like this new idea of just having one menu,' she said.

I found it hard to accept she was Neil Mackay's wife. Standing side by side, their body language was all wrong. Although his expression was grave and his face collapsed like a mournful bloodhound's, his eyes had a twinkle he couldn't quite suppress and his roly-poly bearing was indicative of someone who embraced life with good humor. She, on the other hand, was so rigid in her stance, I couldn't imagine her embracing anything, least of all her husband.

'Not now, Katharine.' Her husband stepped in front of her. 'Melanie's official funeral will be in London, of course, next week. But my mother wants to have a little memorial get-together for her down here later on. We were wondering if we could have it here at The Pelican. We envisaged something along the lines of what you had for Maggie Blair.'

'I'm shattered for your loss,' Sylvia's fake smile was embarrassing in its insincerity, 'but I'm sorry to have to tell you that we can't help you. That was a private party we had for Maggie.'

I could tell we were all stunned by her refusal. Nobody said anything but then, as Neil Mackay began to move awkwardly toward the door, André stepped forward.

'Hold on a moment.' He glanced at Sylvia and then took Neil Mackay by the elbow. 'I'm André Balfour and I'm the chef here. I'd like to do something for you and your mother. How about you have the get-together at your mother's farm and I'll do the catering?'

He was caring, he was genuine, he was everything that Sylvia was not and as he shepherded the Mackays out the door, I sent him a silent vote of thanks for so skillfully averting an awkward moment.

When the Mackays had left and I was paired with Taylor at the sink, cleaning mushrooms and dicing tomatoes and trying not to feel irritated because he was so much better at it than I was, he said suddenly:

'That's not his real wife, she must be a pretend one.'

'What do you mean, Taylor?'

'The lady in the anorak. She's not his real wife.'

'Oh.' I hadn't realized I could rely on a seven year old for village gossip. 'How do you know?'

'Because I saw him kissing his real wife when I was up at the quarry. That one,' he nodded to the *Frampton Gazette* where Melanie's picture graced the front page. 'His wife is the one he kisses, isn't she?'

In my surprise I let go of my paring knife and it clattered into the sink.

'Butterfingers!' said Taylor.

'Taylor,' Wendy muttered a warning from the other end of the kitchen. 'Don't be cheeky now.'

'Are you absolutely sure it was her? The one in the paper?' I bent down to whisper to Taylor.

He nodded emphatically. 'They were going all smooshy-smooshy with their mouths.'

'For a long time?'

He nodded again. 'But then she looked over his shoulder and she saw me. She didn't look pleased so I ran off.'

'Did you see them arrive, Taylor?'

He nodded. 'They weren't together. She came first. I was lying on my tummy at the edge of the quarry looking down. It's exciting doing that! But she walked up and stood right next to me and gave me a big shock. She told me to be off because it was dangerous.'

'But you didn't leave?'

'I just went down the hill a bit and hid behind a bush. I saw him drive up in his car and they had a row. He was yelling at

151

her. But then she started crying so they got all squishy with each other.'

'And then you ran away?'

Taylor nodded. 'But he came down the hill in his car not long after. He stopped and asked what I was doing all alone on the road. He said did I want a ride home?'

'Did you go with him?'

Taylor shook his head. 'My sister says not to go with strange men.'

'Did you tell Wendy what you'd seen?'

'Sort of. Someone told her I'd been up the quarry but I didn't tell her about *them*. I forgot all about it until he walked in here just now.'

I wondered if Jake knew that Melanie was in the habit of kissing her godmother's married son. I wondered if Neil's miserable-looking wife had known he was up at the quarry the day Melanie died. I wondered if *anyone* knew besides Taylor and me.

Gussie was already in bed by the time I got home that night, no doubt catching up on her beauty sleep in preparation for her big date with Mr Wright.

I had it all worked out. I was going to drive Gussie to The Longhouse. We'd get there early and have a drink and then I would find a spot in the pub where I would be hidden from sight but could still watch her meeting with Mr Wright. In preparation I had been reading about cyberdating on the Internet and if the notion had ever intrigued me for a second, I was once again put off by the list of warning questions you were supposed to ask yourself about your potential date.

Is he evasive about his age and marital status? Does he hesitate in revealing his real name? When you suggest a meeting, does he mention issues that have to be taken care of first? Is he reluctant to divulge his phone number? And if he does give you his number, does he speak in hushed tones when you call? Whose voice is on his answering machine? Does he say if he lives alone? But the strongest warning of all was, *Be sure to meet him for the first time in a public place. Tell someone you are meeting him and make sure they have your mobile phone number.*

Well, that was fine, I told myself. From what I'd heard about the popularity of The Longhouse, it was bound to be packed on a Sunday evening and not only would I know that Gussie was meeting him, I would be right there spying on that meeting.

But when Sunday evening came, I didn't feel confident as I drove her across the moors to The Longhouse. She exuded a low-key beauty, having unearthed a slate-blue cashmere turtleneck sweater from the clothes stashed away in boxes in her room that enhanced the length of her neck. The color was subtle, and coupled with the paleness of her skin, it contrived to make her appear especially soft and vulnerable. Tiny sapphire earrings – to match the color of her eyes – and handed down from her grandmother to Aunt Joy, and then to Gussie – were noticeable now that her ears were exposed by her new haircut. Below the waist, however, was another story. Gussie had refused to discard her jeans and sturdy boots.

'It's raining, Lee-Lee. It'll be muddy out there outside The Longhouse. Anyway. He's only going to see my top half so what does it matter?'

I sighed. Gussie really was a country girl at heart.

'Whatever happens, Gussie, you are *not* to leave with him. Promise me.'

'Oh, Lee-Lee, you are such a scaredy-cat.'

'What will you do if it's someone you already know?' I asked her.

'Well, it all depends who it is, doesn't it?' she said, not unreasonably. 'If it's Frank the fish man, I might need you to rescue me right away.'

'And he gave you no description – Mr Wright – so you'd recognize him? Did you even ask him what his real name was?'

153

'No, I never did because I didn't want to give him mine until I'd met him. And he said my red hair would be enough for him to recognize me providing I sat in the corner table at the end. Of course,' she coughed nervously, 'he'll be looking for someone matching Cissie's photo. I hope he won't be *too* disappointed.'

For the umpteenth time I wished Gussie had saved her email correspondence with Mr Wright. Of course it was probably retrievable from somewhere on her hard drive but not by an electronically hopeless person like myself.

The Longhouse was a lone beacon beckoning to us from the depths of a valley as we came down off the moors, driving slowly into the slanting rain. As we approached, I could see it was a long low building with a thatched roof standing right on the road. Warm orange light blazed from a row of mullioned windows and a mass of vehicles outside indicated its popularity.

'Sylvia reckons this place is her biggest competition,' said Gussie. 'In her dreams! It's a different clientele altogether. The farmers come here when they want to give the wife a night out, the *real* farmers, not the newly retired fat cats from London who want to play at it.'

I thought of Jake. 'Well, there's plenty of action tonight.'

'I wonder if he's here yet.' She peered at the cars as I searched for a parking space, eventually settling for the verge further up the road. When I opened my door and plunged my feet into the mud, I could see why Gussie had opted to keep her boots on.

'Which of these cars do you think is his?' She clapped her hands. 'How about that brand new Land Rover?'

'How about that broken down old truck?' I pointed to a pick-up where a sheepdog barked at us from the cab.

Inside we had to fight to get to the bar.

'He's not here yet,' Gussie hissed at me. 'There's no one at the table in the far corner.'

'OK, I'll get you a vodka and Red Bull and you can go over and wait for him.'

'Make it a double,' said Gussie and I could tell she was nervous.

I got myself a glass of red wine and looked around for a good vantage point. But it was going to be hard. There was nowhere I could position myself where I was hidden from Gussie's table *and* see through the crowd at the bar. In the end there was nothing else to do but join Gussie in the dining room. There was a small table tucked away behind a blackened wooden post and I sat down with a look that defied the waitress to move me.

'Did you have a reservation by any chance?' she said breezily, taking a pencil from behind her ear. 'No matter if you haven't. We keep this table for single people like yourself.'

How could she know? Was it so obvious I was on my own? Did I now give out signals to waitresses? Poor hungry polar bear seeks nourishment. Approach with caution. Humor at all times.

I wished she'd move. She was blocking my line of vision to Gussie, which was impeded in any case by the post. I was hemmed in by more black beams in the walls and my only really clear view was of the fireplace at the other end of the room.

'So what'll it be?' she said, pencil poised. 'Roast lamb's nice, providing you don't mind the garlic, of course. But doesn't look as if that'll be a problem for you tonight.' She cackled at her own perception. 'Unless you get lucky, of course.'

Me being a sad creature on her own with no one to breathe on when I climbed into bed. OK, OK, I got it. No need to rub it in. And I was mildly outraged that she felt she could be so familiar with me – just because I didn't have a man in tow.

'I'll have the soup,' I said, 'and then I'll see if I have room for anything else.'

'You haven't asked what it is,' she said. 'it's—'

'I don't mind what it is,' I said, 'surprise me.' I couldn't very well tell her I didn't plan on eating it. I'd be too busy watching Gussie.

It was split pea and ham and it came with warm, freshly baked bread and I enjoyed it very much. Almost as much as I enjoyed the lamb that followed. I had been there for just over an hour and I was running my tongue around my teeth trying to extricate several fragments of rosemary that had been embedded in the lamb, and there was still no sign of Mr Wright. *Oh God,* I thought, *this is what happened with Rosemary Waters. Has something been set up to harm Gussie?*

But Gussie hadn't yet ordered anything to eat. She was concentrating on seeing how many Red Bulls and vodka she could line up in front of her. To begin with she had greeted any man who walked into the dining room with a dazzling smile – until he sat down somewhere else. Now she was focusing on me, pleading with me to go and join her and I figured, *why not? At least she was still alive and whatever Mr Wright's game was, she was well out of it.* I stood up and went over to tell her I was going to make a quick trip to the loo and then I would be joining her.

The crowd at the bar had thinned but not much. I was just threading my way through the drinkers standing behind the people perched on stools, when a blast of cold air pierced me as a new arrival burst into the pub and threw out an arm to waylay me.

'Lee, is that you? Man, it's cold out there. I'm soaked through just running from the car. Gotta get myself a drink. What are you having?'

'I'm fine, thanks,' I said, 'but you could probably get Gussie over there a large pot of black coffee.'

He didn't need to look where I was pointing. Gussie had seen him come in and was on her feet, wending her way towards him and swaying against the tables she passed in an alarming fashion.

'André,' she cried, 'I am *so* pleased to see *you*! What are *you* doing here?' She all but flung herself into his arms when she'd finally made it to the bar.

'What am *I* doing here?' He grasped her round the waist and hoisted her up on to a bar stool. 'I come on over here most every Sunday evening, don't I, John?' he shouted to the publican.

'Andrew comes on over here most every Sunday evening.' John's repetition was dutiful.

'He doesn't believe my name is André. But what I want to know is what are *you* doing here, Gussie? I've never seen you in here before.'

'Waiting for Mr Right,' said Gussie, 'and having a drink with my cousin.'

I couldn't argue with her – on both counts. Except drink*s* in the plural might have been more accurate.

André bought me a glass of the *côtes du Rhône* I'd been drinking and settled himself on the stool between us. It took approximately five minutes for me to realize that he had totally forgotten my existence. Gussie was batting her eyelashes at him, all perked up like Bambi on speed, and he was lapping it up. When he took his eyes off her for one second to signal John for another round, she took the opportunity to look at me and jerk her head several times towards the door.

'Go home!' she mouthed.

'Who me?' André feigned shock.

'No, I think she means me,' I said, slipping off the bar stool. 'Gussie, are you sure? Will you be OK getting home?'

Gussie rolled her eyes and looked away.

'She'll be fine,' said André. 'Count on it.'

But he didn't get her home OK because he never got her home at all.

Chapter Ten

It actually felt a little strange coming downstairs the next morning to an empty house. I was amazed at the extent to which I had grown used to being around people and if you'd told me a year ago that I'd be working every day in a hot and overcrowded space where the noise level was almost unbearable, I'd have told you to have your head examined.

I made a cup of tea and staggered back upstairs with the intention of going back to bed for another couple of hours. Now The Pelican was no longer open for lunch, I didn't have to show up till noon. I threw the ducks' breakfast out the window. Big mistake! They started quacking in gratitude and then squawking when they found there weren't enough stale crumbs to go around. There was a lot of chasing up and down the bank and furious paddling to and fro, and even some outraged flapping of wings.

'Shut up you morons,' I yelled at them, 'or we'll eat you for dinner.'

It was true. Duck was on the menu for later in the week. For a fleeting moment I wondered where André would get it. Maybe I should invite him up to my bedroom with a shotgun.

And maybe I shouldn't!

What did I think about André and Gussie? To my surprise, far from relishing having the house to myself I actually felt a little excluded. All of a sudden I wanted someone to pay me the attention André had lavished on Gussie the night before, not to mention the sex that had undoubtedly followed. New sex was always the most exciting, but then to my horror I found myself thinking, *No, that wasn't necessarily so*. What about the warm familiar embrace of my most constant lover of the last nine years? What did I have to compare to that?

Tommy was a lazy lover, there was no other way to describe him. His love-making was never urgent and this might make it unexciting for some but it drove me wild. His foreplay could take forty-five minutes. OK, maybe it was accompanied by Chelsea playing Liverpool on the box with the sound turned down but the truth was by half-time I was begging for it. And then I'd nestle down again under the blankets beside him as he propped himself up on the pillows to watch the second half. I'd rest my head against his chest – covered in a soft blond fuzz – and feel totally safe with one of his huge arms wrapped around me and his hand idly stroking the hair away from my face. Every so often he would suddenly pull the blankets up over my head and then lean over to rain hot kisses on my face when I came spluttering up for air.

But the best time would be when the game was over and he joined me under the covers. We'd start with our Eskimo kisses, gently rubbing noses and nudging the blankets slowly off the bed with our feet. Then he would examine every inch of my body, prodding me gently here and there.

'Getting to be quite a chubby polar bear. Can't have that.'

At which point I'd wrestle with him and he'd pull me on top of *his* distinctly chubby middle section and this time the foreplay would have his complete attention.

This was the Tommy I had fallen in love with all those years ago. And this was the man I had run away from – twice. First because *he* had called off our wedding but second because I had foolishly imagined myself in love with another man. A man who had not made one move to contact me in over six months, a man I had barely kissed let alone had amazing sex with. What was I thinking? As I snuggled under the blankets on a bitterly cold Exmoor morning three thousand miles away from Tommy, I missed him so much I joined the ducks in some tearful squawking. And I knew that whatever happened I had to get him back.

I wrapped a blanket around me, trailing it on the ground as I struggled over to the table to boot up my laptop in the cold. The Aga had gone out, Gussie wasn't there to light it and I hadn't a clue. Meanwhile I would freeze – but not before I had emailed Tommy. I deleted my first three attempts because even I could see they were too needy. Something along the lines of *Please, darling Tommy, I so need to see you* from the woman who had run away from him and failed to make any contact for six months would surely alarm him. Finally I settled for *Sorry not to have got back to you before now. Yes, I am being a good polar bear but I think I need someone to watch the football with.*

I didn't sign off because that relieved me of having to decide whether to put *love* or *lots of love* or *all my love* and wondering what he would read into it. The very fact that I had mentioned a willingness to watch football should tell him everything. I loathed football with a passion and the fact that I had had to share Tommy's affections with Chelsea FC – in the bedroom as well as everywhere else – had always been a bone of contention between us.

I pressed SEND before I had second thoughts and wondered when Gussie would be home. As it was, when I arrived for work I encountered her sneaking down the stairs from André's lair.

'Gotta run,' she hissed, 'Sylvia'll be here any minute. See you later.'

André appeared not long after and I was secretly impressed by his coolness in not mentioning The Longhouse or Gussie or giving any indication that he had seen me outside The

Pelican. He just nodded hello and disappeared into the larder, reappearing with a container from the freezer.

'I want to send you on a mission,' he said, 'are you up for that?'

'Sounds mysterious,' I said, 'depends what it is.'

'I want to do something for the Mackays, something *now*. Who knows when they'll have that memorial get-together. But I can't leave the kitchen to go pay a condolence call. I want you to take them this casserole. They won't feel like cooking right now but they have to eat.'

I was impressed by his thoughtfulness. 'André, that's incredibly kind of you. It's not as if you even knew Melanie.' When he didn't say anything, I added, 'Did you?'

His answer sounded strangely evasive. 'I never actually met her. So will you take it? Tell her godmother how sorry I am? I called Jake and he's given me directions. It's just over the hill from him. If you leave now, you'll be back in time for the evening prep work.'

On the outward journey I could see a storm approaching on the far horizon but by the time I reached the crest of Dorcas Tor it had changed direction and the sun was winking at me through the clouds. I drove for about two miles until I saw the farmhouse Jake had said to look for nestling into the slope further down the valley. I turned the car down the trail leading to it and parked at the edge of the farmyard.

It was a plain stone house like Jake's but infinitely more welcoming. I crossed the cobbled yard noting that the adjacent barns were in good repair. In contrast to Jake's, the front entrance of the house seemed inviting and I unlatched a well-oiled wrought-iron gate and entered a small walled garden, bare now in the midst of winter but showing evidence of neatly tended borders. The front door opened before I could reach it.

The woman was in her fifties, ruddy cheeked with her hair scraped back in a straggly ponytail. She was wearing a bright red fleecy anorak that gave out a feeling of good cheer totally at odds with the drawn appearance of her face.

'Oh,' she stopped, 'I thought you were my son.'

'Mrs Mackay?'

She nodded.

'My name is Lee Bartholomew. I've brought you this,' I held out the casserole, 'on behalf of The Pelican.'

She looked blank.

'The restaurant in Frampton Abbas? Your son came to see us yesterday about the food for your memorial celebration for your goddaughter.' Damn! Celebration was *not* the right word. I babbled on in an effort at damage limitation. 'André, the chef, he made it specially.' So why was it frozen? 'We're terribly sorry. It's a tragedy.' Cliché, cliché. Maybe I should shut up and make a run for it.

But Marjorie Mackay actually gave me a faint smile.

'Come in,' she turned, 'bring it inside and have a cup of tea. I need company, tell you the truth. It's almost as bad as when I lost my husband last year. Every moment I'm alone I can't stop thinking about her.'

'I don't want to intrude.' I was about to add *at a time like this* but that had to be the biggest cliché of them all.

'You wouldn't be,' she said firmly, 'I told you, you'd be doing me a favor.'

'You farm here?' I said as she put the kettle on the hob. Her kitchen was about as far removed from Jake's as it could be with recently installed Ikea units, a monster refrigerator and a spanking new dishwasher. The stripped-pine countertops and kitchen table were gleaming and the chairs had red and white gingham cushions tied to them. It said Farmhouse Country Kitchen – from a catalog.

'My husband did,' she said, picking up a bag of knitting from a chair and motioning to me to sit down. 'I'm a city girl born and bred. It was just my luck to fall in love with a farmer who dragged me down here to one of the bleakest spots on the planet. I've been here nearly thirty years and I still don't know the first thing about farming. Lucky for me my son and his wife live two miles away. He takes care of everything now. So did you have a problem finding me? Most people do.'

'Jake Austin gave me directions.'

'Old Jake. Did he now? How'd you stumble on him?'

'He's my boyfriend's uncle,' I said without thinking.

'Oh?' Her face brightened for a second. 'You're Max's girl-friend? That's good news. I'd no idea he'd taken up with someone since—' She struggled to find the right words and failed. 'No, well, I mean, poor old Jake, he used to have a lot of—' Again she searched for the right word and came up with, 'Company. Before the tragedy, I mean.'

Tragedy. Good all-purpose word. I was glad to find I wasn't the only one who made free with the clichés.

'Jake's always telling me I'm a silly old woman to worry about Melanie like I do. Do you take sugar at all?'

I shook my head, noting the *like I do,* present tense. Had she not accepted that Melanie was dead?

'But I do worry.' She saw me looking at her. '*Did.* It's all right, love. I know she's dead.' She choked a little and I wondered if I should put my arm around her. 'Her parents live abroad, you see? They flew in last night and they're on their way down here today. Ever since they retired I'm all Melanie's ever had in this country. This was her home when-ever she wanted to come down here. I promised June, that's her mother, I'd take care of her even though June kept telling me she was old enough to take care of herself. But she was-n't, was she? She walked over the edge of the quarry and now—'

She buried her face in her hands and this time I did get up and go over to her.

'You know, she was very lucky to have you. My parents live abroad and I wish I had a godmother who was as caring as you are.'

A Land Rover pulled up outside and a couple of minutes later Neil Mackay poked his head round the door.

'Take those boots off, Neil,' Marjorie cautioned him, straightening and reaching out for the teapot. *Poor man,* I thought, *she still thinks he's six years old.*

'I'm Lee Bartholomew,' I said again, 'I saw you yesterday at The Pelican. André asked me to bring a casserole for your mother.'

Marjorie had been too distracted to put the casserole in the fridge. It was still sitting on the kitchen table, an unappetizing gray mess below cling film beaded with moisture as the meat defrosted with the heat from the Aga.

'Good of him,' said Neil, almost brusquely. He didn't look at me, I noticed. 'June and Roy, Mum, what time do they get in? I was on my way to Tiverton to pick them up when I realized I didn't even know what train they were on. You just said today.'

'Oh it's not till two thirty. You've got a while. Sit down and have a cup of tea.'

'In a minute.' He disappeared through a door and I saw him walking back across the yard.'

'Now where's he going?' Marjorie looked puzzled. 'Always rushing in here one minute and disappearing the next. Just like Melanie. She used to sit in this kitchen and chat to me for hours but about a year ago she went all moody. Every time she came down here she'd go straight up to her room and get on that laptop of hers. Not that I minded, she used to order stuff for me on the Internet. Although I have to say I prefer mail ordering from the catalog. They'll have a bit of a chat with you, often as not, while they take your order. I looked forward to it.'

I felt so sad for her. This would be me, I thought ruefully, if I had succumbed to my romantic notions that life in the country was what I needed for my peace of mind.

'And if Melanie wasn't up in her room, she was out walking the moors. She'd go to that quarry and back every single day, even when it was raining. I said to Neil, I said I don't know why she does it.'

'And what did he say?'

'Not much. He didn't care for Melanie, I'm sorry to say. Never came near here when she was down. I think he was

164

jealous of the attention I paid her but you know, I always wanted a daughter. Ah, there you are.' Neil had come back in. 'Before I forget, could you do me a favor and run upstairs to Melanie's room? I didn't notice it till this morning but she left her laptop on. It's been sitting there all this time and I don't know what to do with it. Go up there and turn it off or whatever you do.'

I was beginning to think I'd better make my getaway soon otherwise I'd never be able to leave. I knew that if I was still there once Neil had left for the station, I'd feel obliged to stay with her until he got back with Melanie's parents so she wouldn't be on her own. She'd barely given me a chance to say two words since I'd been there but I could tell that her incessant chattering was what helped her get through the day. As she prattled on, I thought about what Taylor had witnessed at the quarry. *He didn't care for Melanie, never came near here when she was down.* Poor Marjorie, she didn't have the faintest idea what had been going on between her son and her goddaughter.

'What's he doing up there? I don't know the first thing about them but it can't take that long to turn off a computer. Be a love and pop up there and tell him his tea's getting cold. My bad knee's playing up today.'

There was a bedroom and a bathroom at the top of the stairs with freshly painted magnolia walls, matching floral-patterned curtains and bedspread and piles of pastel-colored fluffy towels. On the walls were several misty blue seascapes by the same artist. A long passage leading to another wing added on to the back of the house had a line of built-in closets. At the end was a guest room as antiseptic as the others and beside it a closed door.

Neil Mackay was inside Melanie's room, staring at the screen of her computer. I reeled at the unexpected smell of stale cigarettes and the sight of an empty wine glass, a mess of clothes and make-up scattered around the room and a DVD player with rentals strewn across the floor.

'Sorry to burst in,' I said, 'your mother asked me to come and get you. Your tea's getting cold.'

He didn't answer me at first. I moved to stand behind him and saw he was reading an exchange of emails.

'Don't tell Mum I'm looking at these,' he said suddenly.

'As if,' I said, surprised that he was asking me to conspire against his mother. 'Are they Melanie's?'

He nodded. 'She met men on the Internet. When I went to shut down her computer, I saw these emails about meeting someone at the quarry.'

'Mr Wright?'

I think somewhere deep in my subconscious I'd known the minute Jake had said Melanie subscribed to Exmoormates.com that she had probably 'met' Mr Wright. And when her body was found at the quarry, I'd probably assumed he was involved. But until this moment I'd suppressed it because I was still resisting the notion that Mr Wright was a killer.

He looked shell-shocked. 'How the hell did you know?'

'I know something else,' I said, making a lightning decision to take advantage of the situation. 'I know you were up at the quarry with Melanie. That little boy at the restaurant, he saw you there.'

I expected him to remonstrate with me, deny it, but he appeared suddenly deflated – almost relieved. 'I know he did,' he said. 'I couldn't place him immediately but last night I remembered where I'd seen him.'

There was a distant creak on the stairs then Marjorie's voice sounded at the end of the passage. 'What in the world are you two doing?'

Neil's fingers hit the keyboard. 'I've got to shut this thing down before she sees it. You won't say a word?' he appealed to me. 'It'd kill her if she found out.'

Unfortunate choice of words.

'I'll make a deal with you,' I said, amazed by my sudden boldness, 'I'll head her off downstairs – and I won't say a word – but in return I'm going to ask you to print out those emails for me before I leave. My car door's open.'

He was too taken aback to argue and when I finally said goodbye to Marjorie and went out to my car, I found a bundle of pages on the passenger seat.

On my way back to The Pelican I stopped to drop the pages off at the house. Gussie pounced on me the minute I walked through the door.

'He's *un*believable!' she said gleefully. 'He's totally divine!'

I'd been so preoccupied with thoughts of Melanie and Mr Wright, I almost said, *Who?*

'All right,' she said, mistaking my silence for disapproval, 'his hands had a tiny whiff of onion but he's so *hot*! I've never had sex like it, Lee-Lee. He flipped me over and over like I was an omelette, told me I was the juiciest thing he'd ever—'

'Gussie!' I reached out and held the palm of my hand to her mouth. 'Go no further! I don't want to know.'

'Jealous?' She sneaked a grin behind my hand. 'I tell you, you'd better be.' She pushed my hand away. 'And one thing I do know, Mickey hadn't a clue. He never made me go the way this guy did. *Never!*'

She calmed down after about five minutes but then came the needling.

'So did André say anything about me this morning, Lee-Lee?'

I shook my head. Of course she thought I'd been there all morning. She didn't know I'd been to the Mackays and I didn't have time to stay and tell her.

'*Nothing?*' She was incredulous.

'Not a thing. But I expect he was being discreet.' I added tactfully. 'Now I've got to get back to work. Maybe I'll have more to tell you by the time I get home tonight.'

André wasn't around when I got back to The Pelican and started work on what would turn out to be my roughest day yet. The trouble began with a man calling for a last-minute reservation. As I answered the phone, André walked through the door with a gigantic leg of lamb on his shoulder and slammed it down beside me. I screamed and the man on the other end of the line reacted in shock. I then had to tell him we didn't have a table for him.

'But it's my wedding anniversary. My wife loves The Pelican.'

Well, then why didn't you make the reservation three weeks go? Because you only just remembered it was your anniversary and you're too scared to tell her you've done nothing about it. 'Sorry, sir,' I said and hung up.

André made me watch while he hacked the lamb into serving pieces in front of me using what looked to me suspiciously like a tomahawk, waving it in the air perilously close to my head and smashing it down through the bone. I kept seeing a human body instead of a carcass of lamb and just the sight of his bloodied apron was enough to make me shudder. He had me label each piece and store it in the freezer. And all the while Sylvia was holding out the cordless to him, trying to make him deal with a supplier, something about an unpaid invoice and he'd been the one who had ordered the produce. Until eventually he lost it altogether, seized the phone from her and smashed it against the oven.

'Well, that's one supplier we won't be hearing from again,' Sylvia said quietly, 'and now we'll have to use the phone on the wall by the fridge. Don't blame me if the cord doesn't reach as far as the stove, André.' And she walked back upstairs, fake smile defiantly in place. I was relieved to see her go. The fact that she and André were barely on speaking terms only served to heighten the almost unbearable tension in the kitchen.

But at the end of the afternoon it was poor Wendy who committed the cardinal sin.

'Where's my knife?' said André suddenly. A slab of meat lay in front of him. The kitchen went totally quiet. Justine froze and Wendy raised her hands to her ears to shut out the inevitable tirade.

'You never – *ever* – take my knife, you dumb bitch.' He had seen the knife fall from Wendy's hand. 'How many times do I have to tell you. *Nobody* touches my knives. And don't tell me you didn't know it was mine. It has my initials carved into the blade. See? *See?*' When she didn't answer, he put the blade within an inch of the end of her nose. 'There, see? Say it, say *I see*.'

He had turned the blade around so it was pointing straight at her cheek and she was trembling, too scared even to cry.

Taylor came out of nowhere, barreling so fast into André's midriff that he almost caused him to stab Wendy's eyes out. His fat little body made enough of an impact that André staggered a few paces.

'Leave my sister alone.' He was pummeling André with his fists.

André's eyes formed the question *What the ...?* but then a grin began to spread across his face. 'Easy, Buddy. You don't want to be going for anyone with a knife in their hand. Now take a closer look, see? This is a really cool Japanese blade and—'

As André defused his own tantrum by taking time out to give Taylor a lesson on knives, Sylvia murmured to me, 'It's one of his many superstitions. He thinks that if anyone touches his knives, it'll bring him the worst luck.'

At that moment André's baggy chef's pants suddenly fell to the floor and I looked at Sylvia, laughing. 'Now that's really bad luck.'

But her face was impassive. She was unlikely to find André amusing at the moment but there were times when I wondered if she was capable of seeing the humor in anything.

'Damned elastic's gone,' André muttered, standing there in his boxers, 'Lee, give me some cling film.' I watched, amazed, as he ripped off a section, pulled up his pants and cinched them back around his waist with the cling film.

And then about five minutes before we were due to open Wendy cried out, 'Where's the bread?', and I realized I had forgotten to go to the baker's to pick it up. Now, of course, they would be closed.

After that things went from bad to worse. A table that had been booked for four turned out to be parents with two brats who screamed for pizza. Without checking with André, Sylvia said they could have it.

'There's no pizza on my menu,' said André, 'If you want them to have pizza, you're going to have to go out and get it.'

'But we're fully booked. I can't leave.' Sylvia shook her wiry terrier's curls.

'Well then go out there and tell them they can't have it.' André turned his back on her.

'Wait,' I caught Sylvia's arm, 'I'll get them their pizza. Just don't ask me how.'

Sylvia opened her mouth but I walked away from her to the phone on the wall.

'Gussie,' I said, trying to make myself heard above the din in the kitchen, 'get in the car, drive to Tiverton, buy two large pizzas with all the toppings and bring them to the alley door. Don't argue.'

If she didn't get the subtext, she was slower than I thought. *You deliver the pizzas, you'll have an excuse to come into the kitchen and see André.*

The pizza family weren't the only problem customers. Even though I'd told him we were fully booked, Mr Wedding Anniversary turned up with his wife all decked out in her best frock and, from the look on her face, the image of a candlelit dinner floating through her head – and there wasn't a single table to be had.

'But it's my wedding anniversary,' he told Sylvia and we could hear his raised voice all the way back in the kitchen. 'I called to make a reservation.' Well, that much was true. 'You can't disappoint my wife.' *You* can't disappoint my wife indeed! Put it all on us, why don't you? I thought.

170

'That guy call to make a reservation?' André asked me.

I nodded. 'But I told him we were fully—'

'Leave it to me,' he said. 'Plate these two pork chops and give them to Sylvia for table four. I'm going out to greet my customers.'

This was a first, and suddenly they had become *his* customers, I noticed. I had always thought it extremely odd that André never made an appearance front of house. Sylvia would refer occasionally to *Chef* but only when she needed to pass the buck. Normally she was the only one schmoozing the diners. She worked hard, I had to give her that. She seemed to have the extraordinary gift of being able to have her eye on every table all of the time. She was on poor Wendy's case the minute a water pitcher needed filling or a plate was ready to be removed. But I had no doubt that she took all of the credit for what went on in the kitchen as well.

So she didn't like it when André suddenly appeared at her side, bending forward, shaking hands, nodding and smiling at everyone like he'd known them all his life. Before leaving the kitchen he had whispered to Wendy to open a bottle of champagne and now he guided Mr and Mrs Wedding Anniversary away from Sylvia over to the hatch where a champagne bucket and three glasses were waiting. He pulled the stools out, motioned to them to sit and poured them each a glass.

'Your table will be ready soon. Meanwhile allow me to propose a toast. So how long have you guys been married?'

He was charm itself and had them instantly engrossed. And of course that's where he was when Gussie came to the kitchen door with the pizzas. I grabbed them from her and mouthed that he was out front and she gave me an incredulous look that said *Oh yeah, right!* before slinking back down the alley. I knew I'd get a mouthful from her later.

I plated the pizzas and left them for Wendy to deliver to the brats. Sylvia had been left standing alone by the entrance and I could tell she was fighting the urge to confront him. But she couldn't argue. André had defused a potentially difficult situation and all she had to do was gently hurry along table six who were already on their dessert, bring them their coffee maybe just a little bit sooner than they might have liked and present the bill along with it. They'd either take the hint or they wouldn't but one way or another Mr and Mrs Wedding Anniversary would have their table soon.

Sylvia didn't say another word to André for the rest of the evening. She made a point of asking me to lock up – something she had never done before – and went home as soon as she had totaled the till. Wendy cleared the dining room and made a half-hearted attempt to help with the final load of the dishwasher but I shooed her away, knowing she wanted to get back to stop Taylor watching DVDs all night. André disappeared upstairs and I assumed he had gone to bed.

But he reappeared ten minutes later as I was gathering the vases of flowers off the tables – something Wendy always forgot to do and I knew Sylvia was meticulous about giving them fresh water every day. *Got to keep them alive, can't waste money buying fresh flowers all the time!* He had a battered spiral-bound notebook in his hands and as he reached the bottom step, several loose pages fell out on to the floor.

'It was terrific the way you sorted out that couple,' I said. I stooped to pick up the pages for him and saw they were recipes, handwritten, the ink fading and grease stains all over the paper. 'Thanks. How long had they been married?'

'Can't remember,' he said, moving to the hatch and laying the book open on it. 'And who cares anyway? He was pretty obnoxious and full of himself and she laughed like a hyena at everything he said. One way to make a marriage work, I guess.'

'Were your parents married a long time?' I asked him. He had removed his skull cap and released his curls from their restraint so that they sprang away from his head in an unruly ginger halo. His green eyes were spectacular but I marveled that Gussie was so attracted to him. For a split second I wondered if it was because his untamed image was such a far cry from Mickey's controlled urbanity. Or maybe it was a question of like attracting like – she was drawn to his red hair that was almost a match for her own.

He had poured himself a large brandy and to my surprise he held up a goblet.

'Don't know. Never met them. Want one?'

I nodded, took the glass and climbed on to the stool beside him. 'What do you mean, you never met your parents?'

'I was adopted at birth, given away – to my grandmother. She was the one who raised me.'

'How come?'

'My mother was only sixteen when she had me and she didn't want me. She took off and never came back. We learned later that she died of a drug overdose.'

'That's terrible. So you were raised by her mother?'

'Well, no, I wasn't,' he grinned. 'Getting a little confused, aren't you? Don't blame you. I was raised by my *father's* mother. He was seventeen years old and he denied he was the father but everybody said yes he was. *His* mother did the right thing and stepped up to the plate to take care of me.'

'And where was all this?'

'Little town of Dublin, New Hampshire. Population under fifteen hundred. Zero crime rate. Lot of snow in winter. A million miles from any excitement.'

I wasn't listening to him. *Dublin*, New Hampshire. On his profile on Exmoormates.com, Mr Wright had said he had been educated in Dublin. On Sunday night, as I drove away from The Longhouse leaving Gussie and André in the bar, I had asked myself repeatedly, *Why didn't Mr Wright show up? Why was it that he made these dates and then failed to keep them? Did it mean that something terrible was going to happen to Gussie in his absence, just as it had with Rosemary Waters?* But then I told myself she was fine, she was with André.

Now I began to put it together. Gussie had been impressed by the way Mr Wright had advised her on how to deal with Sylvia. Who was in a better position than André to give her

173

that advice? Rosemary Waters had opened up to Mr Wright when he had shown himself to be sympathetic and knowledgeable about her peanut allergy. Hadn't André told me that a high-school friend had had a peanut allergy? He had claimed that because of that he wouldn't allow peanuts in any form in his kitchen – but who was better placed to bring in some peanut oil and slip it into the salad dressing?

I looked at André and for a second my heartbeat increased, but he didn't look like he was going to do me any harm. He was clearly drunk and becoming more expansive by the minute.

'My grandmother was the one who got me interested in food.' His expression was soft and sentimental. 'I cook in her memory most every day. See, here I'm looking through her old recipes for something to make with walnuts. She had these walnut trees in her yard and she used to knock the nuts out of them with a pole. I'd run around behind her with a bucket. I couldn't have been much more than seven or eight. Have you ever eaten fresh walnuts? They're moist and sweet.'

I found myself listening to him intently. I have a sixth sense that tells me when someone is relaxed enough that they will reveal who they really are.

'Did she teach you to cook?'

He nodded. 'She didn't so much teach me as *show* me. I watched her do everything and I learned to appreciate food at its best. She'd grown up on a dairy farm and she taught me how to get right up close to a cow and work those udders. Have you ever drunk milk when it's still warm from a cow's body?' His eyes rested momentarily on my breasts and I could feel my face reddening. 'And she knew what to do with a pig. Hey, Lee, this is right up your alley.' He reached out and tapped me on the shoulder and I tried not to flinch. 'She'd boil it all up – the head, the jaw, the liver with a whole load of spices – imagine that pink head bobbing about – and then she'd grind it and make sausage. Maybe that's what I'll do next week right here in this kitchen. How about it?

'Freshness is what's important,' he went on, 'beets, kale, and corn picked five seconds before it goes into your mouth. I've never eaten canned peas in my life. And every Sunday night she used to make a big pot of beef barley stew just like the one I put on the menu the other night.'

'Are you Mr Wright?' I blurted it out, knowing that if I allowed him to go any further down memory lane, I'd lose my nerve.

He was taken aback for a minute, which could have been from my changing the subject so abruptly as much as anything.

'Sure I am.' He fingered the little gold hoop in his ear and gave me his piratical grin. 'I thought you'd never ask.'

Chapter Eleven

'You guys finally figured it out, yeah?' He gave me lazy smile. 'Tell you the truth I was always a little embarrassed about that. I've been wanting to date Gussie since I first got here but I wasn't sure it was such a good idea.'

I was stunned that he would admit it so easily. 'So you pursued her under the cover of Mr Wright?'

'Hey man, I didn't know it was her to begin with. She didn't use her real name on DirtyFarmers.com.'

'Exmoormates.com?'

'Whatever. Everyone round here calls it DirtyFarmers – that's what it's there for, to help all the country boys get laid. But the reason I answered that post in the first place was because the girl in the photo looked just like Gussie, same red hair. It was only when we started emailing back and forth that I realized it really was her, all that stuff about Sylvia.'

'So why didn't you come clean?'

He shrugged. 'Why didn't she? And by the way, she never mentioned she was waiting for anyone on Sunday. I tell you, I've been nervous about starting anything with her. That's why I left it more than an hour before I showed up that night. I figured if she was still waiting, it was meant to be. And then you were there too and the two of you thought it was just a coincidence that I'd turned up to have a drink, I thought why spoil it? But I guess now she knows?'

I shook my head. 'I don't think so. I just worked it out when you said you came from Dublin, New Hampshire. You were pretty crafty on your profile, just saying Dublin. There might be several Dublins in America but over here we'd assume it meant Dublin, Ireland.'

'I was in two minds about how far I wanted to go with this online dating stuff. I never really took it very seriously.' He looked a little shamefaced. 'I guess I always wanted Gussie. How is she? Has she said anything to you about, you know?'

He sounded as needy and hesitant as Gussie. *Unbelievable,* I thought, *all he has to do is pick up the phone.*

'I think she'd like it if you called her,' I said and then mentally hit myself over the head. *What was I doing? If André was Mr Wright, should I really be encouraging a relationship between them?* There was only one way to find out.

But was it wise to probe further? I was alone in a building at one o'clock in the morning with a man who had had a virtual relationship with two women who had wound up dead. Should I not be pleading extreme fatigue and getting out of here as quickly as I could? Except I didn't suspect him of killing them. And the reason I knew this was because I didn't feel afraid sitting here with him. So I was just going to trust my instinct and dive right in.

'But André, what about the other women you found on Exmoormates.com?'

'What about them? Nothing happened.'

'But you set up dates with them?'

He shook his head. 'Gussie was the only one I got as far as inviting on a date.'

I stared at him.

'Why are you looking at me like that, Lee?'

'What about Rosemary Waters?'

He was thrown by that. I saw it immediately. 'How'd you know about her?'

Without mentioning Gussie's involvement, I told him about Gilly Mortimer having Rosemary's laptop. 'You had a pretty long correspondence with her.'

He nodded. *So?*

'And she wound up being poisoned right here.'

'You think I haven't been thinking about that?' He flared at me. 'You think I haven't been asking myself how peanut oil got into the salad dressing in *my* kitchen?'

'But you had a date to meet her here that night. Why didn't you show up?'

Now he looked totally shattered. 'Whoa there, back up. I never agreed to meet her here. It was my night off. I wouldn't bring anyone here in a million years. I like to get as far away as I can. I usually go to Exeter and get drunk and don't get back here till four in the morning. I had no idea she'd even been here till I heard she'd died.'

'I have proof,' I said, aware even as I spoke that I was sounding melodramatic, 'in your emails to her—'

'What do you mean, you have proof? Proof of what? That I invited her to The Pelican on the night of her death? Well, guess what? I have proof too. I was in Exeter getting drunk with – actually I don't remember who with – but the guy behind the bar will remember me, trust me on that.'

'You're trying to tell me you never made a date with her? After all those emails?'

'No, I never did. I'm not saying I feel good about it. Maybe I should have cut off the correspondence way sooner than I did but I felt sorry for her. She didn't sound like she'd had much of a life and from reading her emails, I kind of liked her, she had a good sense of humor, but then she started getting needy and I couldn't handle it. I felt bad about it but I just let my emails peter out till they stopped altogether. She kept suggesting we get together but I never gave her any hope on that – *never!*'

'What about Melanie?'

'Who?'

'Her name was Melanie. The woman who was found at the bottom of the quarry. Don't pretend, André. I was up at the Mackays this morning, don't forget. Neil Mackay was reading emails between Melanie and Mr Wright. Melanie and you! And there was one that indicated she was meeting Mr Wright at the quarry.'

He shrugged. 'OK so we exchanged emails for a while but it was like with Rosemary, I never got as far as asking her out. And if you seriously think I'm going to ask someone to meet me on a date at the quarry in the middle of winter, you're insane. I'm sorry, but you are.'

I hated to admit it but he was right. It didn't make sense. I hadn't actually read Melanie's emails myself yet. Maybe Neil Mackay had jumped to conclusions.

'Lee,' André said gently, 'get this through your head. The only person I ever suggested meeting face to face was Gussie. Isn't that why you're here working in this kitchen? So you can catch me out when I put rat poison in the *salsa verde*?'

I felt totally stupid. 'I'm here because I want to clear Gussie's name and ensure that she gets her job back, and to do that I have to prove she was not the one who put the peanut oil in the dressing. She needs to be able to hold her head up again in Frampton Abbas and not have to hide in her own house. And she needs to be off the hook by the time they have the inquest.'

André shook his head. 'You're nuts, you know that? Sure, it's a mystery how the peanut oil got in here but who says anyone's pointing the finger at Gussie? And as for hiding away in shame, I've seen her walk past the restaurant at least twice today.'

I didn't say anything. He was right, of course.

'But you're right about the inquest,' he said, 'it might not look too good if it isn't all figured out by then. And as for her job, she can have it back tomorrow. I'll call her in the morning and tell her and ask her what she's doing Sunday night while I'm on the line.'

'But what about Sylvia?'

'What about Sylvia? As you may have noticed, I've taken control of running this restaurant and not a minute too soon. Anyway, she'll be pleased. It'll free you up to help her put her boring life story down for posterity. How's that going by the way?'

I was reeling inside. Could I have misread Rosemary's emails? Would he have admitted so readily to being Mr Wright if he *had* asked her – and Melanie – out on dates? It wasn't as if he had denied emailing them. I didn't know what to think.

He was pouring me another drink. 'No comment, huh?'

'Gussie says I should get you to do your story,' I said.

'Gussie doesn't know my story,' he snapped.

The change in tone was scary, coming out of nowhere. I wouldn't have been surprised if he had had a go at me for more or less accusing him of murder but this reaction to Gussie's suggestion startled me. He saw my face and relaxed.

'Hey, I didn't mean it wasn't a good idea. Anything Sylvia can do I can do *better*!'

'Is your grandmother still alive?'

'Are you kidding? She'd be a hundred and ten in the shade. No, she was crippled with arthritis by the time she was in her fifties and I took over the cooking. I was only about twelve but I knew what to do.' He was watching me through half-closed eyes to see if I was listening. 'And then when she died one summer, I took off for the Massachusetts coast and got myself a job as a dishwasher in one of those seafood restaurants floating over the water on rickety pylons. I was just like you, Lee, at the bottom of the heap – peeling potatoes, cleaning shrimp, steaming lobsters en masse. Then the place closed for the winter but they told me if I came back the following summer, I'd be re-hired, maybe promoted to a line cook.'

'And did you?'

'Nope. I went to Europe. Been here ever since, never went back.'

'You haven't been back to America in all that time? How long are we talking about? Twenty years?'

'Twenty-five. I can't go back.'

'Can't? Why ever not?'

He raised his glass to me. 'That's my story. The one Gussie seems to think I should tell you even though she doesn't even know what it is. But I won't, Lee. That's the difference between Sylvia and me. Some of us know when to keep our mouths shut. Drink up, now. We've got to get some sleep.'

As I walked home I knew Gussie was right. I have a built-in antenna that tells me when I'm getting close to a really good story, and by refusing to tell it, André had me all charged up. Whatever happened, before I left Frampton Abbas I was going to get it out of him.

Gussie was on me the second I walked through the door.

'So? Did he mention me? Did he say anything? How could you get me to fetch those pizzas and then tell me he was out front? He never goes out front. Was he avoiding me?'

'Of course not,' I said wearily. 'He went out to deal with some tricky customers. And as for not calling you, you of all people ought to know how frantic he gets in the kitchen. Just as you must know how exhausted I am and how I've got to climb into a hot tub before my body completely seizes up.'

What would she do if she knew I'd just spent an hour chatting to André and sharing half a bottle of brandy with him? I wondered, as I dragged myself upstairs. And as for running a bath, I didn't even have the strength to get undressed before falling into bed.

The next morning Gussie slept through the ducks and I slipped downstairs to enjoy a quiet cup of coffee by myself. I retrieved Melanie's emails from where I had stashed them behind Gussie's Mills and Boons on the dresser and sat down to read.

Melanie had exchanged fewer emails with Mr Wright – whom I now knew to be André – than Rosemary Waters and she was considerably less revealing about herself than

Rosemary had been. Melanie was more probing, often referring to Mr Wright's profile on Exmoormates.com.

You say you love animals. Do you have a pet? André had replied, truthfully, that he didn't. *You say you were educated in Dublin. Are you Irish?* Had I not already known the truth about Mr Wright's identity, I might have paused at André's answer, which was curt and bewildering. *No, and it was only grade school.*

And exactly as it had in the correspondence with Rosemary, there came a point where his interest began to wane. It was clear to me, knowing what I did, but it seemed that Melanie, like Rosemary before her, didn't notice it. It started after she began to quiz him about his ME. *I see you've suffered from ME. Are you fully recovered? I have a friend who has it so I know all about it.* I'd bet serious money André had never had ME. It was just a ruse to avoid having to reveal his identity as the chef at The Pelican. He did not refer to it in his reply, nor did he answer any of her subsequent questions about his illness. In fact his replies became almost perfunctory after that so it was quite a shock when he suddenly emailed an invitation.

Isn't it time we met?

I couldn't believe it. He seemed to know all about her daily walk over the moors to the quarry and looking back through the emails, I found one where she had described them. Now he was suggesting he meet her there on a Sunday afternoon – André's day off – and they could walk down to Frampton Abbas for a drink at The Dog and Frog. It was exactly what you were not supposed to do – meet your cyberdate for the first time alone – and yet Melanie, like Rosemary before her, seemed to throw caution to the winds when the time came. It was as I had always suspected. Once you started down the perilous road of Internet dating, you were drawn to take risks.

I could hear Gussie's voice in my head. *Oh, Lee-Lee, you are such a scaredy cat!* But hadn't I been proved right? Twice?

And then I began to panic. Gussie was hooked on André. André was Mr Wright. He had admitted it. Mr Wright had cyberdated Rosemary and Melanie. Now they were dead.

It was the knowledge of his admission that eventually soothed me. And the fact that Gussie was alive and well and clomping down the stairs at this very minute.

'What are you *doing*?' she said, coming into the kitchen and thrusting the cordless at me. 'Didn't you even hear the phone? Why didn't you pick up? I could have slept another hour! It's your agent, by the way.'

'I couldn't find the phone,' I lied. I'd registered it ringing but had been so engrossed in Melanie's emails, I hadn't bothered to answer it.

'It hasn't exactly got up and walked.' Gussie pointed to the phone on the wall by the Aga and stomped out.

'Genevieve?'

'That's me,' she said, sounding disgustingly bright and chirpy for such an early hour, 'thought it was time I checked up on you. How's your idyllic life in the country going?'

She didn't bother to disguise her cynicism. And I didn't have an instant answer for her. I doubted she'd believe me if I told her the truth. *Well, actually, since I've been down here two women have been killed – one was poisoned by peanut oil and the other was found dead at the bottom of the quarry. Oh, and I've got myself a job scrubbing pans and peeling vegetables. And everything's connected to DirtyFarmers.com.*

'Fine,' I mumbled. 'How are you?'

'You don't sound *fine,*' she said, 'you sound bloody awful. But I'm tickety-boo, thanks for asking. It's so cold and miserable, I'm keeping myself warm by poring through all the travel catalogues trying to find a summer holiday.'

'Well, what about coming down to the country for a breath of fresh air?' I said. 'Didn't you say you knew someone in Frampton Abbas? Who was it, by the way? Maybe I've met them.'

'I doubt it,' said Genevieve with an odd certainty, 'anyway it was a very long time ago. I doubt she's there anymore. Her name's Ann Bates.'

It rang a bell but not a very loud one.

'So the reason I'm calling,' she went on firmly, 'is to tell you about a fantastic-sounding job. Right up your alley. Got a pencil? I want you to take the number and call her right away.'

'Call who right away?' I knew I sounded grumpy. What was the matter with me? Normally I would have been full of excitement at the thought of a new assignment.

'Mary Jane Markham.'

It took me a second and then I remembered. Mary Jane Markham was the name of one of the women I'd read about in the newspaper article Gussie had clipped.

'She got divorced, right?' I said.

'Understatement of the year,' said Genevieve, 'she got divorced *and* she got five million pounds. And there's more.'

'He gave her change for the parking meter and the laundromat?'

'Be serious, Lee. She wants to tell the story of her marriage. Her husband raped her and she was abused as a child.'

'And she's suddenly remembered this?' I was smelling a large rat. 'Sounds highly creative to me. Hell hath no fury and all that.'

'Why are you so skeptical?' Genevieve sounded disappointed with me.

'Because—' I was going to say because child abuse seemed to be the stock ingredient of every other story I heard when I was debriefing potential ghosting subjects, because I knew many of these stories were false and fabricated purely for effect and because I hated the way this somehow detracted from the horror of those stories that were real.

But I could see the potential in Mary Jane Markham's story. Millions of divorced women would want to see how she took her husband to the cleaners. And I knew from experience that once I had a subject engrossed in the telling of her story, I could often steer her away from hackneyed sensation without her realizing it.

'OK,' I said, 'give me her number. You've already told her about me, I take it?'

'I said you were the only person she needed. You'll call her soon, won't you? She's about to go off on a trip around the world spending all her money. On a yacht she's bought.'

'Well, I mustn't keep her waiting.' I wrote down the number Genevieve gave me. 'Don't want her to miss the boat.'

Genevieve groaned and rang off rather abruptly, I thought. I stared at Mary Jane Markham's number for several minutes. It would mean my escape from the drudgery at The Pelican. And, as I'd already admitted to myself, life in the country was not all it was cracked up to be. I was a city girl and this was my chance to get back to London where I belonged. So why didn't I pick up the phone?

It rang before I could even answer my own question.

'We've got a problem here,' said André without preamble. 'Wendy came in and slipped on a grease spill. She's sprained her ankle.'

'So you need me to come in early?' My heart sank.

'No, she's fine sitting on a stool doing prep work at the island. What she can't do is wait tables this evening. I want you to take her place. We're going to have to give you a crash course but you don't need to be here till four. OK?'

I opened my mouth to ask what Sylvia had to say about this but then I shut it again, feeling a little guilty. Sylvia was somehow no longer part of the equation.

'Fine,' I said, 'I'll be there.'

'Great,' said André, 'Gussie there?'

Well, here it was, I thought as I shouted up the stairs to Gussie, he'd offer her her job back and that would be one less reason for me to stay in Frampton Abbas.

I went upstairs to look for my mobile to call Mary Jane Markham. And suddenly I remembered where I had heard the name Ann Bates.

Monica Massey and Ann Bates. I didn't even have their address, just Gussie's description of where they lived: *a rather beautiful Georgian house, set high above the road to Tiverton as you leave the village.* Now that I didn't have to be at work until four, the day yawned before me. I could hear Gussie in her bedroom, still talking in breathless tones to André. I got dressed slowly, a plan of action taking shape in my head. When I left the house a short while later, the piece of paper with Mary Jane Markham's number on it was still lying on the kitchen table.

This wasn't like me at all. I never introduced myself to people unless my work called for it. Or, as in the case of Maggie Blair or Marjorie Mackay, I was on a mission. I was a polar bear whose hackles quivered in protest if anyone even said *You have to meet so-and-so, I know you'd absolutely adore each other.* This was guaranteed to make me resolve to loathe them on sight.

But then, I reasoned with myself, I would be on a mission where Ann Bates was concerned. She had been at The Pelican the night Rosemary Waters had been served the fatal peanut oil.

The house was easy to find because it stood alone on a bank as the road to Tiverton veered out of Frampton Abbas. I walked up a steep flight of stone steps and was suddenly accosted by a Yorkshire terrier streaking round the side of the house. It stood at the top of the steps and yapped at me so ferociously that all four paws shifted this way and that with each sound. I have never got the point of Yorkshire terriers. To me they're nothing more than clutch bags but you can't carry anything in them.

'Trinket! Come *here*!' A woman, squarely built with a face to match, strode after the dog. Her smile was warm and open and I decided I liked her immediately.

186

'Kick it,' she said, pointing to the dog. 'Why don't you? Do us all a favor.'

Now I knew I loved her!

'How could you *say* that?' Another woman, tall, slender and pretty in a fragile way appeared and scooped up Trinket. 'You'd never kick this poor little creature, would you?' she appealed to me.

'Course she would, she looks like an intelligent person to me.' The first woman held out her hand. 'Monica Massey. Actually kicking's too easy. Do you remember Michael Palin in *A Fish Called Wanda*? He ran them over, squashed them, left them flat as a pancake in the middle of the road. That was masterful!'

I giggled. I couldn't help it. Every time I thought of that scene I became uncontrollable. 'I'm Lee Bartholomew,' I managed between convulsions of mirth, 'I'm a friend of Genevieve LaBache's. A client, actually.'

There was an infinitesimal frisson of tension. If I hadn't chosen that moment to take a deep breath to try and suppress my laughter, I think I would have missed it. Then Monica Massey boomed into the silence.

'Cracks me up every time I hear that name. You know what *la bâche* means, don't you?'

I shook my head. I didn't even know why Genevieve had a French name. One of things I liked about her was the fact that she had never felt the need to regale me with details of her personal life. It was all business between us and I relished the fact that whenever we spoke, all the attention was on me. But, I realized with a guilty start, it meant I knew next to nothing about her.

'It means tarpaulin. *Tarpaulin!* Isn't that priceless?' Monica's ample bosom, the only part of her that wasn't particularly square, heaved with laughter. 'I mean, have you ever thought of Genevieve with all her pink and lavender outfits and those frilly blouses she wears – have you ever thought of her as a *tarpaulin*?'

187

I had to admit it was a stretch.

'Anyway, this is Ann, Ann Bates,' Monica gestured to the other woman but she'd gone. 'Oh, well *that was* Ann. Ann-who's-always-in-a-huff. Come inside, it won't last long.'

She led me round to the back door and into a narrow galley kitchen. It was the most modern kitchen I'd seen so far in Frampton Abbas, gleaming stainless steel and granite counter-tops. Trinket was lying on a cushion in a wire filing tray on top of the dishwasher and Ann was tying her – or was it his? – silky hair away from the face with a blue ribbon.

'Tea or coffee?' said Ann. 'What a surprise to have a friend of Genevieve's turn up. She's never sent us anyone before. You'd never kick Trinket, would you?'

'Tea. No, I never would.' I ignored the reference to Genevieve sending me because of course she hadn't.

'I'll get the tea. You put the kettle on, Annie.' Monica squeezed past her and I couldn't help sense the intimacy between them. Kitchens were, I often reflected, especially intimate places. People were obliged to move closer to each other. The preparation of food could be foreplay for the sensual occupation of sharing it. 'You're a client of Genevieve's, did you say?'

I nodded. 'Yes, I'm here visiting my cousin Gussie Bartholomew. And I'm a ghostwriter. Thanks to Gussie I've met Sylvia Leach and she's asked me to help her with her memoirs.'

'Oh, pull the other one,' said Monica, rolling her eyes. 'That woman's much too boring to have a book written about her. You go there for a quiet meal when you can't be bothered to cook for yourself and all you get is her fussing over you and droning on about her banal experiences.'

'Oh, be quiet, Mon.' Ann sounded exasperated. 'You're such a snob. Sylvia's a lovely person and she saves scraps for Trinket so we love her, don't we, Trinket? She's done wonders with that place considering what she has to put up with. That monster of a chef! Why she hired him, I'll never know.'

'Because he can cook and she can't. Bit like you and me, Annie.'

'Well you never give me a chance!' Ann rounded on her. 'And just because I watch what we eat doesn't mean I'm a bad cook.' She turned to me. 'You should see the butter and the cream and the red meat and the barrage of carbohydrates she spreads all over this kitchen! I choose not to poison my body like that and she calls me a bad cook.'

'Speaking of poison,' I said, 'wasn't it awful about that girl dying from her allergy to peanut oil? It was before I arrived but you were at The Pelican that night, weren't you?'

'Were we?' Monica frowned. 'I don't remember.'

'Such a control freak! If you don't organize it, you don't remember it,' said Ann. 'We *were* there that day, but for lunch not dinner. You didn't want to go, Mon, because Sylvia cooks at lunchtime and you said what was the point of paying money for crap? But it was a Sunday and we had nothing in the house so it was a question of eating Sylvia's crap or nothing at all. And we've only got to look at the size of you to know that eating nothing at all is not an option as far as you're concerned.'

They were like a worn-out double act, bickering away from force of habit. Their body language belied their constant barbs, a hand caressing an arm and lingering, a head resting on a shoulder in passing. But I was intrigued to hear what they might have to say about The Pelican, as well as being slightly worried that Gussie had clearly got it wrong about *when* they had been there. What else might she have *mis*remembered?

'Actually, I do remember now you mention it,' said Monica. 'The fire alarm!'

'And the row before it!' said Ann. 'Poor Sylvia.'

'What row?' I was intrigued. 'About what?'

'Who knows?' said Monica. 'He was yelling at her.'

'André?'

'The chef. Is that his name? It's almost a reason to go there sometimes, just for the entertainment of listening to him let rip while you sit there trying to stuff your *gigot au haricots blancs* into your face. You can hear every word through that hatch. *Get out of my kitchen, you fucking stupid cow, how could you forget to put the rice into the risotto!'*

Monica grinned and handed me a mug of tea.

'It was ironic – and now I'm remembering it as if it were yesterday – Sylvia came out and started twittering as usual, acting like nothing had happened, I mean she has to be stupid to think we can't hear – and she apologizes because she says she's got to test the fire alarm and there might be a bit of noise. *Bit of noise!* We've just had ten minutes of her being harangued by chef and she thinks a fire alarm's going to upset us? I did wonder, by the way, why she couldn't have tested it earlier but when it went off, I sort of got the picture.'

I opened my eyes wide in question.

'She obviously hadn't told André she was going to do it,' Monica chuckled, 'because he got the fright of his life. He went berserk, switching off all his ovens and shepherding us all out into the street. I reckon she did it on purpose.'

Ann shook her head. She reminded me a little of Sylvia. Something about the way her lips were pursed in constant disapproval and a worried look played about her eyes. And the total lack of irony. She was the straight guy to Monica's cheerful clown.

'So how long have you lived in Frampton Abbas?' I said. 'What do you do down here?'

'Not a lot,' Monica chuckled. 'I write execrable prose and Annie pretends that one day I'll sell it. But we both know Trinket's got a better chance of a book deal than I have.'

'And you're a writer too?' I asked Ann. Maybe Gussie could start a writing group in the Village Hall.

She shook her head. 'I was a literary agent in London. Gave it up when I moved here.'

'So that's how you know Genevieve?'

This time there was no mistaking it. The silence was almost palpable. And then, after several glances in Ann's direction,

Monica said, 'Genevieve was Ann's partner. Before she met me.'

Partner as in they were literary agents together or partner as in—? I cursed the fact that I knew nothing about Genevieve's personal life.

Whichever it was, the introduction of Genevieve's name had cast a pall over the conversation and shortly afterwards I finished my tea and left.

Back home Gussie was in a state of rapture over André's call.

'He wants to see me again, Lee-Lee. We're going out on Sunday and he's going to speak to Sylvia about me coming back to work at The Pelican.'

'Is that really what you want to do?'

'I'd do anything for him,' she said dreamily while I pretended to be sick. 'Don't you remember feeling like that about Tommy when you first met him? He called, by the way.'

'He did? When?'

'Last night,' she said, not looking at me, 'I forgot to tell you.'

'Where is he? What number did he leave?'

'Oh God! Did I write it down?' Gussie looked mortified. 'Maybe that's it.' She pointed to the piece of paper with Mary Jane Markham's number.

I wanted to strangle her. Instead I went upstairs and checked my email but there was nothing. I sent him another email explaining that I didn't have his number. But I still hadn't heard from him by the time I left for work – with the printouts of the emails I'd read, Melanie's as well as Rosemary's, stuffed in my coat pocket. Before I went back to London, I was going to have one last stab at clarifying their deaths.

'Here,' I thrust them at André as he stood at the island regarding a large ham hock as if unsure what to do with it. 'Read these and tell me you didn't invite Rosemary Waters and Melanie to dinner.'

I expected him to berate me for disturbing him in his kitchen but he took them upstairs without a word, and when he came down again ten minutes later he was uncharacteristically subdued.

'I don't know what to tell you,' he said. 'These are all my emails right up to the point where it looks as if I ask them for a date. But I didn't. I've never seen these emails at the end before. They come from me but I didn't write them and I never saw the ones I'm supposed to have received. And I don't suppose you'll believe this, but I've just checked on my laptop and they're not there. How'd you get these printouts?'

I explained about Gilly Mortimer and Neil Mackay.

'Well, I think you'd better go and ask them some more questions and maybe I'd better be there when you do.'

'When you do what?' Sylvia came in the door to the alley. 'Lee, you've got a lot to learn in a very short space of time so let's get started. Follow me.'

Sylvia revved herself up into terrier mode, barking whirlwind instructions at me over her shoulder as I raced after her.

'Wendy will tell you how to lay the tables, don't forget the flowers. First rule, never argue with a customer. Now when they come through the door I'll meet, greet and seat them and then I'll hand some of them over to you. You take their drink orders first and fill their water glasses. You don't have to take their food orders because there's only one option so you just have to let André know when you need the food. You put it up on the board here, see? Table Five, three starters, Table Two, four venison, right? And you shout it out to him at the same time to alert him. And when it's ready, he'll grab you while you're in the kitchen and tell you or he'll just shout it out – *four venison coming up* – so keep an ear out. There's an area above the oven we use for warming plates. *Always* use oven gloves, those plates will be hot! Now, you're going to have to suggest wines. Always push the local vineyard. They won't go for it unless they're morons but I have to earn my discount. With me so far?'

I was so far behind her, I might as well have been in another room.

That night I screwed up so bad they began keeping score in the kitchen. Right until the moment the restaurant opened, I was kept busy at the chopping block. Then I forgot to take off my apron, the apron splattered with tomato sauce and on which I had recently wiped hands stinking of onion and waltzed out in it to take the first customers' drink orders. I forgot to use oven gloves and let four scalding plates crash to the floor, letting out a howl of pain they could have heard in Exeter. I was so pleased with myself for remembering to tell André about each order that I forgot to listen out for when they were ready. As a result they piled up on the hatch and cooled to the point that four customers sent them back. I wrestled for so long with a newfangled corkscrew that Sylvia had to take it away from me and open the wine herself. And I snapped at a woman who said she didn't want venison, she wanted chicken. *Well then why didn't you go to the pub?* I could have sworn it was under my breath. Apparently not.

The crunch came when a man took out his cellphone and called The Pelican's number. When Sylvia answered not two feet away from him, he demanded to know where his food was.

It was some consolation that it was a relatively slow night and around nine o'clock when I began to serve the first coffees, I started thinking about the bathtub filled to the brim with hot water in which I would soon be soaking my aching limbs. Maybe I'd have had an email from Tommy by now giving me his number and I could have phone sex with him while lying in the tub.

But then André looked up in the middle of plating Justine's *tarte tatin.*

'Oh, shit!'

'What is it?'

'We just got some last-minute walk-ins. We're gonna be here till midnight.'

'Table four needs clearing and re-laying, Lee. Water, napkins, silverware. Hurry! And take their drink orders.' Sylvia's voice grated like chalk on a blackboard.

I stumbled out like an automaton, hoping I wouldn't have to start from scratch with a new tablecloth. I got halfway across the dining room and stopped dead in front of the fireplace.

'Hello, Lee,' said Jake, shrugging himself out of his jacket and loosening his tie, 'got a surprise for you. Just picked him up from the train.'

From the look on Max's face I could see it was just as much a surprise for him.

Chapter Twelve

Max was furious.

Thunder rumbled all over his face and he stared straight ahead, saying nothing. It took one glance in my direction from those hooded eyes – they were like two black grapes, their gaze intense but their expression opaque – to make my heart reverberate inside my chest. Instead of clearing the table and laying it again, I began to back away toward the kitchen. I almost collided with Sylvia who was sallying forth with the menus and a blatantly cranked-up smile.

'Where are you going?' she hissed. 'Where are the glasses and the silverware and the napkins?' She relieved me of the paper overlay under my arm and continued on into the dining room. 'Gentlemen, something from the bar before you order?'

'We'll have two large Bell's and water,' said Jake, 'and the wine list while you're at it. Venison!' He studied the menu and then, ignoring the fact that there were still a couple of other diners finishing their meal, yelled to André in the kitchen. 'Where'd you get it? I've got a saddle or two in my freezer. Why didn't you come to me?'

'Because I wanted a haunch,' André shouted back. 'It's a venison casserole I'm offering. I wanted to teach Lee the basics of a marinade, plenty of juniper berries and red wine and olive oil.' He poked his head through the hatch, 'We've only got one starter left, I'm afraid, Jake. One of you is going to have to go straight to the casserole. Who's your friend? Aren't you going to introduce me?'

'He's my nephew. Detective Super—' Max looked so exasperated at this description that poor Jake shuddered to a halt. 'Max Austin. Old friend of Lee's,' he finished lamely. 'So what is it, the starter?'

'*Pâté de foie de canard avec cognac*,' said Sylvia in probably the worst French accent I had ever heard.

'Blimey,' said Jake, 'what's that when it's at home?'

'Duck liver pâté with brandy.' Max's voice was low and throaty but I could hear the anger.

André noticed me react. 'What's going on?' he whispered to me. 'Jake says he's an old friend of yours but the man's barely glanced at you and you've come scuttling back here like a neurotic rabbit.'

'That's because I barely know him,' I whispered back. 'Jake's got his wire's crossed.'

I was on the verge of tears and I knew André could tell.

'Listen,' he said gently, 'it's only Jake. No one needs to stand on ceremony with him. You've had a rough time tonight. Let's just say you weren't born to be a waitress and leave it at that. Why don't you make some toast to go with the pâté and then take off home? Sylvia can deal with old Jake and his nephew.'

'She'd never allow it.'

'*I'm* allowing it,' said André. 'I don't mind sluicing down the kitchen. You know how I like to have the place to myself and besides, I've got a little helper I can call who can come by to give me a hand." He winked at me. 'Go on, shoo! I'll see you later.'

Because I'd forgotten to go to the baker, we were using yesterday's bread for the toast. So far no one had complained but what was the betting that Max would be the first to detect a little staleness? I popped a slice in the toaster and plated the last portion of pâté. I had watched André make it and it had looked simple enough – fry butter and onions and livers until they were brown, flame with brandy (I'd screamed and reached for the fire extinguisher), and then pound everything into a paste. André had let me do the pounding bit but I knew when I came to make the pâté at home, it wouldn't work. I cut the toast into triangles and arranged it on the plate. I had been anticipating my reunion with Max for eleven months and now that it had happened, I had to face the fact that judging by his silent behavior I was probably the last person he wanted to see.

Sylvia had returned to the kitchen and was gathering napkins, glasses and silver with much sighing. I waited until she had laid the table and then returned to the dining room to place the pâté squarely in the middle of the table with a visibly shaking hand.

After that I ran – through the kitchen, out the alley door and along the High Street to Gussie's house where I encountered her on her way out. *André's little helper.*

As soon as I was inside I knew I should turn right round and go back again. I should re-enter the dining room with a smile and a joke about serving Max to the best of my ability. His wish was my command, ha ha! I pictured him sitting there, his frame so lanky and his legs so long that the tip of his jeans and his chunky boots extended to protrude either side of Jake's chair on the other side of the table. His London detective's wardrobe – always quite formal and any attempts at fashion touchingly apparent in out-of-date designer wear – had clearly been discarded in favor of more relaxed country clothing – the jeans, the boots, a black turtleneck sweater, and an anorak slung over the back of his chair – and it suited him. I imagined the tension in his fierce expression disappearing as the Bell's went down followed by Jake's wine selection. I could see him leaning back, stretching his legs and crossing his ankles in the space beneath Jake's chair. And then he was rolling up his sleeves to reveal the soft black hair on his forearms that had so disturbed me when I had first noticed it and folding his arms loosely over his chest above the slight paunch that was beginning to show above his belt like the startling protuberance of pregnancy in a slender woman.

I imagined Sylvia's expression becoming increasingly pained – she hated it when the customers became noisy with drink – and André urging her to go home. And then I saw André and Gussie joining Jake and Max for more drinks and I began to marvel at the way Max was loosening up and encouraging Jake in family reminiscences so that by midnight his eyes were no longer hard pools of suspicion but were now glistening with amusement.

I say *I imagined* because Gussie's first words the next morning made it quite clear that I had been entertaining fantasies.

'God, what a miserable sod Jake the Rake has for a nephew! He just sat there, not saying a word, barely touched his venison. André was so offended, he couldn't wait to get him out of there. And poor old Jake, he tried so hard to get a conversation going but even he had to give up in the end. So what's up with you? You've got a face like a wet weekend. And why did you disappear like that last night?'

Gussie was my cousin and I loved her. Gussie had had a rough time and I was here to guide her through it and out the other side. I should be glad that she was starting to come back to life and re-establish herself in her chosen rural world.

But the truth was, at that moment I was so bitterly disappointed by my reunion with Max, I wanted to kill her out of sheer envy.

The sound of Gussie and André having sex that morning had been louder than the ducks. It didn't matter that her room was at the other end of the house. They might just as well have been right there in bed with me, so lusty were their cries of passion. And it wasn't as if they were even interesting to listen to. Gussie just shrieked *Yes!* repeatedly and André's utterances were restricted to terrifying heaves that made him sound like a horse straining in the last furlong of the Grand National.

When they climaxed – once, twice – it was even worse. They congratulated each other with over-the-top assurances of *Oh baby, you were the best* and *That was sensational* accompanied by *Shhh!* and muffled giggling. And all I could do was pull a pillow over my head and come to terms with the fact that my dreams of longing for Max Austin over the past eleven months had been forced to evaporate in a puff of smoke when he had barely acknowledged my existence.

'Sorry,' I said to Gussie. 'Rather a lot on my mind. I've got to make an early start this morning.' And with that I left the kitchen, anxious to be out of the house before André came downstairs. I didn't think I could face him after what I'd heard. It was going to be bad enough later on when we would be closeted together for the evening prep work. In the meantime I needed a little time to pull myself together.

'Got to make an early start with what?' Gussie called after me as I disappeared out the front door, slamming it behind me like a rejected teenager.

I had no idea where I was going to go and how I was going to kill two hours until I was due to start work. I crossed the road and was wandering aimlessly along the High Street past Maggie Blair's house when I heard the sound of a heated argument coming from inside. I peered through the window into the living room where I had served Maggie her fish 'n' chips and saw Sylvia and Mona squaring off against each other. I ducked out of sight and continued along the High Street where a large crowd had gathered in front of the Post Office.

'What's going on?' I asked a woman in front of me.

'Oh, hello, Lee,' she said, turning round, and after a second I realized it was Justine, the pastry cook at The Pelican. She pointed to a poster in the Post Office window that read NOTICE OF CLOSURE.

'It's just too bad.' She didn't actually stamp her foot but I could see it going through her mind. 'The Government's getting rid of Post Offices stuck out in the country like this.

They say not enough people use them to make them worth-while and that's bollocks!' She was shaking with indignation. 'They're saying we can get our stamps at the supermarket and have our benefits and pensions paid into our bank accounts and pay for our TV licence on the Internet but what they don't realize is that there's folks living here who are too poor or too old to have either a bank account or a computer.' She jabbed her forefinger at various people in the crowd, most of whom appeared rather startled by the attention. 'You *depend* on the Post Office, you need to know you can walk to it, don't you?'

No one answered her and I winced. You only had to look up and see the proliferation of satellite dishes to know that many people in Frampton Abbas were perfectly well connected to the twenty-first century but from what Justine was saying, once the Post Office went, many of its inhabitants would become as helpless as the ponies on Exmoor. Maybe poor old Maggie Blair had got out just in time, I reflected.

'I've just seen Sylvia up the road in Maggie Blair's house,' I told Justine. 'She appeared to be having a row with Maggie's daughter Mona. I didn't know Mona was back in town.'

I didn't really know why I was telling Justine this. I'd never said more than a few words to her before and these were usually along the lines of *Justine, sorry, could I just squeeze past you?* as we fought for space in The Pelican kitchen. She kept herself to herself and hardly spoke to anyone when she was at The Pelican, which was relatively rare. She prepared her tarts and quiches and cakes at home and brought them in, barely staying long enough to draw André's attention to what-ever it was she had made and where she'd put it. On the odd occasion when she did prepare something in the kitchen, she worked silently in a corner and never engaged anyone in conversation.

But, as I soon learned when she invited me back for a coffee – an invitation I accepted more out of curiosity than anything – she was one of those people who didn't miss a trick and waited until she was one-on-one with someone to indulge in a good gossip. Nor did she have any compunction about extracting information.

'So did you know Maggie Blair?' she asked as she marched me along the High Street and when I nodded 'I didn't know that. Were you friendly with her at all?'

I explained about my encounter on the day I first arrived in Frampton Abbas. 'So what do you suppose they were arguing about, Mona and Sylvia?' Justine still hadn't answered my question.

'Oh, the will, I expect,' she said.

'Maggie's will? Why would Sylvia argue about that?'

'Because she's in it. I dropped off an apple tart at The Pelican this morning. I've got so much going on in my ovens today, I wanted André to bake it in his. And there she was, mad as hell and taking it out on poor André. He looked relieved to see me, I can tell you. He scuttled upstairs as soon as I arrived and I was left with Sylvia. She'd had Mona on the phone asking her to go across the road and meet her at her mother's house.' Justine took my arm suddenly and swung me to the right. 'Here we are, I'm down this lane.'

We'd reached the outskirts of the village and she led me to a thatched cottage on the edge of a field. When we entered I had to dip my head, the ceilings were so low and beams blackened by soot from the fire loomed in front of my eyes every time I straightened up. There was a heavenly smell of baking wafting everywhere as she beckoned me into a kitchen where the far wall was pitted with oblong-shaped recesses housing what looked like cast- iron ovens that had to be centuries old.

'Oh good, these are ready.' She opened one of the ovens. 'You're just in time for some blackcurrant muffins. Now where were we?'

'Maggie's will. Mona and Sylvia.'

'Oh yes. It seems Mona wasn't too happy that Sylvia had even been mentioned in the will. But that was nothing to how Sylvia felt about the *way* she'd been mentioned. I'm not surprised they were arguing.'

'What did Maggie leave Sylvia?'

'Well, nothing as such. What she did was to add a coda saying that Sylvia could continue to manage The Pelican for as long as she wanted. Maggie left the restaurant to Mona, of course, but as long as Sylvia wants to stay there and run it, there's not a thing Mona can do with it. She can't sell it or run it herself. Her hands are tied.'

I frowned. I seemed to be missing some information. 'Maggie Blair owned The Pelican?'

'She owned the building. It was just an empty house until Sylvia arrived and turned it into a restaurant.'

'But Sylvia always made it sound as if *she* owned The Pelican. She always gave me to understand that it was *her* restaurant.'

Justine nodded. 'She acts like it is, sure. And you can hardly blame her given what she's put into it.'

'But why on earth would she be upset with Maggie's coda? Surely she must be delighted she gets to go on running it?'

'You'd think – but from what I could gather from her this morning, she was upset Maggie didn't leave her the building itself. Said she thought it was the least Maggie could have done given all the meals she had given her.'

'*Given* her?' I all but spluttered. 'I understood Maggie had to pay for them. And my cousin Gussie delivered them.'

'And André cooked them,' added Justine, 'and he often delivered them too if Gussie was tied up. He was fond of Maggie, he used to sit and chat to her, which was more than you ever saw Sylvia do. What do you make of her, by the way? I heard a rumor you were helping her with a book she's writing.'

She was good at the sneak question when you weren't expecting it, was Justine.

And I was good at deflection. 'Yes, she's talking to me about her book and I'm learning a bit about her. What do *you* make of her? Do you know her well?'

Justine shrugged. 'Who does?' she said but her tone implied *who wants to?* 'But maybe I know her better than most, now that you mention it. I was the first person she hired and that was well before André rode into town. She leaned on me quite a bit in the beginning and you know something? I found it touching to see how proud of herself she was for starting that restaurant. I have a feeling she's quite a bit older than she lets on, probably well into her fifties, but I had the sense she was spreading her wings for the first time. She's told you about those dreadful parents, I imagine?'

I nodded, hoping Justine would elaborate. 'They sound a nightmare.'

'Well, she was caught between that abusive father – verbal abuse, I mean, I don't think he ever hit her or anything – who yelled at her all the time and made her feel she couldn't achieve anything, and the mother who couldn't say boo to a goose. And then when the father finally croaked, instead of bonding with Sylvia, the mother said *Right, good riddance,* and took off to live with her sister hundreds of miles away in Scotland.'

'No one's ever loved her,' I murmured almost to myself.

'Oh Lord, here we go!' Justine mimed playing a violin. 'Sylvia wants a man, I'll tell you that for nothing. You should have seen the way she threw herself at André when he arrived.'

This tallied with what Gussie had told me.

'But then don't we all?' said Justine, frowning suddenly.

'We do?'

'Well, maybe he's not everyone's cup of tea,' she conceded, 'but I had my eye on him the minute I met him. We'd make the perfect couple, we're both in the business. Believe me, I haven't given up on him yet.'

This was interesting. I watched her as she drew her muffins carefully out of the oven and laid the baking rack on the counter. She was sensationally pretty and not in the stereotypical chubby and cheerful baker mould. In fact her appearance was totally at odds with the traditional cozy atmosphere of the cottage. She was like an exquisite little rat with spiky jet black hair cut almost in a crew cut, dark eyes that darted everywhere and dead white skin. Her thin lips parted to show sharp little teeth and her tiny frame made me feel enormous beside her. She favored modern silver jewelry that I couldn't help thinking was unsuitable for both her size and her line of work. Giant hoop earrings banged against her tiny pointed chin and rows of silver bangles flopped down her skinny wrists, clanging against the baking rack.

I wanted to ask her about her life in Frampton Abbas but I wasn't quite finished with Sylvia yet.

'So what else did you glean from Sylvia about her life?'

Justine regarded me. 'You know, it's odd but once we'd got on to the subject of her parents that was it. She backed away, clammed up, however you want to put it.'

'About them?'

'Well, yes, about them but then about everything, really. I mean, she stopped coming round here, put up a bit of distance between us for no reason that I could see. There was something about her parents, I sensed. Something she wasn't telling me. I asked her if she'd show me a photo of them – you know, like you do, I wasn't really interested but I wanted to show support – and she reacted as if I'd asked her to conjure them up out of thin air in the next ten minutes. She looked shocked and said she didn't have any photos of her parents.' Justine gave me a look that said *Pull the other one!* 'I mean, I ask you. Who doesn't have a photo of their parents? I began to think maybe her mother had got so fed up with her tyrant of a father that she'd stabbed him with the carving knife when he'd said the Yorkshire pudding was soggy.'

I laughed, mostly because Justine appeared to think what she'd said was hilarious and was cackling away herself.

'Anyway,' she said when she'd recovered, 'her and André, she didn't stand a chance really. It was clear to me he didn't want to know. Of course back then he hadn't been separated from his wife for very long and he was maybe a bit tentative about starting a new relationship.'

'His wife? So he's married?'

'So he told me. We had a drunken heart-to-heart one night in the kitchen after everyone had gone home. I'd left my reading glasses in The Pelican when I'd dropped off the desserts earlier that evening and didn't realize it till ten o'clock that night. I went back to get them and there was André clearing up after a slow night. Sylvia had gone, Wendy had gone and Gussie was on her way out. He offered me a drink, you know how it goes?'

Only too well but I had the sense that Justine's 'drink' with André might have gone a bit further than mine had.

'And?'

She caught me looking at her. 'I wish! There was none of that although I don't mind telling you, I wouldn't have said no. You look at him and you think, *red hair, pasty skin, freckles, yuck!* But there's something about him. You kind of know he's a terrific lover.'

I'd had absolutely no idea till Gussie had told me but I grinned and gave her a knowing look. *Yes, I recognize a good lover when I see one*. Although fat lot of good it was doing me right now.

'Anyway,' she went on, 'we had one of those bonding conversations where you bore each other to death about old lovers and then he slipped in the shockeroo that in fact he was married. Didn't say anything about the wife other than that they were separated and he was trying to move on. I have to tell you, I perked up when I heard that.'

'They're not divorced?'

'Not as far as I know.'

Oh dear! What had Gussie said? Justine *reckons* there's an ex-wife somewhere. *Ex*-wife. Not Justine *knows* there's *still* a wife in the picture. I had a feeling Gussie had conveniently forgotten about the possibility of André being married.

'But I could tell he was lonely,' said Justine. 'He's a romantic with a capital R. He's had an awful lot of women in his life but when he talked about them I got the feeling he'd fallen in love, just a little, with most of them. The nature of his work, stuck in a kitchen morning, noon and night, never taking any time off for holidays and that, it's not good for sustaining a relationship, is it? He doesn't have much time. When he meets someone, he's probably trained himself to fall for them hard and fast.' She looked a bit wistful and I imagined she was probably wondering why he hadn't fallen for her. 'But I could tell he wanted someone,' she pulled herself together with a start, 'so I told him about DirtyFarmers.com.'

I plunged my teeth into a muffin so she wouldn't see the jolt she'd given me.

'Is that Exmoormates.com? Did he join it?' I asked innocently.

'Oh, do you use it too? Bit of a laugh but you never know who you might meet. Yes, he made me sign him up for it there and then. Stupidest thing I ever did. I can't stand the thought of him looking for women on it. Can't *stand* it!'

Her vehemence was unnerving. After a second she relaxed and ventured a faint smile.

'He had a new laptop but it was rather sweet, he was so clueless with it. Someone had already shown him how to set up an Internet account and he'd got as far as choosing a password but that was about it. I had to show him how to send an email and we spent half an hour trying to think what his DirtyFarmers name should be. Finally I came up with Mr Wright – with a W, geddit? – and then we had fun coming up with his details.'

As I'd accompanied her along the High Street, at the back of my mind had been the intention to quiz her and see if she had any idea who might have put the peanut oil in the salad dressing. And now, for a brief moment, I toyed with the idea of asking her if she'd known who André had subsequently 'dated' on the Internet, if she'd known about Rosemary and

Melanie? Because what she'd just told me made it clear that she probably knew André's password and could access his email account.

She could have been the one who sent Rosemary and Melanie the false invitations to dinner, posing as Mr Wright. But why would she? Had she been an accomplice for someone else, someone who wanted Rosemary at The Pelican the night she died and Melanie at the quarry?

She was offering me another muffin and I took it, mostly to distract her from what was running through my head, but also because they were delicious, crumbling in my mouth in buttery warmth. Although it was safe to assume that she didn't normally suspect the people she invited in for coffee to sit there wondering if she was a murderer.

Unless she was.

'So do you still look for people on Exmoormates.com?' I said in an attempt to get my thoughts back to normal.

She shook her head. 'Haven't done anything like that for years. Besides, apart from André and a couple of others, they really were dirty farmers. I mean they cleaned up good enough, didn't smell of manure or anything, but their manners and their chit-chat was pretty basic. There were moments when I wondered if they'd have been just as happy with a candlelit chicken or a cow sitting across the table from them. Anyway, I'm getting it regular these days. There's a nice young doctor, Jimmy Jenkins, lives two doors up from the Post Office.'

'But I thought he was ma—' I stopped. Hadn't Gussie said he was in The Pelican the night Rosemary Waters died *with his wife Virginia*?

'Married? Yes, he is but she's a doctor too and she's on nights all the way over in Exeter.'

I was slightly shocked that she didn't make any sort of apology for her behavior. I mean I'm not a saint but on the one disastrous occasion I strayed in this direction, I know my conscience was pricked more than hers appeared to be.

'But you know, I'm open to looking for fresh blood,' she laughed. 'I admit I moved down here from London looking for a quiet life but I'd no idea it would turn out to be this quiet. Fancy going out on the prowl with me one night? Clubbing in Exeter maybe?'

'No!' I said it much too firmly. Maybe it was my vulnerable state of mind following Max's failure to acknowledge me but I had decided that I really didn't like Justine very much. I didn't trust her an inch. I tried to remember what I had said to her during the past half hour because I had a feeling whatever it was would be repeated to the next person sitting in her kitchen.

'I'm spoken for,' I lied.

'Really?' Could she sound more skeptical? 'I thought you lived with your cousin Gussie, all girls together. How's André going to fit into that, by the way?'

I stood up and was at the door before she could get anything further out of me. I thanked her, said goodbye and fled, and all the way back along the High Street I tried to suppress my unease that she knew about Gussie and André. For some reason that I couldn't quite explain, I knew no good would come of it.

André was perched on a stool at the island looking uncharacteristically thoughtful when I walked in. Of course I immediately remembered his frenzied heaving at six o'clock that morning and backed away from him to hang up my raincoat in the cloakroom. I wondered what was on his mind to give him such a faraway look. Maybe he was thinking about Gussie. I made a mental note to tell her. She was bound to be pleased.

But I couldn't have been more wrong.

'I don't know what's going on,' he said as I squeezed past him to get to the sink. 'I called the Mackay farm to firm up plans for that memorial service.'

'Oh,' I said, 'when's it going to be?'

'It isn't,' he said flatly. 'I asked for Neil but the woman who answered, I think it must have been his mother, she was in tears, I could tell, and as soon as I said who I was, she said they weren't going to have it, and then – and this is the weird bit – she more or less slammed the phone down on me. I felt like a telemarketer. No explanation, barely even a goodbye. I've been sitting here wondering if maybe she'd found out I'd had a bit of an online exchange with Melanie.'

'I've just been having a coffee with Justine,' I said. 'She told me how she set you up as Mr Wright in the first place.'

André gave me a wan smile. 'Oh Lord, so she did. I'd forgotten about that.'

'So she knows your password.'

'So?'

'So she could have gone into your computer and sent those emails to Rosemary and Melanie that you say you didn't send.'

'Why on earth would she do that?' he said in such a reasonable tone of voice that I was reminded that I too had asked myself the same question. 'Although,' he added, 'someone did. And I wouldn't put it past Justine to do a bit of snooping into what I've been up to on DirtyFarmers.com. She made it so clear she wanted to start something with me, it was pretty scary. I had to get heavy with her to get her to back off and that's why you don't see her in the kitchen very often.'

I wondered whether I should tell him that Justine hadn't given up on him yet but before I could say anything, he added, 'Didn't you say that Neil Mackay was reading my emails to Melanie on her computer? Looks like he knows how to get in where he shouldn't.'

'Melanie's emails were already up on the screen. He didn't have to do anything more than hit a key to bring them back from standby.' But even as I said this I knew I wasn't entirely sure of this. Neil Mackay was already reading the emails when I walked in. I hadn't thought to ask him how he'd accessed them.

Wendy came in at that moment.

'It's starting to rain,' she said in a voice filled with gloom, 'and Taylor's had the fright of his life so I'm going to have to leave early to be there when he gets home from school.'

I was surprised at the way she was telling André rather than asking him but when it came to anything to do with Taylor, I noticed, Wendy's sense of protection of her little brother seemed to give her extra courage.

'What happened to him?' I asked her.

'That bloke what came in here the other day, that Neil Mackay. He just turns up and bangs on our front door and barges in and says he wants to talk to Taylor. And I say, Why? And he says never mind, it's Taylor I want to talk to and I want him on his own. By this time I can feel Taylor standing right behind me and I can hear him whispering *Don't let him, I don't want to, Wendy, please don't let him near me.*' Wendy shrugged off her coat and advanced upon us, warming to her story. 'Well, I didn't need telling. I mean you don't let a grown man who's almost a stranger be alone with a seven year old, do you. Not with what you hear these days. So I told him to shove off out the door and not come back. I told him!'

She was so puffed up with a sense of having done the right thing, she was positively glowing with righteousness.

'Well done, Wendy,' I said, 'quite right! What could he have wanted to say to Taylor, do you suppose?'

I had a pretty good idea what he wanted to say to Taylor but I was aware that Taylor might not have told his sister all he had shared with me and I didn't want to betray the confidence of a fellow potato peeler.

'No idea but I do know one thing,' said Wendy, 'he was on his way out of town when he stopped by our house. Leaving the area, he was. I ran into old Jake the Rake on my way here and he told me there's all hell to pay up at the Mackay farm. That Neil Mackay's suddenly upped and left his wife.'

Chapter Thirteen

'I've made a dreadful mistake,' said Jake before he'd even got in the door.

It was eight o'clock in the morning, a full three days since I'd had my disastrous encounter with Max and I'd spent the entire time trying to summon up the courage to call Jake on some pretext, in order to find out if Max was still there.

'Bloody hell, what's that racket?' He stamped the mud off his boots on the doormat and raised his eyes to the ceiling at the unmistakable sound of Gussie's bedstead thumping against the wall. A lascivious grin spread across his face in recognition of what he was hearing.

'You should be getting some of that.' He pushed past me into the kitchen. 'Any tea in the pot?'

I must have looked so miserable that he relented and put his arm round me.

'Don't worry, lass. Your day will come. And it's about that nephew of mine that I've come to see you. I want to apologize. I should never have asked him down here. I could tell he upset you the other night. He was—' Jake batted his fingers together in search of the right word. 'He was *uncivil* and there was no excuse. I don't mind telling you, I laid into him the next morning at breakfast, told him what I thought of him.'

'Did he mention me?' I couldn't resist asking.

'Well, no, he didn't as a matter of fact,' Jake looked embarrassed, 'but then neither did I. I thought I'd better keep quiet on the subject of you. You see, I'd got him down here on false pretences. I called him up and said I had a surprise for him, wouldn't tell him what it was, said he should get himself down here for a visit with me when he could spare the time.' Jake's eyes were darting here and there as if he were looking for something. 'I thought the fact that I didn't make it sound urgent would make it clear that it wasn't about Sadie. But I was wrong. I could tell that as soon as he clapped eyes on you in The Pelican.'

I didn't know whether to feel mollified or not. Maybe Max hadn't been angry at seeing me as such – just bitterly disappointed that he'd been falsely summoned, that I didn't represent a cog in the wheel of Sadie's murder investigation. Whatever, it was a straw and I clutched at it.

Jake was still looking around him.

'What do you want?' I asked. 'Sit down. I'll make a fresh pot of tea.'

'Matches,' he said, spying a box by the Aga and grabbing it. 'I'm desperate for a smoke. You don't mind, do you? Don't want me to step outside or something daft?'

'Actually, I do,' I said, 'for one thing it's too early in the morning for me to deal with smoke and for another it's not my house. It's Gussie's and I don't think she'd like it.'

'Oh, come on, she wouldn't mind and anyway she's got other things on her mind at the moment.' He leered up at the ceiling. 'Who is it, by the way? Who's the noisy bugger she's got up there?'

'André,' I said, without thinking and then mentally slapped myself. *That was a bit indiscreet.*

Jake grinned. 'Good old André!' He stuck a cigarette in his mouth but didn't light it. Instead he slipped the box of matches into his pocket. 'Don't mind if I keep these, do you? I lost my lighter about a week ago and I can't seem to find it anywhere. I've been back to all the places I've been – I mean *everywhere* – but I can't find it. And I must. Sentimental value.'

I smiled. His eyes were quite dewy. I wondered who had given it to him.

'I thought you told me you'd given up.'

He grimaced. 'Busted! But I more or less have. I only have one when I'm really stressed out. Like now. Because of Max and the way he's been behaving since he came down here.'

I gave him a quizzical look.

'The day after he arrived, before he even said good morning, he made me draw him a map of where to find the spot where Sadie's body was found. He's been out there ever since, traipsing over the moors, up hill and down dale and across the fields looking for God knows what. It's been nearly six bloody years. Why can't he just let it be?'

I shook my head. Jake was deluding himself. You couldn't lose someone close to you, and on top of that know that they had been murdered, and *let it be*.

'So I heard about Neil Mackay,' I said. I didn't want to dwell on Max and Sadie for too long.

Jake sighed. 'I went over there to look for him. I've got to be away for a day and a night and I wanted to see if he would feed my animals but instead I found Marjorie wringing her hands and wailing and Katharine sitting there saying good riddance!'

'They know about Neil and Melanie?'

'They do now. I told 'em.'

'You *didn't*!'

'Why ever not? Apparently Neil's been behaving oddly ever since Melanie was killed and by that I mean he was over-reacting. According to Marjorie he'd always gone to great lengths to make it clear he didn't have much time for Melanie. Well, now she knows why he acted like that.'

'Was it necessary to tell Marjorie?' I said. Jake seemed to relish forcing the issue in other people's relationship problems

– like summoning Max without telling him about me or me that he was doing so.

'Yeah, I suppose she did get a bit upset when she heard?'

'And you're *surprised*?' Suddenly I was fed up with Jake. 'So you're going away? When? Soon?' I was rude in my bluntness but I didn't care.

'I'm on my way right now. I just popped by to say I was sorry about Max.'

'But why do you have to go away while he's with you? Where are you going?'

His sharp reply set my antennae quivering. 'That's my business. I'll be back tomorrow anyway. All being well,' he added after a beat.

'So did you find someone to take care of your animals?'

'Why, are you offering? Joke!' he added when he saw my horrified expression. 'Max would be the logical person but the state he's in at the moment, they'd starve. No, Marjorie'll send someone over.'

'Well, you owe her an apology as well as me. Sounds like you've managed to make her life even worse than it already was. And you'd better bring her back a nice big box of chocolates from wherever it is you're going,' I said, 'to say thank you. You owe her big time.'

Jake looked quite affronted at my tone but he managed to get his revenge as he downed the last of his tea and stood up.

'I see you haven't bothered taking my advice about tarting yourself up. And you're wondering why Max ignored you the other night and hasn't been in touch since.'

He's got a really mean streak, I thought, not bothering to see him out the door. *But*, I was forced to admit a few seconds later as I pondered his words, *the truth always hurts*.

I found that I couldn't stop thinking about poor Marjorie Mackay and I decided I would drive over and pay her a quick visit in the couple of hours I had free before work. I was still stung by Jake's parting words and as I went upstairs to the bathroom to take the first steps towards repairing my appearance, I acknowledged the real reason I was going to see Marjorie.

The Mackay smallholding was not a million miles removed from Dorcas Farm.

I opened the bathroom door and gasped. André was sitting on the lavatory stark naked. I backed out hurriedly slamming the door behind me and found I was literally shaking. Whether it was from rage or from a kind of old-maidish embarrassment because I hadn't seen a naked man for so long, I didn't know.

'There's a key in the lock,' I shouted from the safety of the landing, 'do me a favor and turn it!' I deliberately didn't add *next time* because I didn't want there to be a next time. Justine had known what she was doing when she asked how André was going to fit into Gussie's and my ménage. I wasn't happy about him being here and it was more than just irritation at being woken up by his resonant sex with Gussie.

Gussie stumbled out of her bedroom with the kind of sheepish grin on her face that says *I've just had the most amazing sex* but, before she could open her mouth, I stomped off to my room fighting back what seemed to be ever-present tears of frustration.

When you've spent months not bothering to watch your weight, get your hair cut or buy new clothes and making do with scooping out the dregs of crusty make-up, it's practically impossible to give yourself an instant makeover, as I quickly discovered. It was only some consolation that my skin was glowing from its uncharacteristic exposure to country air to the extent that I decided that it looked better without any attempt to resort to the dried-up contents of my make-up bag. The less seen of my lank and shapeless hair the better and I scraped it into a ponytail out of sight in the nape of my neck. I spent ten minutes deliberating whether or not I could stand the cold long enough to wear a soft form-fitting sweater and tight jeans. In the end I put on the sweater and negated its curvy effect by piling layers on top of it – a shabby cardigan and a fleece that made me look like the Michelin man. It wasn't as if I was actually going to *see* Max and it was pointless to freeze to death just because I was venturing into his vicinity.

On the way to Marjorie's, I made an unexpected detour. I passed a turning to a dusty trail leading to a field and up a hill and a sign denoting it as a long-distance footpath. But it was the word *Quarry* and an arrow scrawled below that made me halt and reverse to take another look.

It wasn't as if I was going to be looking at Melanie's body, I told myself, as I inched the car gingerly up the trail, which became increasingly muddy as it went on. When it finally petered out into a makeshift car park, I got out and, ignoring the footpath that took off in the opposite direction, I climbed over a gate and continued on foot, as instructed by another sign, across the field to the quarry. The grass track was flattened, making it clear that some people ignored the sign and drove their car across the field.

I was aware that I was climbing all the time, moving toward a head as if I were walking the cliffs and would soon be able to look down and see the sea. And so when I came to the edge and was confronted with the sheer granite drop to the harsh gray stone several hundred feet below, even though I'd known what to expect, it was a terrifying shock.

It was a cold day but a clear one and I could look across the valley to the moors rolling to the horizon. And if I looked to my left, I could follow the crest of the hill all the way to where the road rose up and over the moors to dip down into Jake Austin's property. It was easy to see the daily walk he had said that Melanie made from his farm for her assignation at the quarry.

I shivered and not just because I was cold. Even on a foggy day it was unlikely that anybody would walk over the edge of the quarry by accident, just as people took care not to go too close to the edge of cliffs. And if Melanie had walked here every day then she would know not to walk on regardless, especially on a foggy day. But if she had stopped and stood where I was standing now, and if she had been taken unawares and had staggered and lost her balance, if she had then been given even a gentle push, then it was highly possible that she could have gone over the edge.

I stared at the relentless gravel in the disused pit below me and imagined I saw where it had been disturbed and parted in the shape of a smashed and flattened body. Surely Melanie must have shattered into a thousand pieces on impact. There were probably bits of her still down there spread out like some ghastly mosaic.

I was jolted by the sound of a car approaching behind me. Was this how Melanie's killer had arrived or would they have crept up on her with stealth?

'Good heavens! What are you doing up here?'

Monica Massey's bulky frame lumbered towards me preceded by Trinket bounding ahead of her. I relaxed and then tensed again. *This was probably what had happened to Melanie. She'd seen someone she knew coming towards her up here, someone she trusted or someone totally non-threatening. Like me, she had relaxed, let down her guard before she was taken by surprise and shoved over the edge to hurtle to her death.*

I stepped back hurriedly as Monica advanced upon me.

'What's the matter?' she said. 'You look like you've seen a ghost. Do me a favor, step aside so Trinket can charge past you and shoot over the edge. I bring her up here every day in the hope that she'll commit doggy suicide and we'll be rid of her.'

'You don't mean that,' I said nervously, 'you like Trinket really, don't you?'

'No,' she said firmly, 'I don't like Trinket and no amount of cajoling will make me say otherwise. But it's all right,' she patted my arm gently, 'I'd never do anything to hurt her because that would upset Ann. It's all about Ann, you do realize that, don't you? The reason I wish we didn't have

Trinket is because I resent anyone besides me, be they dog or human, who is the object of Ann's affection.'

I laughed but Monica's face remained serious.

'You think I'm joking but I'm not. I don't mind telling you I had a shock when you turned up the other day. I thought Genevieve had sent you. You would tell me, wouldn't you? Genevieve's not planning to come down here and lure Ann back to her, is she?'

I was taken aback by the naked pain of her love.

'Genevieve wouldn't make a trip to the country if you paid her the national debt,' I said. 'I think she imagines even the suburbs are inhabited by savages.'

'But she told you to come and see us,' said Monica, still not entirely convinced.

'Actually, she didn't,' I confessed, 'that was my idea. She just mentioned your names when I said I was coming to Frampton Abbas. She has no idea we've even met.'

'Don't tell her,' said Monica quickly, then added, 'you didn't know about her and Ann?'

I shook my head.

'In fact, you didn't even know she was one of us, did you?' Monica was looking at me, more relaxed now and slightly amused. 'She didn't tell you?'

'Why would she?' I said, 'it has no bearing on our agent/author relationship.'

'Quite,' said Monica. 'Trinket! Come *here!* Oh my God, what if she really did go over the edge?'

'You come here every day? Rain or shine?'

She nodded.

'And did you see Melanie? The woman who was killed?'

'Haven't a clue,' said Monica cheerfully. 'I mean, I didn't know her from Adam so even if I did see her I wouldn't have known it was her. Depends what time she came up here. I always walk Trinket in the morning. But the truth is I don't see too many people. It's not everyone's first choice for a nice walk, not when they've got the moors so close.'

'Although the view's almost as good,' I pointed out.

'Isn't it?' She seemed pleased that I had something good to say about the quarry. 'It's mostly Frampton Abbas locals you get up here, not the tourists, I'm happy to say. I ran into old Jake Austin the other day. Have you come across him? He was searching for something he'd lost.'

'A lighter, I think,' I said.

'Oh, so you know him?'

'We've met,' I said and left it at that. 'I'd better get on,' I said. I had to be at work in an hour and a half.

'Come and have dinner with us one night,' Monica shouted after me as I made my way back to the car.

What was old Jake doing up at the quarry? I wondered as I drove over the moors to Marjorie Mackay's. *OK, when Monica saw him he was looking for his lighter but what was he doing up there when he dropped it in the first place?* I remembered the wine glasses I'd seen on his kitchen table when I'd gone to Dorcas Farm. Two of them, one smeared with lipstick. And hadn't he told me that Melanie went right past his door on her walk to the quarry, that she'd often come in for a cup of tea? Well, a cup of tea could lead to a glass of wine. He'd as good as told me that as far as Melanie was concerned, he wouldn't say no. Had Jake lost his lighter at the quarry the day she was killed? Had he been jealous of her affair with Neil Mackay? Had he followed her and waited until he'd seen Neil Mackay leave? Had he remonstrated with her, and grabbed hold of her and—?

It wasn't exactly helpful that these thoughts were running through my head as I pulled into the Mackay farmyard. I was here to console Marjorie, not to stir up intrigue.

But as it turned out Marjorie was way ahead of me when it came to stirring. I rapped on the door and entered her kitchen when she shouted *It's open,* and found her leaning against the sink staring at the screen of a mobile phone.

'Come and take a look at this,' she said without even bothering to say hello. Her eyes were bright with tears.

Tears of rage, I discovered.

I don't think of myself as a prude but I'm not comfortable as a voyeur and I was shocked by what I saw. It was a video-phone, a camera, and Marjorie was flicking through the pictures on the screen. The first image I saw was a pair of breasts squashed together by someone's hands to form a massive cleavage. A photo of a girl posing naked on all fours on a bed followed, then she was stretched out on her side with her hair spread out on the bedspread. I recognized it as the patchwork quilt in Melanie's room. Marjorie's thumb was working overtime, flicking through the pictures so fast Melanie appeared to be in motion. She had moved out of her room to run along the passage, opening the doors of the built-in closets to peep out provocatively from behind them.

But it was when she could be seen sitting on the bed in the room with the misty blue seascapes, her legs splayed, her fingers reaching down, that I gave an audible gulp. This had to be Marjorie's bedroom.

It wasn't over. The shot of male genitalia came without any warning that Melanie was now in control of the camera. When Neil Mackay began to walk around his mother's bedroom naked, strutting and clowning for the camera, faking mastur-bation and leering into the lens, I reached out and gently removed the phone from Marjorie's grasp.

'I was probably in Frampton Abbas doing the shopping or perhaps it was when I took the car to the garage in Tiverton for the day.' She was torturing herself, imagining them upstairs. 'That they should be so brazen! That's what I can't come to terms with. I don't go upstairs unless I have to. My knees, you know. I wish I hadn't gone up to clear out her room, then I would never have found this thing under her bed. I was trying to look for phone numbers in her menu and this is what I found. I couldn't—' She turned to me, appealing to me to understand. 'I couldn't stop looking.'

I defy even the most adept diplomat to come up with the right thing to say to someone in Marjorie's position. She was faced with photographic proof of what her son had done. It might not have been so terrible had it just been evidence of his having had sex with Melanie but there was no way she would be able to condone the violation of the privacy of her bedroom. I imagined her trying to get to sleep in the bed on which Melanie had posed.

And then to my horror I had an involuntary flash of Gussie and André taking the opportunity to romp in my room the minute they heard the door slam behind me.

'It's living on these moors,' said Marjorie, slumping on to a chair. 'It does something to a person, makes them behave in a weird fashion.'

'Nonsense,' I said, not reprovingly, trying to humor her, '*you* don't behave in a weird fashion, do you? Let me make you a cup of tea.'

'But I've resisted the moors ever since I came here,' she said firmly. 'I've never stopped thinking of myself as a city girl and I'm going back there as soon as I've packed up the house. Nothing to keep me here now Neil's gone.'

'You think he's gone for good?' I was shocked.

'Put it like this,' she said and I was chilled by the steel in her voice, 'he's not coming back to this house. I've got an estate agent coming this afternoon. Someone ought to buy Neil's farm along with mine. Build a few cottages on the farmland and you'd have a very nice holiday rental property, perfect for the tourists to go hiking over the moors in the summer. I used to tell my husband that's what we should do. Make us a lot more money than farming – but he never listened.' She sighed.

'Both farms?'

'Katharine might see herself as a pioneer woman but I give her one winter trying to run that farm on her own. She'll sell up next year if she doesn't see sense and do it at the same time as I do.'

I could tell Marjorie didn't think much of her daughter-in-law.

'But the worst thing is,' she went on, 'I can't face Melanie's parents. It was bad enough that she died on my watch, so to speak, but if they ever find out about her and Neil.'

'Why would they?' I said. 'Are they still here?' I looked around nervously.

'They were just here long enough to pick up what was left of her body and take it back to London. I was preparing to go up for the funeral when Jake told me about Melanie and Neil. I didn't believe him. I didn't *want* to believe him but then I found that thing.' She pointed to the phone lying on the table.

'Where will you go?'

'Back to Birmingham, where I came from originally. I've still got family there. But what am I going to tell them about Neil?' she said after a moment. 'The shame of it. The bloody shame of it! The only blessing is his father's not alive to see what's become of his son. Or to know that I'm selling the farm he loved so much,' she added softly.

'Do you think Melanie's death was an accident?' I slipped in, equally softly.

Her head jerked up and I saw that I had totally taken her by surprise.

'What else could it have been?'

'She could have been killed.' I didn't like saying it so bluntly but I was beginning to realize that Marjorie Mackay was a whole lot tougher than I had first thought and if I didn't ask now, I probably wouldn't have another opportunity.

'She *was* killed,' said Marjorie, puzzled.

'I mean, someone could have killed her.'

'Like someone killed Sadie,' was Marjorie's surprise reply.

I didn't know what to say. For a start it reminded me of Max less than half a mile away. And I realized that Marjorie Mackay must have gone through all this before at one remove when Sadie died.

'What is it about these moors?' she said again. 'Is it the winds that turns women's heads up here if they're not looking out for themselves? Is it the bleakness or what?'

222

'What do you mean?' I didn't understand what she was talking about.

'Well, Sadie had someone, I'm sure of it.'

'Had someone?'

'Jake said Max was here on a visit,' she said, switching tracks abruptly. 'You must be pleased. You're on your way to see him, I expect. I mean, I probably shouldn't mention it, seeing as he's your boyfriend, but I got to know Sadie a bit when she was here that time. Those months before she was killed, she practically lived down here at old Jake's and she used to take that stupid little dog of hers for walks. If the wind was blowing in the right direction, I'd hear it yapping a mile away. I don't know how Jake stood it.'

'She used to come and visit you?'

'She did.' Marjorie nodded. 'She was lonely. And before you ask, she didn't talk to me about her marriage. She never mentioned Max. Jake dropped the odd hint that all was not well between her and his nephew but she wasn't the sort to go on about her private life. Besides, as I said, I think she had someone.'

'Someone?' I still didn't quite get it.

'Like Melanie had Neil. She found someone down here.'

'And you think whoever it was killed her? Did you tell the police?'

'They never asked,' said Marjorie flatly.

I stared into space, trying to take in what she had just said, trying to assess the ramifications of her having kept quiet all these years about the possibility of Sadie having had an Exmoor lover.

And then my eyes focused on the digital clock on the console of a DVD player. Eleven fifty-eight gleamed in luminous green and I leapt into action. I was due at work in five minutes.

'I'll be back soon,' I told Marjorie, secretly thinking it highly unlikely.

'It was nice to have met you,' she said, sounding genuine and surprising me yet again.

As I came to the end of the lane leading to the Mackay farm, I paused at the edge of the moors road. I could turn left and within minutes I would be at Dorcas Farm.

I turned right, heading back to Frampton Abbas and congratulating myself on resisting the temptation to stray in Max's direction. I was going to be late for work in any case.

I drove fast, relieved that there were no other cars on the road. But then, as I dropped down into the valley and was forced to slow down as I approached the narrow bridge over the River Exe, a Land Rover came hurtling out of nowhere towards me to cross the bridge before I could.

I slowed to a halt to let the Land Rover squeeze past me and through the windscreen my eyes came face to face with Max's as he leaned forward, his lanky frame hunched over the steering wheel.

I shot over the bridge away from him, acting on instinct. I didn't want him to see me, to assume that I had been looking for him. I sped along the river, picking up speed but when I glanced in the rearview mirror, I nearly careered off the road and into the water.

He was turning the Land Rover around and now he was crossing the bridge. He was coming after me. Within seconds he was right behind me, bearing down upon me, hounding me.

I put my foot down on the accelerator and shot away from him. But he came right up on my tail and this time instead of staying behind me, he pulled out and drove alongside me, gesticulating with his arm, waving at me to stop, to pull over.

I felt like a criminal. But was that because I knew Max represented the police? Would I have automatically felt so guilty and assumed that I had done something wrong if a total stranger had flagged me down?

He cut in front of me and I had no option but to stop on the verge. He climbed out of the Land Rover and advanced on my car, his face as furious as ever. He opened my door and looked as if he was going to reach in and pull me out.

Shaking and almost sobbing, I got out of my own accord and then, before I could say a word in my defense, he took me roughly by the shoulders and pressed me against the side of the car.

Then he leaned in and kissed me hard on the mouth, moving his lips against mine so forcefully that I parted them and gave myself up to him until gradually I felt his anger begin to subside.

Chapter Fourteen

The rain that had been threatening all morning began to pelt down on us. Max's face was pressed against my cheek and his eyes were closed so that when I opened mine his long eyelashes, soaked and glistening, appeared in giant close-up.

He pulled away from me as abruptly as he had taken hold of me.

'OK, you lead the way back to Jake's farm. I've done nothing but get lost on these moors ever since I arrived here.'

These were the first words he'd spoken directly to me since he'd arrived in Devon. Normally I don't do meek, but I obeyed Max instantaneously and tottered to my car, my heart still reacting violently in my chest to his unexpected show of passion. The road was too narrow for us to turn around so we had to drive for about two miles until we came to The Longhouse where there was room to pull in. Max was so close behind me that every time I glanced in my rearview mirror, I could feel his intense gaze upon me.

It scared me. When I drew into the parking lot of The Longhouse, I had the ridiculous instinct to leap out of the car and call for help. *This man is following me, give me shelter. Please, call the police.* This man, for whom I had been longing for months. This man who *was* the police. This man whom nothing would have stopped me accompanying to Jake's.

When we got to Dorcas Farm, I had the presence of mind to stop at the cattle grid. The rain was coming down in such torrents that the mud was literally running down the hill from the farmhouse. The Land Rover had four-wheel drive so I flagged Max down and mouthed *Let me in,* pointing to the passenger door. Even then, though he pulled up as close as he could to the front door, when I got out I sank ankle deep into a scratchy mix of mud and stone chippings. Dorcas Farm was in a hollow and the rain was driving everything down off the moors to settle into a pool around it.

I ran into Jake's house, drenched and shivering and wondering what was the point of trying to maintain a glossy appearance in such foul weather. I made a mental note to challenge Jake the next time I saw him. *How could a woman ever look good in the country?* I took off my mud-caked shoes and placed them in the hall and padded into the kitchen, flinching at the cold touch of the flagstones, icy even through my woolen socks.

Somehow the kitchen was even more gloomy than on my first visit. It had been tidied – presumably Jake had made an effort in honor of his nephew's visit – but the absence of clutter deprived the atmosphere of what little warmth it had ever had. Loneliness pervaded the air and the only sign of life was several meals' worth of dishes dumped in the sink and an overflowing trash can with a pile of empty packets of TV dinners propping up the lid.

A slight sound made me start and then I looked under the table and saw a black and white sheepdog in a basket on the floor. Willow's arthritis must have worsened for her to have been brought into the house. Her ears pricked slightly and she lifted her long snout, her liquid eyes full of reproach. I reached down to pat her and she whimpered a little. Poor Willow. Old and in pain and destined to end her days in Jake's forlorn environment.

Suddenly I wanted out. This wasn't the place for my reunion with Max. Already I could feel my shoulders hunching in protest at the mood of depression that was creeping over me.

I rushed to the door to escape and ran headlong into Max who confirmed my fears that it was all wrong. He had me in a confined space. If the passion he had unleashed upon me so recently was still there, surely he would waste no time in gathering me once again in his arms.

But he merely stood his ground until I was forced to turn around and re-enter the kitchen. He followed, not bothering to discard his wellington boots at the door as I had done and he trailed mud everywhere. I waited for him to take my coat and offer me a cup of something warming but he didn't. He stomped around for a bit and then stood awkwardly in total silence.

What can he be thinking? Is he wondering how to get me upstairs? Should I help him out, go over and put my arms around his neck? Or should I put the kettle on?

'I've been thinking about you,' he said suddenly and it gave me almost as much of shock as when he had grabbed hold of me and kissed me.

I felt an inane sentence forming – *Oh have you? that's nice* – and fought to conquer my nerves.

'Even before Jake called and suggested I come down. I had no idea you were here. Jake never said.'

'Oh, I know,' I said and allowed the floodgates to open with a stream of chatter. 'I met Jake at a funeral and for a second I thought it was you – you look so alike – but then I remembered you had said you had an uncle who lived here. I told him I knew you and I had a feeling he might try to get us together. He kept saying I had to do something about my appearance for you but you didn't seem to be put off back there by the—'

'Stop! Why are you twittering away like this?'

His tone was gruff but I breathed an inward sigh of relief because I knew that with this typical Max reprimand the ice had been broken. It might seem odd to talk about ice after someone had kissed you with such fervor but his awkward silences could cause the temperature to plummet in seconds.

'Shall I make a cup of tea to warm us up? Where does Jake keep it?'

He looked around helplessly then opened several cupboards at once, rifling through the contents and knocking several packets on to the counter. I was surprised to see that Jake had quite a collection – Earl Grey, Lady Grey, English Breakfast, Irish Breakfast, Tetley's builder's, Darjeeling, Assam Leaf and even some Green Tea.

Max stared at them, seemingly bewildered. 'These aren't teabags,' he said. 'Why can't he have teabags?' And I watched in horror as he emptied the contents of an entire packet into the teapot and walked over to the Aga to place the kettle on the hob. His domestic incompetence was one of the things that had first drawn me to him – apart from the magnetic sexual attraction. I had been touched by his grocery shopping for one and his futile attempts at managing his laundry. Now the evidence that he barely knew how to make a pot of tea brought his lonely widower status sharply into focus once again.

I tipped most of the contents of the teapot into the garbage, hoping he wouldn't be too offended, and out of the corner of my eye I saw him take a bottle of brandy out of a cupboard in the bottom half of the dresser. He brandished it at me. 'This'll warm you a whole lot more than a cup of tea. Want some?'

I nodded and took the kettle off the hob. 'So what have you been thinking about me,' I said playfully, watching him seek out a snifter into which he poured an extremely generous measure. He handed it to me and I downed a large gulp, feeling the nausea rising up the minute it hit my empty stomach.

'Richie Cross – you remember him? My sergeant as was, he's Detective Inspector Cross now. He mentioned you were back in England.'

I seethed with tacit annoyance. *Of course* I remembered Richie Cross. Max knew perfectly well that he was married to my best friend Cath. I had sat across from Max at Richie and Cath's dining table. Why did Max always have to be so formal, to put so much distance between us, to act as if we barely knew each other? It was almost as if he were ashamed of having kissed me.

'Back from America,' he added needlessly.

'I came back months ago.'

'You didn't call.' He sounded quite petulant.

'Well, you knew from Richie I was back in London and you didn't call either,' I pointed out as gently as I could.

He looked quite surprised. 'I suppose you're right,' he said after a moment, 'I guess I just didn't – I mean, I – you know—' now he turned to me looking distinctly put out. 'I'm quite busy. It's not like I sit around all day.'

Was he implying I did?

'People get themselves murdered a lot more often than you probably realize and it's not like they give me any notice.' His growing agitation was apparent and it was clear we were not going to sit down for a cozy chat at the kitchen table. He had got me here but now he didn't know what to do with me. This was how he'd always been with me and I don't know why I had imagined he would be any different now. His fierce looks and the fact that he was always so wired signaled to me the presence of a highly passionate nature lurking within him but on the surface he was often gauche. He never seemed to be able to convey to me what he was really thinking. At times I was touched by his awkwardness, at others it unnerved me.

He moved to the sink and began running the hot tap, filling the washing-up bowl with far too much detergent, plunging the dishes into it and whipping them out and stacking them un-rinsed in the wooden rack.

'No one calls up and says "Hello, how are you? I'd like to make an appointment to slaughter someone next Tuesday at three in the morning, would you be available to be woken up and dragged to the crime scene? I was thinking Clapham Common but I could make it somewhere a little closer to your neck of the woods if that's more convenient?"'

I hadn't forgotten his sarcasm, it was part and parcel of him, but it was always a bit of a shock when he chose to bite. I could feel my face going red and I moved to his side and handed him his brandy. Then I removed the plates and mugs from the rack, ran them under the hot tap and re-stacked them.

'I hear you got a promotion. Congratulations,' I said, hoping to steer him in a more amiable direction.

Fat chance!

'It's been a bloody nightmare ever since I got that promotion,' he said. 'I'm too far removed from the action. My desk work has doubled. Just as well Sadie's not around to complain about it. It was bad enough when I was out all hours after a villain – and then I'd need a bit of time to put it all behind me before I went home,' he held up his glass by way of explanation and mimed throwing a drink down his throat, 'so that by the time I finally walked through the door, dog tired and ready to hit the sack for even an hour or so, she was on my back before I'd even taken my coat off.'

I didn't say anything. I was struck dumb by the fact that he was talking, unprompted, about Sadie. Was that what was making him so nervous? Sadie's ghost was there hovering between us? I wanted him to focus on me, not her, but at the same time I was riveted by the possibility of gleaning information about her.

'The thing about Sadie is that she was gregarious. And I'm not. She said I used my work as an excuse not to go out and about with her. No matter how much I tried to deny it, she always said my job meant more to me than she did. She went on and on and on about it. I sometimes wonder,' he gave me a bleak grin, 'if she didn't get herself murdered on purpose – because she knew that would get my attention.'

I must have looked shocked because he smiled a little. 'You always did take everything I said so literally, didn't you?'

'So when Jake called you,' I said, 'did you come down to see him or to try and uncover something about her death? Hasn't too much time passed for you to find out anything new?'

'Not really,' he said, 'not as far as I'm concerned. They put a total idiot in charge of the case, wouldn't let me near it. I'm always trying to figure it out in my head. I came down because I thought Jake had something to show me and I was ready to punch his lights out when I realized it was you.'

'Thanks a lot.' I smiled to show I understood. 'But you're still here.'

'I've got about ten years' vacation time owed to me and those moors are good for walking and sorting things out in your head. Don't you find that?'

I had expected him to tell me he was still here because of me and the surprise direct question threw me.

'I don't actually,' I said, 'I mean, I haven't tried. The country's a bit of a disappointment to me, tell you the truth. It's not what I expected, not as quiet and peaceful as I thought it would be and there's too much—'

'Mud?' he said and grinned and I wanted to fling myself into his arms. His lips were thin and cruel and when he gave them an infinitesimal tweak to form a smile, it was almost more than I could bear. 'So anyway, I've been walking the moors, trying to trace her path from here to where her body was found—'

'Where was it found?' Now I was curious in spite of myself to hear the details. 'Who found it?'

'It's weird to think of her in this house,' he said, ignoring my question, and there was a catch in his voice. I looked at him sharply and he turned away from me. But I'd seen that his eyes were watering and I was astounded. Was Max, the sardonic hardened detective, really on the brink of tears? 'Jake said she cooked for him while she was here – in this kitchen.' He waved his arm around, seemingly in control of himself once again. 'She always liked old Jake, God knows why. He's a pretty hopeless old bugger but they hit it off from the start when he came to our wedding. He always came out with that ridiculous garbage that she liked so much – *you've had your hair cut, it suits you, there's not many women that can wear red like you do, how much did you have to pay for those sensational legs?* She lapped it up every time she saw him.'

'She came down here for a holiday?'

'So she said,' Max's tone was suddenly curt. 'A four-month holiday. All right for some.'

'But what did she do down here all that time?'

'How the bloody hell should I know? I was a little preoc-cupied with a man who went off on a cruise with his mistress and left his wife to starve to death locked in the basement. Her body had been decomposing for four months by the time we found her. And a sixteen-year-old boy who found his stepfa-ther's gun in a drawer in a Willesden flat and shot him with it just because the stepfather wouldn't give him any of the crack he was dealing. No, there's more.' He held up his hand when I opened my mouth to say something. 'Although it was never proved, someone trained his Rottweiler to attack his neighbor and kill her because she complained about the wretched dog barking all night. I remember telling Sadie on the phone that I was quite depressed when they put the Rottweiler down, couldn't make them understand they'd got the wrong guy, that the dog was only an accomplice. I thought it'd make her happy to hear that I was on the dog's side. She was always accusing me of cruelty towards dogs, just because I couldn't take Pixie seriously.'

'Pixie?'

'Her poodle. Her *miniature* poodle. A bit of gray fluff on legs, never stopped yapping. The baby she said I wouldn't let her have.'

I was uncomfortable. The brandy was enabling him to work himself up into an anguished state and on top of every-thing else I recalled what Gussie had told me about Pixie being butchered and I had a sudden flash of bloody poodle segments scattered around a field. I looked at Max, wondering if I could handle much more of this.

But it seemed I had no choice. He carried on without waiting for me to speak.

'I never said I didn't want a child. But she never became pregnant and she got it into her head it was my fault. And who's to say she wasn't right given what happened.' He sounded so bitter I was shocked.

'But how could the fact that she was murdered make it your fault she couldn't get pregnant?'

'BECAUSE SHE WAS PREGNANT WHEN SHE DIED!' He saw my face. 'Doesn't look like old Jake told you that?'

'I'm sorry,' I said. It was inadequate but I was intent on treading carefully while he was in such an explosive state.

'If she said it was my fault she didn't get pregnant and then she comes down here – *away from me* – and suddenly, guess what, she's expecting a baby, what does that tell you? Do I have to spell it out? I was devastated.' The word *devastated* came out like a groan.

I thought about it for a split second and decided to tell him but before I did so, I sat down. I felt unsteady on my legs, either from the brandy or shock at the turn the conversation was taking, I wasn't sure.

'When you met me on the road back there,' my voice was a little squeaky and tremulous and I cleared my throat in an attempt to gain control, 'I wasn't coming from here. I hadn't been looking for you. I'd been at the Mackay farm. I went to see Marjorie Mackay, she's a friend of Jake's.'

He shrugged his shoulders. *So?*

'She was telling me about how Sadie used to come and visit her, how she took Pixie for walks and used to drop in for tea or whatever.'

'And she told you Sadie had a lover down here?'

'Oh,' I said, thoroughly deflated. He knew. I felt like an idiot. 'She said she *suspected* Sadie had someone. How did you know?'

Now he looked at me with undisguised contempt. 'What have I just told you? Sadie was pregnant and she hadn't been near me in months.'

'I thought Jake said she went back to London soon after she arrived and then came down here again?'

'How much time have you spent sitting here nattering about me with my uncle? And if it's not with old Jake then you're digging up my private business with some woman on another farm? So did she tell you who the lover was?'

'I didn't go to see her about you. Or Sadie. I went to see if she was OK. Her goddaughter's just died and her son was having an affair with her and now he's left his wife and gone to London.'

'Spare me the soap opera,' said Max. He had propped his ungainly frame against one of the wooden posts either side of the Aga but he was too tall to fit into the alcove and had to stoop uncomfortably so that he didn't bang his head on the beam above. He rested his brandy glass on the top of the Aga and I wanted to shout at him that the heat would probably cause it to shatter. Willow clambered out of her basket and stretched her stiff hind legs. She pressed her nose into Max's thigh and he reached down with one of his long arms to stroke the top of her head. Rather tenderly, I noticed. The most unlikely people had an affinity with animals.

'It's *not* a soap opera,' I exclaimed, aware that I was becoming as agitated as he was. 'Melanie died and it was totally and utterly real.'

'But she was having a number with this Mackay woman's son? Sounds like a soap opera to me. Or are you leading up to telling me that he was the one who was screwing my wife as well. The local Lothario?'

The thought floored me for a second. It had never entered my head. Maybe he had something there. Who knew what Neil Mackay was capable of?

'Did you—' I wasn't sure how to phrase the question. 'Did you try to find out who Sadie's—'

'Who got Sadie pregnant? Of course I bloody did. That was where I really came to blows with the man leading the investigation down here. I wanted him to get DNA samples from every man who could get it up between here and Exeter but he didn't even test one.' Max snatched his glass up in a violent action and a drop of brandy flew out and sizzled on the top of the Aga. 'Can you believe it?' he yelled. 'Can you bloody believe it? Sadie'd had a basin full of whisky poured down her and enough barbiturates to knock her out cold and then she was strangled. And she was pregnant. So maybe the guy who got her pregnant wasn't the one who killed her. But it was just as likely that he was. Or he'd at least have been able to assist the investigating team with their half-baked inquiries. I think I'd better go and have a word or two with this Mackay woman about her son.'

'No,' I cried, 'she isn't ready for that yet. She's had too much to face what with Melanie's death and the fact that they were carrying on right under her nose. She found pictures of them on Melanie's phone and—'

Max rolled his eyes in exasperation. 'Why do you keep going on about this Melanie woman? Was she a friend of yours?'

'I never met her.'

'So she died. I'm sorry. But my *wife* was *murdered!*'

And then I lost it.

'So was Melanie!' I yelled back at him. 'And Rosemary Waters. Everyone's saying their deaths were accidental. No one's even considered they might have been murdered but I know they were. I just don't know what to do.'

There was an awful silence while he pondered what I had just said. His gaze was focused on me now and his eyes had acquired a familiar gleam.

'So OK,' he said after a moment and his tone was quite gentle, 'calm down, you think they were murdered, whoever they were. What did the police do when you told them? Although if you landed on that useless jerk who was in charge of Sadie's case, I'm not surprised you're getting nowhere.'

'I haven't been to the police,' I said quietly and braced myself for the inevitable retort.

'Well, don't sound so pleased with yourself,' he said. 'You assume we're all psychics, do you? That it's not necessary to actually tell us when a murder's been committed? Oh no, we've got plenty of time to go combing the countryside to see if we can stumble over a body? Give us something to do.'

'I don't have any proof,' I shouted back at him. I hated it when he was contemptuous of something I said to him, mostly because he was usually justified. 'And besides there are no bloody police to go to. There's not a police station for miles and everyone says that if you do call them, they don't come for days.' 'Everyone' being Gussie, of course, but I didn't mention that.

'You may not have proof but you have suspicion,' said Max, 'and as for the police not coming, you know perfectly well they'd respond to a suspicious death. So how are these women supposed to have been killed?'

I told him about Rosemary Waters' peanut poisoning and Gussie finding a bottle with traces at the bottom and how André didn't allow peanuts in his kitchen.

'But they haven't had the inquest yet.'

He nodded. 'So how did Melanie die?'

'She fell over the edge of the quarry in the fog.'

'But you think she was pushed?'

I nodded.

He sat down opposite me at the kitchen table and to my surprise he reached across and took both my hands in his. Just for a second, and he was still scowling as he did so, but it was enough to fill me with longing once again.

'Why don't you tell me absolutely everything you can remember about what's happened since you came down here, starting with the day you arrived? I want to know about everyone you've met and what you've observed about them. Take your time.'

I took at least half an hour during which time the level in the brandy bottle went down. When I'd finished he seemed – not surprisingly – to be most interested in Mr Wright.

'This André guy actually confessed to being Mr Wright?'

'It wasn't a matter of confessing – as if he'd done some thing wrong. He was quite open about it because he didn't actually invite either Rosemary or Melanie on a date.'

'How do you know that?' Max was regarding me with a look of skepticism.

'Because he told me. When I showed him the printouts of the emails to Rosemary and Melanie from Mr Wright inviting them to meet him, he was completely mystified. He actually went upstairs to check on his computer but they weren't there.'

Max continued to stare at me as if he couldn't believe what he was hearing.

'Because he told you? He didn't send those emails *because he told you*?'

I had taken André's word because I wanted to, because Gussie was falling in love with him and I couldn't bear it if he turned out to be unworthy of her. But as Max shook his head in mock despair, I knew I'd be doing her a greater favor by facing up to reality.

'How do you know he didn't go upstairs to *delete* those emails, to get rid of any proof that he'd invited those women out on a date?' He wasn't exactly sneering at me but he might just as well have been. How could I have been so gullible? 'But hold on, hold on,' he said quickly when he saw my look of misery. 'It *is* possible that someone who had access to his password might have used his computer to send the emails on his behalf.'

'Justine!' I said. 'It's obvious! She could have popped up from the kitchen at any time.'

'Justine,' Max repeated wearily. 'You never mentioned her. Fill me in.'

I told him about my coffee morning beside her antique ovens. 'But they don't necessarily have to use *his* laptop, do they?' I said. 'It could be anyone who knows his password using a computer anywhere.'

'Sure,' said Max cheerfully, 'it could be old Jake. He's got a computer up in the attic. And what about that Neil Mackay bloke you've just told me about. He seemed to have no problem getting into Melanie's computer. I don't buy that it'd been left on since she died. He could have manufactured those emails to show you on her computer to frame André.'

He drummed his fingers on the table but it wasn't from annoyance. He was excited.

'Because maybe he knew about her correspondence with Mr Wright,' he said, warming to his theme, 'or maybe he was jealous. Jealous enough to pose as Mr Wright and lure Melanie to the quarry and push her over. And that's why he's taken off. Although,' he shrugged, 'it could be anyone who logs on to DirtyFarmers.com. God, the thought of impounding all those hard drives. How many people do you know of in that godforsaken hole of Frampton Abbas who uses a computer, let alone has a cyberlover? Have you encountered many?'

'I saw one within half an hour of my arrival,' I said, and told him about the laptop I had seen in Maggie Blair's outhouse.

'Maggie who? I thought I asked you to tell me about everyone you've come across. How many more people are you going to come up with?'

Maggie's story, especially Jake's revelation that she had had an illegitimate baby, seemed to intrigue him more than anything I had already told him and he didn't laugh when I told him of Mona's bewilderment at discovering her confused and near-demented mother had an email account.

'Her son-in-law?' he repeated slowly. 'She said it belonged to her son-in-law? You're quite sure of that?'

'Oh yes, and she was adamant. But she was also gaga as I later discovered and her son-in-law has been dead for four years.'

'Yes and no,' he said mysteriously.

'What do you mean?'

'Yes, he has and no, maybe he hasn't,' he said and I was none the wiser. 'Do me a favor.' He passed a small gray notebook across the table to me and a pen. 'Write down Maggie's full name and Mona's and the address of the house if you can remember it.'

Why was he asking for these details, I wondered, glancing at the pages of spiky black jottings that constituted his own notes. His handwriting was microscopic and its economy made me embarrassed to add to it with my extravagant scrawl. And he appeared to have lost interest in me because he was on his feet again and pacing to the end of the kitchen and back.

When his fingertips rested on my shoulders, I thought it was a fly and reached up to brush it off, wondering if I was being too pedantic when I wrote *Maggie Blair, daughter Mona, née Blair, don't know married name. 142 High Street, Frampton Abbas.*

Then I realized with a supercharged electric jolt that he was standing behind my chair and now he was massaging the back of my neck and then his hands came over my shoulders to plunge down under my sweater and cup my breasts. I felt his breath in my ear as he whispered *Let's go upstairs.*

The staircase running from the hall up the center of the farmhouse was too narrow for the two of us to mount it clasped to each other, so I watched him kick off his boots and then followed him. His long legs loomed above me like stilts until he collapsed on the top step and pulled me to him. I stood a few steps down, leaning into him between his open legs, my arms up in the air as he ripped off my sweater and tossed it behind me down the stairs. I tried to dismiss Jake's pestering in my head – *What's he going to think of your boring old sports bra? You should have gone out and got yourself a lacy push-up, God knows you need it.*

'What's the matter?' said Max, sensing my hesitation as he undid my front-fastening bra and grazed his flattened palms lightly over my nipples, a gesture that would ordinarily have made me squirm with pleasure.

'Nothing. It's a bit cold.'

'Well, take the rest of your clothes off and let me warm you up,' he said and unzipped my jeans. He had long bony fingers and they were ice cold as he tried to slip them inside me. I flinched and he laughed and gave me a quick slap on the behind.

'Come on,' he said and pulled himself up by the banister, almost pushing me down the stairs in the process.

We were an odd pair. He was still fully clothed and immaculate whereas I was a mess with my jeans halfway down my hips and my bra flapping untidily open over my breasts. He was sleeping in one of the cell-like bedrooms I had seen on my previous visit. I stared in horror at the narrow iron bedstead and the striped ticking of the mattress that had been rolled out but left bare.

'Jake didn't give you any sheets?' I looked at the blankets crumpled into a ball at the end of the bed.

'Sure he did,' said Max, pointing to a pile of linen placed on a chair.

'But why haven't you—'

He shrugged. 'I'm hopeless at making beds. Now take those jeans off and lie down.'

His voice had an urgency now that I couldn't ignore and as I wriggled out of my jeans, he sat down on the mattress and reached out to touch me. He examined my flesh with wonder, his fingers resting on a blemish on my abdomen, a tiny scar on my thigh. Then he placed his hand firmly in the small of my back and drew me to him. He pressed his face into the crevice between my breasts and kept it there for a long while so that I hardly heard him when he whispered.

'Have you any idea how long I have wanted to do this?'

You could have fooled me! was the first thought that came into my head and I banished it guiltily. How could I possibly have known from his angry, dismissive behavior in The Pelican that he had been harboring these kind of feelings for me?

'Well, have you?' He looked up at me fiercely. 'Do you have any idea what you've put me through?' He sounded angry and accusing as if it were all my fault he'd had to wait months to get his hands on me.

'Sorry,' I murmured because I couldn't think what else to say.

'Lie back,' he commanded, and placed his palm flat on my chest until I lay prone beside him. I could feel stray tufts of horsehair protruding through the mattress, piercing my bare skin and I knew I would be marked with unsightly red scratches. He didn't lie down beside me but continued to sit on the edge of the bed looking at me before swooping down without warning to take my left nipple in his mouth.

I looked down on the crown of his head, the bridge of his hawk-like nose, as he worked away and idly stroked his thick black hair. Out of the corner of my eye I could see a little hold-all on the floor. The zipper was open but very few of the contents had been unpacked. Other than that, besides the bed, there was practically nothing in the room except for a chair and a couple of empty coat hangers on the back of the door. There were cobwebs in three of the four corners of the ceiling, dead flies on the windowsill and grime on the panes. There was dust on the floorboards, and no mat and I was glad I'd kept my socks on. It was monastic and desolate and utterly devoid of romance but Max didn't seem to notice. He had lifted his head and was gazing down at me and I should have been in total ecstasy.

I was – and I wasn't.

I was totally and utterly confused. My body was beginning to awaken from its lengthy slumber of enforced sexual absten-tion and the effect was electric. But in my head there were warning bells ringing and until I could figure out what they were trying to tell me, I knew I should slow down.

And my heart? My heart was running this way and that. Try as I might to deny it, there were two other people in bed with us. I was appalled to discover that at the revival of my sexual

242

feeling, even though he wasn't there in person, Tommy's comfortable presence embraced me as if he were right beside me. He was snuggling up to me and gradually forcing Max to the edge of the bed on my other side to the extent that I half expected to hear the thud as Max hit the floor.

But the biggest hindrance of all was the ghost of Sadie hovering between us. However scathing he might be about her memory, she was still there lodged in his head. But more than that, I knew that the way Max had captured just a tiny bit of my heart was via my sympathy for him and his eternally lonely state. We had too much in common, Max and I. We were both loners by nature, perfectly capable of dealing with people when it came to our work but shunning parties and the superficial social behavior most people relied on to relax. And we needed partners like Tommy and Sadie, who were our polar opposites, to keep us on the straight and narrow.

'Relax.' His voice in my ear was hoarse with desire and I could feel him hard through his jeans against my bare thigh. He drew my hand to his crotch. 'Unzip me,' he whispered.

'Kiss me,' I replied, hoping that this would help me overcome my confusion. His first kiss months before, and again against the car only a couple of hours ago, had been intoxicating. He obliged by letting his tongue wander languidly around the inside of my mouth and I felt myself melt a little. I pulled him on top of me and clasped him to me, sliding my hands inside his jeans and over his buttocks.

And then I heard a creak on the stairs, and then another. Someone was on their way up here.

I threw him off me and leapt up, grabbing my clothes and rushing to hide behind the door before Jake appeared.

But it was only Willow, nosing open the door and padding stiffly into the room. She buffeted her body into Max and began to bark incessantly.

'Well, that's it,' he said. 'I'll have to take her out. That's what she wants. She won't stop until I do, will you, girl?' He patted her head and nudged her towards the door. 'I won't be long. Don't move,' he pointed his finger at me. 'I'll be right back.'

But I did move because I couldn't stay in that miserable room another second. I put on my clothes and made a trip to the bathroom where I studied Max's electric toothbrush and razor as if the intimacy of such articles would give me some insight into this strange man who was causing such disruption in my life. I had a quick pee, yanked the long chain hanging from the ceiling to flush and wandered back via Jake's bedroom. On impulse I opened his closet door to take a closer look at the pin-up I had caught a glimpse of the last time I had been there. But it had been torn down, the drawing pins still embedded in the door with remnants of the photo's corners attached.

I could see Max through the window in the bathroom. He was swaying like a long tall tree in the pelting rain and wind. Willow's arthritis had prevented her from moving swiftly enough through the mud to evade being sucked into it and I watched him bend over and pull her upright, guiding her back inside. He was gentle with her. He was a gentle man, I realized, but he seemed to prefer to keep it a secret.

I returned to the monastic cell and made up the bed. I stole a couple of Jake's satin pillowcases for good measure as well as a bedside rug, worn but soft to the touch. To offset the gloom, I took the lamp from Jake's nightstand and placed it on the floor to give the room a token warmth.

I heard Max come in downstairs and this time he remembered to remove his boots. I stood at the top of the stairs and listened to him settling Willow back into her basket, talking to her in soft calming tones.

I'd had time to think and I knew I had to be cruel to be kind. When he came into the room and saw me standing fully clothed by the window, his face fell.

'I'm sorry,' I said, 'please don't ask me to explain – at least not right now. I just can't. It won't work. It's – I don't know, it's the wrong time, the wrong place, the wrong—'

'Man?' He looked sad but also strangely relieved.

'I'm truly sorry,' I said, and I was. 'It's nothing to do with you, it's just—'

'Of course it's to do with me,' he said, his voice hoarse and achingly sad. 'Don't blame yourself for one second. You're right not to want me. I'm a disaster, I know I am.'

'No! You're not. Really!' I went to him and made to embrace him but he caught me and held me at arm's length.

'Come and lie down,' he said suddenly, 'no hanky-panky, I just want to hold you and talk to you. You know,' he said when we were lying side by side again on the mattress, 'I miss Richie. Since I was promoted, I barely see him. I could talk to Richie, I could unwind with him, let go of some of the horror we witness. I know I'm awkward to be around, I've always been like that.' He squeezed my hand as if trying to make me understand. I squeezed back to show that I did. 'I just don't trust people naturally. There are very few people I can let down my guard with. Richie was one. And you're another,' he said after a beat. 'I knew that as soon as I met you. I feel as if I can say anything to you.'

You could have fooled me. 'But Max—' I began.

'Sadie was right.' He didn't seem to have heard me. 'It must have been a nightmare being married to me. Everything she said about me was true. I didn't pay her enough attention, I did hide behind my work and it probably was my fault that we couldn't have a baby together. I'm a misery to be around and when I can face thinking about it, it amazes me that she didn't leave me way before she did. And it's probably a good thing if you don't want to get involved with me either. I couldn't bear it if I inflicted the same torture on you.'

'Sometimes you do behave as if I'm the last person on earth you want to be around. When you first arrived – that night in the restaurant. I couldn't believe the look you gave me.'

'I know,' he said. 'I always seem to act the opposite of how I feel. All I wanted to do was leap up and crush you to me but I'm hopeless at showing people how I feel in private, let alone in such a public place as a restaurant. Just as well since now you don't want me—'

'I didn't say that,' I said. 'I do – want you. I'm just not sure—' I hesitated because what I was about to say sounded pathetic. But I felt I owed him the truth. 'Because I'm not sure I can handle you. Sometimes I'm frightened of you, Max.'

He began to stroke my hair. 'That's truly awful to hear. The last thing I want to do is frighten you.'

'You're so *angry* all the time. Have you ever thought of talking to someone?' I tensed, expecting him to treat the suggestion with derision.

But he surprised me. 'You mean a therapist or someone? The truth is I have thought about it once or twice. It's got that bad. But thinking and doing are two different things. Cold day in hell and all that.'

I knew I should reassure him that it would be different between us, that he should trust me to endure whatever he put me through, that we would come out the other side. But what I had finally worked out in my mind was that I knew I couldn't help him until he was ready. He probably didn't realize it but while his widower status made him available, in his own mind he was still Sadie's dysfunctional husband and as such he would never allow himself to be claimed by me. Maybe the time would come when he would be free, but who knew where I would be when that time came.

It was terribly sad and as darkness fell early on the wintry afternoon and the light from the lamp on the floor threw up indistinct shadows on the wall, he went downstairs and made me the most inelegant sandwich I had ever seen, fashioned out of chunks of bread too large to fit in my mouth and dried-up ham curling at the edges. And he brought the rest of the brandy, which he bade me drink and he held me in his arms and talked and talked but I was so woozy from

246

the brandy that I couldn't make out much of what he was saying.

Eventually I drifted into sleep and when I awoke it was nine o'clock at night and he wasn't there. As I sat up, I saw the hold-all on the floor was gone and looking out the window, I saw the Land Rover was no longer there.

Downstairs in the kitchen he had left a note – for Jake.

Recalled to London unexpectedly. Will leave the Land Rover at Tiverton station.

Chapter Fifteen

Gussie's front door would hardly budge an inch when I put my key in the lock and tried to push it open. I yelled her name through the crack but there was no reply and in any case the house was in total darkness. I slid my hand in and found the light switch on the wall.

Now I could see that the hall was crammed with furniture and for one ghastly moment, I thought that maybe she had invited André to move in. But then I remembered his pathetic collection of belongings in the room above The Pelican. I could see what was blocking my path and I was able to bend over, stretch my arms out and push away the chair that was behind the door. I squeezed into the hall and stared at the furniture, which stretched into the empty sitting room to the right of the hall. I recognized some of the items – the wing chair with the outscrolled arms, the mahogany cabinet, But what on earth was Maggie Blair's furniture doing in Gussie's house?

I stood in the hall, aware that I was making a terrible mess. To reach my car on the other side of the cattle grid at Dorcas Farm, I'd had to wade through the mud, sinking almost up to my calves in some places. My shoes, socks and the bottom half of my jeans were now reddish brown in color and I squelched every time I moved. Knowing I couldn't trail mud any further into the house, I undressed in the hall and climbed the stairs to my room.

Gussie had left a note pinned to my door.

Where the hell *are you? They're going mental at The Pelican, André's been calling every five minutes. No one can get hold of you, your mobile's sitting on the kitchen table. I've gone in to cover for you. Get there as* soon *as you can.*

Well, I wasn't going anywhere till I'd had a bath, I reasoned, and anyway it was already nearly ten o'clock. By the time I'd wept with frustration at Max's disappearing act, returned the various things I'd purloined from Jake's bedroom and laid out some food for Willow, it had gone nine thirty when I finally left Dorcas Farm.

I tried to relax in the bath, sinking down until my chin rested on the hot water. I could feel my face going bright red and I closed my eyes tight to clamp down on the tears that were poised to flow. Why had I allowed Max to get away? Why had I let him scuttle away once he had emerged from his defensive shell to engage me in intimacy? Should I have tried harder to coax him into analysis? Would there have been any point?

To my surprise, as I lay there in the bath tub, I began to remember snippets of the turbulent outpouring of words he had kept up while we were lying on the narrow bed, pressed together with our limbs interlocked. I could still feel the rangy extent of him stretched out against me, his chin resting on the top of my head as he talked, my face buried in his chest, my toes jutting into his shins. I had been asleep and then I had been awake. It had been like when I watched television in bed and often dozed off in the middle of a program, only to jerk awake to try and pick up the plot.

He had been talking mostly about Jake, I remembered with a start, and that had surprised me.

'You asked me who found her,' he had said, suddenly picking up on our conversation in the kitchen. 'Well, it was Jake, of course. Jake said she was missing and went to look for her and found her in a field. *Strangled!*' He had said the word strangled as if he didn't believe it. And then he had shaken me fully awake. 'So what do you think of old Jake? What do you make of my uncle? Fancy him, do you? Ever wondered if maybe old Jake was Mr Wright? What have you heard about my uncle? What do they think about him down here?'

By that stage I had heard enough to know that much of what he was saying to me was rhetorical and it really didn't matter if I drifted in and out of sleep. He was speaking out loud but he was talking mostly to himself as one might address a dog. Indeed he was stroking me as if I were a pet, affectionate fondling punctuated by the odd half-hearted slap on my rump.

Now I wished I had been sufficiently alert to talk to him about his relationship with Jake. After all I had gossiped with Jake about *him*. It seemed only fair that I find out what *he* thought about 'old Jake', as he had repeatedly called him. Maybe he was frightened that he was destined to wind up lonely and embittered like his uncle or maybe he was envious of Jake's alleged prowess with women? But whatever he felt about Jake, and even though I knew I didn't have the right to hold on to him, I still wished he hadn't run away without saying goodbye.

I was still brooding on this when I heard Gussie come in, slam the door and start climbing the stairs, shouting my name. There was a full-length mirror on the floor of the bathroom propped up against the wall and it reflected Gussie as she entered through a haze of steam.

I felt defenseless lying naked in the bath tub as Gussie stood over me, preparing to rant.

'What are you *doing*?' she yelled and I winced. A headache from drinking too much brandy was pounding in my head and I contemplated submerging myself completely to shut her out. 'Have you spent the evening taking it easy while I've been slaving away? And by the way, if you have, you can get used to it because André is so angry you didn't show that he says he no longer wants you to work there. I'm taking your place permanently. I'm reinstated as of tomorrow. So where were you?'

I didn't have an answer for her. I'd never mentioned my association with Max to her and given the fiasco at Dorcas Farm it seemed pointless to enlighten her now.

'What in the world is Maggie Blair's furniture doing in the hall?' I said by way of retaliation at her outburst. 'I could barely get in the door.'

'She left it to me in her will.'

'You never told me that, nor that it was being delivered today and doesn't the will have to go through probate or something?'

'What's it to you?' Gussie's face was becoming a little pink from the steam. 'I agreed with Mona that I would store it here so Sylvia wouldn't get her hands on it.'

It was just as well Justine had already filled me in on the provisions Maggie's will had made for Sylvia. So Maggie had left Gussie her furniture. Well, well, well. Three holes in the ground. I giggled at the memory of my childhood joke.

'What are you bloody laughing at, Lee? I *need* furniture. André's coming round tomorrow to help me move everything into all the rooms.'

'So long as he isn't coming round tonight,' I muttered.

'I heard that. How could you let him down so when he's been so good to you?'

'Good to me?'

'Letting you work in his kitchen.'

I couldn't believe what I was hearing. 'Gussie,' I said, struggling to my feet in the bath and trying not topple over as I reached for the towel I'd lodged on the windowsill, 'you seem to have forgotten why I was working in – *his kitchen*. I didn't get a job there for fun. I went there to try and find out who put the peanut oil in the dressing, to clear your name. And then,' I wrapped the towel around me and stepped out of the bath, 'I went *on* working there so as to earn money for you, the money you lost when Sylvia let you go. I haven't spent a penny of what I've earned. Come with me,' I marched out of the bathroom and along the freezing corridor to my room where I rummaged in the drawer of my bedside table. 'Here!' I flung a load of cash at her, 'this is for you. So you can pay the bloody mortgage. So the bank won't foreclose, so you can stay in your house. I've been saving it for you.'

'How do you know about the bank?' No word of thanks, I noticed, just as there had been no concern as to what might have happened to me when I didn't show up for work. 'You've been snooping, Lee. How *could* you?'

'I wasn't snooping. You just left everything lying about on the kitchen table, I couldn't help seeing it.' Not strictly true but still. 'So you take this, Gussie, and put it in the bank and use it to back pay the mortgage and if you get into that kind of trouble again, for God's sake tell me and let me help you.'

'I don't *need* your help!' she shouted at me, every inch the outraged little figure she'd presented in our childhood, 'My situation's not *completely* hopeless, you know. André will take care of me. I know he will.' She didn't sound terribly convinced.

'You can't be sure of that, ' I said as gently as I could. It was so alien to me, this concept that a man would automatically take care of you financially just as independence was equally inconceivable to Gussie. 'You can't expect him to pay your mortgage. You're not – you're not even his wife, Gussie. Are you?'

'Not yet,' she said.

'Oh Gussie,' I said and the despair I felt for her eternal false hope must have been evident in my voice because she frowned. I took care to soften my tone. 'You mustn't raise your hopes for anything like that. It's much too soon.'

'But Lee-Lee, I just *know* that's what's going to happen. I feel I'm meant to be with him.'

I shook my head. 'No, Gussie, it can't happen. At least not for a while.'

'Can!' said Gussie, pouting like a two-year-old. 'Don't be such a spoilsport, Lee-Lee.'

'Gussie, I'm going to say this as gently as possible. He obviously hasn't told you this but he's already married.'

There was tiny flicker of doubt in her eyes before she said firmly, 'You're just jealous!'

'What?'

'Yes you are. You're just jealous because I've got André and you haven't got anyone.'

I was speechless – at her playground level childishness, at her gullible conviction that she wanted to marry a man she'd spent only a couple of nights with but most of all because I knew deep down that what she said had more than a shred of truth in it.

I would have let it go had she not begun to taunt me in a ludicrous sing-song voice. *Lee-Lee needs a boyfriend! Lee-Lee needs a boyfriend!*

I was tempted to shout at her. *You wanted to know where I've been. Well, I'll tell you. I've been with a man I've been dreaming about for months. Not a ginger tom cat reeking of onions who knows his way around a kitchen. I've been with a fascinating complicated challenge of a man, a man whose unpredictable behavior makes him a magnet for my neurotic and pathetic needs.*

A man who has buggered off without even saying goodbye.

'Listen, Gussie, André is definitely married. He has a wife somewhere. He's not divorced. Justine told me and how does she know? Because he told her. You said as much to me your-self when I first arrived. You know André's married. You're just in denial and you should snap out of it.'

'What have you got against André?'

I wanted to throttle her. How could she persist in missing the point.

'I don't have anything against André except that he makes a godawful noise when he makes love to you. Even the ducks stopped to listen.'

She giggled. 'Sorry, Lee-Lee.' She pretended to look guilty and I relented a little. That was the thing about Gussie that I remembered from when we were growing up. It was hard to stay mad at her for long. 'Friends?' she said. I nodded. 'Friends for life?'

'Don't push it,' I said.

'So where were you?' she persisted. 'Tommy said he'd been trying your mobile too.'

My heart and my stomach lurched simultaneously. Tommy, Tommy, Tommy, Tommy! How could I have forgotten about him? 'Tommy called?'

'Yes, I told you. Several times, always when you were at work but we've been having some nice chats. I've never understood why you aren't nicer to him, Lee-Lee.'

'*Some nice chats,*' I repeated after her slowly. 'How many *nice chats* exactly?'

'Oh, I can't remember. He's been calling every day, at least twice a day, but you've not been here, have you?' She looked at me archly. 'Anyway when I spoke to him earlier just before I went off to fill in for you, he said he was coming to London. He said he'd been looking for an excuse and he decided to come for that woman's birthday. She's having a celebration of some kind because it's the big four-oh.'

'What woman?' I was mystified.

'Well, you must know all about it. She's supposed to be your *best friend.*' Gussie spat out the words. 'Cath Clark.'

Well, yes, Cath *was* supposed to be my best friend although it had always been a case of opposites attract. We couldn't be more different and Cath never missed an opportunity to point this out, usually drawing attention to the fact that I was a hopeless case and it was just as well she was around to sort me out. Gussie loathed her, which was unusual in itself in that Gussie was basically too good natured to harbor ill feeling toward anyone. But, try as I might to tell her she was wrong, she had always maintained that Cath was not worthy of my friendship.

'She's always so critical of you, Lee-Lee. She never seems to be able to accept you as you are. She's not a real friend for you and she's, I don't know, she's *treacherous*.'

It had stayed with me because it was such an unlikely word for Gussie to use. I felt rather disloyal for remarking on it even to myself, but it was true, Gussie normally stuck to a simple vocabulary.

I didn't say anything because I was shocked that I had forgotten Cath's birthday – it was tomorrow – as well as being hurt beyond belief that she hadn't asked me to whatever celebration she was having. Although it was unlikely to be a rip-roaring affair. Cath was an alcoholic and ever since she had come out of rehab, she had steered clear of parties and any social gatherings that were likely to include alcohol. But if she was just planning to have cake and coffee at one of her meetings, how come Tommy was flying in for it?

'So did anyone else call?' I asked Gussie as a way of avoiding further conversation about Cath – or Tommy.

'Only your agent, Genevieve. She said to tell you she's going to have Mary Jane someone call you direct and you'll know what that means. I hope you've bloody well left me some hot water, Lee-Lee. We were rushed off our feet tonight and I ache so much I didn't even want to spend the night with André.'

'That's because you're out of practice,' I said. 'Off you go and have a nice long soak.'

It took me a long time to get to sleep but I more than made up for it in the morning. André wasn't there to rouse me with his moans of passion and even the ducks had drifted further downstream although the thundering of the rain on the roof above me made me wonder if perhaps that had drowned out all other sound.

When I finally stumbled downstairs it was almost noon and Gussie had left me a note saying she had gone to The Pelican to make an early start with the prep work. Prep work that involved sharing a confined space with André, I couldn't help

255

thinking. I had a feeling that Gussie would be going to work earlier and earlier in the future if André had not spent the night with her.

My phone lying on the kitchen table peeped and I snatched it up. Max, please let it be Max.

It was a text – from Tommy. He hadn't signed it but I knew it was from him because of the plethora of acronyms he always persisted in using. I'd managed to train him not to do it when emailing me because I could never figure out what they meant but they always resurfaced in his texts.

Am in London Where RU? Tried to reach you OTP. RU going Cath's B day 2NITE? WYCM KFY

I got as far as *London Where R U?* That was easy enough but after that I drew a blank. What on earth was OTP and WYCM and KFY? Tommy's passion for country music made me wonder if that was what CM stood for but somehow it didn't seem likely unless he was planning to run the karaoke for Cath's birthday. I smiled in spite of myself, picturing him lumbering around the stages in Long Island clubs where he was a karaoke DJ, burbling into the microphone with a loopy smile on his handsome face, as if he believed every word of the trite and sentimental lyrics he was singing.

As I stared at the text message, I made a spontaneous decision. I would go back to London and I would leave immediately. There was nothing left for me in Frampton Abbas. Gussie had her job back – and her reputation would surely follow – and I was no longer needed at The Pelican. I could surprise Cath on her birthday and she would be none the wiser about my having forgotten it. And I couldn't put off dealing with Mary Jane Markham any longer, even if all it meant was having one interview with her and then saying I didn't want the job. Rather guiltily I realized I was abandoning Sylvia's book and would have to explain this to her.

And there was one other thing. When I left her, Marjorie Mackay, in a fit of remorse for her fury at her son, had told me that Neil had almost certainly gone to London. He had a cousin there on his father's side and Marjorie was sure that was where he had gone even though the cousin had denied it when she had called. *But that's probably because I was shouting at him down the phone.* She had given me the address and phone number and begged me to track Neil down and confront him when I went back to London. 'Make him get in touch,' she had said, 'or I'll never forgive myself.'

I had almost thrown away the number – why would Neil Mackay talk to me? Why would I even think of getting in touch with him? – but I hadn't and now I knew why. There was something I was leaving unresolved in Frampton Abbas, something that I had a disturbing feeling would draw me back here one day, and that was the truth about the deaths of Rosemary and Melanie. Max had pointed out that Neil Mackay had been Melanie's lover and that he had been up at the quarry the day she died. Maybe I should use Marjorie's request as an excuse to contact Neil and quiz him further about what exactly *had* happened up there at the quarry.

But, as I packed, I pushed to the back of my mind the most urgent reason for my departure. Max had gone back to London.

And every now and then a tiny nagging detail would surface in my thoughts: *And don't forget Tommy will be there.*

I bundled my bags into the car with one hand, holding an umbrella above me in the other. The rain was coming down so hard it bounced up again as soon as it hit the pavement. The front door of the house next door was open and the woman who lived there was on her knees in the entrance, trying to fix some sort of gate into a hollowed-out space either side of the door. 'Try and talk some sense into Gussie,' she said looking up at me and smiling. 'I've told her time and time again to get floodgates installed but will she listen? Ah,' she wrestled the barrier into place across the threshold, 'that does it!'

'That's a floodgate?' I said.

'Just a precaution at the moment. I'm just checking it fits. And I've got Gussie between me and the river but what's she got?' She jerked her head in the direction of the bridge.

'You think it's going to flood?'

'It's been raining for days. You never know.'

Her ominous words taunted me as I finished loading the car and splashed down the High Street to The Pelican. André was at the stove, stirring a huge pot.

'Nettle and garlic soup,' he explained, when I peered at the drab green liquid.

'Don't worry, you won't miss out, Lee. There'll be plenty left,' said Sylvia emerging from the pantry. 'No one who chooses to dine at this restaurant will want to eat nettles.'

'Course they will,' said André, 'it's perfect for country folk.'

'That's my point,' said Sylvia. 'Ever since you started changing things around here, ever since you started catering to what you call a more upmarket clientele, that's exactly what you've got. They're not country folk you're cooking for anymore, it's *moved-to-the-country* folk. They just want what they're used to in London and I doubt they've ever gone foraging for nettles in Hyde Park.'

'Well, I love nettles,' said Gussie staunchly, rallying to André's defense, and I almost burst out laughing. I doubted Gussie could even recognize a nettle let alone eat one but I was struck by the way she challenged Sylvia so confidently, something she would never have dared to do when I first arrived in Frampton Abbas. She had, I realized, established her standing in André's kitchen and Sylvia had been subtly relegated to less important status.

'Gussie,' I said, 'I've come to tell you that I'm going back to London. You don't really need me here anymore, do you? And I've got a ton of work waiting for me.' Slight exaggeration of the truth but I couldn't very well say I had to go running after Max.

Gussie looked momentarily shocked. 'Oh Lee-Lee, you *can't* leave me.' She was at her most beseeching. 'I won't be able to manage without you.'

'Of course you will,' I said, wrapping my arms around her and kissing her on both of her pink cheeks, 'you're not *completely* hopeless. And besides,' I whispered in her ear, 'now you can move André in and he'll look after you.'

Even as I said it, I wondered if I was setting her up for disaster. Hadn't Max suggested that André could easily have gone upstairs and deleted his emails inviting Rosemary and Melanie to their fatal dates? Was I mad to leave Gussie alone with him in the house?

'But why do you have to go to*day*?' she whined.

'You know why – for Cath's birthday. And Tommy will be there.' Could I get any more hypocritical? 'And since I'm going, I might as well stay. I was always going to have to go back some time, Gussie. You know that.'

Sylvia hovered nearby. 'Did I hear you say you're leaving us?' She gave me one of her wan smiles, her eyes sending out a cold hard message that didn't match that of her upturned mouth.

'Sylvia, I'm sorry. I confess I was never going to stay here forever and maybe I should have made that clear when I said I'd help you with your book. But we never made anything more formal than a verbal arrangement and based on what you've done so far, I'm sure you'll have no problem with the rest of it.'

I wasn't sure of anything of the sort. I might be prejudiced, but I had never subscribed to the maxim that everyone had a book in them. What I was prepared to admit was that the books many people – Sylvia included – *thought* they had in them were likely to be unreadable. I braced myself for her insistence that I continue to work with her in some way.

But she startled me with her reply.

'Oh, that was just a bit of fun. I had a good time going down memory lane for a while but I'm going to put the book idea aside for the time being. I'd no idea it'd be so time consuming and I have got a restaurant to run, you know.'

I breathed slowly in and out. Had I heard her correctly? Was she actually admitting there was something more to writing a book than she had first envisioned? Yet there was something different about her voice today, something just a little defeatist in her tone.

And then something happened that made me do a serious doubletake.

'Sylvia, are you going to go across the road and pick up the bread? It's nearly noon and we don't want the baker to run out of those wholewheat rolls.' This was Gussie talking, Gussie tossing out what was almost a command to Sylvia. And even though her mouth gave a little twitch of protest, Sylvia turned to go upstairs.

'I'll just get my coat. Anything else we need while I'm out?'

Wendy was at the sink, she could have sent her. I wouldn't have put it past her to ask me to run the errand even though I was no longer part of the kitchen staff. But she submitted to Gussie's request like a lamb and it was almost spooky.

'I'll walk out with you,' I said but when she went upstairs, André caught my arm and led me into the pantry.

'Sylvia may not want to tell her crappy little story anymore but I've been thinking about my own. I'd like to run it past you, if you're still interested?'

'You want to do a book?' I'd had a hunch about André, that he did have a story to tell and that it was probably worth hearing – if only because it might throw up the truth about his wife.

'I'm not sure about that,' he looked a little coy, 'but who knows, maybe you'll persuade me. But it'll have to wait until Sunday, when I'm off.'

'André, you just heard me tell Gussie, I'm on my way to London.'

'Well, you'll just have to come back then, won't you?' He patted me on the back and pushed me gently into the kitchen. 'I'll be waiting for you.'

I'd said goodbye to André and Sylvia and Gussie and even to the ducks but there was one person I hadn't seen, I thought as I drove away along the Exe Valley. By the time I hit the M4 I couldn't get the picture of Jake out of my mind.

I imagined him coming home from wherever he'd been – where *had* he been? – and finding Max's note. I imagined him swearing when he found he had to get someone to drive him all the way to Tiverton to pick up the Land Rover from the station. Would he sense I had been there? He'd call Max and yell at him about the Land Rover but would Max mention that he'd brought me back there? Somehow I doubted it.

The torrential rain petered out as I approached London but even so it had taken its toll on the traffic. A lorry had skidded out of control on the slippery surface near Slough, causing a back-up for several miles so that by the time I came off the Hammersmith Flyover and doubled back up Shepherds Bush Road it was after four and getting dark.

I was making for Blenheim Crescent but it occurred to me that I was about to go right past Cath's house in Shepherds Bush. My plan had been to surprise her by showing up at her party but I realized I had no idea what form that party was going to take, or even where it was to be held.

I drove around until I found somewhere to park and then forked out for an extremely expensive amaryllis planted in a heavy terracotta pot. I had them tie a bit of ribbon in a big bow around the pot and then I struggled back to the car with it. I'd surprise her early, present her with it, say hello to my godson Marcus and scrounge for information about the party. Maybe even get a cup of tea into the bargain.

Cath and Richie lived in a little gem of a Victorian cottage in a quiet street off Goldhawk Road. Hard to imagine anywhere could be quiet off Goldhawk Road but somehow their little backwater managed to be even though it was close to the hustle and bustle of Shepherds Bush, which probably made it a pretty valuable property. Or it would have done if they had owned the whole house. Every time I visited Cath, I never ceased to marvel at the way someone had turned what was ostensibly a two-up two-down cottage into two flats and a bedsit.

Cath and Richie had the ground floor so at least they had access to a postage stamp of a garden but even so it was daunting to accept that they – plus three-year-old Marcus, not to mention his newborn sister Jacqui – had to squeeze into such a small space while I had my parents' four-storey mansion all to myself. It was something Cath rarely let me forget.

I hefted the amaryllis up the steps and almost broke the pot when I ran out of steam and let go of it too quickly outside the front door. There was no answer when I rang the bell. I wasn't going to lift the bloody plant all the way down again so I padded round the back where I knew Cath kept a key on a hook in a shed. I sensed movement as I passed her bedroom window and prepared myself for the names she would call me if I had awakened her from one of the rare naps she snatched once she'd got Jacqui down.

I let myself in and waded through the contents of an over-turned crate of toys scattered all over the kitchen floor. I wondered why there was no sign of my godson who usually announced his presence by clawing something sticky on to my knees. Maybe Cath had taken him into bed with her in an attempt to get him to nap beside her.

I nudged open her bedroom door and sure enough there she was in bed. But she wasn't asleep. Her eyes were wide open and boring into mine but if she wanted me to be quiet, she had another think coming because the body slumbering in the crook of her arm with his head on her shoulder wasn't her scrappy little son. It was a large and cumbersome shape that took up half the bed as it usually did and its name was Tommy.

Chapter Sixteen

I wrestled for several minutes, trying to fit my key in the lock of the front door at Blenheim Crescent before I realized it was the key to Gussie's house in Frampton Abbas. But apart from the key to the car, it was the only one I had in my bag and it slowly dawned on me that in my haste to get to Gussie several weeks ago, I had rushed out of the house leaving my only means of entry to Blenheim Crescent on the hall table. If I peeked through the letter box I would probably be able to see it lying there just inside the door.

I kicked the door in frustration. I had taken one look at Cath and Tommy snuggled up to each other and made a run for it, ignoring Cath's cries of *Lee, where are you going? Lee, come back!* My fiancé and my best friend! OK, my *ex*-fiancé and my best friend. And what kind of an expression was *best friend* anyway? It made it sound as if we were still at school together. You didn't have a *best* friend when you were grown up, did you? You had loads of friends but even I knew that, whatever you called them, they weren't supposed to sleep with your fiancé. Ex or otherwise.

I kicked the door again and jumped back when it opened suddenly.

'What *are* you doing? Stop it at once, you'll scuff the paint-work.'

I stared in total amazement. 'What are you doing here, Mum?'

'I live here. It's my house. And before you start arguing with me, I *know* it's your father's name on the deeds but I'm the only one who takes an interest in its maintenance.'

'Oh God, Mum, please don't tell me you're doing some remodeling?' It was my mother's favorite trick. She'd wait until I was at a crucial stage in the writing of a book, with a deadline looming, and then she'd bring in a crew of the noisiest workmen she could find and tell them to knock down a wall or something. Although since she and my father had moved to New York a year ago, I'd been spared any such intrusion. Not that I had any work to interrupt. 'And what are you doing in London? Why didn't you let me know you were coming?'

'Why didn't you let me know *you* were coming?' countered my mother. 'I thought you were safely out of the way in Devon. I did call you, as a matter of fact, and Gussie told me you were on your way to London. You could have warned me.'

It was typical. Most mothers who were separated from their only child by an ocean would cross it in order to see that daughter, but mine had clearly intended to take advantage of the fact that she was unlikely to find me home.

'Anyway, come in, darling, and tell me how you are. Don't stand there letting the cold air in.'

I staggered through the door and put my bags down, and my arms up, for her embrace – and put them down again in a hurry when I realized my mother had disappeared into the kitchen. Again typical. She always makes all the right noises but never follows through.

'So what brings you from New York?'

'I'd make you a cup of tea but I can't find it,' she said, ignoring my question. 'I don't know what you've been doing in this kitchen, Lee. You've put everything back in the wrong place.'

I reached for the kettle with a sigh. She'd been gone for a year and she expected everything to be exactly as she'd left it. Besides, as far as I could remember, she'd never made me a cup of tea in her life.

'I'll have Lapsang Souchong,' she said, 'and I'm here for a benefit I'm giving at Grosvenor House for Phil's foundation. I'm the President, you know?'

I didn't know. Phil was Philip Abernathy, the man who for a tragically short time had been the love of my mother's life. Indeed he had been the only person to whom she had actually managed to demonstrate any love as far I could see. My father and I understood that she loved us but we were rarely the recipients of any outward displays of warmth and affection on her part.

She had found Philip Abernathy, an American billionaire whom I had always called the Phillionaire, during the few months she had been separated from my father following my father's misguided affair with Josiane, a young French divorcée. But the Phillionaire had been killed when his chauffeur had a heart attack at the wheel on the Long Island Expressway, and my father had tired of Josiane, and in the aftermath, my parents had somehow resumed their marriage. Only this time it was in New York where my mother had inherited property – and, apparently, a charitable foundation.

'No biscuits,' she said, not that I'd offered her one. 'I'm so mindful of what I eat these days when so many people in the world are undernourished. Do you know, Lee, ten million children die every year and it could so easily be avoided. I feel that all lives – no matter where they are being led – have equal value.'

There was something vaguely familiar about her last sentence. I had the distinct feeling I'd read it on someone's website recently – Bill Gates' probably.

'So is Ed here too?' Ed was my father. I never called him Dad or Father or anything like that. 'Where is he? Upstairs? Does he want a cuppa too?'

265

'Your father's staying in New York. He's totally useless at charity. Oh, he's still sending his little checks for $1500 to Médecins sans Frontières every now and then but he's a dead loss when it comes to the big stuff.'

Only my mother could dismiss a check for $1500 as little. I felt rather sorry for my father. He'd inherited a small amount of money as a young man and had proceeded to lose it steadily but surely via his antiquarian book business, a business that had brought him constant pleasure. I imagined that, for him, $1500 was no small sacrifice and I knew *every now and then* actually translated into several checks a year.

'You had a few phone calls. I took messages.' My mother made it sound like an extraordinarily onerous task. 'An utterly charming woman, Mary Jane Markham.'

'You know her?'

'Well, I've never *met* her face to face but I feel like I know her now. We had such a lovely chat. Seems like you didn't bother to tell her you were coming to London either. She had to find out where you were from Gussie.'

'What did she want?'

'You *know* what she wants. You're writing her book.'

'Mum, I haven't even had an interview with her. I'm not at all sure she'd be my cup of tea.'

'Why ever not? No! Don't put milk in mine. Just a slice of lemon. I tell you, my dear, I took the opportunity to get as much out of her as I could and she was *so* helpful. Marriage is a partnership, of course, and a judgement for the abandoned spouse has to recognize the sacrifice they've made. You know, she was only married for four years and she didn't have any children but she said she knew she had to get the court to look at the standard of living *during* the marriage rather than the hopes and expectations at the beginning of it.'

'Mum,' I said, smelling a rat as I invariably did when my mother suddenly showed an interest in something totally unexpected, 'why do *you* want to know about divorce settlements?'

'Well, you never know when you might need the information.'

I laughed. 'If Ed divorced you I doubt you'd get five bucks out of him, let alone five million!'

She didn't smile. 'But if *I* divorced him and he came after *me* for a settlement, right now he'd be looking at a lot of shared income! I just wanted to know what I should be prepared for and your Mary Jane Markham pretty much set me straight.'

'She's not *my* Mary Jane Markham,' I said angrily, more to cover my sudden unease than anything else. Surely she wasn't planning to divorce my father? 'You said I had a few phone calls. Who else was after me?'

'Cath. She called just before you turned up and left you a message I can't make head or tail of but maybe you can. She said to tell you that when someone asked her what she wanted for her birthday, she decided the best present in the world would be four hours' unbroken sleep so this person came and took Marcus and Jacqui away so Cath could climb into bed – and, just as she dropped off, Tommy turned up from the airport and he was as exhausted as she was and—'

The crash of the doorknocker drowned out the rest of her sentence.

'Speak of the devil,' said my mother, clapping her hands and literally skipping out into the hall.

'Mum!' I hissed. 'Come back here. *Please!* If it's him, you can't let him in.'

'Of course I can,' she said, 'he's staying here.'

'WHY?' I literally screamed.

'Because I invited him, of course. He called here looking for you, probably redirected by Gussie as well, and I asked him where he was staying and he said he hadn't got that far so I said *Look no further, we've beds all over the place.* I've put you on the top floor, by the way.'

'Not *together?*' I grabbed her arm but it was too late. She shrugged me off and opened the door.

267

To my intense annoyance, the sight of Tommy standing there clutching a laptop flat against his chest with one of his huge paws and hefting a rather smart black leather carry-on bag in the other made my heart give a familiar lurch. He had an infuriating habit of somehow managing to be at his most attractive when he knew he'd done something wrong. Wariness added a boyish vulnerability to his handsome wide-planed face and rather than berate him, it always made me want to rush and console him.

'Tommy, darling, this is just glorious!' gushed my mother. 'What a wonderful coincidence that we're both in London at the same time. When did your plane get in? You must be exhausted.'

She aimed a peck at his cheek as she ushered him through the door. More than she'd done with me. Once inside the hall, Tommy planted himself squarely in front of me. *Don't say it,* I whispered to myself, *don't tell me it's not what I think.*

'It's not what you think, Lee. Honest. She was having a kip while the kids were out and I'd just come in off an overnight flight and I flopped down beside her and passed out.'

I wanted to believe him. There was no reason why I shouldn't but if there's any excuse for me to fret about something, I'll use it. Cath had once been in love with Tommy. OK, so she'd found Richie and married him but who was to say she didn't still have a hankering after Tommy? And why had she told *him* she was having a birthday party and not me?

'Tommy, do you want to take your stuff, and Lee's, up to the top floor?' My mother had failed to detect the note of tension between us. 'The beds are made up in both the rooms up there so pick which one you want.'

This was suitably ambiguous as far as the two of us bunking up was concerned, but I had suddenly woken up to the fact that if my mother was suggesting *I* sleep on the top floor as well as Tommy, then she must have thrown me out of the master bedroom one flight up that I now thought of as *my* room. I was pathetic, I truly was. At almost forty I was still living at home and being moved about the house by my mother as if I were still a teenager with no rights.

'Take whichever room you want,' I said to Tommy, 'I'm going out.'

It was a childish and cowardly gesture and utterly futile because, as soon as I was outside, I had no idea what I was going to do or where I was going to go. I waited for Tommy to open the door and rush after me but he didn't and that made it even worse. When a drop of rain fell on my nose, I all but stamped my foot in infantile frustration and made a run for the car.

Although he was no longer standing right in front of me, I could now see Tommy more clearly. Back in the house my vision of him on the doorstep had had one of him in bed with Cath superimposed over it and in addition all clarity was blurred by the confusion of seeing him for the first time in nearly a year. Sitting miserably in my car I was struck by how much weight he had lost and the rather cool three-quarter length leather coat he'd been wearing. And he'd had a bit of blond stubble over his chin, which could have been the result of getting off an overnight plane rather than any kind of fashion statement – but it suited him. It brought out the penetrating turquoise of his eyes in the way that lipstick could often enhance the color of a woman's.

I saw the blind go up in the bay window of my mother's kitchen and there he was, outlined like a male model in a chocolate commercial, watching me. All I had to do was calm down, get out of the car, run back to the house and apologize for jumping to the wrong conclusion.

I gunned the car into action and shot out into Blenheim Crescent, turning left into Ladbroke Grove and down the hill towards Notting Hill Gate. I was starting to cry, mostly because I was so angry at my total inability ever to do the right thing and I reached into my pocket for a Kleenex. Before I realized what I had in my hand, I was trying to blow my nose on a scratchy bit of paper. I could barely see out the wind-screen, the rain was suddenly coming down so hard and leaves trapped underneath the wipers had ground them to a halt. I turned left into Westbourne Park Road and pulled over outside a wine bar.

The piece of paper had Neil Mackay's address on it. It wasn't in the immediate vicinity but it was close enough and suddenly I needed a mission to take my mind off Tommy and Cath and being hounded by Mary Jane Markham and my mother's sudden preoccupation with fending off non-existent divorce settlements. Resisting the temptation to go in and drink the wine bar dry, I nudged the car back out into Westbourne Park Road.

It took me about ten minutes to find the seedy run-down square on the wrong side of the Harrow Road where Neil Mackay's cousin lived. The tall stucco houses with their impressive porticoes had probably been the residences of the wealthy when they had been built in Georgian times but now they were crumbling and smothered in graffiti. There was an illuminated strip comprising twelve doorbells at the number on my piece of paper, a sure sign that the once magnificent house had been carved up into a dozen bedsits.

Neil's cousin was lucky. His room was on the first floor and the floor-to-ceiling French windows leading out on to the balcony above the entrance were still intact, bringing in plenty of light. But the room itself – with a living room and a kitchen area and a bathroom crammed into what had once been a drawing room – was but a travesty of its former splendor.

Neil answered and he wasn't pleased to see me.

'I'm Lee Bartholomew,' I said, holding out my hand. 'We met at your mother's when—'

'I know who you are, I remember you.' His tone was curt. He had turned his back on me to wander into the room, leaving me to follow. My stomach turned over at the smell of last night's takeaway curry.

270

'What do you want?' It was late afternoon but he was in a toweling robe over his pajamas and bare feet. The cheerful burly impression he'd emanated at our previous meetings was nowhere to be seen. He seemed to have shrunk several inches.

'You mother gave me this address, she thought you might be here.'

'And I am.' He didn't ask me to sit down, not that there was anywhere that wasn't piled high with clothes, old newspapers and the odd plate of congealed food. There was no armchair, no sofa, just a bed pushed against a wall, a table and chair and an air mattress on the floor. Empty beer bottles were lined up on the floor. Everything told me that Neil's cousin was a bachelor considerably younger than he was. I doubted Neil would be able to stomach it for long, arriving here from a country farmhouse run by a wife, a settled ordered existence – at least I imagined that's what it must have been.

'She's been trying to reach you, your mother.'

He eyed me skeptically. 'What's her problem? She never liked Kathy anyway. That's why you're here, I assume. You've heard I left her. Big scandal down in Frampton Abbas, is it? Hot gossip at The Pelican?'

By way of reply, I pulled his phone out of my pocket and handed it to him.

He looked at it in astonishment and his mouth flickered in a smile.

'I don't believe it. Is that mine? I figured I must have left it at home. Where the hell did you find it?'

'At your mother's,' I said. 'She found it, not your wife.'

'Well, thanks anyway.' He picked it up.

'And she looked at the photos on it.'

He paused. 'What photos? I know it's a videophone but I hardly ever use the camera.'

'You used it,' I said, 'take a look.'

He reacted so badly, I almost wished I hadn't told him. For a second I thought he was going to cry, then he just slumped down on the air mattress. I felt a bit foolish towering above him so I picked the plate with the remains of a takeaway off the only chair and sat on it.

'It was Melanie's idea,' he said although it was clear from the look of shame on his face that he didn't expect me to absolve him of guilt. 'It was the sort of madness she liked getting into. I admit it felt weird doing it in Mum's room let alone taking pictures but it was the fact that she was so wacky that got me hooked on Melanie in the first place.' Now he seemed to be appealing to me to understand. 'She was just so different to what I was used to and it woke me up, made me realize I could still have some fun in my life.' He stared down at the screen on the phone. 'But I did wonder at the time if these pictures would backfire on us. I've been worrying that Kathy would find the phone. It never occurred to me that I might have left it at Mum's.'

'She knew anyway,' I said. 'Jake Austin told her.'

'About me and Melanie?' He looked at me, astonished.

I nodded.

'Fucking creep!' he exploded. 'What in the world did he have to gain by telling her a thing like that? Although it's obvious, isn't it?'

'Is it?' Now that I thought about it, it was a spiteful thing for Jake to do. Why *had* he told Marjorie something that would undoubtedly upset her? After all, Neil's affair was over. Melanie was dead.

'Of course it is. Old Jake had been lusting after Melanie for years. He wanted her for himself. He kept following us around like a perverted Peeping Tom.'

And he was up at the quarry the day Melanie died, I thought, *that's why he'd been there. He'd been spying on Neil and Melanie.*

Neil lumbered to his feet and shambled in the direction of the kitchen area. He flipped the top off a beer and drew on it without offering me anything.

'Why are you really here?' he said suddenly. 'You didn't drive all the way up to London just to give me my phone back. What did you do with those printouts I gave you from Melanie's computer? You're here because of her, aren't you? Because she died?'

Until he said it, I hadn't realized that was why I was there. But he was right.

'Do *you* think Melanie went over the edge of the quarry by accident?' I asked him. 'In the fog?'

'Or do I think Jake was up there spying on us and that he waited until I'd left and then tried his luck with her and while she was resisting him, she fell over the edge? Or maybe he pushed her in a fit of jealousy?'

Or maybe you lured her there with an email posing as Mr Wright, and you were the one who pushed her over the edge in a fit of jealousy? This was one of Max's theories. But I abandoned it as what Neil had just said finally penetrated.

'We used to laugh about old Jake,' he said. 'It wasn't the first time he'd followed us up there. It was a good place for us to meet. Melanie could walk there easily from Mum's and no one would see her – except Jake, of course. She had to go right past Dorcas Farm. I think we even put on quite a show for him one hot day last summer. We reckoned if he wasn't getting any himself these days, he might welcome a bit of vicarious action.'

I held up my hand to show him I didn't want to hear any more.

'But, you know, it turned out I was making as big a fool out of myself as he was. I heard it in a pub in Tiverton, these blokes were talking about their conquests on Exmoormates.com. *Have you tried Mellow Yellow yet?*'

I understood the bitterness in his tone. *Mellow Yellow* had been Melanie's Exmoormates name. I'd seen it on the printouts he'd given me.

'Of course they could have just seen her profile.' He nodded as if trying to convince himself. 'Maybe they hadn't even contacted her but the fact that it was up there – I checked it that night – meant that she was on the lookout for other men. Mum was always telling me she was never off her computer. I should have put two and two together long before then. We'd arranged to meet up at the quarry as usual and when I asked her about it, she didn't like it, said I didn't own her, that we couldn't go on much longer anyway. She felt bad about deceiving Mum.'

He raised his eyes at what he obviously felt was the irony of it.

'She'd been *deceiving Mum* as she called it for two whole years; why it had suddenly got to her was a mystery to me. And if she felt so bad about it, why didn't she have a problem using Mum's bedroom?'

And how come you were deceiving your wife with no qualms whatsoever? I thought but didn't say anything.

'But we'd been here before a couple of times,' he said. 'She'd say she thought we ought to knock it on the head – but a few days later she was always up for it again. So I left her up there at the quarry. I went to my car and drove away, thinking I'd give her a few days to consider her position, as they say. I didn't see Jake, to be honest. But I did see that kid, the one in The Pelican.'

'Taylor. Wendy's little brother.'

'Yes. *He'd* been spying on us, I could tell, the little devil. I offered him a ride home but he refused although I don't know why.'

'What do you mean?'

'Well, he accepted a ride from someone else not long after. I was quite a long way away but I stopped and looked back because I wanted to see if Melanie had started walking back across the moor. I confess I was a little worried about leaving her there in the fog. I couldn't see her but the boy was running down towards Frampton Abbas and a car overtook him and slowed down.'

'And he got in *that* car?'

Neil nodded. 'I remembered this and after I saw him in The Pelican and found out who he was, I went to see him but his sister wouldn't let me near him.'

'Who was in the car?'

'That's just what I wanted to ask him.' Neil sounded exasperated. 'It was too far away for me to see but it was a blue car, looked like a Nissan.'

'So it was someone he knew? Someone he wasn't frightened to accept a lift from? He didn't know you so he wouldn't have got in the car with you. Wendy told him not to accept rides from strange men.'

'But not from strange women,' Neil said simply. 'Katharine drives a blue Nissan. I always take the Land Rover because it's what I need on the farm and the Nissan is what she uses as her runaround. Maybe *she'd* found out about Melanie, maybe she'd followed us.'

There was an awful logic to his theory. If Jake had told Marjorie, who was to say he hadn't already told Katharine?

'That's why I left Kathy,' said Neil, looking suddenly even more wretched than before. 'I couldn't bring myself to confront her. Melanie's dead. Kathy being arrested for her murder won't bring her back. I've screwed up Kathy's life enough as it is. If that kid keeps quiet, then she may get away with it.'

He was sitting there in front of me blatantly accusing his wife of murder.

'But why are you telling *me*?'

'Because you're the only one who seems to think Melanie's death wasn't an accident. You'd have figured it out sooner or later and now you've turned up here, I have to deal with it. Better to tell you and beg you to keep quiet.'

'You're forgetting something,' I said. 'We both know Jake was up at the quarry. Wouldn't he have seen the blue car too?'

'So why hasn't he told anyone about it?'

Neil was right. If Jake had seen Katharine, wouldn't he have told Marjorie – or even me?

'So you'll call your mother?'

He gave me a look. *What do you think?* And in the light of what he had told me I could see it was pointless trying to persuade him. But when, as I was leaving, he tried to make me promise not to say anything to Marjorie about the possibility of Katharine being at the quarry, I walked out the door without giving him any such reassurance. Maybe Melanie had walked over the edge in the fog, but she'd been going to meet Mr Wright, and the peanut oil that had killed Rosemary Waters hadn't walked into The Pelican by itself. I knew I had to delve a little deeper before giving up on the notion that the women's deaths were not an accident, and that might well include quizzing Marjorie Mackay about her daughter-in-law.

Outside I was suddenly sickened by my visit to Neil. Maybe there was something to what Marjorie Mackay had said about the moors having a destructive influence on people living in their shadow. Neil Mackay could still rescue his marriage and his livelihood down there if he contacted his mother soon but somehow I couldn't see him doing it of his own free will.

And I could still rescue my situation with Tommy. I fished out my phone and called Blenheim Crescent but my mother reported that he'd already gone over to Cath's for her birthday celebrations.

Once again I climbed the steps to Cath's front door, wondering why I couldn't hear the sounds of a party coming from the house. I had to ring twice before anyone answered – I wasn't about to go round the back and set myself up for any more surprises – and when it opened, Richie stood there in his pajamas.

'Hello stranger,' he said, stepping aside and jerking his head in an invitation for me to come in. 'I heard you were here earlier and caught them at it. Thought you'd see if I wanted to shack up with you in retaliation, did you?'

'As if!' I said, patting him on the cheek and then moving the palm of my hand to his forehead. 'You're boiling up, Richie, did you know that?'

'Hadn't a clue,' he gave me a weak grin, 'and I'm always in my jim-jams by eight o'clock in the evening. I suppose you've come to see the birthday girl but you're out of luck. Tommy's taken her out to celebrate while I babysit. I ate a sandwich for lunch that had been sitting on my desk for God knows how long and now I'm paying for it. I'd be puking all over you except I don't think there's anything left in my stomach to come up.'

'I thought she was having a party?' I said, slightly uneasy at the thought of Tommy and Cath out on the tiles together. Cath's crush on him was old history, and I knew for a fact that he had never been remotely interested in her *that* way, but could I trust her not to entice a special fortieth birthday kiss from him?

Of course I could. She was my best friend, even if Gussie loathed her guts. And Richie clearly trusted them together.

'What is it with this alleged party? Tommy had convinced himself there'd be a knees-up. He even tried to pretend that was why he came to London although Cath and I both know it's more likely to be because he wants to see you.'

'So there's no party?'

'Cath said the last thing she wanted to do was draw attention to the fact that she was turning forty.'

'So where have they gone? Maybe I could join them.'

Richie threw up his hands. 'No idea. Tommy sounded like he had an agenda. He made her go upstairs and get dressed up is all I know. I hadn't seen her look so good since Jacqui was born. Made me quite upset I wasn't up to treating her myself. Oh damn! Who's that?' He beckoned me into the kitchen as he went to answer the phone.

'Hello? *Hello? Sir?* I can't hear you, sir, you're breaking up. Sir? Maybe he'll call back.' Richie put the phone down and pushed a half-empty bottle of wine and a glass towards me. 'Help yourself. Hope he does. We don't get to talk much any more since he got his promotion.'

'That was Max?' I sat down suddenly and reached for the bottle.

Richie nodded. 'Believe it or not, I miss him even though he could be a miserable old sod. I learned a hell of a lot working with him and I know he was probably responsible for my promotion being fast-tracked.'

'Oh my God, Richie, I didn't realize. Cath never said anything about it.'

'Detective Inspector Cross,' he puffed out his extremely large chest to ridiculous proportions through his pajama top, 'at your service.'

I giggled and gave him a mock salute. He was a good-looking man even in his current state and I could understand why Cath had fallen for him. For a start he was a similar type to Tommy – big and burly with an open friendly face. But whereas Tommy was fair-haired and normally overweight, Richie Cross had thick floppy dark-brown hair and probably didn't have an ounce of flab on him.

'Congratulations,' I said, 'really, that's wonderful, Richie, although I suppose it might mean you won't see too much of little Jacqui and my godson. I bet Max misses you. I've just seen him, as a matter of fact. I've been in Devon with my cousin and he was there visiting his uncle, taking a little holiday.' I said it casually, hoping that Richie would continue talking about Max and let slip a nugget or two.

'Don't you believe it,' he said, 'Max doesn't take time off. If he went haring off down to Devon, he'll have had an agenda.'

Seeing me. I smiled to myself, feeling smug and warm for about twenty seconds before Richie added, 'Murder related, no doubt.'

His phone rang again and he snatched it up.

'That's better. What's that? She's not here at the moment, gone out to celebrate. Yes. Well, thank you, sir, I'll tell her.

She'll be sorry to have missed you. It's good of you to remember. No, no I'm staying in tonight, bit of food poisoning but Lee Bartholomew's here. I hear you've just seen her down in Devon, sir. She's keeping me company. Yes, yes I will sir, but don't you want to tell her yourself? She's right here.'

I held my breath but he didn't hand me the phone.

'Yes, of course I can, sir. I understand. No trouble at all. Registry of Births and Deaths. Hang on, I'll just write all that down.' He scribbled away for quite some time but I couldn't see what he was writing. 'Would that be *or* at the end or *our*? Right, sir. What? Oh, I'm sorry to hear that. Yes, I'll pass that along as well. She knows him, does she, sir? What a shame. Yes, *I'm* keeping very well, thank you for asking. Except for the – yes, but I'm on the mend. Get back to Lee? I suppose I should,' he winked at me, 'but we'll have a jar soon. Yes, I'd like that, sir.'

He hung up, shaking his head. 'I keep on forgetting, he hates me calling him sir but I can't shake the habit. And now we no longer work together he keeps suggesting we have a drink and talk shop but the only time we did it, he was on my back all the time just like he always was. *Why didn't you do this, why didn't you do that?* When we're face to face, he seems to forget I've been promoted.'

'So he didn't want to talk to me then?'

Richie stared at me for a second or two and from the expression on his face I couldn't make out what he was thinking. Then he smiled and said, 'No, he didn't want to talk to you but I don't think you should take offense at that.'

'You don't? Why's that?'

'I'm not a detective for nothing. The slightest hint of abnormal behavior and I'm on it.' Now he was grinning at me. 'Is there anything you want to tell me about you and Max?'

I could feel the flush rising all the way from my chest up my neck and flooding over my cheeks.

'Thought so.' Richie was triumphant. 'Cath and I always knew he had this unholy crush on you and just then I could tell he'd rather have had my food poisoning than talk to you.'

'Richie, you're not making much sense.'

'Well, it never did make much sense but it's what he does. Every single time, not that it happens very often. Cath and I have never been able to understand it. He'll meet someone, he'll fancy them – he's not too subtle about showing it although he thinks he's being cool as a cucumber. He'll take them out and then when they call the station, he'll run a mile rather than talk to them. He's one of the best they've got on the Met but he can't handle intimacy to save his life. Cath thinks he should talk to someone about it.'

'A counselor?'

'Yeah. Don't look at me like that. I know as well as you do that he'd rather slit his own wrists than see someone. I tell Cath, I say *you* tell him that's what he should do and see what you get for your trouble.'

He mimed ducking a blow from Max and I couldn't help laughing. I was half inclined to tell him that I'd brought it up with Max and that Max hadn't thrown it out of court entirely. But I had a feeling he would not want Richie to know this.

'But listen, he wants me to tell you a couple of things,' said Richie. 'One, his uncle's sick and he wasn't sure whether or not you knew. He's just spoken to him about the hospital tests, it wasn't good news apparently. Won't be long now.'

I was surprised at my reaction. I hadn't thought I had any feelings about 'old Jake' one way or another but learning that he must have been away in hospital while I was with Max at Dorcas Farm gave me a jolt.

'You wrote down a name,' I said to cover my shock, 'was that for me?'

'Yes it was. Here it is. He said to tell you he'd checked out the son-in-law – the one who had the computer in the outhouse. Does this make any sense to you? He said he went to the Registry of Births and Deaths and Maggie Blair's illegitimate daughter did get married. He thought you'd be interested in knowing who to.'

He handed me the slip of paper where he had written down the name and when I read it, it gave me a far bigger shock than learning about Jake's illness.

André Balfour.

Chapter Seventeen

Tommy insisted on driving.

He swore he knew the way to Devon, had been there count-less times and I nodded yes, OK, fine, knowing everything he said was a total lie.

But the morning papers, which he had brought up to me at the ungodly hour of six thirty – I had a terrible feeling he had run outside in his pajamas and stolen them from other people's doorsteps – had reports of massive flood damage in the West Country slapped across their front pages and Tommy said he didn't trust me on wet roads in Somerset. Why Somerset in particular I had no idea since water levels were dangerously high in Wiltshire and Dorset and – Oh Lord! – in parts of Devon.

I had gone straight back to Blenheim Crescent from Richie's, suddenly exhausted from the long drive up to London and the subsequent stress of my fleeting encounters with my mother and Cath, not to mention the shock effect of seeing Tommy again. I could hear Parkinson's familiar Yorkshire tones echoing through the house as I let myself in the front door and I fully expected to find my mother glued to the TV in the kitchen. But I had to mount the stairs to trace the sound coming from her bedroom – *my* bedroom – and I found her slumped against the pillows, her mobile still in her hand

and a glass of wine balanced on a book on the bedclothes, miraculously still upright. Until I turned off the blaring television – was she going deaf? – I couldn't hear her soft snoring, which sounded more like whistling. I removed the phone from her hand and bent over to brush her forehead with a kiss.

I didn't cry, something I would have done a few years earlier under the circumstances, because it was only at moments like these that I was able to feel really close to my mother. She murmured something as I raised the blanket up to her chin and I leaned over, hoping to hear my name.

· 'Mary Jane,' she whispered and I tiptoed to the door and left her.

Somebody, Tommy most likely, had brought my bags up from the hall and deposited them in the largest of the two bedrooms on the top floor. It had been my bedroom while I was growing up in the house and I'd had my own bathroom beside it, but an all-encompassing fire had necessitated renovations that had moved the bathroom down to what had once been a little box room on the half landing and left two antiseptic modernized rooms on the top floor. I resented being bounced upstairs to this room, partly because it increased the nostalgic longing for my teenage clutter. But my only option was a similarly barren room next door or going down and climbing into bed with my mother. So I undressed, slipped between the sheets and clenched my eyes shut, focusing on banishing from my mind sleep-denying thoughts like *Maggie Blair's baby was a girl* and *André is her son-in-law* and *why wouldn't Max speak to me?* Needless to say all attempts by Richie to get him back on the phone had failed. Richie said it was probably because he was out of range. *Yeah, right! More like he saw Richie's name on his caller ID and let it go straight to voice mail because he knew I was there.*

I must have fallen asleep eventually, otherwise how could Tommy have woken me up? Tommy is invariably at his loudest when he's trying to be quiet. I was jolted into consciousness by the sound of the front door slamming. Then

I distinctly heard him say *Oh shit!* even though he was two floors below me. It was only a matter of time before a series of agonizing creaks reverberating upward signaled that he was hefting his 200 lbs up the stairs towards me.

I knew what would happen when he got here. He was undoubtedly slightly drunk – maybe *very* drunk – and he'd stumble through the door and across the floor to flop down beside me. Even though he would think he was being careful, the springs would react to his weight causing the mattress to bob up and down in alarm. He would slide under the covers fully clothed and then attempt to undress himself, one item at a time. His rationale for this bizarre behavior was that it made less noise than if he hopped about the room on one foot, crashing into the furniture while he tried to take his pants and socks off.

There's a funny thing about familiarity. After a long period of absence, I maintain it breeds anticipation rather than contempt. To my surprise, I found I was lying there waiting for the moment when he would be beside me, the contact with my breast or hip as he endeavored to slide his pants down his legs, the inevitable *Oh sorry*, followed by the hopeful *Are you awake?*

Part of me wondered whether I wasn't trying to reclaim him just in case he'd felt the temptation to succumb to Cath's wiles. Not that she would have tried anything, would she? Was I *ever* going to stop driving myself into a state about this? I thought as I rolled into Tommy's embrace.

It wasn't urgent passionate sex, the frenzied reunion of a couple parted for nearly a year. It was the well-remembered moves of a pair of ballroom dancers proceeding comfortably to a standing ovation. And I was astonished at how satisfying it was. Only later, much later once it was over and he was snoring cheerfully away beside me – Tommy was the only person I've ever met who slept with a smile on his face and not only when he'd just had sex – did I allow myself grudgingly to admit that Tommy's very presence, clumsy and overweight though it might be, always made me feel relaxed and safe.

Tommy awoke disgustingly early, bouncing out of bed and whistling his way to the bathroom while I lay there thinking that I had to get back to Frampton Abbas as fast as possible. But even though I sent Tommy stumbling downstairs to make coffee – and steal newspapers – at six thirty, by the time we actually left the house, it was almost eleven o'clock. Tommy made breakfast and burned it and re-made it and had his bath and sung the complete works of Dolly Parton in it – repeating his favorite *Jolene* five times – and that took two hours. And then my mother wanted me to go through her entire wardrobe with her to find something she could wear to her benefit, although of course in the end she said she'd have to go out and buy something new and I knew that was what she had intended all along.

As we were finally leaving the house, with my mother remembering rather belatedly to ask after Gussie before disappearing upstairs without even saying goodbye, we encountered a pleasant-faced woman coming up the steps to the front door. She exuded the same kind of casual chic my mother had adopted when the Phillionaire started paying her bills. On a shopping trip in New York, I'd once had a disastrous conversation with my mother about the price of clothes and it had dawned on me that when she said *I don't want to spend more than fifteen,* she was talking thousands, not hundreds. Although to someone like myself, to whom a splurge meant ordering the most expensive item in the Boden catalogue, even fifteen *hundred* pounds was a serious stretch.

Tommy followed me out of the door carrying far too much stuff and inevitably his laptop and the sweaters he was clutching to his chest began to slip from his grasp. The woman caught the laptop just in time before it smashed to the pavement, and dropping her own capacious bit of Prada to the ground – I could recognize quality even if I couldn't afford it

285

– she even managed to break the fall of the sweaters. I relieved her of the laptop and carried it to the car.

'Beautiful cashmere,' I heard her say and, turning, saw her raise the sweaters to her cheek. She mentioned a designer who was clearly so far out of my price range I didn't even know the name and, to my amazement, Tommy nodded. 'This man has great taste,' she told me as I returned to the steps, 'you'd better hang on to him. If he's yours, that is?' She was smiling and it was clear that she was joking but I could tell she was waiting for my answer.

I didn't give her one, because what could I tell her? *He was mine but I let him go*.

'Not going to tell me?' She was going to play this out for as long as she could. 'You're off on a trip somewhere? Together? Not together? He's taking six hundred pound cashmeres, you're wearing five-year-old jeans. One of you is more interested in money than the other. That has to be *your* car?' She pointed at my mud-spattered little Renault Clio, 'because I'd put *him* in an Audi at the very least.'

It was odd but I wasn't offended. In fact I liked this woman's nosiness, I understood it. Being a ghostwriter, you have to be interested in other people and what makes them tick. You have to be prepared to subsume your own personality under someone else's and the fact that this woman was not afraid to point out the kinds of things I often longed to draw to people's attention about my own subjects, but rarely dared to, was refreshing to me. I wondered who she was.

'Can I help you?' I asked her.

'I'm here to see Vanessa Bartholomew. I think I have the right address. We spoke last night and she said to come round for coffee.'

I was about to say *I'm her daughter* but something stopped me.

'And you are?'

'Mary Jane Markham.' She held out her hand and I was surprised she could hold it up given the weight of the diamonds and sapphires dotted across her fingers. I liked her smile and the way she was sizing me up with a knowing look. I had a feeling she knew exactly who I was.

'I'll just give her a yell,' I said without identifying myself, 'she's upstairs but she'll be right down. Forgive me for not taking you in but we're late leaving as it is.'

'Not a problem,' she said, 'I can take care of myself.'

Understatement of the year, I suspected. 'Mum!' I shouted again, realizing too late that I'd just given myself away. 'Mary Jane Markham's here.'

'I get it,' she said, 'this was just a fleeting visit to see your mother and you're on your way back to Devon. But don't think you're getting away from me!' She laughed and wagged her only ring-free finger at me in mock severity. 'Seriously,' she added, 'I'll do what I can to help your mother even though the boot's on the other foot, so to speak. That's why I want to do a book. All women going through a divorce can learn from my experience.'

Something struck me. 'Your divorce lawyer,' I asked Mary Jane Markham, 'it wasn't Mickey Beresford by any chance, was it?'

'No way!' She shook her head vehemently. 'He's a complete shit – and unethical too, so my lawyer told me. I'm thinking of including a few telling details about him in my book if I can get around the libel aspects.'

Are you? I thought. *That's interesting. Maybe Gussie can help you with your research.*

'Well, goodbye,' I said, passing her on the steps. 'Tommy! What are you doing in the driving seat?'

'Hang on to him,' I heard her say again and the urgency in her voice made me turn back to her. This time she wasn't smiling. 'He's a keeper,' she said, 'and not just because of the cashmeres. You only have to look at him. My guess is you're the one who's trouble.'

I let Tommy drive because I wanted to make a speedy getaway before my mother appeared and detained us. I spent the first hour yelling at him to stay on the left-hand side of the road – a year living in America had programmed him to veer to the right – and by then I was so exhausted, I started nodding off as we began to cruise smoothly along the motorway.

I slept for a long time and awoke to find we were now driving through Somerset on the A303 approaching Wincanton. I studied Tommy's profile for a minute or two before he noticed I was no longer asleep. I couldn't quite say how exactly, but he had definitely changed. It was probably a figment of my imagination but I felt his face had hardened somewhat during the year we had been apart. He was wearing an American baseball cap pulled down low over his forehead so I couldn't really point to additional lines there. It was more the firm set of his mouth and the fact that although he was still pudgy, he had definitely lost weight so, instead of his jowls descending into the flopping dewlaps I remembered, his profile now presented the distinctive jut of his chin.

He'd made love to me the night before but we hadn't said a word about it this morning. We'd be at Frampton Abbas in an hour and I still hadn't told him what had been going on there. For all he knew we were on our way to hang out with Gussie, no particular agenda. I hadn't even told him about André and the fact that we might find him ensconced in Gussie's house when we arrived.

And what was I going to do about Max's bombshell? I had to tell Gussie as quickly as possible but it was going to be hard if she were still in a state of obsession about André. Maybe it would help if Tommy knew what was going on and could back me up.

He listened carefully as I filled him in on everything that had happened since I first arrived in Devon. It was typical of him that he barely reacted to the news that two women had died and I suspected they had been murdered, didn't express the kind of shock/horror protest that I would have made under the circumstances but merely nodded his head and glanced at me a few times. The only thing I left out was the time I had spent with Max at Dorcas Farm, although I told him of Max's visit to Jake and how he had thrown up Neil Mackay and André, and even Jake, as possible suspects. And then I explained about Neil Mackay's own theory that his wife could have been responsible for Melanie's death.

'But what would be *her* motive for killing Rosemary Waters?' I said. 'The fact that the two women were both lured to their deaths by emails from Mr Wright – there *has* to be a connection there.'

I waited several minutes for Tommy's take on the information I'd given him. He was a bit of a slowcoach when it came to sharp insights, but I'd come to the conclusion that by this stage any fresh view was worth hearing. But when he finally spoke, what he said was so unexpected, it almost gave me a seizure.

'So did you sleep with Max Austin?'

I was so shaken, I failed to fully react. I didn't come out with a string of *What are you talking about? Why on earth would you think that? Of course I didn't sleep with him.* I just answered simply – with the truth.

'No.'

'Aren't you going to ask me why I wanted to know that?'

Tommy's question was maddening in its accuracy at reading my mind, something in which he had always managed to excel. I was tempted to just say *no* again but of course I couldn't.

'Don't bother, I'll tell you anyway,' he said and this infuriated me even more. 'I didn't have sex with Cath yesterday despite what it looked like—'

'I know,' I said. I was convinced by now that nothing had happened. 'It was—'

'Don't interrupt, let me finish for once in my life.'

I looked at him, astonished. This forcefulness was unlike Tommy.

'I was so tired coming off that overnight flight and Cath and I – we didn't even have a chance to talk before we both fell asleep – but that doesn't mean we *haven't* talked. Before then. Over the phone. You know something, Lee? I was wretched when you walked out on me in America and came back here. I needed someone to talk it over with, someone who knew you as well as I did, someone who could help me figure it out.'

'She never told me.' I stared out through the windscreen. Why did it always come back to Cath? She might have got over her infatuation with Tommy but she still managed to reach out with her tentacles and draw him into her orbit. It was the fact that she did it behind my back that disturbed me. 'And anyway there was nothing she could tell you about Max and me because until last week I hadn't even spoken to him.'

'No, but you wanted to, didn't you?'

I couldn't work out where Tommy was going with this. He wasn't taunting me with the bitterness of a jealous lover. He sounded quite relaxed as if he might have been teasing me about hankering after another piece of forbidden chocolate cake.

'You think I don't know anything about Max Austin,' he went on, 'but Cath and Richie used to joke about the crush he had on you and then she told me you'd seen him when you went back to London to sort out your visa, had an intimate lunch with him, she said. Anyway she picked up on something then and it was right after that visit that you left me and came back to London for good. I'm not a fool, you know, Lee.'

He reminded me of Gussie and her eternal attempt to persuade us that she was not *completely* hopeless – except that there was something in Tommy's voice that told me he was *telling* me, not trying to persuade me.

'OK, I saw him, and yes, OK, I *wanted* to see him.' Suddenly it was important to make Tommy understand there was nothing going on between Max and me. Before I knew what I was doing, I was telling Tommy about running into Max at the bridge as we were both about to cross the river, about the kiss and the subsequent return to Dorcas Farm.

Resisting the temptation to go into too much detail, I took him through the episode on the staircase and then into the sparse little bedroom and on to the scratchy horsehair mattress. I couldn't look at Tommy. I just had to get it all out. I felt the need to be brutally honest with him.

'But when it got to the crucial moment,' I said and I could sense Tommy leaning away from the wheel towards me because my voice had dropped to a whisper, 'nothing happened.'

'Not even a little—?'

I raised my hand.

'That's it, Tommy. I'm not going into it any further than that. You'll just have to take my word for it.'

He pursed his lips together in an exaggerated clamp down and we drove in silence for a few miles. A silence I broke, as I'm sure he'd known I would.

'There's no need for you to be jealous,' I burst out, 'none at all.'

'I know,' he said, sounding annoyingly smug. 'Even if something did happen, from what I've heard, he's not right for you anyway.'

I was so angry at this – partly because there was a certain amount of truth in it – that I opted to change the subject altogether before I totally lost it with him.

'So, what brought you over here? Apart from Cath's birthday, I mean. Are you taking a break from karaoke?'

'Oh, I've been taking a break from karaoke for quite a while,' he said. 'I quit Long Island and that whole beach/bar/karaoke scene. I'm living in New York these days. I thought you knew. And I'm over here because my visa ran out. I have to leave the country every three months – last time I went to Canada and back but this time I thought I'd take advantage of Cath having a big birthday to come to London.'

No mention of wanting to see me. 'Except you missed the part where she said she didn't want to do anything for that birthday. So what in the world are you doing in New York? I don't know how I'm supposed to know you've moved if you didn't bother telling me.' I was aware I sounded waspish but I was furious. He must have let Cath know in one of their little transatlantic chats. Couldn't she have told me?

'I'm working in artiste management, learning the ropes.'

'You're *whaaat*? How did you manage to get a gig like that?'

'Don't sound so surprised. I think I'm going to be quite good at it actually. There's this woman out on the island, she heard me doing karaoke one night, told me I had a sensational voice—'

'Tommy,' I said carefully, not wanting him to take it the wrong way, 'you have an OK voice. I admit I was amazed at how good you turned out to be at karaoke, but having listened to you singing in the bath for almost nine years years, I'm here to tell you, you do *not* have a *sensational* voice. Not by any stretch of the imagination.'

'No, well, OK. You're right. I think she was probably shooting me a line but we got talking and she bought me a drink—'

'*She* bought *you* a drink?'

'That's what I said and she told me she was in artiste management, had her own business in New York—'

'And she wanted to know if she could represent you?'

'Well, no, she didn't actually. She never mentioned that.' It was hard to tell from his profile under his baseball cap but I thought he looked a bit crestfallen that she obviously hadn't thought his voice was *that* sensational. 'But we chatted and the more she told me about her job, the more I liked the sound of it, you know, working with singers and that. By the end of the evening I was asking her if there was any chance it might be something I could get into.'

'How long—'

'Six months now. I'm just a lowly dogsbody at the moment, running errands for the artistes, meeting them at the airport, accompanying them to rehearsals, dry cleaning, coffee, that sort of thing. But Shannon says she's got plans for me.'

'Shannon. Like the river in Ireland?'

'Yes,' he beamed at me, 'Shannon Sonnenschein. Melodic, isn't it?'

Not to me, I thought uncharitably. 'So she owns this business?'

'She's mega successful,' he said with a reverence that for some reason annoyed me intensely. 'You should see her apartment on Central Park West. It's got rooms she never even goes into, and she's got a place out in the Hamptons for the summer. Must be worth millions. She was out there when she saw me singing—'

This didn't sound at all like the Tommy I knew. I'd never heard him bring up real estate before. One of the things I'd always found so refreshing about him was his total lack of interest in status. He was secure enough that he never bothered to think what his car said about him – or his home or his clothes for that matter. I liked that about him and now it seemed his year in America had transformed him into a yet another lifestyle-conscious clone.

'So have you slept with Shannon Sonnenschein?' Let's see how he liked it when the boot was on the other foot.

'Just the once,' he said and I wished I hadn't asked. 'Just that first night. We were both pretty drunk. I mean she's quite a bit older than I am but she's amazingly well preserved. She was telling me all about the work she's had done, she's not in the least ashamed of it. She even said maybe I ought to think about getting—'

'Tommy,' I said firmly, more to stop him divulging further details of Shannon Sonnenschein's anatomical adjustments than anything else, 'you do not need cosmetic surgery. You're just fine the way you are.'

He preened in the rearview mirror and I clenched my fists.

'So you're not mad then, about me and Shannon?'

'I don't own you, Tommy.'

'I wish you did.' He said it very quietly and he reached over to cover my hand with his. 'I'm going to come clean and admit there were other girls – younger – every now and then. They came up to me at karaoke, what could I do? You were gone and I'm a bloke.'

'Are you sure, Tommy? I thought you were an ape.'

'Don't tease me, Lee. This is serious. Even though you walked away from me, every time I sleep with someone else I feel like I'm being unfaithful to you.'

This was presumably what Mary Jane Markham had meant by him being a keeper.

'I'm not like your dad,' he looked at me, 'I couldn't be married and have affairs all over the place.'

His hand was still covering mine but I pulled it away. What on earth was he trying to tell me? That he felt like he was married to me so that was why he felt guilty when he had sex with someone else? But why bring my father into it? Unless—

'Is my father having an affair?'

'I didn't know whether you knew? I didn't know whether I should tell you.'

You just did, Tommy. Mr Blurt-it-out strikes again.

'Who is she?'

'Oh, I don't know *that*. I'm not sure your mother even knows who it is. She just called me up a couple of weeks ago and asked me to have lunch with her. She said she'd seen them in Central Park walking hand in hand round the reservoir. I mean, is your father stupid or what? He and your mother *live* on Central Park. Couldn't he have taken it to another part of town?'

'So it's OK by you if he has an affair providing he takes it *to another part of town*? You feel bad when you cheat on me and you didn't sound too happy about Max and me even though I've told you nothing happened, but my father's adultery, that's a whole different ball game?'

'Your mother said you'd take it badly. That's why she's come to London, to tell you she's going to ask him for a divorce.'

'She never said a word about it,' I said. *Oh God, it was all my fault. If Mary Jane Markham hadn't called me – but wait a second, my mother had told Tommy she wanted a divorce before she came to London.* 'Maybe you shouldn't have told me, Tommy. And besides, seeing someone holding hands with someone isn't grounds for divorce. My father might have been comforting the woman about a bereavement or something. You shouldn't get so worked up.'

'I know,' he said, surprising me, 'but I've got this thing about fidelity. I want someone who'll be the *only* one for me. It doesn't do anything for me, this running around. It never did. I suppose I'm not like most blokes, I'm a bit weird in that respect but I can't help it.'

'If my dad's up to his old tricks again then he's an idiot. You'd think he'd give it a rest now he's in his seventies,' I said, wishing I hadn't left my mother all alone with Mary Jane Markham. 'But I can't believe Mum would want a divorce at this late stage.'

'Unless she doesn't love him anymore,' said Tommy and again I wished he'd kept his mouth shut. There were times when I wondered if she'd *ever* loved my father but it wasn't something I liked to dwell on.

'Stop the car!' I said suddenly. We had long since come off the motorway and were bowling along the top of Exmoor.

'Why?' Tommy didn't even slow down.

'Please, Tommy! I want you to turn around and go down that track on the other side of the road.'

It was the road that led off the crest of Exmoor down the valley to Dorcas Farm. Seeing it had reminded me of Max's message to me about Jake being sick. It made sense to take this opportunity to pop down and see how he was.

Nothing to do with the fact that he might have news of Max. Nothing at all.

I made Tommy stop the near side of the cattle grid to avoid the Renault getting stuck in the mud. Although from the way the rain had almost flooded the area around the house, I discerned that only an amphibious vehicle could have made it through.

'Where are we?' Tommy sounded suspicious.

'Dorcas Farm, where Jake Austin lives. He's ill and I want to pay him a quick visit.'

'Well, you're on your own. I'm staying put. That's where you spent the night with whatsisname, isn't it?'

'But nothing happened. I told you.'

'OK, so maybe you didn't have full-on sex with him but don't kid yourself nothing happened – because I know you too well. I can tell from your voice that there was something going on. But, given the way you were with me, I'm OK with it because I can tell it's over. I just don't want to go poking round there like it's open to the public or something.'

I was secretly relieved. I didn't think I could face Jake's inevitable dissection of my relationship with Tommy. I opened the car door and gingerly began to lower my feet but I saw instantly that I would be up to my calves in mud.

'Oh for God's sake, my shoes are sturdier than yours.' And without a second thought he leapt out of the car, waded around to my side and plucked me from it into his arms. He carried me up to the front entrance, deposited me on the doorstep and marched away again. I watched him squelching through the mud, aware that his shoes were probably ruined, and hoped they hadn't cost the kind of money that would give them the Mary Jane Markham stamp of approval.

Jake didn't answer the door but I'd seen the Land Rover by the side of the house so he had to be there. I tried the handle, hoping I wouldn't have to summon Tommy to carry me round the back. But it turned and I stepped into the hall.

'Jake!'

I wandered into the kitchen calling his name. His wellingtons weren't by the door so maybe he was out in the barn. Well, I wasn't going to struggle out there and contend with chickens' blood and whatever other gory country details I might encounter.

For some reason, try as I might, I couldn't conjure up Max's presence in the kitchen. I sat down at the table and tried to picture his stooping frame in front of me, trying to fit itself into the alcove around the Aga.

But I couldn't. My mind refused to dwell on his image long enough for me to relive our conversation, let alone how he'd looked. Instead the vision of a burly cuddly figure loomed before my eyes, resting his butt on the Aga and leaping away like a scalded bear when the heat seared through his jeans.

Tommy.

I went upstairs, shouting Jake's name as I did so just in case he was up there. I wanted to see if I could summon up Max in the sad little bedroom and I didn't want to have to explain to Jake what I was doing in there.

But my phantom Tommy followed me there too. He lay down on the mattress with me and the horsehair scratched the butt he had just burned on the Aga and he maintained that he was just going to have to lie on top of me to protect his soft and sensitive skin and I laughed and drew him down into—

I leapt up and ran out of the room feeling very confused. The door to Jake's bedroom was open and I wandered into it without thinking. His bed was unmade, the gaudy satin bedspread pulled aside to reveal less than pristine sheets. His pajamas were on the floor lying next to a pile of washing waiting to be taken downstairs. The trousers and jacket he must have worn for his trip to hospital in Exeter were hanging in a haphazard fashion over the bedstead. They were good quality, I noticed, not up to Mary Jane Markham standard, but not cheap.

Somewhere at the back of my mind I recalled that Jake was sick and had more important things on his mind than taking care of his clothes. So, wanting to try and do something for him, I picked up the jacket and the trousers and moved to the closet to hang them up.

The poster of the naked woman had been restored to its place on the inside of the door, the four corners showing evidence that it had been once been torn down in a hurry. Jake's clothes dropped from my hands as I stared at it, taking in the details I had not had time to register before.

The woman was naked and she was lying across the bed in a highly provocative position. It crossed my mind that she was trying to recreate the famous photograph of Marilyn Monroe stretched across a red satin bedspread.

A *satin* bedspread.

I turned and looked at Jake's bed and knew immediately that this was where the woman had been posing and that Jake had taken the photograph. The woman was pouting suggestively at the camera and a hand was cupped under one of her breasts, pointing the nipple at the camera.

But it was the caramel color of the woman's skin that caught my attention more than anything else. I felt myself reaching out to touch it as I studied the almond-shaped eyes, the slight thickness of the lips and the wide and flaring nostrils of the woman's Afro-Caribbean face.

I never imagined she would be this beautiful, I thought as I heard the sound of Jake's footsteps on the stairs.

It was bad enough that he caught me in his bedroom but I could feel myself blushing scarlet with shame when he entered the room before I could shut the closet door.

But he seemed almost resigned to the fact that I had seen what I had.

'That's Sadie,' he said and his voice was sad and on the point of breaking. 'Max ripped it down, of course, but I can have her back there now he's gone.'

Chapter Eighteen

'Looks like you've had some sex since I last saw you.' Jake didn't miss a trick. 'Your skin's glowing and you look like a different woman.'

Of course he'd hit the proverbial nail on the head and I could feel the flush spreading across my face.

'Come downstairs,' he said, grinning. 'I'll make you a cup of tea and you can tell me all about it. I have to say I didn't expect any visitors on a day like this. Not that I get visitors at all these days, as you know. But this rain, it never stops and I admit I'm worried. It gets to the point where you begin to think the earth won't be able to contain it and it's going to come back up and sweep you away.'

'The river will flood?'

'Undoubtedly. I heard it was about ready to burst its banks down in Frampton Abbas anyway.'

And I'll bet Gussie's done nothing about installing flood gates, I thought as I followed him down the narrow staircase where I finally had an unwelcome flash of Max unhooking my bra.

'But it's not just the river,' he was staring out of the window at the rain coming down, 'it's the streams and all those springs hidden away that nobody knows about. Everyone's attention will be on the river and they'll forget about those sneaky trickles running outside through their backyards, being fed by some source that's probably overflowed long before the river. That water's probably already rising up under floorboards and into cellars in Frampton Abbas. So who's the lucky fellow, eh?'

'Tell me about Sadie,' I said sharply, shaking my head to show him I wasn't about to give him any details of my night of passion.

He turned his back on me to put the kettle on the hob.

'Sadie,' he repeated. He must have dropped a million hints but never would I have dreamed that he was her mystery lover, the one who – and here I flinched at the awful realization – must have made her pregnant.

'Sit down.' He motioned to a chair. 'I'm going to tell you everything whether you want to hear it or not. I've been wanting to tell someone ever since she died.'

I hadn't bargained for this. I had come to see Jake because I had learned he was sick. I wasn't even sure whether I was here out of genuine concern for his welfare or because he was Max's uncle, but whichever it was I seemed to have blundered into an area where I might find myself totally out of my depth.

'I couldn't help it,' said Jake. 'I admit I always nurtured a bit of a hankering after her, she was so gorgeous, and when she called up out of the blue and asked if she could come down and spend some time with me, it just sort of went to my head. I told myself she wasn't interested in *me*, that she just picked me to visit because she could talk to me about Max. But once she was here, upstairs, sleeping in the next room,' he raised his eyes to the ceiling, shaking his head, 'I couldn't help myself. We'd sit up late, drinking, with her pouring her heart out about Max and me listening and wanting her more and more every time she opened her mouth. And then we'd go upstairs to bed and about a week after she'd arrived we were standing in her doorway, saying goodnight and she flung her arms around me – *Thank you for being so understanding* – all that sort of thing. What was I supposed to do?'

'But she must have been so vulnerable,' I said, horrified. 'You took advantage of her.'

'You're right.' He made no attempt to deny it. 'But – and I'll never understand why – she didn't fight me off. She came into my bedroom willingly, that night and the next and the next until she moved in altogether. She was literally *craving* affection. Max had been starving her. I'm telling you, *starving* her.'

'Still,' I said.

'Still what?' he said angrily. 'Those months we were together we gave each other a lot of comfort, I know we did. I'm not saying she loved me but I'd never had warmth like that from any woman. OK, so it was probably my own fault. I didn't earn my reputation for nothing and Exmoormates, it's nothing but an online knocking shop if you ask me. But she was different. She responded to my heart and my mind as well as my decrepit old body. Goodness knows what would have happened if she hadn't—'

He stopped because of course as far as he knew I hadn't a clue about the baby.

'Become pregnant?'

He was pouring boiling water from the kettle into the teapot and he almost scalded himself. 'You knew?'

'Max told me she was pregnant when she died. But he doesn't know who the father was. Or did you tell him?'

'No,' Jake looked at me, 'no, I never did. But I've had that photo up inside my closet ever since she died and he could have seen it. The day after he arrived I came home and found it ripped down. There was a strong wind blowing outside and I'd left the window and the closet door open. The photo was lying across the other side of the room. He could have come in and seen it, torn it off the door, or it could have blown down. All I know is the next day he went stomping off across the moors every day. That's Max for you. If he did see it, he wouldn't challenge me, well not immediately anyway.'

'But he doesn't know who killed her.'

He looked at me without saying anything and I saw that his eyes had gone dead.

'Jake,' I said, 'do *you* know who killed her?'

Again he was silent, his face frozen. Then he began to speak, very fast and very softly so I had to lean forward to catch what he said.

'What is it about you, Lee? When I first saw you at Maggie's funeral I had you pegged as someone who wasn't going to go away. I knew it was only a matter of time before you got it all out of me.'

'I haven't got anything out of you,' I said. 'I'm still waiting.'

'I'd gone to Exeter for the day,' he said, 'and I came back and found an empty bottle of pills right there where you're sitting. And half the contents of what had been a full bottle of whisky gone. I don't know if she was trying to get rid of the baby or if she wanted to kill herself because of it. *She never told me she was pregnant.*' Now his anguish was apparent but he recovered almost immediately.

'She killed *herself*?' I hadn't seen that coming. 'You found her upstairs?'

He shook his head. 'She wasn't in the house. I went out and searched for the rest of the day, roaming the moors. I blame myself—'

'You didn't call the police?' I interrupted.

'I found her just as it was getting dark and I had no idea how long she'd been out there. She'd crawled under a bale of hay to die, not far from Marjorie's farm over the hill.'

'You should have gone for help!' I shouted at him. 'Why didn't you call someone, the police, anyone, even Marjorie?'

'She'd left her little dog shut in the house here,' he said, not answering my question. 'If she'd just gone out for a walk, she'd never have left Pixie behind.'

'But they said she was strangled.'

Jake didn't say anything for a while. Then he got up and walked into the larder, returning with a biscuit tin. He opened

302

it and took out a cigarette from what must be his emergency stash and lighted it.

'She was. I strangled her.'

'What do you mean? She died from an overdose, you just said so.'

'She took an overdose. She didn't die from it.'

'Well, then why didn't you rush her to hospital when you found her?'

'BECAUSE I THOUGHT SHE WAS DEAD!' Now he was yelling at me, on his feet and stabbing his cigarette so that the ash floated towards me.

'When I found her lying there unconscious, I went berserk. I don't know what came over me but I lost control. How could she do this to me, to Max? I didn't realize what I was doing. I clasped her by the head and shook her, trying to bring her back to life and my hands slipped down to her neck. I was trying to shake her awake and I went on and on and there were these great red weals all over her throat. I had these gloves on that were made of some coarse material and they did more damage than anything else.'

I couldn't help glancing at his hands. I'd noticed before how large they were – not soft fleshy paws like Tommy's but strong-looking with wide palms and long fingers and thumbs that I could picture encircling a throat and pressing on a wind-pipe. I'd read that it takes only ten seconds of pressure on the carotid arteries for someone to lose consciousness and a further fifty seconds before they suffer fatal oxygen depriva-tion. And from the sounds of things Jake pounded her for well over minute.

'But how—' I began.

'SHE WASN'T DEAD!' he said. 'I was shaking her and yelling at her for what she'd done. I could have saved her but instead I killed her without even realizing what I was doing. I didn't even know I'd strangled her until all the details came out afterwards.'

'What do you mean?'

'The pathologist wasn't happy with his autopsy findings. He said they were inconclusive. The toxicology report showed that she'd swallowed the pills and the whisky but apparently he wasn't entirely convinced that that was the cause of her death. Max was feeding me information on an almost hourly basis.'

'And then they found that she'd been strangled?'

Jake nodded. 'They discovered that a tiny bone had been broken in her neck and that was what killed her. Death by manual strangulation. I'd throttled her.'

I could barely look at him. How did I know he wasn't lying? How could I be sure he hadn't strangled her, intentionally, right here in this kitchen and taken her broken body out to the fields and dumped it there?

'So if it was an accident,' I said, 'did you rush back here and report it?' Max hadn't said anything about Jake being the one who had found Sadie's body.

'No,' he said.

'You didn't do *any*thing?' I hoped he could see how appalled I was from the look on my face.

'I panicked. When I realized what I'd done, that she really was dead, I left her where she was. I'd as good as murdered her and I thought they would know it was me as soon as they found her because it was no secret she'd spent so much time with me. I thought they'd come for me. I sat here day after day waiting for the knock on the door. But that detective who headed up the investigation, he was worse than useless. When he came here to question me, I left the gloves I'd had on lying right here on this table. I *wanted* him to notice them. I must have left fibres or something and I know Max had his suspicions.'

'Well, why didn't he do something?'

'I'm his uncle,' said Jake simply. 'We're all the family we've got – each of us.'

'And you're bloody lucky to have him,' I shouted. 'He cares for you a damn sight more than you seem to do for him.

304

He made sure I knew you were sick. That's why I'm here. You went away to hospital, didn't you? For tests?'

He nodded, his face betraying nothing. 'It's my pancreas. Could be just a matter of months. It's the real reason I got Max down here. I didn't tell him, well not until this last hospital visit. When he saw you at The Pelican, he assumed that's why I'd called him and I let you both think that. Anything happen, by the way, while I was gone?' There was a trace of a smile on his face.

I ignored his question. 'I'm very sorry, Jake.' I forced the words out because I wasn't at all sure that I *was* sorry.

He shrugged. 'We've all got to go sometime and since Sadie went I haven't enjoyed a single moment of my life. Max says he'll take a break, come down here to be with me, you know – at the end.' He looked at me and nodded when he saw the amazement on my face. 'Yeah, I know. Took me by surprise and all but he offered. Shows there's something human buried in there somewhere. Said he'd even take poor old Willow if she doesn't go before me, although what kind of a life she'd have with him out chasing killers all day and night, I dread to think.'

His mention of Willow made me remember another grisly detail of Sadie's death.

'Her dog. I heard it was cut up into pieces and scattered around the field where they found her.'

To my utmost horror, he nodded. 'I left her body and came back to this yapping creature in my kitchen. I shut it in the barn but I could still hear it in here. I couldn't take it anymore so I got blind drunk and I gave it a chop to the neck just like Maggie tried to teach me to do with the rabbits when we were kids. She must have taught me well even though I didn't have the guts to follow through back then. I dispatched Pixie with the first chop then I had to dispose of her body.'

I was sickened by the slight gleam in his eye. I had the distinct feeling that he was enjoying telling me about Pixie.

'I carried her out into the yard, thought about throwing her into the log splitter but it would have been too bloody. So I took her into the barn and butchered her just like I do the rabbits and the hares, only smaller pieces. Chop, chop, chop, all neat and tidy and then I gathered her up into a plastic bag and took her back to be with Sadie. Just emptied the bag and the wind did the rest.'

I stood up. I couldn't take much more of this. 'You're a coward and you're a miserable bastard. A *murdering* bastard. Even if it was an accident, you still killed her by not going for help.' I knew part of me was berating him for what he'd done to Max, for the tragedy that had turned Max into the way he was. 'You've ruined Max's life!'

'I never meant it to—'

'You're despicable,' I said and I ran to the back door because I knew I had to get out of there as fast as I could. Before he had time to stop me, I had slipped out of my flimsy shoes and climbed into his giant wellington boots standing by the door. It would be a lie to say I made a run for it. Jake's boots were so big, all I could do was hobble around the side of the house, lugging my feet through the mud and across the yard to the cattle grid. Jake wasn't likely to follow me in his stocking feet and I was banking on making it to the car before he found another pair of boots. What he'd done to Sadie's dog confirmed what I had always suspected – that he had a sadistic streak in him. And if he hadn't intended to kill Sadie, why hadn't he called for help?

Tommy was asleep at the wheel with his mouth hanging open and his breath misting up the window. I climbed into the passenger seat and pummeled him, shouting at him to drive away.

'What happened, what's the matter?' He was alert in a matter of seconds, almost bludgeoning me with questions as he reversed the car back up the track to the road. 'Why are you in such a state? Those boots are not a good look for you, by the way.'

I didn't answer him. I was in a state of shock over what I had learned.

'All right, don't talk to me then,' said Tommy, his voice showing signs of descent into one of his huffs. 'I fly all the way across the Atlantic to see you, I drive you all the way down here at the drop of a hat and what do you do? Ignore me. How to make a bloke feel special the Lee Bartholomew way.'

'Shut up, Tommy,' I said, rising to the bait as usual, although I was so edgy that anything he said was bound to wind me up. Was Jake telling the truth or had he meant to strangle her? Had Sadie really taken an overdose or had he killed her in a crime of passion? And would anyone believe me if I told them what he'd said?

There was only one person who might take me seriously and that was Max and I couldn't see myself getting hold of him in a hurry.

'I'm bloody starving.' Tommy's voice penetrated my thoughts. 'I hope Gussie can rustle up something to eat as soon as we walk through the door.'

'I wouldn't count on it,' I said without bothering to tell him that, without me there to fill it, Gussie's fridge was bound to be empty. 'But hang on, I see light at the end of the tunnel. Pull in over there.'

We had arrived at Frampton Abbas and were driving slowly down the High Street. It was Sunday and The Pelican was closed but there was a light on. Leaving Tommy to follow, I crossed the road and walked in to find the restaurant empty. But a mouth-watering aroma of lamb and herbs – I detected rosemary and thyme – and butter and onions wafted toward me and I saw André in the kitchen beaming happily at the contents of a giant skillet.

'Hey!' He appeared delighted to see me and even went so far as to mouth an air kiss in my direction. 'Just in time to help me clear up.' He nodded at the grimy collection of pots and pans that had accumulated over every available surface. 'We're closed but as you know, I never take a day off and I've had this earth-shattering idea. I'm going to serve shepherd's pie. We won't be able to keep them away – it's the *perfect* winter dish. I don't know why I never thought of it before. You take a lamb shoulder and some—'

'I know what shepherd's pie is, André,' I said dryly.

'Not how I make it, you don't, not with herbs and nutmeg and lashings of butter in the mashed potatoes. Of course the trick is in the packaging. I'm going to serve it with a loaf of crusty bread and the freshest greenest salad you've ever seen. Anyway,' he saw the skepticism on my face, 'it's worth the old college try at least. So I guess you've come back to hear my story? All the way from London. I'm impressed.'

He was right – but not in the way he imagined. I wanted to know how in the world he came to be Maggie Blair's son-in-law and why he'd never mentioned it? But then hadn't I always had a sneaky feeling that André's was the story I wanted to hear? Probably because up to now he had refused to tell it but then who knew? Maybe what he would divulge would turn out to be the basis of my next ghosting assignment.

'I need a drink,' I said, 'and don't ask me why.'

André shrugged and pointed to the bar – *help yourself* – but he did raise his eyebrows a little when he saw me pour myself a large Scotch.

'You're Maggie Blair's son-in-law,' I said. I was hoping to catch him off guard and I succeeded. He gripped the handle of the skillet, holding on to it as if he needed it to anchor him.

'There's someone trying to get in the door. It must have slammed and locked behind you. Go tell them we're closed on Sunday, will you?'

He was buying time, clearly wondering how to deal with my discovery, but when I turned, Tommy was indeed standing outside and making the kind of idiotic faces you do when you're shouting at someone and don't realize they can't hear you.

'Oh, that's Tommy,' I said, 'he's my—' and I stopped because what role should I give Tommy in my life? He was no longer my fiancé. Boyfriend sounded too lame, as if we'd known each other a year instead of nine. Friend implied a platonic relationship and that didn't quite work after last night. 'He's with me,' I said finally as I moved to let him in, 'and he's starving.'

'Well, he can be a guinea pig for the first batch I'm about to get out of the oven. Does he like shepherd's pie?'

'He'll eat anything.' I said. 'He'd be happy if you just scraped the mashed potato off the top and gave him that.'

'Not exactly a man after my own heart then.' André's face fell. 'OK, I'll feed him – and you too, if you like –and then you and I will talk. Alone.'

I made Tommy remove his shoes encrusted with Dorcas Farm mud before he came in and devoured the shepherd's pie as if he hadn't eaten anything for days, and he downed several beers along with it. He was still jet lagged, I realized, when instead of chattering away like he usually did when he met someone new, he appeared sluggish, even a little morose.

'It's time we got you to Gussie's so you can go back to sleep,' I said. 'Is she at the house, André?'

'I guess she must be,' he said. 'I ran into Sylvia on my way here and she said she was popping by to give Gussie a lesson on how to instal her floodgates.' He chuckled and patted Tommy on the shoulder. 'You want to stay out of that one, but if you want some shuteye, why don't you go upstairs and lie down on my futon while Lee and I have a chat down here?'

Once we'd got Tommy settled, upstairs and out of the way, André made me a cappuccino and led me into the restaurant. 'Let's sit in here and pretend we're customers for once. So how did you find out – about Maggie being my mother-in-law?'

I told him as quickly as I could, feeling uncomfortable under the steady gaze of his green eyes. Sitting close to him at a table in the window, I could smell both the pine-scented bath essence that Gussie never quite managed to erase from her tub and the slight onion tang that lingered on his fingers.

'I never exactly hid it from you,' he said, 'that Maggie and I were related. I was at her funeral and Gussie must have told you I used to take her meals now and then. I just didn't spell it out. Look.' He leaned toward me and very gently rubbed my cheek. He wasn't making a move on me. I suspected it was just a gesture intended to bring us together and it made me think that he was preparing me in some way, that what he had to tell me must be very serious. 'Let me start at the beginning and then you'll get the whole picture.'

'OK,' I said.

'You remember what I told you about how I was raised by my grandmother and how she taught me to cook. And then when she died I left New Hampshire and got myself a job as a dishwasher in a seafood restaurant on the Massachusetts coast?'

I nodded. 'You said you were just like me – starting out at the bottom of the heap. But you said that they told you if you went back the following summer, you'd be re-hired and promoted to a line cook. Is that what's going to happen to me?'

'You don't want that to happen to you,' he said, not really answering my question. 'But if you remember that then you'll also remember that I didn't take them up on their offer, that I came to Europe and never went back to the United States. Not once.'

I did remember. That's when I had sensed he had a story. I raised my eyebrows at him. *Why?*

'I killed a man.'

He had a good sense of timing, I noticed. Instead of charging ahead with his story, he sat back to gauge my reaction. My mind was reeling – *He'd killed a man. He was a killer. Did this mean that he'd killed again right here in Frampton Abbas, Rosemary Waters, Melanie?* – but I maintained an impassive front. For some strange reason I wasn't frightened and it wasn't just because Tommy was only a shout away.

'It was an accident,' said André and I breathed a secret sigh of relief, 'but I can't prove it. It happened at the end of the summer season. All summer long there'd been this friction between me and this line cook from Mexico.'

'Is that significant? That he was from Mexico?' I said.

'Kind of. He had a real chip of resentment on his shoulder, used to taunt me about the color of my hair. He hated me, he was always yelling at me. He worked the French fry station and I had to peel potatoes and keep 'em coming. And as far as he was concerned, I was always way too slow. But then I caught him stealing.'

'French fries?'

'Steaks – from the walk-in freezer. We were a fish restaurant, right? But there's always going to be some jerk who doesn't eat fish so we kept a few steaks and hamburgers for them. And this guy lifted them from the freezer, I saw him.'

'Did you report him?'

'Not exactly. I pointed out to the owner that it would be very easy to steal from the freezer room and that we should get a padlock put on the door and the last person to leave at night should lock it up. But first you had to check there was no one inside. There was a kind of forked arrangement that clasped the door shut, a safety latch that could be pulled open from the inside. And there was a switch inside the door that turned a light on outside, above the door, so you could see there was someone inside.'

'So anyone who went inside flicked the light on to show they were there, so no one would shut them in.' I knew what was coming but I didn't see how.

André nodded. 'Unless you didn't want anyone to know you were in there. This Latino knew I was the one who had foiled his thieving and he really hated my guts. If it hadn't been so close to the end of the season, I'd have quit, he made my life so unbearable. You've seen what it's like to work at close quarters in a kitchen, imagine what it's like when you've got someone who never speaks a civil word to you. But there were only a couple of weeks to go so I stuck it out.'

'But you'd put a stop to him stealing?'

'So I thought. Right at the end of the season a team of us – this guy included – were clearing out the place ready for the big winter shut-down. We were hosing everything down, putting stuff in storage and finally we were done. The others all left about a half hour before me. I said I'd take care of the final lock-up but I was running late for a date with a girl I'd met so I took off before I was done with a plan to go back later and finish the job.'

'And when you went back you found the Mexican?'

He shook his head. 'That's the whole point. I *didn't* find him. It never even occurred to me that he might be there. I assumed he'd left along with the others. The freezer was cleaned out but I guess he didn't know that. The place was way out on a spit of land, perched on pilings. There was always a bunch of beat-up trucks parked in a rusty lean-to. I guess his must have been one of them and I never noticed. I just raced through the place locking up. If the light had been on outside the freezer, I guess I might have gone in – but it wasn't. I padlocked the door and left.'

'And he was inside?'

'For the whole winter!'

'He was never discovered?'

'Not until they opened up the restaurant the following May. If it had happened now, he'd have summoned help on his cell-phone but back then—'

'And nobody reported him missing?'

'He was an itinerant cook, an illegal. He went from place to place looking for work. He'd made sure he was under the radar.'

I wasn't sure I wanted to know but I had to ask. 'And you never told anybody?'

'Everyone witnessed the hostility between us. By the time I heard about his death from a friend, I'd been working in

France for the best part of a year. And he told me it'd been ruled a tragic accident. No questions were being asked and for good reason.'

I must have looked amazed because he leaned forward. 'Think about it, Lee. The owners didn't want it investigated. They'd hired that guy illegally. They figured that if any of the guys working at the restaurant were blamed, they'd blow the whistle on what went on there to the INS.'

'But you've never gone back to the States?'

'I know I killed that guy – through carelessness or whatever. I know it's crazy but I still feel so guilty that I can't stop myself thinking I'll be nabbed the minute I step off the plane. Even with my new identity.'

'What's new about it?'

'I changed my name to André Balfour when I came to England. I'm not even going to tell you what my real name is. I'd been working in France for a few years, in country restaurants, moving from place to place, just like the guy I killed.'

'You *didn't* kill him. Not intentionally.'

'Sometimes I wonder if I did. Whether not checking if there was anyone inside was one of those Freudian slips you hear about. I didn't know he was in there – but I didn't know he wasn't. And I spent quite a long time in Europe trying to be invisible to the authorities, I know what that's like. That's why when I came to England, when I had a chance to make myself legal by getting married, I took it.'

'You married Maggie Blair's illegitimate daughter?'

'Yes,' he smiled, 'I did. I met this woman in Bath. I was working in this really upscale place as a pastry cook. It's not what I like doing and believe me, I'm more than happy for Justine to do her stuff here but at the time it was the only job I could get that I thought would enhance my résumé.' He gave me a rueful grin. 'Anyway, there was this woman who used to come in on her own now and again, older than I was, bit mousy but not bad looking and I wouldn't have paid her much attention except she was interested in cooking and food and kept hanging around at the end of the lunchtime shift and pestering me with questions.'

I smiled. My guess was the woman had probably been more interested in André than cooking and food.

'As it turned out she was looking for someone to cook for her, undercover so to speak.'

'Undercover?'

'She wanted me to prepare food she could serve at dinner parties and pass off as her own.'

'And did you?'

'Sure. And it escalated from there. Her friends, the ones I cooked for, only they didn't know it, they told her *she* was such a good cook she ought to open a restaurant, like it was the easiest thing in the world.'

I smiled again but André was giving me an odd look.

'Lee, you haven't asked me where my wife is now, you haven't even asked me *who* she is.'

'I know who she is – the baby Maggie gave away. Jake told me about her.'

'Your friend Max, he didn't tell you her name, did he? Well, he couldn't have done otherwise that would have been the first thing you would have said when you came in here today.'

'No, he didn't, now you mention it.' He may have said it to Richie, I thought, and Richie omitted to pass it on to me. 'But I'm sure he knew. You see Maggie Blair told me it was her son-in-law's computer in her outhouse and I told Max that. But we knew Mona's husband had been killed in the car crash so Max must have worked out that Maggie was talking about her *first* daughter's husband. Are you still in touch with your wife and did you tell Maggie where to find her?'

He was shaking his head in exasperation. 'You just don't have a clue, do you? My wife was adopted at birth and she had managed to trace her biological mother just before I met her. When I started cooking for her she'd already been here, to Frampton Abbas, and been reunited with Maggie. She'd

314

discovered that Maggie had a bit of money. When her stupid friends started putting ideas into her head about starting up a restaurant, she asked Maggie to loan her the start-up funds. *Give* her, I should say. I don't think she had any intention of paying it back. Maggie owned this building and it had the perfect space. And to answer your question, yes, of course I'm still in touch with my wife. I see her every day.'

Suddenly it made awful blinding sense. The taunting, the shifting of power, the way Sylvia had laughed and called him a *naughty boy* when he attacked her – it had had all the undercurrents of bickering between husband and wife but I just hadn't seen it at the time.

And then everything fell into place very quickly and I realized with mounting horror just how far Sylvia had taken her marital grievances.

'André,' I said, 'that was your computer in Maggie's outhouse.'

'Sure,' he said, 'Sylvia used to have her office over there before she moved it upstairs. I used to spend quite a lot of time at Maggie's because Sylvia was setting me up on the Internet, showing me what to do. She had this fantasy that I'd help her out in the office. I'd go over and practice and Maggie would make me cups of tea. Only she'd forget to put the teabag in.'

'Sylvia set you up on the Internet,' I parroted.

'It was great! We used Maggie's name on my account since the outhouse was at her address.'

'And you had a password?'

'Sylvia thought it up for me.'

'So she could read your emails—'

And invite Rosemary Waters and Melanie to dinner on his behalf.

And she was all alone with Gussie down the road.

Chapter Nineteen

While I had been listening to André, I had been aware of a certain amount of activity outside in the High Street. It was Sunday, normally the sleepiest day of the week in a place not known for its frenzy at any time, and yet there had been people running down the street. *Running!* Normally the only figures who remotely bestirred themselves were cats scampering out of the paths of oncoming delivery vehicles and tractors as they rumbled through the center of Frampton Abbas. But I had been so absorbed by André's revelations that I had not registered what all the excitement was about.

Now, as I ran to the door, having first summoned Tommy, I saw with mounting alarm what had caused the commotion.

The drains below the pavement on either side of the road were overflowing and erupting underneath parked cars. Channels of water were flowing toward me down the middle of the road from the bridge.

The river had finally burst its banks.

Up ahead, I could see André wading ankle deep as he tried to reach Gussie's house while all around him people were carrying children to safety. Now I could understand the absolute necessity of the floodgates fitted across the lower parts of the doors of the houses situated down the street, near the river. Until the water reached at least three feet and could seep in through a window, they denied it access to the ground floors. All along the High Street the inhabitants of Frampton Abbas had already retreated to the upper floors of their houses and a line of Georgian sash windows was being thrown open as the occupants leaned out to check how far the water had risen.

I had changed out of Jake's boots in the car on the way into Frampton Abbas but now I thought to retrieve them as I remembered his words. *It's not just the river. It's the streams and all those springs hidden away that nobody knows about. That sneaky trickle running outside the backyard, being fed by some source that's overflowed long before the river.* How long would it take for all the melting snow and overflowing springs flowing down from Exmoor to fill up the valley and drown us all?

I had to lean from the pavement, over the rushing stream, to open the car door and even as I was reaching for the boots, the water showed signs that it would soon rise up into the car. I returned to The Pelican to put on the boots but Tommy grabbed them from me as soon as I got inside the door.

'Those'll fit me better than you,' he said and he was right. 'And I'll put them to better use.'

He picked me up in his arms and waded along the High Street, just as he had carried me over the mud at Dorcas Farm. André was already banging on Gussie's front door, which had a floodgate installed across it. When there was no answer we peered into the kitchen window from the street but could see no immediate sign of water inside. The overflow from the river was only about six inches deep but it was moving so rapidly that we saw it knock someone down across the street.

'I can't see her or Sylvia but it looks like the floodgates have done their work.' André's wet hair was plastered to his face and neck and the soaking rain had turned it a dark orange. 'Let's hope they have had enough sense to go upstairs. I'll find a way to get her out. Go back to your car and get out of here.'

'No,' Tommy yelled back. 'That's the last thing we want to do with the water rising so rapidly. If it keeps on like this it's going to reach two feet pretty soon and that's all it takes to float a car.'

A man leading a group of people toward the bridge called over his shoulder. 'If you can get to the other side of the bridge, you can walk up out of Frampton Abbas to higher ground. That's what we're trying to do.'

As he spoke, a tractor lumbered over the bridge, it's giant tires navigating the water and three children were lifted up to clamber around the driver, hanging on to him as he endeavored to steer.

'Take me up on the bridge,' I beseeched Tommy. He probably thought I wanted to escape to higher ground but it wasn't that. I was frantic at the thought of Gussie alone in the house with Sylvia, and from the highest point of the bridge I could look down on the side of Gussie's house overlooking the river and see what I hadn't been able to before. I could see my bedroom window from which I had thrown bread to silence the ducks and I noted with shock how fast the water was rising up the wall below it.

And then I saw a movement at the rear of the house as Gussie came out of the back door followed by Sylvia who was pointing at the river. Gussie nodded, *Yes!* then ducked under the washing line, ran across the yard and hopped up on to the low stone wall to look down at the river. She seemed utterly impervious to the fact that at any minute the water would inevitably rise up over that wall and flood her backyard on the other side of it. The road at the front of her house was already under water and from there the house sloped downward so that the yard at the back was on lower ground. It was only a matter of time before the low wall was breached. If anywhere, this was where the floodgates were needed the most, to stop the water flowing into the back of the house as well as the front.

For the first time I thought that Gussie might actually *be* as completely hopeless as she always protested she was not. She had appeared to be responding to some suggestion of Sylvia's but it was an insanely stupid thing to do, leaping up so close to danger.

But as I was about to call out to her, a greater danger loomed.

Sylvia was climbing almost casually on to the wall behind Gussie. She crouched for a moment like a giant squirrel in her gray duffle coat, her wiry gray hair framing her face as it poked out from the hood. She gazed down at the swirling river below her as if mesmerized before straightening up. And then I realized Gussie had no idea that Sylvia had silently crept up and joined her on the wall, was in fact poised right behind her.

It would look so like an accident. All Sylvia had to do was give Gussie a surreptitious push and Gussie would be bound to fall in. Afterwards Sylvia could say she had been reaching out to restrain her, to persuade her to come down, away from the danger.

'Tommy,' I screamed at him, 'get along that wall and tell Gussie to get down before Sylvia pushes her in. Don't ask another question. Just do it, *please.*'

As he ran down from the bridge towards Gussie's house, I saw Sylvia's arm reach out and I screamed as loud as I could.

'GUSSIE! LOOK BEHIND YOU! GET DOWN NOW! SYLVIA'S GOING TO PUSH YOU IN!'

Gussie reacted to the sound of my voice, looked up, saw me gesticulating furiously on the bridge and waved. She had felt Sylvia's presence now and had turned to face her.

And Sylvia's hands gripped her shoulders.

There was a low parapet running off the end of the bridge and along the side wall of Gussie's house to where Sylvia and Gussie were perched so precariously at the back. It was still just above the water line and Tommy climbed down on to it, flattening himself against the wall as he inched his way along

319

it. The breadth of Jake's cumbersome rubber boots exceeded that of the parapet and at any moment it looked as if he would overbalance and tumble into the river.

Sylvia saw him approaching. She let go of Gussie and jumped into the river just as Tommy made it on to the low wall and moved to grasp Gussie.

Sylvia floundered and thrashed about so violently that I wondered if she could even swim but then it became clear that the waters were moving much too fast for her to keep her head above water for longer than a second.

And then, to my utmost horror, Tommy shed Jake's boots and dived in after her. He was a strong swimmer and he fared better than she did against the surge of the river. He reached her in a few swift strokes and began to pull her towards the river bank.

But she continued to fight him, flailing and kicking as he tried to hoist her to safety. He was on his back, carrying her along with him and he had almost reached the bank when, with some kind of superhuman effort, she managed to lean forward and extend her face out of the hood of her duffle coat and sink her teeth into his hand, a ferocious little terrier to the last.

I could see that it required all of Tommy's strength to wrestle with her and maintain a hold on her struggling body. Her bite gave him a shock and he released his grip just for an instant but it was enough for her to slip out of his grasp.

By the time Tommy had recovered enough to reach for her, she had been swept away under the bridge, the river carrying her furiously downstream and out of sight.

Five months later Tommy was back in the river below Gussie's house, stripped to his ample waist and wearing a pair of ridiculous baggy shorts that flapped around his thighs in the mild, summer breeze. He was paddling barefoot in water that barely covered his ankles and, as I watched, he kicked out at several ducks floating past him.

They bore no resemblance to the raucous birds who had deprived me of my sleep back in the winter. These were of the bright yellow plastic variety and Tommy had been in a state or rapture since the minute he had first laid eyes on them.

He was standing in the shallows along with several children in their swimsuits, paddling and splashing about. They were gathered at the finishing line of the Frampton Abbas Duck Race that took place each year on August Bank Holiday Monday. Some two hundred plastic ducks had been released from a net further upstream, each with a number painted on its backside, and they had just rounded the bend in the river to flow en masse under the bridge toward Tommy. He was frantically searching for the duck with his number on it. If it was the first duck to float past him, then he was in line to win a free cream tea at the baker's. Scones and raspberry jam and Devon clotted cream had featured largely in his reveries of late.

I was sitting on Gussie's wall – the same wall from which Sylvia had jumped – with my legs dangling over the edge. The river had dwindled over the summer to a narrow channel trickling between the stony riverbeds below the banks and it was almost impossible to reconcile it with the churning waters of the winter flood.

Sylvia's body was found washed up on a bank along with that of a dead sheep and, with her death, I knew that I had probably lost all concrete proof that she had killed Rosemary Waters and Melanie. But over the months that followed, and with André's help, I gradually worked out what must have happened.

Ironically, it was a barrage of phone calls from Genevieve that reminded me of something that helped to slot the first piece of the puzzle into place.

'I hear you came up to London recently.' Genevieve sounded as if she were accusing me. *You came to London and you didn't tell me.* 'Did you see Mary Jane Markham?'

'Yes,' I said simply. Because it was the truth. I had seen her. I just hadn't talked to her about her book project.

I fudged the rest of the conversation, knowing perfectly well I wasn't fooling Genevieve for a second. But just as I thought she was about to pin me to the telephonic wall and tell me to find myself another agent, her voice changed and in a soft, almost coy tone she asked, 'You haven't by any chance run into Ann Bates while you've been down there, have you?'

And that started me thinking about my visit to Monica Massey and Ann Bates, and what they had told me about their lunch at The Pelican.

'André, do you remember the lunchtime service at The Pelican the day Rosemary Waters died? Not the evening when she came in, but the lunch that day?'

He looked at me suspiciously. We were sitting in Sylvia's old office above The Pelican, something we'd done a good deal in the months since her body had been found. In a sudden remorseful change of heart, André blamed himself for Sylvia's death. *If I hadn't made her keep quiet about our marriage, if I hadn't joined Exmoormates.com, would those women still be alive? Would she still be alive?* Over and over again he pounded himself with recrimination.

'The marriage was a big mistake,' he conceded when we began meeting for a couple of hours every day to unravel his story, 'although I did fall in love with Sylvia briefly. Don't look so surprised.' He could see the disbelief on my face. 'As you must know by now, chef work doesn't give you much time off and I always fell for women much too quickly whenever I had the opportunity – and then I'd repent at leisure.' He grinned. 'But there was something about Sylvia. I was touched by the way she was so thrilled to be giving dinner parties, to be finally accepted into the kind of social milieu to which she had always aspired.'

He was smiling now, albeit wistfully.

'And she was so thrilled by what I was doing for her. I had never had anyone be so appreciative of my efforts before. It was – how can I put it? It was heartwarming. Literally. We did have a love affair and I let it go too far because she got me to the altar, or the registry office at any rate. I suppose we were happy for a while but I soon began to realize what a terrible mistake I'd made. By the time I'd made myself legal by marrying her, I didn't need her anymore so inevitably I started making noises about splitting up.'

He threw up his hands as if in despair. 'She wouldn't hear of it. She would not even begin to discuss it. I was just about to get up and walk out on her when she began to talk about a job I really liked the sound of.'

'The Pelican?' I said.

'Right. She'd told me about her reunion with her birth mother – that was something we bonded over in the beginning, the fact that we never knew our biological parents – and about her plans to open The Pelican. She had it all worked out. She'd even persuaded Maggie to keep quiet about the fact that Maggie was her mother. Her plan was to chip away at Maggie so she could do Mona out of Maggie's money when Maggie died. Maggie letting her use this building for the restaurant was only the beginning. Sylvia was banking on Maggie leaving her everything.'

'So how did you come in, apart from being her husband?'

'The thing about Sylvia is that she's not—' he frowned. 'She *wasn't* totally stupid. She could see that I had the potential to be the kind of chef she needed to draw people to her restaurant and she knew I was ambitious. Plus I'd made the mistake of telling her about why I would never go back to America. She knew she could pick up the phone and embellish that story to my disadvanage any time she wanted. So she made me a deal. She agreed to the end of the marriage and she said she'd leave and move to Frampton Abbas to start up the restaurant.'

'But there was a condition.'

'I had to follow her there and become her chef. My cooking would make a name for The Pelican and together we'd build up its reputation until it became a pretty valuable commodity, by which time she'd assumed she'd own the building. Then we'd sell, split the profits and I'd have the cash to start my own place, which of course had been my dream since I first started cooking.'

'And you insisted she keep quiet—'

'So I could move on. So I could date people, find someone else. We knew it wouldn't look good for business if people knew she was my wife and I was always seen to be cheating on her. And besides we were married in name only. She said she'd give me a divorce as soon as we had sold The Pelican and we were poised to go our separate ways.'

But of course she didn't and the more I thought about it, the more I realized that Sylvia had never had any intention of letting André go, whatever she might have told him. She had never stopped loving him and she had obviously hoped to lure him back to the marriage eventually. The discovery of his activity on Exmoormates.com must have come as a bitter blow to her.

'There was one good thing to come out of the marriage,' said André. 'I got to know Maggie, bless her. She was such a sweetie, her eyes used to light up when I ran over the road with her dinner. Not that she ate much in the end, poor love. Sylvia doesn't know this but I told Maggie I was her son-in-law.'

Now it all made total sense. That first day when I arrived in Frampton Abbas and met Maggie, she hadn't seen Mona's husband in over four years, had probably forgotten his existence. As far as she was concerned, André, whom she probably saw every day, was her son-in-law.

I had stayed in Frampton Abbas after the flood because Gussie had begged me to. In his tormented state, André had distanced himself from her and she couldn't understand why. I couldn't bring myself to explain to Gussie that he held his relationship with her responsible for driving Sylvia to her death. All I knew was that with the rapidly approaching inquest hanging over her, and in her shock at learning that André had been married to Sylvia, she was suddenly in danger of slipping back into the unstable state in which I had found her when I had first arrived in Frampton Abbas. I had every reason to believe that André would come to his senses eventually but until that happened, I had to stay and support Gussie.

But it was hard. I had no work and nor did Gussie. With Sylvia gone, Mona closed The Pelican and put it up for sale. André too was out of a job and in a curious reincarnation of Sylvia, he now hounded me to help him with his story, hence the almost daily meetings upstairs at The Pelican, where Mona had said he could stay until it was sold. I was going along with him for one simple reason: his story would incorporate his marriage to Sylvia and her subsequent death and within it I could build up a strong case for her having killed Rosemary Waters and Melanie. It would be speculation, of course, but it would be the closest I would get to pointing the finger with any conviction.

But of course it was André's finger that would have to do the pointing – I was only his ghost – and here I had a problem. André's guilt over Sylvia's death was causing him to rewrite history every other day. One minute he was blaming himself for giving her a reason to go after Rosemary and Melanie in the first place, and the next he would be waxing sentimental over Sylvia and denying that she could possibly have had anything to do with their deaths.

'If she'd actually pushed Gussie into the river and Gussie had been the one who had drowned, would you be whining like this?' I yelled at him one day, driven to near distraction by his constant ambivalence.

'But maybe she was trying to save Gussie, trying to persuade her to come down off the wall because it was dangerous,' he responded.

'So why did she jump into the river when she saw Tommy coming towards her?' I countered.

'She slipped,' he said, but he didn't sound entirely convinced.

It was that day that I pressed him further on what had happened at The Pelican when Monica and Ann had been there for lunch only hours before Rosemary Waters had ingested the fatal peanut oil.

'It was the day Sylvia tested the fire alarm,' I prompted him.

'Oh God!' He rolled his eyes. 'How could I forget? The least she could have done was to warn me before she set the damn thing off. I was mad at her anyway.'

'You were? Why?' I recalled Monica and Ann talking about listening to a huge row going on in the kitchen.

'Because she'd got me out of bed on a Sunday – my day off – and made me come down and make sixty pancakes for dinner that night. It was something she had said she'd do after the lunchtime shift but she suddenly decided to take off for the afternoon. You remember? She didn't even get back in time to open for dinner in the evening. Gussie had to do it on her own.'

And she served Rosemary Waters salad dressing with peanut oil in it.

'So then what happened?'

'Well, I made all the pancakes and she never even said thank you so I yelled at her, told her she was an ungrateful cow. And she ignored me, didn't react at all and of course that made me even more mad. It always did. She knew just how to press my buttons. And then before I could make another attempt to get through to her, she walked away from me into the dining room and started talking to the customers. So that really tipped me over the edge. I'd set the pancakes aside ready for Wendy to wrap in cling film and put in the fridge and when she wasn't looking, I picked them up and chucked them out the alley door into the garbage can.'

'You didn't!'

'I absolutely did. But even though Wendy didn't notice, Sylvia did. She was standing in the dining room talking to those two old biddies who live at the end of the village and she was facing the kitchen. She watched me without making any attempt to stop me, and then she took her revenge.'

'How?'

'She went upstairs and hit the fire alarm and I'm pretty sure she did it to get back at me. Everyone had to get out fast, including me, and I had something in the oven that was completely ruined.'

'André,' I said, 'listen to me. I don't think she hit the fire alarm to get back at you. At least not in the way that you think. You used to leave your laptop on all day up here,' I nodded towards the landing, 'and as we've already established, Sylvia knew your password. I think she popped out of her office one day while you were busy working in the kitchen downstairs, and she logged on to Exmoormates.com on your laptop and sent an invitation to Rosemary Waters *from you* to meet you for dinner here at The Pelican. And that Sunday lunchtime, by hitting the fire alarm she made sure everyone was out of the building for a few minutes, which gave her time to go downstairs and add some peanut oil to the salad dressing. Then she joined you out on the street until you all realized there was no fire. It was a false alarm.'

I watched him process the information. 'It's possible,' he conceded. 'If she'd read my email exchange with Rosemary, she'd know Rosemary had a peanut allergy. But how did she know Rosemary would order a salad?'

'Because Rosemary said so. It's all there in the emails – the ones that were deleted before you ever saw them. Rosemary discussed with Sylvia – thinking it was you – what she was going to order. So that gave Sylvia the idea to spike the dressing.'

'And I suppose you've got an equally credible scenario for how she killed Melanie?' André's tone was grudging in its reluctant acceptance of my theory.

At the time I wasn't able to come up with a plausible link from Sylvia to Melanie's death. Once again it was another small detail niggling away in my mind that led me to place Sylvia at the quarry on the day Melanie died. My mind went back constantly to my visit to Neil Mackay in London and his horrifying admission that he believed his wife Katharine might have been responsible for Melanie's death. His basis for this had been because he had seen Taylor getting into a blue Nissan driven by a woman.

And Katharine drove a blue Nissan.

But there was something that didn't fit. When Neil and Katharine had come into The Pelican to talk about the catering for Melanie's memorial service, Taylor had recognized Neil but not Katharine. Surely, if he could remember the man he had seen only from a distance arguing with Melanie at the quarry, he should have been able to recall the woman who had allegedly driven him all the way back to Frampton Abbas?

Wendy actually seemed quite pleased to see me when I knocked on her door. We'd run into each other a few times in the High Street and she'd nodded to me and I'd seen her stacking the shelves in Spar, where she now worked.

'If you're collecting for something, I've nothing to spare,' was how she greeted me but she smiled as she said it.

'Actually it's Taylor I'd like a word with, if that's OK?'

'He said he was going upstairs to do his homework, which means he's playing video games. But he might come down, seeing as it's you. He mentions you now and then, Lee, which is pretty amazing for him. I think it means he likes you.'

'Oh, I like him too!' Well, I didn't *dis*like him.

'TAYLOR!'

I covered my ears with my hands. Wendy had a voice like a sergeant major on parade. But it worked. Taylor's head appeared on the landing.

'Look who's here,' said Wendy. 'Come down and say hello.'

'Can I have an ice cream out the freezer?' Taylor wasn't born yesterday.

'Go on then,' said Wendy.

'I just want to ask you something about that time you were up at the quarry,' I said gently when Taylor was licking the remains of a choc ice from the corners of his mouth.

'You've not been back up that quarry *again,* you disobedient little monkey,' Wendy's hand reached out to tweak his ear. 'I told you to stay away from there.'

'No, I meant the time he saw Melanie up there, before she died,' I said hastily. 'Taylor, I want to know how you got home from the quarry. Did someone give you a lift?'

'Well, I'd have known about it if they had,' said Wendy. 'He knows not to accept lifts from strangers, don't you, Taylor?'

Taylor nodded.

'So did someone you know give you a lift?' I repeated, wishing I could get Taylor on his own.

Taylor hesitated. He glanced at Wendy. His eyes were wide with apprehension and when he didn't respond, I leaned forward and put my hand on his knee. 'Taylor?'

'Well, answer her, Taylor. If you took a lift off someone and never told me, it's too late to bother about it now. What's done is done. So who was it?' To my relief, Wendy's tone had softened.

'Her at the restaurant.' Taylor jerked his head in the direction of The Pelican. 'Where you worked. She drove past me in her car right up to the edge of the quarry. You're not supposed to take your car up there, are you? You're supposed to leave it in the field and walk up. But I don't think she expected anyone to be there.'

'And was there anyone there – besides you?'

'That woman was still there. The one who had the row with the man. He'd been gone for a bit but she was still there.'

'Did you see Sylvia – from the restaurant, did you see her with the other woman?'

329

'No, I didn't. I had my back to them. I was walking home by that time.'

'But you got a lift in Sylvia's car?'

Taylor nodded. 'She drove back down pretty soon after she'd got there and when she saw me, she slowed down and opened the door and asked me if I wanted a lift. When I got in she made me promise not to tell anyone she'd taken me home. She said she knew I shouldn't accept lifts from strangers but I looked so tired, she had to stop for me. I said I wouldn't tell anyone if she bought me a Cadbury's Flake. I'm not so keen on them now but back then I thought they were wicked!'

It was smart of Sylvia, I thought. She knew Taylor had seen her anyway and it was better to buy his silence than to leave it to chance that he might remark on it to someone.

'One more thing, Taylor. What color was her car?'

'Blue,' he said. 'Can I go now?'

Later that day I asked André what kind of car Sylvia had driven.

'A crap car,' he said helpfully. 'It was on its last legs. I kept telling her to get a new one but she always said what did she need a new car for? She hardly ever went anywhere. She left it to me along with her pathetic collection of useless possessions – useless to me, that is. What am I going to do with a closet full of a middle-aged woman's clothes, a ten-year-old radio, five self-help audiobooks about how to change your life and a clapped-out car? When I tried to sell it, the garage told me it didn't have a hope of passing its MOT. But what I keep on thinking,' he said with his eyes downcast, 'is that it's just so sad that was all that was left of her.'

'What color was it?' I asked quickly to ward off a further bout of sentimentalism, although I was secretly shocked at how little Sylvia's life had amounted to. She didn't even own a house. She had put all her savings into The Pelican, I realized, and had rented the cottage where she lived. She had banked on Maggie Blair coming through for her and it must have been a crushing blow when she didn't inherit The

Pelican. And Maggie leaving her furniture to Gussie couldn't have helped either.

'Gray,' he said.

'*Gray? Not blue?*'

'Well, I supposed you *could* call it blue but it was a sort of sludge blue. Looked more gray to me but maybe that's because she was sort of gray herself.'

'What do you mean by that?'

'I feel bad saying it but she was a different person to the woman I met in Bath. Maybe she was older than she let on.' He looked at me, raising his eyebrows, *What do you think?* 'But when she moved to Frampton Abbas she just seemed to turn gray. Gray hair, that gray duffle coat she always wore. I didn't notice what I was doing at the time, but looking back I realize I stopped looking at her as a woman, especially as a woman I had once been attracted to. She just became invisible – I mean I could hear her all right, hard not to, that chirpy voice with its constant undercurrent of menace – but for the last six months before she died, I just couldn't seem to *see* her anymore.'

I'd heard that this happened when a woman reached a certain age. Gussie and I had discussed it and I had spent a long evening persuading Gussie that she wasn't there yet, not by a long stretch. And she had repaid me by remarking that as a fully paid up member of the Polar Bear Club, I was probably looking forward to reaching such a stage. But faced with the reality of it from a man's point of view and the effect it had had on an already desperate woman, I knew Gussie was wrong. I was dreading it.

For a while I wondered whether Sylvia would have jumped into the river whether Tommy had gone after her or not. And, like André, I started to question whether she could have been capable of cold premeditated murder and eventually I settled on a compromise.

I decided that she had only intended to scare Rosemary Waters. She had probably assumed that someone in

331

Rosemary's situation would be sure to have an emergency kit in case she went into anaphylactic shock. But I became convinced that Rosemary's eventual death had given Sylvia the confidence to go after the other women André targeted on Exmoormates.com.

I marveled at how terrifyingly easy it was for her to kill two women with relatively no violence on her part. If Melanie had been standing at the edge of the quarry, lost in thought as she pondered the argument she had just had with Neil Mackay, then all Sylvia would have had to do was walk up close to her, engage her in casual conversation and wait for the right moment to catch her unawares and push her over the edge. Weren't most murders supposed to be committed by someone known to the victim?

But however much he might be avoiding Gussie on a day-to-day basis, André came through for her at the inquest. He testified that there had been a Thai evening at The Pelican some months prior to Rosemary's Waters' death. He claimed to have discussed it with Sylvia who, he said, had conceded that there might have been a trace of peanut oil left in an empty bottle in one of the kitchen closets. And if Gussie had used olive oil that had later been stored in that bottle, then it was entirely an accident that the peanut trace had been transferred to the salad dressing, an accident, he stressed, for which Sylvia would undoubtedly have held herself responsible, had she still been alive.

The ease with which he lied scared me and I wondered what else he could have lied about. I seethed as I listened to him. I wanted to stand up and yell *Sylvia was responsible because she deliberately spiked the peanut oil,* but I held my tongue because I could see Gussie's eyes pleading with me, *Please don't spoil it, please let's just get it over with.*

And after that I left André alone for a while and closeted myself in my room at Gussie's house to begin transforming his story into the first draft of a book. I had already mapped out the early chapters when Gussie – whom I had finally trained not to interrupt me unless it was of the utmost importance – burst into the room.

'Old Jake's dead,' she said. 'Apparently he's been ill for a while but he didn't tell anybody. Anyway his funeral's tomorrow. I just thought you'd like to know.'

Like wasn't really the word. I had been avoiding thinking about Jake and I felt as ambivalent – and as guilty – about him as André did about Sylvia. Whether he had deliberately murdered Sadie or not – and I was still in two minds on that score – his affair with her, and her resulting pregnancy, had contributed to her death, of that I was sure. And his gleeful recounting of what he had done with her dog had disgusted me. I hadn't gone near him for that reason, even though I had known that he was dying a painful death.

He'd said he'd have Max to tend to him at the end. Yet had he? I had jumping butterflies in my stomach as Gussie and I walked along the High Street to the church the next day, wondering if I would encounter Max at the funeral.

He wasn't there and that was when I began to wonder if he had abandoned his uncle altogether, taking his revenge for what had happened to Sadie. I pictured Jake, and Willow, wasting away together on a satin bedspread, all alone in a weatherbeaten Dorcas Farm.

But however his demise had manifested itself, Jake had a massive turnout at his funeral, most of whom, I couldn't help noticing, were female. They were a teary-eyed lot and some of them were quite young, evidence, I suspected, of his former patronizing of 'DirtyFarmers.com'.

The person I was most surprised to see was Marjorie Mackay. I had felt guilty about not going to see her either but I had consoled myself with the assumption that she had undoubtedly sold up and left the area, as she had said she wanted to do.

'Oh, I decided to stay in the end,' she said, making a beeline for me the minute Jake's body had been lowered into the ground. 'I know I said I wanted to get away but the more I thought about it, the more I realized what a wrench it would be at my age. I decided it was a question of better the devil you know so it was Neil and Katharine who left. She took him back – can't say I'm happy about it, but she did – on condition that they move and start afresh somewhere else. So do you know what I did?'

I shook my head, aware of Gussie coming to stand beside me and slipping her hand into the crook of my elbow.

'I took my own advice – that which I'd given to Katharine. I bought their farm and I'm turning the house and the outbuildings into holiday cottages. Have you heard about these working-farm holidays? They're going to be popular now that people are trying to reduce their carbon footprint or whatever you call it. They can come and spend two weeks on the farm and the children can muck out the barn and help me feed the animals. It'll be ever so organic. What do you think of that?'

'I think it's a wonderful idea,' I said and I did. She was a brave woman.

'Well, you'll have to come and stay – although,' she gave me a rueful grin, 'I imagine you'll go to Dorcas Farm. Old Jake left it to his nephew but I expect you already know that?'

'He's not here, I see.'

'Big case in London, so I heard,' said Marjorie, lowering her voice somewhat conspiratorially. 'Teenage stabbing in Peckham. Didn't you read about it in the papers? I don't suppose they can spare him. But he was ever so good at the end with old Jake, came down as often as he could. I did my bit, of course, popping over there every day but Max was his main support. It's good when you can depend on your family, isn't it? Wonder what'll happen now though, whether he'll keep the farm or sell it?'

My eyes filled with tears and I gulped at the discovery that even though I hadn't seen it – and probably never would – there was a soft side to Max. Surely he couldn't have known

334

about Sadie and Jake if he'd made the effort to come down and be with Jake at the end.

I had been aware of Gussie's ears flapping at Marjorie's association of me with Max and I tried to guide her away before Marjorie could enlighten her further. But she resisted my attempts to move her on and as I moved away, I heard her say, 'So, Marjorie, we've never really met. I'm Gussie, Lee's cousin and—'

But Marjorie put out a hand to stop me. 'Just a minute, dear. I've got something for you.' She handed me an envelope with my name on it. 'Max found this at Dorcas Farm after Jake had passed on. He asked me to give it to you.'

It was sealed and I slid my fingernail under the flap to open it as I walked back to Gussie's house leaving Marjorie and Gussie ensconced in a huddle. Inside were two pieces of paper. The first one I unfolded was a note in an almost illegible hand, the words sprawled along the page as if the writer had barely had the energy to put pen to paper.

Jake, don't hate me but I can't have this baby. Max will know it's not his and it would destroy him. I can't do that to him. Look after Pixie for me. Don't let Max have her. He hates her. Sadie

The first thing that struck me was that she'd used the word hate twice. I wondered if she'd been trying to abort the baby or kill herself? Or both?

When I read the second note I suspected I had been meant to read it first.

Lee, I wanted you to see this, in case you didn't believe me when I said she was trying to kill herself. I'll leave it up to you whether you want to show it to Max. Jake

Damn you, Jake, for putting this on me, I thought. Would the realization of what his uncle had done allow Max to put

Sadie's ghost to rest? Or would it plunge him into an even greater despair?

But worst of all was the dilemma I now faced. The news was bad enough but did he need to hear it from *me*?

And the more I thought about it, the more I wondered: *Did he need to hear it at all?*

Chapter Twenty

The next day Gussie was in for a shock.

While the majority of Frampton Abbas inhabitants had been attending Jake's funeral, André had packed his bags and left.

Gussie was inconsolable but after a day or so I managed to calm her down and get her to accept that his hasty departure was no reflection on her. He'd had a complicated life up to now, I explained, without going into too many details, and a transitory one, and even if he had tried to make a life with Gussie in Frampton Abbas, the chances were always going to be strong that he would move on eventually.

But then, just when she had begun to get through the day without bursting into tears, he telephoned her and asked her to join him in America.

America! It seemed they hadn't nabbed him as soon as he got off the plane, as he had been anticipating all these years. I admired him for facing up to his past. And I blessed him for the return of a jubilant Gussie into our midst. What, I wondered, would she do now?

More to the point, what would *I* do now?

About a week after the flood, Tommy had turned to me as I was driving him to the station so he could take the train back to London.

'So are we a couple again?' he asked.

He must have known it was a dangerous thing to say to me. I never liked being put on the spot about our relationship. It was something of a miracle that we had twice managed to get within a whisper of marrying each other. Now, as usual, I evaded the issue.

'Hard to know how we can be given that we'll be on different sides of the Atlantic.'

'Oh, I'm not going back to New York,' he said to my astonishment. 'I've decided to stay here and become an artistes' manager in London.'

Just like that! Tommy's problem was that he never foresaw any complications in his life. I loved him for his uncluttered optimism but at the same time I knew that someone had to pick up the pieces if his fantasies evaporated into thin air, which they sometimes did, and he came crashing back to reality.

'Shannon Sonnenschein's sending me the names of some contacts in our business to get me started.'

He's going to wish he hadn't added that, I thought grimly. *In our business!* Who does he think he's kidding?

But as the months unfolded Tommy was proved right in one thing. One way or another we became a couple once again. I stayed in Frampton Abbas with Gussie and he moved into Blenheim Crescent, taking a rather suspect job flogging what sounded suspiciously like dodgy sound equipment – something he knew a lot about as a former sound engineer – from a basement somewhere in Notting Hill. Every now and then he went off for an interview at some artiste management firm and every now and then he never got the job.

He came down to Frampton Abbas most weekends even though it was a four-hour drive from London (he had acquired a second- hand Ford Fiesta – actually I think it was *twenty*-second hand by the look of it, so much for Mary Jane Markham's assessment of him as an Audi man), and I was forced to admit that I looked forward to seeing him on Fridays.

Until the day when he turned up with my mother.

'Now don't blame Tommy,' she cried as she came flying through the door to flop down on a chair in Gussie's kitchen. 'The first he knew I was in England was when I called him and told him I was on my way in from the airport. Then when he told me that he'd be driving down to see you I made him bring me along. I knew if I told you in advance, you'd make a fuss. Anyway, I haven't been to Devon for thirty years and it's high time they saw me again. Gussie, my darling, it's sweet of you to have me and – Gussie, what's the matter?'

Gussie had been on the phone when my mother had banged on the door and I had come downstairs to let her in. Now, as she dissolved into my mother's outstretched arms – outstretched to her but never to me – we could see she was fighting back tears.

André, I thought, he's changed his mind. He doesn't want her to join him, the bastard! I had spent the morning moving the pages I'd written of his 'story' round and round my makeshift desk, trying to face up to the fact that there was not much I could do with them now. Not that I had seriously believed they would ever be published. I had embarked on the task of debriefing André more as a deterrent to my brain turning to mush from exposure to too much country air than anything else. I had delayed my move back to London following André's hasty departure back to the States and Gussie's subsequent collapse. But now she had recovered a little, I was itching to get back there.

But it wasn't André.

'I've just been talking to Mum,' wailed Gussie. 'I called her because I needed—' she hesitated and I knew that for Gussie to ask Aunt Joy for anything would require an almost superhuman effort on her part. 'I needed money.'

'Oh Gussie, why didn't you come to me?' I was saddened that she hadn't thought of it. 'I'm here to help you out, you know that.'

'I don't mean just a few quid to help with the bills,' said Gussie. 'You're wonderful about that in any case, Lee-Lee. I'm talking about serious money. I think it's called start-up money?' She looked at us as if for confirmation. 'I want to start a business with someone.'

'*You?* Start up a business?' I stared at her in total shock and in reply she burst into tears.

'See! None of you take me seriously. You're just like Mum. She said I hadn't a clue what I was talking about, that I was barely capable of starting up a car let alone a business and she'd have a better return on her money if she lent it to a chicken about to hatch an egg. She thinks I'm completely—'

'You're not hopeless, Gussie, you know you're not. And you know that we don't think you are either. In fact how can we think anything when we don't even know about this business you're starting up?' And then, rather late in the day, I remembered something. 'And what about America – and André?'

'I'm not going to America.' She looked quite defiant as she said it, as if she expected us all to tell her she was making a big mistake. 'I've thought about it *very seriously*.'

I tried not to giggle. Gussie was always endearingly child-like in her earnestness when she was stressing something important.

'Despite all that's happened, I've found something here in Frampton Abbas that I never thought I would,' she said. 'I'm happy here. I don't want to move and that's why when Marjorie told me about her holiday cottages, I begged her to let me become involved.'

'Marjorie?'

'You friend, Lee-Lee. And mine now. I met her at old Jake's funeral, remember?'

I did remember. I'd walked away assuming they were talking about me and Max. Well, that would teach me to be so self-absorbed.

'But why would you need money from Joy?' asked my mother in a surprisingly patient tone given that no one had so much as offered her a cup of tea after her long car journey.

'Marjorie doesn't just want me to be a cleaner or something. She's asked me to be a proper partner. I put money in and I reap the profits, same as her.'

'Assuming there are any,' muttered my mother and I could have hit her because I thought it was possibly the best idea I'd heard in years. I remembered what André had said about Gussie, that if she was left to get on with it, she was a good organizer. I'd seen enough of Marjorie to know that she would have the upper hand and would undoubtedly take care of the overall running of the business but even so, if she was prepared to cut Gussie in, then it was a wonderful opportunity. Briefly, I outlined as much to my mother.

'It's a truly beautiful spot up there on the moors,' I concluded, 'and these working farms are really popular.'

'I see,' said my mother and then without any warning she took her mobile out of her handbag, searched through the numbers on her screen and started dialing.

'Joy? Is that you? Listen, we haven't been in touch in quite a while and I'm only sorry I have to contact you about something as sordid as money. What? Well, just listen and I'll tell you. I have to say I think it's truly disgusting that you won't help Gussie get started with her holiday venture. Yes. Yes, I'm with her now – in Devon, yes. I happened to be in the country and I've come down from London to give her my support.'

Tommy, who had been coming in and out of the house fetching the bags from the car, caught the tail end of what my mother was saying and stopped to look at me, widening his eyes in bewilderment. *I'm going upstairs for a kip,* he pointed to the ceiling as he mouthed at me.

'I don't care, Joy. Your daughter has come to you for help and I think you ought to listen to her. God knows you can afford it! And from what I hear, you'll get a pretty good return on your investment. Gussie'll make those holiday cottages irresistible. Have you been down to visit her here in Devon? No, I didn't think so. Well, you should see how beautiful she's made her house. The decoration is a triumph. I had no idea she was so gifted—'

My mother had been no further than the kitchen, a corner of which was piled high with laundry. The paint was peeling off the walls on the damp river side of the house and the chair she was sitting on was held together with masking tape. But who cared? She hammered away at Aunt Joy for another five minutes and then handed the phone to Gussie.

'Take her for everything she's got,' she whispered.

Gussie was ecstatic when she came off the phone. 'Aunt Vanessa, I can't thank you enough. You shamed her into helping me. Do you know what she said? *Just work out how much you need and let me know.* I just can't believe it. Will you forgive me if I rush off and tell Marjorie?'

'Thanks, Mum,' I said when we were alone. I tried to give her a hug to show her how much what she'd done for Gussie had meant to me but she tensed as I approached and reached out for the kettle. 'Tea. I'm gasping. And I have to confess that I'll take any excuse to have a go at your Aunt Joy. God, she's a silly bitch!'

'Why do you hate her so much?' I had always been curious. It had to be more than just envy of Aunt Joy's looks.

'I suppose, deep down, it's because of your father.' My mother wouldn't look at me as she said this.

'Ed? Oh my God! He didn't have an affair with her?'

'Not since he's been married to me,' said my mother, and then she stared at me. 'At least not as far as I know – and I usually do. No, he was the first one to meet Joy, long before I came into his life. He wanted to marry her but she fell in love with his brother instead. So you see there's unfinished business between your father and Joy and I know it's stupid, but I can't get it out of my mind that one day he'll do something about it.'

Her vulnerability was tangible. Suddenly I found myself wondering what she'd had to put up with married to my father all these years. He wasn't a blatant philanderer despite Tommy's view that he should have played away further than Central Park when indulging in his latest adventure. He and I despaired over my mother's inability to show warmth and affection but maybe it wasn't surprising given that she couldn't be sure of receiving a 100 per cent share of his.

'How is Dad?' *And are you still thinking of divorcing him?*

'We're fine. In fact we're more than fine. We're actually pretty close at the moment.'

It wasn't what I'd asked but I could usually count on my mother to bring herself into everything. And she'd answered what I'd really wanted to know.

'He's sorry not to be here to tell you about Blenheim Crescent but there didn't seem much point in both of us traipsing all the way across the Atlantic.'

'What about Blenheim Crescent?' Suddenly I was nervous. I had been looking forward to the day when I could return there. Was I now about to be thrown out?

'Your father and I have decided to make it over to you and Tommy. We want to do it now to avoid death duties.'

'To me and *Tommy*? You've giving it to him as well?'

'Well, he'll be family after all.'

'He will?'

'He'll be our son-in-law.'

'Mum, we're not getting married.'

'Yes, you are. He's going to ask you this weekend. He told me all about it on the way down. In fact,' and now she did look a bit guilty, 'he told us on the phone last week and that's what gave us the idea about giving you the house. Look upon it as a wedding present.'

I shook my head in wonder. Only Tommy could manage to propose to me via my mother.

And she was right. He did ask me that weekend, although if I hadn't been expecting it, I would never have recognized it as a proposal. He'd brought a load of overdue bills down from Blenheim Crescent and late on Saturday night, after my mother and Gussie had gone to bed, we sat at the kitchen table while I went through them.

'I'd like to contribute,' he said, getting out his checkbook. 'I'll take Thames Water and the council tax. You do the electricity and the gas. You know,' he pushed a couple of envelopes across the table towards me, 'it'd make more sense if we had a joint bank account.'

'I suppose it would,' I said without thinking.

The next minute he was on his feet, rushing out of the kitchen and yelling up the stairs.

'Vanessa! Gussie! Are you asleep? Guess what? She said yes! SHE SAID YES!'

I don't know why I didn't set him straight, tell him I hadn't really been listening, ask him what on earth had given him that idea?

I don't know why I didn't say *What are you talking about?* when Gussie and my mother spent most of Sunday discussing where the wedding would take place. Not something in which I would have a say, I noticed.

Nor did I say anything when Tommy kissed me goodbye on Sunday evening, telling me that he had an interview during the coming week that was as much of a cinch as anything could be. When he told me I was going to be married to the future manager of major recording artistes, I just nodded, kissed him back and walked around the car to bid my mother farewell from the considerable distance she normally required.

But this time she reached out of the car window and clasped my hand.

'This'll work,' she whispered. 'He's not like your father. You'll never have any trouble with him.'

I was touched. Should I take advantage of her unexpected softening to lean in for a kiss? Better not push it, I decided almost immediately. Quit while you're ahead.

Had I finally grown up, I wondered, as they drove away? There had been a time when the words *You'll never have any trouble with him* would have been a death knell for me. I'd deliberately courted trouble when it came to men – look at Max. Anything to give the relationship an edge.

But I'd changed. I was saying yes to Tommy by taking the line of least resistance. The way things were going, with Gussie and my mother in charge of operations, I could just sit back and do nothing and find myself getting up one day and walking up the aisle at some point in the not too distant future.

It could be next month for all I know, I thought now as I dangled my legs over the wall and watched my future husband struggling to arrest a few renegade plastic ducks, which were floating rapidly downstream toward a weir. But while I might decide to absent myself from all the wedding plans, there was something I knew I did have to take care of. Once again Tommy hadn't even made it through the interview before they told him they didn't think he was a good fit for them. He remained optimistic that it was only a matter of time before he found his niche and I didn't have the heart to tell him to get real. We might be fortunate enough to be given a four-storey house in the heart of Notting Hill but we'd still have to pay its bills.

So much for the *joint* account. Another one of Tommy's fantasies.

Wearily, I climbed down off the wall and went indoors to extract Mary Jane Markham's number from my wallet where I'd stashed it for a rainy day.

Watch out for Lee Bartholomew's next adventure in
HELD TO RANSOM,
now available from Piatkus Books:

Newly married and excited about honeymooning near her family in the Hamptons, ghostwriter Lee Bartholomew isn't prepared for the disasters that happen when she arrives on US soil. Not only has her husband had to stay behind in London, but very soon Lee finds herself at the centre of a crime investigation that seems to get more tangled – and more sinister – as the seconds tick past.

A botched ransom attempt on her stepbrother's adopted son brings horror into her family's midst. But when a body is found close by, followed by a further kidnapping of a little boy, the fear escalates as Lee begins to suspect a link between the crimes. Until it seems that almost everyone in Lee's circle *could* be involved – and could even pose as a very real threat to her life . . .

978-0-7499-0903-1